Southern
Solstice

Southern Solstice

A Novel

Sarah Sadler

Blue
French Press

In memory of Minnie Ora Strother Sheppard Staton—the Carolina girl that started it all. You are still charming us through the legacy of love you left behind.

Acknowledgments

I would like to thank: Gary and Debra Sadler, my parents, for their unending support and encouragement (Dad, for your gift of music and words and Mom, for instilling in me the importance of heritage, family and food made from scratch); my husband, Jim Butler, who I get my beat with and who I love so much he's nearly southern; Leah Sadler Armstrong ("Lolly"), my sister, for believing the best in me—always; Samantha (Sadler) Moorhead for loving these characters as much as I do and urging me to finish their story; Yvonne Sheppard Petty Pepper, my grandmother—so many expressions I learned from the stories you whispered over sweet tea and gossip; Lynzie Gillespie for years of waving your red ink across the chapters of this book like a wand; West Jameson, my son—for changing my perspective on everything when you rewrote my role in life to play your Momma (I am honored).

CHAPTER ONE

Snow Globe

"Don't make this harder on me than it already is, Larken. I didn't plan it this way. Sometimes these things happen and you just have to see where it goes before you plan the rest of your life based on obligation."

A hot, round tear began to blur the vision in her right eye—making the scene in the kitchen seem as though she were watching it through a snow globe. She tilted her head, repositioning the blurriness.

"She and I have something special," he continued. "I can't explain it. It's just…right." David bit his bottom lip. "You remember what it's like to be in love—you would do anything to be with that person. Well, Lark…that's how I feel about her."

Larken watched as David paced anxiously around the sink, balancing on his heels and leaning on the counter. He, a man that had hated conflict and confrontation looked relieved to be saying all of this to her. His words sounded rehearsed—almost made up.

"I love you, but…we promised each other in the beginning we would always be honest. No matter what."

Remember what it's like to be in love? The realization that she had been in love by herself would not register. David's words rang in her head, but they did not find a place to settle. *How long?* She wanted to ask, but did not. The tears in her eyes stung more than the silence, but she refused to release them.

The wedding is in 4 months. Friends and family from Charleston would be coming to Seattle—bringing gifts and well wishes with them like a caravan of happiness. There would be wedding showers and bridal parties—toasts made in their honor and childhood reflections displayed on a projection screen, Sinatra playing in the background. It would have been so wonderful.

"What am I supposed to do?" she blurted out in a frail voice from the bar stool where she sat, repositioning her hands underneath her legs. "I mean, we have the wedding and the house and we've got the party that your friends are throwing us next month and—"

David cut her short. "Larken, listen. I'm sorry. I don't know what else I can say. It's better now than later." His voice was warm, but tight, pleading her to believe him.

Her thoughts drifted to their wedding registry and the words *"David Maddox and Larken Devereaux – Holy Matrimony – July 18"* burned inside of her mind. She visualized the china pattern they had chosen the week before—bone white with subtle gold inlay and muted blue rim, delicately understated but "appropriate for all forms of entertaining and dishwasher safe," the store clerk had told her. "China reflects its hostess exactly," the woman had said. "The pattern you choose speaks volumes to the style of life you'll have and the friends you will entertain. I can tell everything I need to know about someone by their china pattern." Larken flashed back to the fervent retail smile of the woman who had presumable summed her up so completely and wondered if she'd predicted this in her future.

Walking into the store that day, David had said, "Why don't we wait on the china? One pattern for the rest of our lives seems like a pretty big decision." She waved his plea off with a kiss, not seeing through the implication. She supposed now that he wasn't referring to china. He could have told her then, but he didn't. He only wrapped his arms around her and walked down the aisles, scanning cookware and linens, never saying another word about china.

"You can stay in the house until you're set up on your own," David continued. "I'm going away for a while anyway. I need to…regroup." His eyes drifted to the floor as he adjusted the edge of the rug with his foot. The boldness in his words had begun to dissipate and a deep, unacknowledged guilt was evident in his voice.

Larken's attention moved to a burgundy duffle bag lying on the floor beside the island butcher block. "That's my bag," she said without inflection.

"I'll make sure you get it back." David's voice was soft. He fidgeted again uncomfortably.

"No. You can keep it." Larken shrugged without looking up. "I don't use it anyway." The amount of civility she projected stunned her. She stared down at the bag, wondering if she could have ever known it would be the object of such an arctic conversation. She didn't even remember where she had gotten it, only that it had sat in the closet, unused for years.

David picked up the duffle and adjusted the canvas strap over his shoulder, keeping his thumb looped beneath it. She noticed for the first time that he had been holding his keys throughout their conversation, gripping them like they were a lifeline.

A yellow mini-van pulled in front of the house and parked on the street, the well-worn brakes grinding to a halt. An eager cab driver promptly got out and stood door-side—hands crossed in front of him, waiting to handle the new passenger's luggage.

Larken's attention went back to David and she sat looking at him for a moment. She didn't focus on any one part of him, but glanced across him as if he was behind a one-way mirror. He was undeniably handsome with striking features and moody, blue eyes. His composure is what she'd always loved most about him though. He was strong and steady, never wavering because of fear or doubt. Those same qualities were betraying her now.

She watched as a bead of sweat slowly dripped down the side of his face and agitation grew in his stance. Was he waiting for something? Was he waiting for her to say it was okay to leave? Waiting for her to beg him to stay? Waiting to change his mind?

The taxi in the driveway sounded its horn, warning David of the time.

"I told you I love you and I mean that." David tugged at his sweater and stood up straight and tall, not allowing concern to interfere with the delivery of his words. "I know you can't, but...try to believe me."

Somehow, saying "I love you" and "I'm leaving you for someone else" in the same conversation almost cancelled each other out. Almost.

He didn't apologetically kiss her goodbye or touch her arm in failed regret. He repositioned the duffle bag strap on his shoulder, flipped the keys in his hand and set for the door, locking it behind him out of habit.

Larken sat still, listening to his footsteps down the front steps, across the walkway and onto the street where the taxi waited for him. She heard the driver offer to help with his bag, but he declined.

The gliding sound of the mini-van door opening felt like a tear in the center of her heart. A few seconds went by before the door zipped closed again and the van accelerated down the street. It was only then that she could hear the lonely sound of her heart beating, deep and hollow.

She inhaled sharply and began to let out all of the tears that she had kept David from seeing. She wanted so badly for him to hear her, to understand the pain that she felt. She couldn't think about how she had just been betrayed, the mess left to clean up, how she would explain what had happened and how she could ever start over. She only felt the cold stillness of a lonely house and a broken heart.

*

It was four in the afternoon by the time she was able to collect herself enough from crying to see that it had been a crisp, sunny day in the stereotypically overcast Seattle. Her head pounded from trying to understand what had happened. She couldn't help but replay the scene in her head, over and over, unable to determine the actual words from the ones she thought she had heard.

She remembered that it must have been mid-morning when David met her in the kitchen. With no alarm in his voice, he said that he needed to talk. It wasn't until he asked her to sit down that she felt panic catch in her chest.

"Is everything okay?" She asked, taking a quick sip of her coffee. "Did you put my jeans in the dryer again?" She smiled at him jokingly, trying to lighten the mood. David, famously, had a flare for the dramatic, especially on the weekends when they were both home and had no plans. It would not have been unlike him to have planned an impromptu sailing trip with friends to the San Juan's or to book a Bed & Breakfast for the night on Friday Harbor. When they'd first met, he had bragged that surprises were his specialty and had undisputedly owned up.

She remembered how David's eyes had left hers and in that moment she felt an incredible sinking feeling. She sat there silently, waiting for him to begin.

"God, this is really hard to say," he said. For a second she thought he looked like he was going to cry, but he quickly forced himself to go on. "When we met, I knew right away that you were special. I knew you were someone I could spend the rest of my life with. We got engaged really fast, you moved in, we started making all of these plans and before I knew it, it felt like my whole life was planned—just like that." He took a deep breath and continued. "I just don't think this is what I want right now."

She blinked at him, confused. "Are you saying you want to postpone the wedding? I mean, we both agreed we wanted a summer wedding and it's been over a year since we got engaged." She inhaled deeply as his words slowly began to register.

"I don't—" He looked at her sharply. "We're not getting married." David shifted his weight and began shaking his head in confirmation. "I met someone. I wanted to tell you so many times, but I had to be sure it was for real before I did this to you. You have no idea how hard it's been for me to watch you plan this wedding knowing that it was never going to happen."

She remembered how her face had flooded with heat and the kitchen went swirling around her. She grabbed on tightly to the counter and glanced down at her engagement ring, suddenly feeling the weight of it on her finger. How could she have not seen this? Nothing in David's behavior had alarmed her—no working later than usual, no last-minute business trips or late night phone calls worth sneaking away to take.

*

Larken snapped back to reality, rubbing her face in her hands and making a congested grumbling noise. She had so many questions she wanted answers to, but for now, she just needed the pain to remind her it was all real. She wanted to start hating him, but couldn't. She only missed him—something she felt weak and stupid for.

She had been lying on the sofa in the living room for what seemed like days. The quiet rustle of a Saturday afternoon lulled in and out of the house from the outside world. Dedicated joggers and little dogs barking at cats provided enough occasional distractions to keep her lying there, listening and remembering.

David's house had never felt quite like home, but it suddenly felt like she was just a visitor now, urged to leave. The first time David brought her here, she was charmed by the statuesque rows of established town homes gracing the steep slope of E. Highland Drive in Seattle's eclectic Capitol Hill neighborhood.

Even though she was a newcomer to the Pacific Northwest, there was a cadence that she immediately felt connected to. David, an entrepreneur in his early thirties, started his own advertising firm and had done well enough to reside and work in Capitol Hill. He was on the fast track to the top and had recently expanded his firm—his success seemingly effortless.

Though his appearance was clean-cut, she somehow still expected David's house to be messy, with no sense of style or color scheme. She was surprised to find that he had thoughtfully decorated with cool silvery blues and even had art hanging on the walls, contemporary and inexplicable as it was.

There was a tastefully placed ceramic pot of wheat grass beside a juicer on the kitchen counter, an orchid perched on an orderly stack of unopened coffee table books in the living room and royal blue damask throw pillows for the light blue sofa and arm chairs. There was a calm masculinity in the house—nothing screamed of boldness and disorder except the dishes toppled together in the sink. It was in that mess that she felt she could be needed here. The soft edge that was missing from this street, this house, this man—she could provide.

The energy she felt was not warm like the rich, inviting drawl of Charleston. It was conflicted—ushering in insecurities and imbalance. Motivated people with direction and ambition set the tone for Seattle's heartbeat. Everyone was going somewhere, becoming something, but Larken wondered if they were actually living.

Before meeting David, she had done little venturing outside of the suburban Bellevue part of town after taking a Public Relations internship with a water trust conservation group based in Puget Sound. Larken was three months into a six month internship when David's company offered the conservation group a pro-bono ad campaign on water usage.

Larken had thrown herself so far into the internship that she hadn't had time to make friends or learn the city in her short time there. After all, she wasn't planning on staying. Seattle was a short-term solution to a long-term vocational problem. David was instantly taken with her southern charm and fluent beauty and he had no problem talking her into going on a tour of the city with him.

Before long they were inseparable. With all of the working together and sleeping together, it only felt natural to live together. After a few months, even that didn't seem like enough, so David proposed by the water on Alki Beach after Larken's last day at the Water Trust. Larken said yes faster than she could think about it and she only remembered feeling happier than she had ever felt in her twenty-four years.

Being with David made the last fifteen months of her time in Seattle fly by and only occasionally did she think about what she'd left behind in South Carolina. And who had left her behind.

*

It was getting dark outside now. The last glow of the late-winter sun was disappearing behind E. Highland Street, sinking deep into the earth and bringing with it the misty chill of a Pacific Northwest night. Her eyes were heavy and swollen, but she dreaded sleep. Not because she knew how hard it would be to be alone, but because she knew that she would awaken countless times, startled by her recall of what had happened. The idea of the projected pain was piercing and exhausting.

She didn't consider sleeping in the master bedroom, as if it were magically off-limits now that she was an unwelcome guest in this house—like Goldilocks. She changed out of the pajamas she had worn all day and put on a pair of well-worn yoga pants and a tank top and crawled beneath the sheets of the guest bed down the hall.

CHAPTER TWO

Moonshine

"Ohhh. You look terrible." The southern drawl spoken above a velvet voice and elongated vowel usage was distinctive to only one woman Larken knew—Elizabeth Ashby Devereaux Caldwell Blaine Vasser Dabney. Affectionately called Bunny.

"Hey, Momma," Larken greeted her, getting off the couch and forcing a smile.

Bunny was a slender, tall woman with shoulder-length dark hair, almost mahogany in color. Even in her fifties, her beauty was striking and accentuated by her vivaciousness and poised demeanor.

Bunny swooshed through the doorway, bringing with her a wave of sweet perfume and clinking pearls. "I brought Priss with me, of course," she said with a draft of enthusiasm and extended arms towards Larken, embracing her for a tight hug. "That ought to cheer you up if anything could. She's always been my beacon in times like these. Couldn't have done without her and Lord knows we both know how you feel right now."

Larken held back a small smile at the reference to her

mother's almost countless marriages. Her divorce attorney was on speed-dial and the role of the mourning widow had been mastered, warranted or not.

"Priss! Get on in here. Larken is dyin' to see you." Bunny spoke in a loud voice to the direction of the street where Priss sat in a rented Town Car, driver's door propped open, hastily applying Coral Rose Estee Lauder lipstick and trying to manage her mountain of salt and pepper curls in the damp Seattle air. "She just looks terrible though, bless her little heart."

Larken squeezed her eyes shut. Her mother always had a talent for talking about her as if she wasn't there.

"I'm comin', I'm comin'. Oh ohhh, I can't wait. I don't care what she looks like—I'll take her anyway I can get her," Priss said, bouncing up the walkway with a butterfly print carpetbag and matching pop-up umbrella.

Priscilla Alston Winslow Thompson had always been in Larken's life and rarely left Bunny's side. She was a staple in all of Larken's childhood memories and one of the only constants in Bunny's life. Men had come and gone, but Bunny and Priss always had each other.

"Oh, Sweetheart," Priss whispered with all of the delicacy in the world. She hugged Larken, stroking her hair while simultaneously observing the living room and kitchen. "Everything is going to be just fine."

Priss held Larken back at arms length, looking at her as if she were her own. "You're just as pretty as a picture. A little skinny, but that's understandable. Nothin' here that can't be fixed, huh Momma?" Priss looked over at Bunny who agreed with one proud, solitary smile.

Bunny and Priss had grown-up together in Charleston's Battery Park area and were second-generation best friends. They'd attended Ashley Hall School for Girls before going on to The College of Charleston together and had spent the past thirty-five years "surviving," as they called it, seven marriages and five children between them. They were true Charlestonians—steeped in the south and proud of their rich family histories.

"Now, Larken," Bunny started in her business tone, "I know you've been through a lot and I don't want to upset you, but you know why we are here—to take you home. There is *nothin'* here for you anymore. And if you ask my opinion, which I know you won't, you had no business bein' out here in the first place. All this rain and fog and gloom, well, it's enough to make anybody depressed." Priss stood beside Bunny, nodding in calm agreement.

"I know you thought he was the one, but he just wasn't, sugar," Priss said in a sweet voice. "It's like carrying an egg from the refrigerator to the counter, only to drop and break it on the way there, but then realizing it was rotten all along anyway. It doesn't get you any closer to finishing the recipe, but at least you know that you would have needed a different egg."

Bunny rolled her eyes at Priss' flowery metaphor.

It had been twelve days since David had left. Larken had waited as long as she possibly could to break the news to her family. Almost as if she had done something to be ashamed of.

After three missed phone calls from her older sister, Larken knew she would have to break the news sooner rather than later. To her surprise, she felt a huge sense of relief in telling Caroline the news, but knew it would only be a matter of days before Bunny showed up in Seattle, script in hand, determined to save her.

Larken knew there was nothing left for her here except false hope for David's change of heart. Still, she felt unprepared for the ensuing changes and the tightness in her chest was growing.

"I know how you are feeling, Lark. I do. You might have been too little to remember—you were maybe no more than five, but Cal Stewart did the very same thing to me right before our wedding and I–was–devastated." Bunny closed her eyes and clenched her chest for dramatic effect. "It was about a year after your Daddy died and before I married Marshall Caldwell. Or was it after I divorced Marshall and before I married Roger Blaine?" Bunny looked at Priss for verification.

"No, it was before Marshall," Priss stated, not even looking up from the purse she was rifling through.

"Well, anyway," Bunny continued, "I'm here to tell you that life does go on, baby and you will meet someone else, someone smart enough to stop looking when they find you. Someone who deserves you. And God willing…a southerner." Bunny closed her eyes as if she were praying. "And besides," she continued, her voice perky, "you know I need you back home. We can be lonely together!" Her eyes twinkled at the prospect.

"Oh, isn't that nice?" Priss said sweetly.

The tightness in Larken's chest increased and she swallowed hard. So far, her life was setting up to look a lot like her mother's. A fate she had dreaded since she was old enough to know what normal was supposed to look like.

"I don't wanna be lonely." Larken began to cry. "I want to be with David." She felt ridiculous for saying it out loud, the residual toxins of heartache poisoning her sanity.

"Prissy, I think we're gonna need something with some grit to fix this one up," Bunny instructed as she stroked Larken's hair. "How 'bout some of the good stuff?"

Priss winked in agreement and walked quickly out of the kitchen and into the living room where her butterfly carpetbag was propped against the sofa. She smiled as she unzipped the top and reached inside, pulling out a red flask. "Ta-da! The potion for your emotion. And just wait, 'cause I perfected this batch. You'll be saying 'David who?' in no time flat."

"Jewels on your crown," Bunny said out of habit. The saying had become her official tag line—whether for feeding the homeless or fetching her coffee, jewels on your crown was Bunny's heavenly promise for a job well done here on earth.

Larken sat up, blowing her nose into a Kleenex. She smiled at Priss' homemade moonshine and her attempt at making everything better. "You remember the time Sylvia and I got into this stuff when we were twelve?" she asked.

"Oh, I'll never forget!" Priss exclaimed. "There I was, watching you and your sister for the week your Momma was on her honeymoon with—humph, who knows who…and I go outside to find you and Sylvia laid out by the pool like a cold supper, drunk as a couple of skunks. Oh I coulda' died. I would have never forgiven myself if somethin' had happened."

Sylvia was Priss' youngest child, older than Larken by two days. She had been like another sibling to Larken and her older sister Caroline. Their mothers had given them no choice but to be inseparable growing up. Sylvia looked every bit like Priss— proportionally fluffy and mountains of hair, but with biting, cynical humor.

"Well, I knew right away that the twins had given it to you," Priss said, shaking her head. "I have never been as mad at those boys as I was that day. You were still a little wrong side up the next mornin' and I had to keep you outta school. You remember that?" Priss took a quick swig and passed the flask to Larken, scowling from the taste.

Priss' twins, Jackson and Taylor, were the oldest of all of the children. They were only a year older than Caroline Devereaux, but because there were two of them and their presence so concentrated, it seemed as if they were much older than the four years that separated them from Larken and Sylvia.

They were always into something—catching frogs and crawdads—climbing trees and planning sabotages of the girls' sleepovers.

For most of her childhood, Larken had dreaded the twin's presence with everything in her. Priss blamed their daddy, Tip Winslow for their ruckus behavior. Tip's family was from Rock Hill, on the edge of North Carolina, far inland. Priss called them "outdoorsy type people." She wouldn't admit that she had married into a clan of hillbillies, but knew all along that they were and secretly cherished the rebellion of it all.

Priss loved Tip every day that they were married. He had loosened her from the aristocratic tangle of Charleston and taught her to love life. When Tip died six years earlier due to complications after a car accident, Priss became determined to carry on the traditions she had so adamantly frowned upon in the beginning of their marriage, moonshine being the first. She had gotten rather good at making it now though and enjoyed bootlegging it all over the Lowcountry.

When Larken was seventeen, she had been crazy for one of Priss' twins. Jackson was irresponsible and remote, but handsome as the devil. When he came home from Auburn over the holidays during his senior year of college, Jackson was enamored with how beautiful Larken had become in the time he'd been away at school. She was fair and thin with delicate features and hazel eyes framed by wavy auburn hair.

Somehow, the subtle sensuality Larken had unknowingly inherited from Bunny had gone unnoticed by everyone until that point, but she had indeed blossomed into a superb creature—despite being planted in the shadow of her mother's extravagant presence.

As was tradition, their families went to Edisto Island together for Christmas Eve through New Year's Day to stay at Will-o'-the-Wisp, the Ashby family's house. Will-o'-the-Wisp was named for the eerie pixy lights that flicker off the water and was a massive colonial house positioned on an estuary where the black water from the Edisto River would amble tirelessly until it disappeared into the great Atlantic, disregarded.

Larken and Jackson kept their feelings a secret from the family—neither of them could stomach the thought of Bunny disapproving.

In between helpings of molasses pork tenderloin and squash casserole at supper, Jackson reached for Larken's hand under the table and told her with a devious, intense smile that he had a Christmas present he wanted to give her when they were alone.

In an effort to divert him from the scandalous plot that he most certainly had devised, she refused to make eye contact with him for the rest of the evening and even offered to read the Christmas story from the book of Matthew, just in case there was any chance for deliverance.

Savoring the last of her innocence, Larken found every excuse she could to postpone going to bed that night, but long after everyone had hugged goodnight and the house was dissonantly quiet, she finally accepted her fate and walked upstairs to the far side of The Ashby House to find Jackson leaning against her bedroom door. The glow of a waning moon seeped through the windows and a damp mist draped like a quilt over the ocean. Somehow, after all the trepidation of knowing Jackson would come through on his promise, she was relieved that he had.

To her surprise, Jackson held an actual Christmas present out to her, wrapped messily but finished with a bow. It was a first edition Chapman & Hall copy of *Great Expectations.*

"You are my Estella," Jackson said after she opened it and thumbed through the antique pages. I have to have you."

Larken, still finding it important to make Jackson think she was more prudent than she had implied, tried not to look as pleased as she felt, but her delicate face gave her façade away.

Their first time together would have been madly romantic if she hadn't been scared to death of getting caught. Jackson, on the other hand, didn't seemed to mind the risk that was tangled in their juvenile affair, only that that past few weeks of being teased by Larken's eager kisses behind doors and in hallways had been vindicated by her willingness to finally oblige him.

Immense guilt coupled by utter shock flooded her conscious the next day as they celebrated the birth of Jesus by opening presents and singing carols around the Christmas tree. Larken was disappointed in her lack of remorse and Tip's speech about everyone being "one big happy family" didn't bring much comfort either—especially as Jackson burned a hole straight through her, mentally making plans for an afternoon of debauchery. She nearly fainted.

The guilt eventually melted under the pleasure they found and she gladly granted his frequent requests.

"I think we should tell 'em," Jackson whispered the night before he returned to Auburn.

"No. What's wrong with you?" Larken felt frozen with fear from the idea of their families knowing. She sat up, pulling her shirt on over her head.

"But I wanna be with you, Bird. And I don't care if everybody knows." Jackson kissed her while he buttoned his shirt. "I'm moving back after graduation anyway."

"So we'll talk about it then," Larken said, hoping to delay him.

But they never talked about it again. And he never came back after graduation.

*

"Go lay down for a while," Bunny instructed Larken as she capped the moonshine and handed it back to Priss. "A little cat nap would do your complexion good, I think."

Larken didn't need any convincing of the need for sleep. Nodding in agreement, she slowly stood up from her chair, dizzy from the burly moonshine and shuffled down the hall to her make-shift space in the guest bedroom. Somehow, having her mother there felt strangely comforting and she was thankful for some serenity after nearly two weeks of emotional chaos.

As she drifted off to sleep, she heard the women verbally dissecting David's decorating. Their voices dissipated into the back of the house while Larken fell asleep, comforted to know that she was not alone anymore.

*

Hours and what felt like a lifetime later, Larken woke up to rain on the window and laughter drifting in and out of the guest bedroom. Judging by the bird songs outside, she could tell it was morning. She got out of bed and walked sleepily down the hall to find Bunny and Priss in the kitchen, flipping through magazines and catalogues.

"Well, there she is," Priss said, getting up from her stool at the kitchen counter and greeting Larken with a hug.

Bunny was fully dressed with hair and make-up already done.

"What time is it?" Larken asked, stretching.

"Its noon already, well…it's 9 o'clock here, but we're still on Eastern Time," Bunny replied matter-of-fact, pushing the sleep-flattened hair out of Larken's face.

"You must have been absolutely exhausted," Priss cut in. "I almost put a mirror under your nose to make sure you weren't dead. I told you this batch of moonshine was a good one." Priss winked at Larken and let out a giggle. "Didn't know it'd make you sleep all night and half the day though. Not to worry. Being back home will build your tolerance."

"Hope you don't mind," Bunny said, handing Larken a cup of coffee, "but Prissy and I have taken the liberty of packin' up all your little things."

Larken looked around to see boxes stacked up near the

kitchen island.

"We thought about shreddin' some of you-know-whose shirts and linens—maybe the mattress, but thought that might be tacky. You think that's tacky?" Bunny looked at Larken inquisitively, hoping she'd say no.

"No, Momma, that's not necessary." Larken tried to hide that she was amused by the idea. She could tell by the look on Priss' face that she too was disappointed that they wouldn't be demolishing anything.

"Well, if you change your mind, we came prepared," Priss offered, motioning to a large pair of Fiskar gardening sheers that gleamed with the anticipation of hacking more than azaleas.

"How'd you get those through airport security?" Larken asked.

"Honey, that's why her hair's so big," Bunny said, taping a box closed. "It's full of secrets."

By now, Bunny had memorized a retribution ceremony for cheaters. After years of unfaithful men and a lot of practice, revenge came easy to her. As in all things, she was elegant in her approach and between her and Priss there was no evidence of recourse ever left behind. They were a force to be reckoned with, delighting in the punishment.

Larken remembered when Bunny found out about her third husband, Roger Blaine, having an affair with some woman from New Jersey. Unfortunately, Roger hadn't been very tactful with his infidelity and when Bunny found pictures of him and his mistress in compromising positions on the desk of his state run office, she had them published in *The Post and Courier*.

Elected officials don't fare well with public disgrace and Bunny, naturally, played the part of an unknowing, horrified wife.

Roger never knew it was Bunny who had sold him out to the public. The thought crossed his mind, but he assumed that she would never have put herself or family name through that level of public humiliation. He had severely underestimated her. After all, she'd been awarded more than half of *The Post and Courier* in her divorce settlement from Marshall Caldwell years earlier and had worked diligently to increase the gossip columns, firmly believing that the southern art of slander would sell more papers than how the stock markets were falling. The story on the Roger Blaine affair alone tripled the circulation and increased readership by forty-five percent all that quarter. From Bunny's perspective, their marriage had been a success after all.

Larken knew her mother had been deeply hurt by what Roger had done, but she also had too much pride to let anyone see it keep her down for long. After that, she swore off all politicians and Yankees saying, "It's that damn Northern aggression."

Larken and Caroline's father, Charles Devereaux, had dropped dead of a heart attack on the thirteenth hole of Oak Point on Kiawah Island when Larken was four and Caroline was seven. Larken wished so much that she could remember more of him than the plaid golf knickers he was known for, but Bunny's way of dealing with his loss was to move on and not speak of him.

As far as Larken knew, her father was the only man that Bunny had ever truly loved and everyone that came after him was a disappointment. Even though Bunny continually remarried after every failed attempt, she justified it to her daughters by saying, "Sometimes you only get one person that loves you enough to last a lifetime. I'm just makin' sure there aren't two."

Currently, Bunny had just finalized a divorce from Coy Dabney, possibly the strangest man Larken had ever met. Standing only five foot-four he was the shortest of all of Bunny's husbands and at just under one year long, their marriage was also the shortest in her catalogue of nuptials. She didn't win anything in terms of a settlement because she had more money than Coy and theirs was the only marriage she had to site "irreconcilable difference" as opposed to the usually more theatrical "infidelity" or "death." After the divorce, Bunny told Larken's unwilling ears that the irreconcilable part had been Coy's, "inability to perform where it counts." Having heard enough already, Larken did not push for the details behind that statement.

Before Coy, Bunny had been married to a lovely older man named Jesse Vasser, a yacht designer in his seventies that Bunny affectionately called "Sailor." Sailor was sick for most of their four-year marriage, but he was crazy about Bunny and said that she kept him young. The whole family felt like they'd lost a dear friend when Sailor died, so Bunny founded the annual Sailor Ball in his honor, one of her many philanthropic undertakings that just happened to involve ungodly amounts of alcohol and designer gowns.

Larken knew that it wouldn't be long before Bunny would fall head-over-heels again—especially since Priss had happily remarried a few years ago to a very nice man named Hank Thompson. Hank often joked that he had married two women when he married Priss. In many ways, he still didn't know how true that statement was.

*

The rain began to subside outside. Only a sleepy drizzle collected on the windows now. Larken ate two bites of a sandwich that Bunny and Priss had gotten earlier, but she hadn't felt much like eating anything since David left.

Bunny left her position at the kitchen table and walked over to Larken, looking down at the sandwich. "Honey, I hate that son-of-a-bitch that left you. Usually I think women have something to do with a man's leaving, but I blame him. For absolutely everything. I always say you never can trust a man that asks a woman live with him before marriage anyway."

Bunny's morals were sporadic, but the ones she followed were highly coveted and closely adhered to when convenient.

"It must be poor breeding and all this rain that left him without the capacity to love you good enough." Bunny looked out the window and scowled. "His loss 'cause you're really something, Lark. I mean that. Really something."

Larken hugged her. It felt nice to have her mother's support.

"Alright. Let's talk business," Bunny said with a satisfied smile, fully recovered and back to plotting. "We have FedEx coming later this morning to pick-up the boxes we packed. They're shipping them home." Bunny checked Larken's reaction to the reference of home and when she did not seem opposed, continued. "We packed you a suitcase to hold you over 'till then and we have a flight home later tonight. It's a red-eye, but I've got a charity ball committee meeting and a thing with some godforsaken property in the Lowcountry that I've got to get back for. That all sound okay to you, shug?"

"Yes. Thank you," Larken replied. "You two have thought of

everything."

Bunny and Priss nodded in agreement.

"All you have to do is get on that plane and forget this ever happened." Priss winked, glowing with accomplishment. "Speaking of forgetting, I promised Hank I'd bring back one of those little Space Needle magnets from the airport gift shop. He just loves tacky things. Guess that's why he ended up with me!" Priss threw her head back, laughing.

Larken was resolved at the idea of returning home, even though she'd have to explain a million times to a million people what she had been doing for the past year and a half. She thought that getting married would take the emphasis off the fact that she still hadn't decided on a profession. Or a life.

Since college, she'd finished several internships without any clear direction as to what she wanted to do. Now she was single, or worse, un-engaged and still couldn't answer the "what do you do?" question. The friends she'd made in Seattle were all David's friends. She cringed at the thought that all or some of them had known about his affair. She didn't have anything to say to any of them now. Bunny and Priss were right, there was absolutely no reason for her to stay there a second longer.

"By the way," Bunny said, taping up a box, "I took the liberty of having Carrie in my office order some 'Cancel the Date' cards to let everyone know the wedding is off. Hope you don't mind? No need for this to drag out like week-old road kill," she said, scrunched her nose up at the implication of the impending awkwardness Larken was yet to endure. "We'll finalize the wording before they print."

"I didn't know there was such a thing," Larken said, surprised.

"I don't even know how to begin wording something like that. I guess 'picked the wrong guy, gave the wrong finger' works."

They all let out a good laugh.

"Sounds good to me, sugar," Bunny said, thumping a stash of magazines down and tidying up. "Let's get this show on the road. My body's not used to this elevation."

CHAPTER THREE

High Cotton

After four hours of flying through the night and a bothersome layover in Chicago that she could barely remember, Larken opened one eye to find an excitable Priss, her voice sounding miles away. "We're here, honey. Wakey-up. Laaaaark, Lark, Lark. We made it."

Larken closed her eyes again, making a grumbling noise that sounded a lot like, "Uhhhh." It's always easy to forget how grueling red-cye flights are until the next morning, but still, she didn't remember ever feeling like her eyes were sealed shut and her limbs were too heavy to move. She could tell by the sudden quiet that the plane was empty for the most part and only the last few passengers struggling to dislodge their too large carry-ons remained.

"Bunny," Priss hissed from her seat beside Larken, eyes narrowed. "How many did you give her?"

"I only gave her a little bitty blue one," Bunny said innocently. "And just a teensy green and white one."

"Are you *crazy*?" Priss chided, her voice squealing with accusation. "Did you want her to sleep through the rest of her twenties?"

By now, Larken was starting to make sense of her mother and Priss' conversation and the realization was helping her come-to. She quickly remembered the "vitamins" that Bunny had offered her upon take-off when the water works started after the reality of actually leaving Seattle set in. Judging by Bunny's description, Larken assessed that she'd unknowingly taken an Ambien and a Prozac—one of the many prescription staples in Bunny's well-stocked medicine cabinet. Bunny viewed drug interaction warnings more as suggestions than instructions and enjoyed making her own remedial cocktails. "I know my own body better than some doctor," she would say.

After a few minutes of patting, from Priss, and slight smacking, from Bunny, Larken was conscious enough to stumble down the narrow aisle of the plane and let the annoyed service crew tend to the cabin before the next load of travelers boarded.

"Before you say anything," Bunny defended to Larken, "that was a mercy coma and you're welcome."

Larken rolled her eyes. They were back on Bunny's turf and playing by Bunny's rules.

Though the last effects of the Prozac was partly to blame, walking through the terminal of the airport felt good—slightly unfamiliar, but welcoming all the same. "High Cotton" by Alabama was playing over the airport sound system, unnoticed by Bunny and Priss, but more evidence of the southern hospitality Larken had missed without knowing it. Maybe three thousand miles away from David would make her heart hurt less after all.

"Lil just texted me and said that she's waitin' curb side for us and if we hurry, she won't have to circle," Bunny said as she quickened the pace, kitten heels clicking louder underneath her.

"Since when does Lil text?" Larken said, trying to imagine her grandmother's long manicured fingers typing out messages on tiny buttons.

"Oh, honey," Bunny leaned her head back, "she texts more than any teenager I've ever met. She texts when she's going to bed, when she wakes up, while she's shopping—she's got a smart phone. She's on the Twitter, too. Can you believe it?"

Larken's grandmother, Lillian Middleton Ashby was an elegant, quick-witted woman. She was buoyant and unflappable and weaved her charm through old family stories that went back as far as Charleston itself. She was the quintessential matriarch and the elementary pillar of the family.

Lil was all that Larken knew for a grandparent since her father's side of the family was estranged. Except for high school graduation and a few major holidays, Larken never saw them. Charles Devereaux was an only child and after his untimely passing, his parents maintained only stoic interaction with Bunny and the girls.

When Bunny remarried to Marshall Caldwell a year after Charles' death, the Devereaux's, feeling betrayed, withdrew almost completely from Caroline and Larken's lives and moved from Charleston to the mountains of North Carolina. Bunny was relieved to see them go as she did not endorse the Devereaux's stiff and overly formal airs and they in return had never warmed to having an Ashby for an in-law.

Luckily for Caroline and Larken, Bunny's side of the family alone was more than they would ever need. More than anyone would need, really.

As Larken, Bunny and Priss emerged from the sliding glass doors onto curb side pick-up, Lil stood waiting for them, propped against a pale yellow Cadillac wearing a flowing pantsuit with a botanical print scarf tied around her pale blonde hair.

Lil clapped her hands together and looked straight at Larken, absolutely smothered in admiration.

"There's my girl," Lil said, the honey of her sweet, rich voice lingering on every consonant. She hugged Larken and kissed her cheek, leaving distinct outlines of red lip marks on her face.

"Tell me all about it. Tell me everything, all of it." Lil glowed. "I'm tickled pink to have you home. Isn't this wonderful, Bunny? All of us together again. Wonderful. Wonderful."

"Thanks for coming to get us so early, Momma," Bunny said, tossing her Berkin bag into the back seat.

"I'll put it on your tab." Lil turned, winking at Larken jokingly. The four women loaded up into the car and set off for a quiet ride to the Battery.

Mid-March in Charleston was delightful. Even though the evenings were still relatively cool, many of the trees had hopeful buds painting a pastel hue at the end of bare branches, beckoning warmer days.

For the most part, this time of year was void of vacationers who usually waited until the hottest parts of the summer to visit and even then, most of them stayed around Foley Beach or Isle of Palms, renting waterfront homes large enough to sleep twenty people.

Larken rolled down the window of Lil's Cadillac as they exited US 17 South onto Smith Street. The earthen smell of oak-lined marshes and salt water from Charleston Harbor coated everything with a patina of distinction. Lil watched in the rearview mirror as Larken closed her eyes in the back seat, letting the chilled breeze blow through her hair and then taking in a subtle, deep breath of brackish air.

Lil drove slowly down Smith Street to Priss' house, waving at early morning joggers and old men with pipes. Priss' house, The Alston House, had been in the family for over a hundred years. It was a colonial brick building glazed with moss and a massive, unforgiving magnolia shading the portico. The Alston House was beautiful— modest in terms of other Battery houses, but the garden was the envy of even the most prestigious horticulturist. Priss said the difference between her garden and all of the others was that she did the gardening and no one was allowed to prune anything without her saying so.

Lil rolled the car to a stop on the cobble stone driveway of The Alston House. Hank emerged from the front door with a hot cup of coffee and a fluffy white dog wiggling under his arm. Priss had been busy applying her lipstick and messing with her hair since they'd left the airport.

She smiled ear to ear when she looked up and saw Hank with Iris, an apricot colored Havanese that Bunny had given her as a birthday present years ago.

Priss collected her butterfly carpetbag and took one final swing at her hair before getting out of the car. "Love y'all," she said, leaning beside the window. "Glad you're back, Larken." Priss smiled, knowing the bitter sweetness of her coming back home. "We kidnapped her good, didn't we?" she asked, wrinkling her nose at Bunny.

"Sure did, babe," Bunny replied, smug with accomplishment. "See you tomorrow. Give Hank our love."

Priss leaned up, waving at Hank and Iris as she started down the walk way towards them. "Oh. Almost forgot," Priss squealed, quickly turning around and walking back to the car. "Jackson just got back into town," Priss said, leaning beside Larken's window. "He's staying with us. I'm sure he'd love to see you. So would Sylvia, of course. She's living in a condo up on Palmetto. Taylor lives in New York, but he'll be back to visit this summer. Stop by anytime." Priss stood back up and set off again for Hank and Iris, who was now barking wildly with excitement.

Lil gave two goodbye honks at Priss and Hank as she backed out of the driveway. Larken, Bunny and Lil drove quietly as the massive Cadillac turned by Colonial Lake and then onto Rutledge Avenue for the five-block drive to The Ashby House.

Larken let out a deep sigh when they turned onto Tradd Street from Rutledge Avenue and the gold-sphere on top of the cupola of The Ashby House was visible through the tree tops. The house was built in 1782 by Colonel John Ashe, a cotton farmer and major contributor to Charleston's then booming shipping industry.

After slavery was abolished in the mid 1800's, Colonel Ashe, for obvious reasons surrounding the source of his wealth, became known as John Ashby to avoid any negative repercussions associated with his name. The farmlands, dotting the country from Georgia to the Lowcountry, were still owned by the Ashby family's trust though the majority of Ashby wealth was now obtained through a textile company and a farm equipment manufacturer. Bunny's advantageous marriages had also thickened the pot with the wealthiest of husbands dying and leaving her as sole beneficiary. "Old is gold," she would say.

Bunny always insisted that the Ashby family had never owned slaves and Lil would tell stories passed down from her mother-in-law about the generations of black help that stayed on to work for the Ashbys even after slavery was abolished.

When Lil did some ancestry work for her involvement with the Historic Charleston Foundation, she came across legal name change certificates of employees that requested to take on the Ashby surname after the ratification of the Thirteenth Amendment.

*

At the press of a button, Lil opened the menacing wrought-iron privacy gate surrounding The Ashby House and ascended the driveway into the courtyard. Larken looked up above the garage to the bronze plaque that read through the Latin verdigris inscription, "Aedes Mores Juraque Curat" and recited from memory the meaning in English, "She Guards Her Buildings, Customs and Laws." Such an appropriate caption for a house run by women.

No matter how many times Larken saw The Ashby House, it never grew boring. Every architectural detail of the building's four stories was exceptional. The pale yellow building stood tall, dominating even the most esteemed homes in the Battery with three levels of pristine porches and massive windows adorned with black, hand-carved shutters. The Ashby House was originally a colonial-style building, but in the late 1800's it had been revamped with heavy Italian Renaissance influence.

All three piazzas showcased panoramic views of ancient church steeples: the Charleston Harbor, the Sullivan's Island Lighthouse and Fort Sumter. The interior of the house was no exception with a graceful staircase that ascended three of the four floors, ornate dentil ceiling cornices, decorative mantles with original wainscoting, six grandiose fireplaces and imported, handmade tiles.

In the sitting room, an 18th century Italian landscape painting over the mantle and a Walnut Bosendorfer Grand Piano that Lil played a Cimarosa or Cherubini piece on almost every day were the most praised visuals in the home. *Garden & Gun* and *Viranda Magazine* had both featured The Ashby House in beautiful detail, an accomplishment that Bunny took full credit for after the last major renovation of the East Wing and the completion of the Orchid Garden Room behind the nursery.

Lil always felt that The Ashby House was too ostentatious and intimidating to keep up, so when Bunny and Charles were married, the house was gladly taken over by Bunny who was eager to take on the societal demands of a building of its importance.

After they relinquished The Ashby House to Bunny, Lil and Larken's grandfather, Alistair "Al" Ashby, moved to a brownstone on Laurens Street in the French Quarter. Al died during the summer of Larken's sophomore year of high-school and Lil made the decision to move back onto The Ashby House property with a then single Bunny. Depending on Bunny's marital status, Lil floated gracefully between the main house and the carriage house.

Larken always loved the carriage house for its location and charm—through the enormous backyard, around the marble fountain and past the private garden and gazebo. Larken felt such a huge sense of relief with Lil living on the grounds. It was nice to have an adult present and after Caroline left for Vanderbilt, Larken wasn't alone in the massive place.

Most nights during her childhood, Larken stayed in the carriage house with Lil who would make late-night snacks of warm crepes filled with fresh fruit while Larken finished homework or while Lil told stories and read out loud. Larken wanted to stay there forever—she felt like she had deep running roots when she was with Lil, like she knew who she was. She preferred a night in the carriage house with Lil to any night out with her trivial friends from school.

To Bunny's dismay, Lil had encouraged Larken to see the world, do everything she wanted to do and to always, always remember that Charleston was home, even if she didn't live there.

After high school, Priss' daughter Sylvia and Larken attended Anderson University together, three and a half hours from Charleston, where she earned a degree in Communications with a minor in Public Relations. Bunny and Priss drove up once a month, bringing clothes, food, magazines and gossip, paranoid that they would become obsolete to Charleston society.

"I still don't know what's wrong with the College of Charleston," Bunny would whine. "It's so much closer, Larken. Your grandmother and I both went there. It's tradition. And what on earth are you going to do with a Communications degree anyway?"

"*You* have a Communications degree, Momma," Larken reminded her.

"Yes. Exactly. But from the University of Charleston—and now I own and run a successful publication." No one reminded Bunny that it was the divorce settlement from Marshall Caldwell and not her educational background by which the *Post & Courier* had come under her control.

After Larken's sister Caroline married her college sweetheart

Aaron Harrington in a lovely garden ceremony at The Ashby House and Larken was finishing school at Anderson, Lil applied for an auditing course at Le Cordon Bleu in Paris. After eight months of flambéing, poaching and souffleing herself into culinary genius, Lil returned to Charleston and began cooking masterpieces for the patients at Kindred Hospital where, after a routine knee surgery months prior to her Parisian adventure, she was appalled by the cuisine and felt compelled to do something about it.

After graduation, Larken was hired on as a freelance publicist by Bunny's various society friends to pitch their luxury events from waterfront condos to art gallery openings. Bunny couldn't help herself from interfering though and managed to overtake each project.

Realizing her mother's involvement would always be a hindrance in both her personal and private life, Larken sought out the internship in Seattle, as far away as she could go. Bunny cried for three days and then met Coy Dabney and seemed to forget the whole thing.

"Sugar," Bunny said, snapping Larken out of her glaze of reminiscence, "you coming inside or are you gonna take up residence in the Caddy?"

Larken shook her head and smiled intently. "Nope. I'm comin' in."

*

Bart Wheeler emerged onto the circular travertine parking area through the back gate entrance of the house, offering to take hand bags, carry-ons and crinkled magazines read in flight. He was a slim, one-quarter Thai man in his early fifties with short black hair and kind, handsome features. Bart had worked at The Ashby House for fifteen years as Estate Manager after his wife died. The fact that Bunny had inexplicably not run him off proved his high tolerance to her particular style of management. From day-to-day household accounting and oversight of domestic employees to extravagant party planning and travel arrangements, Bart handled all of Bunny's tasks stylishly.

After exchanging pleasantries and welcome home greetings, Bart took the belongings inside where he would identify and distribute each item to the correct bedroom without question.

The house was quiet. Bart had placed an all green flower arrangement and set an assortment of fresh baked goods and a French press of coffee out on the kitchen table. Bunny's itinerary for the day sat beside it, her appointments highlighted in yellow.

Land development meeting at 11 o'clock, fitting with seamstress on Market Street at 12:30, lunch at Piper's with Muttie Halloway to discuss the annual Parade of Boats at 1:30 p.m., massage with Inga at 3:15 and interview with new head gardener at 5:30

Larken had forgotten how someone could be so busy with absolutely nothing of real importance.

Bunny had changed into a silk robe and breezed into the kitchen, pouring coffee while simultaneously reading her itinerary. "Sorry to be so busy your first day back, honey. I'm sure you need the rest anyway. And Lil will be here."

"Oh, no I won't," Lil corrected, her voice singing from the hallway outside the kitchen. "I've got a dozen casseroles I'm cookin' over at Kindred today, but I was hoping Larken would come with me. I could use a sous chef." Lil reached for a piece of banana bread and winked hopefully at Larken. "Grab me a cup, would ya, baby doll?" Larken reached up into the mug cabinet for Lil, who was checking to make sure she hadn't forgotten her way around the kitchen.

"Oh, well—long as you're home by seven," Bunny said uninterested in getting involved. "I'm cookin' supper for us tonight. Bart's picking up triggerfish from the dock later this morning. Oh, and y'all let him know if there's anything you want while he's out." Bunny poured a cup of coffee and puffed at it, tiny steam curls billowing up into her face.

"I can't think of anything," Larken replied with raised eyebrows, faking enthusiasm. "What time are you going to Kindred, Lil?"

Lil looked up from buttering her banana bread. "Whenever you're ready, sugar." It was hard to tell Lil no when she made everything so easy.

"You do remember that I can't cook, right?" Larken reminded her, hoping for a downgrade in her level of expectation. "I'd hate to ruin your good deeds by giving somebody food poisoning."

"Mmmmm, I know that you *think* you can't cook and I love you anyway," Lil said smiling. "Besides, *I'm* doing all the cooking. *You're* doing all the slicin' and dicin'." Lil grinned wickedly and reached for the current copy of the *Post & Courier* before collecting her coffee and heading upstairs.

"Alright, I'm goin' to put my face back on," Bunny said, placing her coffee cup in the sink and sweeping at banana bread and croissant crumbs. "You know where I am if you need me."

Larken sat down at the round mahogany table in the suddenly quiet kitchen and glanced at the clock. It wasn't even 9 o'clock and she was exhausted—mentally, physically and emotionally.

She calculated that Lil would be ready to leave in an hour and there was no denying the need for a shower and some decent clothes.

Larken evaluated herself sitting in the oval backed armchair—slumped over, wearing three-day-old yoga pants and what used to be a white cashmere hoodie, expressionless, drained of color for nearly two weeks, dry complexion from abandoning her skincare routine and rail thin from being heart sick.

Larken brushed the hair out of her face, stood up from her chair and walked sloth like through the wide hallway to the base of the enormous staircase. She stopped short of the first step, staring straight up through the top of the cupola where the gold dome refracted the morning light like a spotlight down and over the banister.

She couldn't help but catch a glance of her greasy hair and sullen face in the wall of countless antique mirrors of all shapes and sizes that decorated the three-story staircase wall. What a terrible chore for the cleaning staff to endure, not to mention a less than pleasant experience when scaling the stairs late at night.

Larken wound her way up the stairs, blinking from the gold light shining above her. Once at the top of the second floor landing, she walked to the East end of the house where her bedroom was. Bart had placed her carry-on bag and purse just inside of the French doors leading into her pale blue room. The balcony doors overlooking the edge of the gardens had been opened and a smaller arrangement of the same greenery from downstairs sat on the console table. A light breeze disturbed the butter colored silk taffeta drapes, waving in a fresh scent of peninsula air, humid and succulent.

Larken peeled her hoodie off, repositioning the camisole underneath and wheeled her carry-on to the bathroom. She stopped at the walk-in closet, opening the pocket doors and peeking inside. Bunny had taken the liberty of re-stocking Larken's closet—top to bottom and left to right. Nanette Lepore jackets, KENZO skirts, Abi Ferrin dresses, Rebecca Taylor tops and Coclico shoes gleamed with newness. If there was one thing Bunny didn't skimp on, it was fashion.

"Knock, knock," Bunny said softly from outside the bathroom entryway. "I thought it'd be nice to start fresh. I hope you like them." Bunny was dressed in a dove gray suit with a white silk camisole plunging below the top button, her hair pinned back loosely with a mother of pearl clip and bright red lipstick accentuating her pristine face.

"Oh, they're great," Larken said, emerging from the closet. "You didn't need to, but I won't say no. The style in Seattle is different than the style here." She thought about how it had been nice to have the weight of social responsibility lifted off of her.

"Oh yes I noticed that." Bunny smiled tightly. "Well now that you're back there will be more things to dress up for than you can shake a stick at. Oh! Speaking of which, the Bakers have asked us to join them for the kick-off of Charleston Fashion Week this Friday night. I said we'd love to."

Larken shuddered.

Bunny glanced down at her watch. "Well, I've got to get a move on, but you and Lil go have some fun today. And sugar, please do change into something else. I can't look at those spandex britches one more day. You really should fix yourself. It'll make you feel like a million bucks."

Bunny kissed the air and set-off for her day of pointless appointments, leaving Larken standing in a fog of her Coco Mademoiselle perfume and cloud of unspoken expectation.

*

After Larken showered and washed her hair twice, she dragged herself out of the hot water and halfway dried her hair, leaving plenty of interpretation for it to style itself. Taking Bunny's advice to wear actual clothes for the first time in two weeks, Larken pulled on a soft pink silk knit v-neck dress that, except for the bust, fit like an hourglass, shaping around her waist with perfect precision and hitting shamelessly in the middle of her thigh. Larken had never done hospital volunteer work before, but she had a pretty good idea that she was already completely overdressed for a sous chef. Still, she felt good for the first time in what felt like forever and unpedicured toes and all, slipped into camel colored strappy heels with a peek-a-boo toe.

As Larken doused a generous helping of moisturizer on her face, ten chimes from the grandfather clock downstairs drifted throughout the house.

Larken grabbed her purse, one that David had given to her for her birthday the year before. She remembered opening it on Friday Harbor as the sun sunk down at Sunset Point and how, even though it was just a purse, it was so much more in that moment.

Larken tossed it on the floor, punishing it for reminding her and taking one small step away from her life in Seattle.

*

When Larken got to the bottom of the stairs, she could hear Lil talking from the kitchen table. "Yes, and if you wouldn't mind seeing about getting me rhubarb next week, I have a recipe I thought I'd try," she said, her voice pleasant and warm. "Well, if they aren't ready yet, the apples will be fine. Don't worry about it either way. We'll just see what we get. Well, thank you, Bart. Oh. Lark just came downstairs and goodness gracious you should see her. She's *gorgeous.*

41

Alright—we're off. Thanks for bringing the eggs by. Yes, yes we are on our way there right now. Okay, you too. Bye now."

Larken stared in amazement at her grandmother. Lil stood cross-legged, phone in hand, simultaneously texting and talking on her Bluetooth.

Lil took the device off her ear and pushed her phone aside, pursing her lips with review of Larken's appearance. "Oh Mylanta." Lil gawked. "Larken Lillian Devereaux. You *are* a vision. Spin around. Let me get a look at you."

Larken put her hands up in the air, turning around like a Lazy Susan for Lil to see all sides of the ensemble. She was relieved to see Lil in a similar outfit, wearing a long tunic dress with a triple set of pearls.

"I know it's a little much," Larken said, picking her feet up and showing Lil her high heels.

"Nope. Not a bit. It's wonderful. And you never know who you might meet." Lil winked. "There are plenty of eligible bachelors at Kindred. Some of them aren't even on life support yet." Lil let out a giggle. "Come on. Bart's coming straight from the market to meet us."

*

Larken worked her loosely curled hair into a ponytail on the three-minute drive to the hospital, swooping up the long layers in the front to hopefully resemble a hairstyle. Lil pulled the Cadillac into the parking garage of the hospital and turned into a handicapped parking spot front and center of the elevators leading into the main building.

"I know, I know," Lil admitted, pushing her sunglasses over her head before Larken could say anything. "The Chief of Medicine insists that I park here though – handicapped or not."

Larken rolled her eyes playfully. "I'm sure he does."

Following Lil down the sterile white hallways of the hospital, Larken juggled casserole dishes, mixing bowls and measuring cups as they weaved through nursing stations and treatment wards. As they reached the main reception area in the center of the complex, Lil gracefully greeted acquaintances and strangers alike with the same cordial tone and pleasant smile. Lil introduced several of the nurses as well as the activities director to Larken in passing, beaming with pride.

Lil turned down another unmarked hallway and entered a large door into a commercial-grade kitchen. The remaining kitchen crew had just finished cleaning up what looked to be a breakfast of scrambled eggs and bacon, with empty orange juice and milk cartons spilling out of the large trashcan.

"Well, hey lady," a raspy voice from the walk-in freezer said. Claire Donelson had spent the past twenty-five years as kitchen manager for Kindred Hospital. Claire was a pear shaped woman with large, unsupported breasts and thin bird legs. She had shoulder length coffee-colored hair with lightning gray streaks framing her tired, kind face.

"Well, good morning, Ms. Claire," Lil responded, finding an empty space on a stainless preparation table to place her things. "I brought my granddaughter to help me today. Larken, this is Ms. Donelson."

"Happy to meet you, Larken. Call me Claire. I feel like I already know you. Your grandmother has told me a lot about you. We sure do love having her come and give us a break a couple times a week when she can. She's a real lifesaver. Fine cook, too."

"Ohhh, hush. I get more out of it than you do," Lil said

bashfully.

"Well, I doubt that." Claire smiled. "What do you have on the menu for us today, Ms. Lillian?"

"Well, I'm still on my quiche kick," Lil answered. "So Bart's bringin' some fresh peas and smoked ham from Donahue Farm. Let's see... What else?" Lil pouted her lips out while she mentally scrolled through her internal recipe book for the day's menu. "Oh yes, fresh pureed apple sauce, steamed green beans with slivered almonds and a little cucumber salad. Nothin' fancy."

"Nothin' fancy," Claire mimicked. "Well, it beats the meatloaf—if you wanna *call it* meatloaf—and boxed mashed potatoes I was gonna fix. Sounds delicious. I'm sure everyone will love it."

The door creaked open and Bart entered, carrying a produce box piled high with cucumbers, onions, all-purpose flour and cartons of farm fresh eggs.

Larken could tell by the effortless way Bart placed the groceries around the massive, stainless steel kitchen that this was a weekly routine for him. Bart and Claire exchanged a sterile, routine goodbye before he disappeared again.

"Well, I'm gonna go on and get outta your way, too," Claire said playfully. "You know where I am if you need me. Thanks again, Lil. And nice to finally meet you, Larken." Claire waved at them both as she walked out of the door.

Lil turned back to Larken and tossed a ruffled apron with a smocked top at her. The magenta fabric corresponded perfectly with Larken's pale pink dress, making the ensemble look ridiculously coordinated. Lil walked behind Larken, pulling either side of the ties together into a big bow then fluffing the ruffled edges out so that they lay right.

"Okay, sweet pea, let's get cookin'," Lil said as she finished tying her matching lavender apron and walking toward one of produce boxes that Bart had dropped off. "We've got three hours before the lunch crew comes in to start filling up the delivery carts, so I'll start rollin' out the dough if you can start chopping some veggies for the quiche fillin'."

Lil found ten large Vidalia onions from the produce box and rolled them down the surface area to where Larken stood waiting with a cutting board and knife.

Within minutes, Lil had the sixty-quart mixers full of flour, salt and olive oil, churning together rhythmically. The stockpots were boiling rapidly, waiting to envelope the freshly peeled apple slices.

Lil hummed a melody from a section of Rhapsody on A Theme of Paganini, something that she always hummed when she was being very diligent. Larken hadn't missed hearing her grandmother hum until that very moment that she heard her voice again, subtle and sweet.

Larken had diced a mountain of onions and celery by the time Lil was rolling out the dough for the quiche. Lil brought fluted tart pans from Paris with her, all in pastel colors. As with everything Lil did, her culinary skill was a beautiful, luxurious art that spared no expense.

The hospital kitchen sounded like a symphony of kitchen appliance motors, metal blades on wooden blocks and the occasional clicking of high heels on the discolored floor.

"I think it's more about intuition than formula sometimes," Lil said with self-approval as she set several of the tart pans with dough, crimping the edges. "It's important to be happy with what you're doing, even if you aren't doing it perfectly. Of course, everyone has their own idea of what perfect is..." Lil raised her eyebrows for emphasis. "But I'm pretty sure everyone would agree this is as good as it gets." Lil held up a completed pan to Larken before sliding it into the oven with authority.

Suddenly, Larken's heart sunk for the first time all day. She didn't know what triggered it or how it dropped so quickly, but she was suddenly overwhelmed with uncertainty. She thought about David and what she would be doing right now in Seattle if nothing had gone wrong. She winced from the pain of missing him—it was numbing and sharp at the same time.

"Larken?" There was slight alarm in Lil's voice. "Are you okay?"

"Yes. I just started thinking about everything and—oh God, it hurts, you know?"

"Well of course it does, Lark," Lil squealed as she ran to Larken's side. "You dropped a big ole knife on your toe! How could that not hurt?" Lil clenched her chest as she moved closer. "Oh God. It's worse than I thought."

Larken and Lil looked down, horror stricken. A large cutting knife stood straight up, impaling Larken's open-toed shoe, its sharp edge piercing the tip of her unpolished pinkie toe. Larken almost laughed when she realized the pain wasn't from thinking about David at all, but quickly collected herself when a puddle of blood began forming on the linoleum floor beneath her.

"Ohhhh, no. I'm so, so sorry, Lil," Larken wailed. "I don't know how it happened. Oh, this is so *stupid.*" Larken took her plastic gloves off and rubbed her face fretfully.

"Uh uh, none of that now," Lil said shaking her head, refusing to let Larken blame herself. She mumbled something about Bunny over medicating her on the flight and cursed. "Don't move. Dear God, do *not* move, Lark," Lil instructed adamantly. "I'll be right back with help."

Lil moved quickly out of the kitchen, removing her apron in one motion, leaving Larken propped against the stainless steel work table in the utter silence of the kitchen.

Larken focused on regulating her breathing and not looking down. With light-headed clarity, she thought about the reprieve that physical pain was to emotional pain.

A few moments later, Lil returned with a plump, gray-headed nurse pushing a wheelchair. Larken's foot was prickling with pain, but she was in too much shock to move or even speak.

The nurse quickly wheeled the chair behind Larken and with Lil's assistance helped her sit down so that the placement of the knife didn't move. For only a pinkie toe, there was an unsettling amount of blood. As soon as Larken realized she was safe from falling over, she gracefully lost consciousness.

CHAPTER FOUR

Sycamore

Larken squinted under fluorescent lights in a quiet, sterile room. It took only a second to remember what happened as she propped her head up, looking for Lil. She was still in the wheelchair— the knife standing upright in her toe and the same nurse who was in the kitchen sat in a rolling chair beside her.

"You're fine," the nurse said smiling when she saw Larken was awake. "Probably just got a little woozy when you saw all that blood. It happens. Nothing to be embarrassed about. I understand you've been under some stress lately, too. That may have had something to do with it, bless your heart." The nurse got up and opened a cabinet that stored medical supplies.

"Your grandmother went to finish up lunch prep – she didn't want to leave you, but I told her you just needed a couple of stitches and not to worry."

"I didn't…cut it off?" Larken asked, biting her lip from the pain. "It sure felt like I cut it off."

"Oh goodness, no," the nurse said chuckling. "It looks like a real clean cut. The doctor's just gonna remove the knife very carefully and put a couple of stitches in. It shouldn't be too bad."

The nurse finished arranging a metal tray full of items needed for sutures and handed Larken a clipboard of forms to fill out.

"Someone will be in to fix you all up in a minute or two. I'll come back later to get your paperwork finalized."

The nurse closed the small examination room door and Larken listened as her rubber-soled shoes squeaked down the hall, back to the nurse's station.

The room felt more like a private doctor's office than a hospital and Larken felt relieved that she was spared the embarrassment of the emergency room. She looked around slowly at the pinstriped wallpaper and inspirational artwork hanging on the walls. A streak of pain zinged her toe when she heard the customary rat-a-tat-tat announce the arrival of a visitor.

A tall, flaxen man with light brown hair and deep brown eyes swung the door wide open, ushering in a gust of stale hallway air. He stopped at the clipboard on the wall, tilting his head sideways to read the nurse's notes. Larken noticed immediately that he wore dark navy scrub pants and a light gray jaspé T-shirt, but no customary white medical coat.

The doctor reached for the back of a rolling chair, spinning it around forcefully before sitting down and rolling towards Larken with a dazzling, engaging smile.

"Ohhhh, that's a new one," he said, looking down at the knife in Larken's foot. "Were you making anything good?"

"What?" Larken asked, dazed by his sudden presence.

"Well, you don't look like the knife throwing type, so my

guess is you were cooking?" The doctor kept his eyebrows raised in question. "Plus your apron gave it away."

"Oh. Right," Larken said, looking down at the pink ruffles on her apron and suddenly feeling self-conscious. "I was helping my grandmother."

"Looks like you were doin one hell of a job," the doctor said, hesitating on Larken's face for a second before looking away again. "Lucky for you I do better sutures than anyone." He bit at the side of his lower lip before releasing a full-fledged smile, like he knew something that she didn't. "Let's take a look at your handiwork here." For the first time, Larken heard a southern drawl leak through his otherwise non-regional accent.

The doctor leaned over Larken's foot, pursing his lips together in review and glancing side to side at the entry point of the knife.

Larken sat impossibly still, not wanting to interfere with the inspection. She was unable to help from noticing his shoulder blades though—perfectly muscled through the stretchy T-shirt fabric. She noticed the way that his arms were built, long and lean with visible definition on his biceps, more like the arms of a surfer than those of a hospital doctor. Though his complexion was fair, the golden hues that shimmered across his skin were evidence of spending time in the sun.

His hair was short and thick, strands of it looking naturally highlighted in flecks of gold, maybe remnants of being blonde as a child—a few gray pieces serving more as a testament to stress than age. Trying to practice some restraint, Larken leaned a little closer and subtly hovered over him. He smelled ruggedly delicious like fresh air and sycamore.

"One, two, three," the doctor said quietly, applying pressure with his hand to the top of Larken's right foot. His palm was warm and soft on Larken's cold, bloodless foot. In one smooth, piercing motion, the doctor pulled the knife out of Larken's toe and immediately applied gauze to stop the bleeding.

"You alright?" he said, looking up at Larken intently. He held the gauze in place and stretched his other arm to the metal tray, laying the knife down with a careless thud.

"Fine, thanks," Larken lied, sitting back as far as the wheelchair would allow. His face was so close to hers that she thought he might kiss her. Or worse, she might kiss him.

She felt ashamed for being so attracted to someone else. Maybe it was the pain in her foot that distracted her, but she noticed that the constant throbbing in her chest was gone, at least temporarily.

"I think you only need three or four sutures," the doctor said reassuringly.

"Is it gonna hurt?" Larken asked, feeling immediately childish. She glanced down at his hand to look again for a wedding ring.

No ring.

"Nah, I'll numb the area really well first. You'll barely feel a thing." He watched the skepticism on Larken's face. His eyes went dark, silky brown as he stared straight at her. "You should trust me. I'm really good."

I bet you are.

Larken's thoughts caused a streak of red to flash across her cheeks. She suddenly felt desperate for trying to find hidden meaning in his words.

"Wonderful," she said, pretending to have not read into any innuendos.

He reached down to Larken's shoe and unbuckled the clasp with one try before gently removing the shoe from her foot, careful not to graze the wound. He propped her foot up beside his leg on the chair and moved closer to examine the cut under the gauze. He gave her another big smile and wheeled over to the metal tray.

"Now, I'm great at sutures, but needles are a passion of mine," he said, reaching for the syringe that was pre-filled with the clear, numbing liquid. "I won't hurt you a bit."

"Should I be alarmed at how much you seem to enjoy this?" She bit the inside of her cheek for flirting with him.

"Hey, what can I say?" he defended. "I'm a surgeon. I love it all. I mean, most days I don't have pretty girls with kitchen knives stuck in their designer shoes, so maybe I'm a little more eager than usual. This is as exciting as my day's gonna get."

"Surgeon, huh?" Larken asked. "You don't have anything better to do? I mean, stitching up a pinkie toe seems trivial in comparison to surgery. There's no one to slice and dice today, Dr.—?" Her voice was a little too high to pass for relaxed. "I'm sorry. I didn't catch your name."

Larken wanted to take it back immediately. She didn't want to know his name. She didn't want him to even have a name. You can't be hurt by someone whose name you don't know.

"Nope, all I've done is check new patient charts and advise the first-year residents on things they should already know," he said shaking his head. "And it's Miles. I'm sorry, I should have introduced myself. Apparently bedside manner isn't my strong suit."

Shit.

Now she had a name to go with his engaging smile, the shoulder blades that could open a tin can, his subtle, undeniably sexy scent and those deep, soulful eyes. At least she didn't know his first name. He would remain as "Dr. Miles" in her fantasy.

Shit. Memory, not fantasy.

Dr. Miles repositioned her foot on the chair beside him and approached her pinkie toe with the needle.

"Oh, you might not want to watch," Dr. Miles cautioned through a grimace. "I hear you've been known to get a little queasy…"

Larken rolled her eyes in agreement and changed her gaze to the ceiling. After about thirty seconds, she felt pressure on her pinkie toe. She looked down to see him gently squeezing her foot all over, surprised to not feel any pain.

"Anything?" he asked casually, surveying her face.

Larken slowly shook her head, amazed that she hadn't felt even a needle prick.

"I think you got it," Larken said, rotating the ankle that she'd kept motionless.

"I thought so," he said happily. "I'll give you a couple more minutes to numb up completely and then we'll start the sutures." He stood up quickly and opened the examine room door, disappearing in only a couple of strides.

Larken untied the apron in the back and slipped it over her head before laying it over the back of the wheelchair. She caught a reflection of herself in one of the framed inspirational posters—her hair must have taken the brunt of her unconsciousness. Most of her ponytail had fallen out, she had frizzy flyaways on either side of her temples and the top of her hair was about three inches too high, resembling a rat's nest. It was a miracle that no one had checked her for electric shock.

Larken loosened the pony tail, flipping her hair over and shaking it all out into one mass of loose curls before collecting it all again and smoothing it down. She pressed the wrinkles out of her dress and unsuccessfully repositioned the top of the dress to reveal any cleavage that was available.

Pointless.

She was wiping at the mascara creases under her eyes when she heard Dr. Miles. He knocked and opened the door simultaneously then stopped cold when he saw Larken.

"Ha," he said, continuing into the room. "I thought I had the wrong patient for a second."

Larken laughed resentfully.

"Alright," Dr. Miles started, "let's do this."

He began to walk towards her and then stopped again, crossing his arms and looking her over thoughtfully.

"What is it?" Larken asked. She smoothed her hair again.

"You are wearing a dress and… I'm trying to figure out how to get you on the exam table so I can do the sutures properly." He rubbed at his face in thought.

"I can get up there fine," Larken said, looking at him puzzled.

"Well, I'm sure you can get *on*, but I need your foot to be flat and I'm not sure how you'll sit without—"

"Oh," Larken cut him off, "without flashing you?"

"Bingo," Dr. Miles said, eyebrows raised. To Larken's surprise, he actually looked embarrassed.

"I've got it," he said after thinking for another couple of seconds. "If you don't mind sitting on the end of the table, you can just put your foot on my leg. I think that will work for me. If…that's okay with you."

"Sure." She stood up from the wheelchair, putting the pressure of her right leg onto the heel of her foot.

"You got it?" Dr. Miles said, watching to make sure. "Let's not take any more chances."

Larken reached for the arm that he extended and steadied herself before beginning the four-foot walk to the exam table.

Before she could contest it, he had his arm under her right elbow and was lifting her up like a human crutch to compensate for the injured foot. She could feel the muscle in his arm flex with each small step they took and noticed how her head came exactly to the top of his shoulder. The delightful fragrance that she had smelled earlier was intensified now, sweet in a masculine sort of way.

The table was low enough for her to climb on without his help and once she was settled on the edge of the table, Dr. Miles sat down on the exam chair and wheeled over to her, bringing with him the metal tray of medical supplies.

He adjusted his chair up and down until he found the perfect height for Larken's foot to fit on his leg. He reached out for her foot, pulling her ankle closer to him and placing it firmly on his thigh.

Being this close to him made her heart race a little and she once again steadied her breathing, telling herself how immature it was to read into anything.

Dr. Miles fell silent, moving in close with needle and thread in hand, concentrating on his work. Larken felt only pressure in her foot again and kept her eyes on the ceiling, uninterested in the doctor's self-proclaimed skill set.

Five minutes later, Dr. Miles tied the last suture and snipped the extra material off.

"Good as new," he said, proud of his handiwork.

"Except for the scar I'll have for the rest of my life, this wasn't too bad," Larken said, shrugging.

"Scar? Ehh. You won't have one," Dr. Miles said matter-of-factly. "I don't leave scars." He smiled arrogantly.

"Oh, it's okay. It's just a pinkie toe," Larken said, lifting her foot up enough to see the stitches. "Besides, I might need a permanent reminder of kitchen safety from time to time."

"Naw," Dr. Miles corrected her, "it would be a shame to leave a scar on such a pretty foot." He carefully wrapped her foot with gauze and bandage tape before washing his hands.

"I hope that you learned your lesson with knives though," Dr. Miles said as he reached down for Larken's right shoe. "No future in the circus for you."

"I'll try to stay out of the kitchen from now on," she said, hopping off the table and taking the shoe, inspecting the damage.

Dr. Miles smiled. "The numbing agent will begin to wear off in about thirty minutes and you'll want to keep that foot elevated. Do you have someone to pick you up?"

His eyes searched her face, waiting for her answer.

Larken nodded.

"Well, then," Dr. Miles said, turning for the door, "that's my cue. It was a pleasure meeting you today." He sounded so professional now, but his eyes were the same friendly, chocolate brown as before.

"Thanks," Larken said sarcastically, "I had a great time…"

Dr. Miles let out a muffled laugh and closed the door behind him.

She felt a dipping feeling in her stomach and the fracture in her chest was noticeable again. For a brief second she wished her broken heart was visible—maybe then he could suture it up so David wouldn't leave a scar either.

*

Nurse Jenkins knocked on the door and came in quietly. "Did you survive, honey?"

"Oh, yeah, I'm fine," Larken said, blowing the stitches off. She sat down in the wheelchair, placing the shoe in her lap.

"Well, you sure got lucky in the surgical department," Nurse Jenkins said. "We only have that doctor here every once in a while when our Chief of Medicine is out. We call him the 'phantom doctor'."

"So…he doesn't *work* here?" Larken asked, trying to veil her disappointment.

"Nope," Nurse Jenkins shook her head. "But even an old gray mare like me can appreciate a man like that." She handed Larken her bloodied shoe.

"Oh, really," Larken teased. "Guess I didn't notice."

Nurse Jenkins shot her a look over the frames of her reading glasses, acknowledging the lie. "Oh come on, now honey. You hurt your toe—not your head."

*

After Nurse Jenkins gave Larken some topical medication for the stitches, instructions on how to clean the wound and a date to come back for a check-up, Lil scurried into the room.

"Well, isn't this par for the course," she said looking at Larken's bandaged toe, shaking her head. "Can you believe all this? Your first day back and we've got you sliced up like a spiral ham. Some welcome home, huh babe?"

"Awww, its fine, Lil," Larken said convincingly, "these things happen. At least to me they do."

"Not for long. It's all gonna turn around. It's just got to." Lil squeezed Larken's hand and sighed deeply.

"Well, I've got a couple of things left to do in the kitchen, but Bart should be waiting outside for you. Nurse Jenkins will roll ya on out there."

Nurse Jenkins nodded in agreement and pushed Larken's wheelchair out of the door and down the hallway.

Just as Lil had said, Bart was there to greet Larken when Nurse Jenkins wheeled her outside. Larken once again thanked the nurse while Bart helped her into the passenger seat of his Mercedes CL550 Coupe.

"Maybe I should work for my mom," Larken joked with Bart, touching the buttery leather seats of the black car and carefully placing the damaged shoe in the floorboard.

"Yes," Bart agreed. "Your family has been very good to me over the years."

Bart didn't talk much. All the same, he communicated well without words and Larken had always appreciated that about him. She had never lingered much on the fact that, in some strange way he had been the father figure in her life. There was no doubt that Bart was part of the family.

"Speaking of work," Bart said in a calm, lucid voice, "have you had much time to think about what you might want to do now that you are back?"

Larken swallowed hard. "Hmmmmm, no, not really," she said. "It might be good though…to stay busy—focus on something other than… To focus on something else."

Bart nodded at her from the driver's side. "Certainly," he said.

Larken quickly scrolled through the Rolodex of possible job options in her mind, but every single one stemmed from Bunny or worse, Bunny's friends.

"Thanks for coming to pick me up," Larken said casually, changing the subject. "This whole foot thing, it's really not as bad as it looks." She leaned toward the floorboard, inspecting the bandage once again.

"Well, you'll need to convince your mother of that," Bart said stoically as they crossed over Gibbes Street. "She came home as soon as Lil called her."

Larken immediately slouched in the passenger seat.

The Mercedes purred into the driveway of The Ashby House, quickly pulling to a stop once Bart positioned the car in its usual location by the urn-shaped water fountain.

It took less than five seconds for Bunny to dramatically cascade down the back steps when she heard the car pull in.

"Lark," she pleaded, running to her daughter's side, "this is just the last thing you need right now. Are you in pain? How bad is it? Can you wear heels?" Bunny held her hand to her head, letting out an exasperated sigh.

"Momma, please, I'm fine," Larken said, beginning to laugh at the ridiculousness of the situation. "It's just a scratch. It really wasn't all that bad." She tucked the bloody shoe behind her back.

"Who was the doctor on-call?" Bunny asked. "Hopefully someone that's been thoroughly vetted…"

"I don't know. Some guy." Larken thought about Dr. Miles, saddened by the fact that she might not see him again.

"I want you to get straight in bed and rest," Bunny said sternly. "That's what you should have done today anyway. Oh, how careless of me to think that you were ready for the real world so soon. I blame myself."

"I blame you, too, Momma," Larken mocked.

"Bart," Bunny said, turning quickly toward him. "I need you to have Carrie clear my schedule for the rest of the week. I have more important things to tend to right now and, well, I'm sure everyone will understand. They'll just have to."

Bart nodded in agreement. "Consider it done."

"'Cept for my spa day at the club," she added, patting at her skin. "And see if they can add Larken, too. She needs a full workup."

Larken was walking better on her injured foot now, keeping her toes up and applying all of the pressure from her right leg to the heel of her foot. The numbing medicine was beginning to wear off though and small tinges of pain were rippling through her toe.

With Bart's help, Larken climbed the stairs up to her bedroom, careful not to seem too dependent on his help. He would never say anything to imply it, but Larken felt badly that he had been pulled away in the middle of his daily tasks to play nurse to her. Once Bart was convinced she could maneuver in her own bedroom, he closed the door quietly behind him.

Larken searched through the closet again, pulling out a pair of sweatpants and a paper thin T-shirt that had somehow managed to escape the wardrobe massacre that Bunny had ordered.

After Larken maneuvered the bandaged foot into bed, Bunny brought her a mysterious little white pill that she promised would rid her of any pain and then kissed her forehead before apologizing yet again.

Larken, exhausted and drugged, replayed her time with Dr. Miles before falling into a deep, dreamless sleep.

CHAPTER FIVE

Avery

Well into the early part of the evening, Larken felt a rustling at the edge of her bed and heard a small, callow voice.

She looked up from her pillow to see a cherub smile and bright blue eyes watching her—the last of the afternoon sunshine dancing through blonde, translucent hair.

Larken's sister Caroline had a three-year-old boy, Sam. He was a stout, well-dressed child that had his father's quiet temperament and chubby fingers.

He watched Larken for a couple of seconds in silence before climbing up on the bed to sit beside her.

Larken had never spent much time around children, but Sam didn't seem to notice. She was amazed at how trusting he was and thought about how lovely and simple it must be to be only three.

"Are you awake?" he asked through short, shallow breaths, leaning closer to her face.

Larken nodded sleepily. "Do you know who I am?"

"Uh-huh. Yes ma'am. You're Lawk," Sam said, beaming with pride for answering correctly. "Can I see where you hurt your foot, pweese?"

"Who told you about that, huh?" Larken said playfully as she sat up.

"Nanny," Sam said matter-of-factly. "She said you bwoked your hawt, too. And that you live hewer now."

"Yep." Lark blinked, blindsided by his awareness of the situation. She pulled her foot out of the covers and showed the child the bandage.

"That must have hurted real, real bad," Sam said, grimacing.

"Looks like you have a boo-boo, too," Larken said pointing to a Bob the Builder bandage on his knee.

"No. Not yet. It's for just in case," Sam explained, patting the bandage flat against his chunky knee.

Larken felt like an immature, inadequate adult beside this well-prepared and confident child. Even at three, he was expecting to fall and was already armed with the equipment to patch things up and carry on, bandage and all.

He wiggled off the side of the bed, grunting with difficulty as he maneuvered his husky frame off the pillow-top mattress.

"Lawk?" he asked, landing with a thud. "You can sit beside me at dinnah."

Larken nodded her head in agreement, smiling at his sincere, round face.

With that, Sam ran out of the room making siren noises followed by crashing noises and then his deliberate, heavy footfalls disappeared down the last flight of stairs.

Larken threw the covers off and sighed. She could smell the aroma of Bunny's supper coming from downstairs and heard waves of voices, none distinguishable, drifting in and out of the doorway that Sam had left flung open.

The pain in her foot hadn't started again, but the pain that intensified in her chest as evening fell was sinking like a stone now, revealing the ache that daylight seemed to conceal.

She did her best to shake the feeling off. She knew how important it was for Bunny to see her on the mend. And in so many ways she was. Larken quickly remembered Dr. Miles from earlier in the day and let a small smile creep across her lips.

"Hey, sugar," Bunny said, sweeping through the doorway, chardonnay in hand. "You feelin' better?"

"A little." Larken nodded. "Sam came to see me. I can't believe how much he's grown since I was home last."

Bunny smiled ear-to-ear. "He's something, isn't he? Little spitfire." Larken watched Bunny's entire countenance change as she thought about Sam and his lively, certain nature.

"Well," Bunny said, sipping her wine, "supper's 'bout ready and there's a whole house full waiting to see you, little Calamity Jane."

"Oh God, Momma," Larken fussed. "Did you have to?"

"Honey you know I'm kiddin'. You aren't really Calamity Jane. Everybody has an accident now and then."

"No," Larken corrected her, walking towards the closet, "not about that. About the house being full of people. I just don't feel like putting on a show tonight."

Bunny let out a hearty, three glasses of wine laugh. "Judging by the lingerie we discovered, or should I say *didn't* discover in Seattle, you don't *ever* feel like puttin' on a show."

Larken peeked her head around the closet door, eyes slit in a stiff glare and lips pursed disapprovingly.

"Oh, Lark," Bunny said, adjusting her tone, "people love you here. It's not like Seattle, baby. You can just be yourself. You can be an Ashby." Bunny watched as Larken considered the idea. "C'mon. It'll be fun."

Larken dove back into the closet, ruffling through her assortment of new clothes, looking for a pair of jeans. ·

"Fine," Larken said tersely, her voice muffled in the closet. "I'll just sweep my heartache under the rug and throw my emotions into the wind and—."

"Oh that sounds wonderful," Bunny cut her off, obviously not listening. "Oh, and no blue jeans, Lark. Jackson is downstairs."

Larken's jaw fell open. Jackson Winslow was not someone she was ready to handle right now—maybe never.

"Why is he here?" Larken asked, poking her head out of the closet to find that Bunny had conveniently left the room.

Larken stood in front of the floor-length mirror. *Oh, hi, Jackson,* she said to herself. *Remember when we used to sleep together? Thanks for avoiding me for the past seven years. This isn't awkward at all.* She forced a fake smile in preparation.

Her hair was salvageable if she could smooth it down and put it in a ponytail. In the closet, she found an indigo dress with a square neckline and a slit up the side of the straight skirt revealing most of her left thigh. She found a pair of gold gladiator wedges that she managed to squeeze the bandaged foot into without discomfort and after wanding on some mascara and lip gloss, she was only slightly inappropriately dressed for dinner.

She took a deep breath and began her descent down the stairs, voices from the dining room growing louder and louder with each step.

When Larken got to the bottom of the staircase, Sam ran to greet her. "Lawk," he said with big eyes, "Nanny got ice qweem for dessert, just for me, but you can share it." And then he ran off again like a terrier, landing in the living room in front of his fleet of Tonka trucks and army men.

Larken tugged at her skirt and walked as confidently as possible into the dining room. She took in a table full of faces—Bunny and Priss Velcroed at the hip as usual, gossiping—Lil and Bart discussing a broiled bananas recipe—Hank telling Caroline and her husband Aaron stories about Iris the Havanese and his latest deep sea fishing adventure, but there were no signs of Jackson.

Larken felt her entire body relax. She could only hope that he had decided to leave, realizing the uneasiness his presence would cause.

"Lark," Caroline called. She stood up from the table and wrapped her arms around Larken, rubbing her back and squeezing tightly. "Welcome home."

Caroline never changed. She had always been an old soul, but her face remained youthful and vibrant, always smiling and rosy. She had Bunny's coloring exactly—fair skin, dark hair, deep blue eyes.

"Sam told me that he woke you up," Caroline said laughing. "I guess Aaron let him sneak up there."

Aaron stood up from his chair and gave Larken a side hug, welcoming her back. "Yeah, sorry 'bout that. He's like holdin' on to a greased pig."

Larken walked toward Bunny and Priss, hugging Hank on the way.

"Now, that's what I'm talking about, sugar," Bunny said proudly, admiring Larken's ensemble. "Doesn't she look like a catch, Prissy?"

Priss nodded her head adamantly. "She *is* a catch, Momma. Good grief. Look at that backside. Buns of steel magnolias." Priss gave Larken a playful pat on the backside and winked as she popped a lobster cream-puff in her mouth.

"Why don't you pour yourself a glass of wine while we wait," Bunny suggested. "There's a bottle of white and a bottle of red already open in the kitchen, but I'd go with the chardonnay."

Bunny's advice on food and wine pairings were more like orders, so Larken set off for the kitchen for a glass of (white) wine. The fish was still in the oven, bubbling cheese sauce under the broiler and filling the kitchen with a gourmet dill and lemon fragrance. Orzo and currant salad sat steaming in the warming drawer alongside asparagus and dinner rolls. Though it was rare, Bunny did know how to prepare a lovely meal and as with everything, she spared no opulence.

Larken poured a generous glass of wine and tipped it up, taking several large gulps before re-filling it again.

"Hey, Bird," a liquid, baritone voice boomed from behind her.

There was only one person to ever call Larken "Bird." Hearing it again resonated through her entire body, jolting her back in time.

Larken whipped around, wine glass and wine bottle in each hand—some of the wine sloshing out onto the floor.

Jackson Winslow stood with his arms crossed, propped against the cabinet across from her with a devious smile on his face. He wore fitted navy suit pants with a silver blue crewneck sweater that pressed against his athletic frame, sleeves pushed up to his elbows. His brown hair was short on the sides with enough length on the top to still require styling.

From things that Priss had said over the years, Larken knew Jackson had worked as an investment banker and had seen a fair amount of success. Seeing him stand in front of her now, it looked like a role he played perfectly.

"I didn't mean to startle you," he said, walking dangerously close to Larken. He motioned at the wine bottle in her right hand. "Could I get some of that?"

Larken carelessly placed the bottle in his hand.

"You look good," he said, pouring the wine slow and steady. "Sorry to hear about what brings you back home, but... It's good to see you." He stood back again, admiring her.

Larken could hardly breathe, let alone speak. Jackson was all the ways she had remembered him being and then some. He was still charming and attractive in an unattainable way, but was more polished now than when he was twenty-one. And at the same time, he still had all of the button-pushing qualities as when he was a ten year old— hiding in the garden and sabotaging tea parties.

Larken immediately recomposed herself and took a casual sip of her wine. She seemed to remember with Jackson, bullying and seduction were one in the same.

"Ah. Good to see you're still lurking around, Jackson." Larken kept her eyes glued on him now. "Guess some things never change."

"Ouch," Jackson said, clutching his chest. "The way I remember it, you and me did a whole lot of lurking around together once upon a time."

"Mmmmm. That's right," she said, narrowing her eyes. "I haven't thought about that in years." Larken felt her façade slipping away the longer he stood in front of her.

"Really?" Jackson asked, leaning in closer. "'Cause I think about it all the time." He let a wide smile cover his face as Larken blushed in the wake of his words.

"Lark," Bunny called as she entered the kitchen. "How's that fish lookin'?" She smiled widely when she saw Larken and Jackson together. "Oh, good. I found you both. C'mon. Y'all help me set this out."

Bunny pulled the fish from under the broiler and quickly transferred it to a serving platter. Larken and Jackson each took a dish from the warming tray and walked silently into the dining room, placing them on the table.

Larken eyed the only two available place settings at the far end of the dining room beside Sam, side-by-side. The idea of choking to death was more appealing than sitting beside Jackson at this point.

Larken calmly accepted her fate and walked around the table to sit down between Sam and the empty chair that Jackson would soon occupy.

Larken took her chair with a thud and unrolled her silverware, smacking her napkin against the air with a pop before placing it in her lap.

"Everything okay?" Priss asked.

Larken looked up to see a table full of curious eyes on her. Jackson leaned back in his chair, enjoying the awkwardness.

"Yes. Sorry." Larken forced a smile. "Must be the wine." She let out a small laugh and everyone went back to their merriment of talking and passing the food around the table.

It was uncomfortably evident that no one wanted to ask Larken the wrong questions over dinner. Hank made a few jokes about her clumsiness and the unfortunate accident at the hospital, which Priss playfully reprimanded him for.

After a few more glasses of wine, Larken relaxed. Sitting beside Sam gave her every excuse to ignore Jackson, who seemed to be deep in conversation with Aaron anyway.

Sam was a wonderful conversationalist, telling Larken about the things he loved at the zoo and showing her some of the silly faces that he could make. Larken loved how natural talking to him was. She cringed at the thought that one day he would grow up and maybe break someone's heart.

Caroline monitored Sam closely, correcting him easily with just a look when he got too loud or too boisterous.

After dinner, Bart brought out a homemade key-lime pie that Lil special requested he make. An exhausted Sam was given his ice cream as promised before being ushered upstairs to Caroline's old room, now a lavishly redecorated playroom with a cowboys and Indians theme.

Lil brought out after-dinner coffee for everyone and intuitively brought Larken some Advil and a glass of water for the toe that was once again throbbing.

"And how is that darling Avery doing?" Bunny asked Jackson as she passed him a slice of pie.

Jackson nodded proudly and settled the plate down in front of him. "She's great. Turnin' seven in August."

Larken felt a pull in her chest at the mention of Jackson's daughter. She'd never met her, but she figured that was as intentional as Jackson's avoidance of her for the past seven years. She'd stopped counting the times that he'd made a whirlwind visit to Charleston without as much as a hello from him. For several years, part of her held out hope of him returning to Edisto Island for the tradition of vacationing together, but he never showed. She didn't know what she would have said to him anyway.

"She lives in Alabama with her mother," Jackson said, turning to Larken to explain the situation. "Her mother and I... Kayla... well, me being back here is a recent development." Jackson seemed modest now, his arrogance humbled at the admission to his personal life.

Jackson and Kayla had never married, Larken knew that much. She also knew that based on Avery's arrival into the world, Kayla was in Jackson's life well before her time with him that Christmas break.

"We really should catch up sometime, Bird," Jackson said. "I mean, if you want." He smiled.

"Yeah. Sure. It's been years." Larken shrugged, hoping to seem indifferent.

"Alright." He shook his head slowly. "I leave for New York tomorrow, but maybe next week? I'll give you a call or swing by or somethin'."

Larken agreed with a nod—the wine sloshing her thoughts around arbitrarily.

"Bunny," Jackson said, standing up from the table, "dinner was wonderful as always. Thank you for the invitation. If you don't mind though, I'm going to excuse myself. I've got an early start."

Bunny got up from the table, hugging Jackson and offering to send him home with leftovers.

"Don't you want a ride home, baby?" Priss asked.

"It's such a nice night, I think I'll walk," Jackson reassured her with a smile. "I'll see you back at the house." He waved goodbye, showing himself to the door and closing it quietly behind him.

After the last crumb of pie was gone and conversation had lulled, Lil and Bart cleaned up the dishes, leaving a fair amount for the housekeeper to deal with in the morning.

Priss and Hank hugged everyone goodbye after Caroline and Aaron brought a sleepy-headed Sam down the stairs.

Bunny, Lil and Larken stood on the front porch, watching everyone get into their cars and leave. The night air was still and crisp. Even the harbor was quiet—with only the occasional wave audibly hitting the barrier wall.

Bunny turned to Larken, wrapping a silk chiffon shawl tighter around her. "That wasn't too bad now was it?"

"No," Larken admitted. "It was actually really nice. Thank you. I know you're trying to make things easy for me."

"I don't know if I can make things easy," Bunny said seriously. "I guess some things are just hard until they aren't anymore. I want you to know that you have all the time you need, though. I am not going to rush you through this."

Larken threw her arms around Bunny. Somehow having permission to not be okay made her feel like she would be okay.

"Well," Bunny said, brightening her tone, "tomorrow is a whole new day full of wonderful possibilities. But today was long and hard and I'm beat."

The three women walked back in the house and Bunny kissed Lil and Larken goodnight before shuffling up the stairs, stilettos in hand.

"Alright, sugar," Lil said through a yawn. "I'm gonna hit the hay, too... You gonna be alright tonight?"

Larken twisted her lips together, looking up the dark staircase lined with mirrors.

"Actually, I was thinking you might need some company in the carriage house..."

"Oh, goodie." Lil laughed. "I was hoping you'd come and keep an old lady company. How 'bout some butter and cinnamon crepes before bed like old times?" Lil's eyes twinkled with excitement. "Go get your jammies on and I'll fire up the griddle."

Larken felt like a child running up the stairs to grab her freshly laundered yoga pants and cashmere hoodie. She hopped barefoot across the garden to the carriage house with her toe elevated, ducking inside the door just before the sprinklers turned on.

CHAPTER SIX

Phantoms

Six weeks had passed since Larken had returned home from
Seattle. She was beginning to feel like an inferior version of her old self
now, slowly readjusting to the slower pace of Charleston and finding a
rhythm in her day-to-day life at home.

She occasionally caught herself enjoying simple things again—
a morning walk to Waterfront Park, running errands with Bart,
cooking lessons with Lil and late-night porch talks with Bunny.

Her mind, weakened by a helpless state of sleep, would dream
of David's house. In some dreams she'd just stand outside, watching
his shadow move inside. In other versions of the dream she'd find a
house key and let herself in, trying not to be found out. All versions
made her feel empty and lost.

Charleston was in full blossom now. The first of many annual
festivals celebrating blooming flowers were underway, and brightly
colored window boxes draped wave petunias and lobelia down house
fronts. A blanket of warm, salt water and gardenias perfumed the
streets, intensifying with the unpredictable coastal breeze.

A week after the unfortunate knife accident, Larken returned to the hospital to have her stitches removed. She was filled with irrepressible disappointment when an expressionless, middle-aged nurse walked in to perform the procedure. Somehow she knew it was not as pleasant of an experience as it would have been if Dr. Miles had been there to do it.

She ran into Nurse Jenkins on the way out of the exam room and asked, as casually as possible, if there had been any "phantom doctor" sightings. Nurse Jenkins shook her head, apologetic for not knowing more. Larken, then feeling ridiculous for wearing three-inch heels and a silk halter dress in hopes of seeing Dr. Miles, walked briskly outside where she cried for five minutes. Bart pretended not to notice the smudged mascara when he arrived to pick her up and they rode silently back to The Ashby House.

Jackson extended his New York trip after the stock-market took a tumble, but he called Larken as promised to let her know he was still looking forward to getting reacquainted when he returned. She hoped he meant it in the most platonic of ways.

Larken was also spending most nights in her own room in the main house now. She was easily persuaded to stay in the carriage house though when Lil presented the offer of late night bananas foster or blanc manger. Larken listened for hours as Lil retold stories of when she first met Alistair and their whirlwind love affair. Lil's eyes twinkled as she remembered how they drove to North Carolina on a dare and eloped in a small chapel in the mountains months before their planned wedding.

Priss' daughter Sylvia went to dinner with Larken a couple of times—Larken quickly discovering that they had very little in common. Sylvia was ambitious and abrupt and Larken found herself struggling to keep her side of the conversation interesting to her.

Caroline and Sam picked up Larken twice a week for a day of adventures. Sam was always full of information about wild animals and fictitious creatures and loved collecting shells on Kiawah Island. He gave even the broken ones to Larken as if they were diamonds, fragmented and tattered as they were.

When Sam would finally pass out from exhaustion for his afternoon nap, Caroline and Larken would talk for hours about everything from their capricious childhood to the downfalls of their relationships, past and present. Larken told Caroline about her short-lived fling with Jackson Winslow years earlier—the burden of the secret somehow alleviated. Larken began to appreciate her sister more than she ever had, finally understanding their difference as experience instead of hereditary.

As it turned out, Caroline and Aaron had endured a great deal of marital strife early on. Living within a budget proved strenuous, even for someone as undemanding as Caroline. Aaron made it very clear that Bunny's monetary influence was not permitted, so Caroline took a job at a high-end ladies boutique in town to off-set her customary living expenses.

Bunny begged Caroline to let her help them, but Caroline grew to love making her own money. Eventually accepting that Aaron and Caroline wouldn't take handouts, Bunny found a way to persuade the store owner to sell the boutique to her and Caroline became the highest paid store manager in retail history.

By the time Sam was born, Aaron's residential renovation business had taken off astronomically, much in part to Bunny hiring him for project after pointless project at The Ashby House. Bunny always found a way around the rules, but Caroline was more than happy to be a full-time mother and Aaron accepted that Bunny was irrefutable.

"There are certain things you don't ever, ever have to think about when you grow up the way we did," Caroline told Larken. "This sounds ungrateful, but in many ways I feel as though I was at a disadvantage. I feel like I became confident when I became self-sufficient, out of necessity I guess."

Larken considered the idea of self-reliance and what it would be like to live independently of Ashby money. There was no denying she was a hard worker, but all of her work experience had been as unpaid internships or worse, secretly funded by Bunny.

*

Bart was gentle yet relentless in encouraging Larken to find something she enjoyed doing. He saw how tirelessly Bunny worked to keep a busy social calendar for her when she wasn't with Lil or Caroline. Bart also saw how Larken didn't know how to tell her no. Despite his loyalty to Bunny, he knew that Larken needed to get out from under her thumb if she had a chance at a normal life. Because of her name alone, Larken would always be taken care of, but becoming emotionally independent of Ashby money and social status under Bunny's reign was vital.

Larken had difficulty sleeping much past daybreak anymore, whether in her room or in the carriage house with Lil. She seldom dreamed about anything that she could remember the next day, but she would awaken with both her heart and mind racing, unable to stop the feeling of disorientation. Before the sun had melted through the fog that enveloped the harbor, hovering above the placid water, Larken would go for a run through the Battery, sometimes running for an hour before she had collected her thoughts enough to stop.

By the time she returned home, Bart had coffee brewing and the morning paper placed on the kitchen table, job opportunities highlighted in yellow for Larken. Most were outlandish manual labor jobs like "deep sea fishing vessel first mate" or work at home opportunities promising takers to get rich quick. Bart's subtle sense of humor let Larken settle into the idea of working again and the daybreak routine became a welcomed joke between the two of them.

It infuriated Bunny that Bart would imply that Larken needed anything more than what she could offer, though she never said anything. She would just wad up the newspaper after Larken was done with it and throw it in the trash, leaving it displayed on top for visual evidence of her disapproval. Bunny considered canceling the classified section in the paper altogether since she owned over half of the *Post & Courier*, but quickly changed her mind when the Board of Directors informed her that it was the classifieds paying the staff's salary.

Lil thought it was a wonderful idea that Larken wanted to work. "Don't rush into anything, but I do think the right opportunity will be really good for you, honey," Lil said, encouraging Larken over a tomato sandwich. "Not that she would ever tell you this, but your Momma knows deep down that it's a good idea, too." Lil winked at Larken knowingly. "There are only so many brunches and tea socials you can take before that pretty little head of yours might explode. I've seen it a hundred times."

"Maybe I should move away again," Larken said. The thought alone stung.

"Well, if you do, just take me with you." Lil laughed.

Larken went back to the hospital with Lil on the days that she volunteered her culinary creations, but for liability reasons was assigned to tasks that didn't include knives or other sharp objects.

Nurse Jenkins still had no news of any "phantom doctor" sightings, so embarrassed and annoyed at the same time, Larken stopped asking about him. She began resenting him for not being more obtainable and decided, officially, to not care anymore after she couldn't find any listings for a "Dr. Miles" in the business pages of the phone book. He was a phantom indeed.

*

It was the first day of May, murky and shadowed with cloud cover when Larken woke up. The windows in her bedroom were covered with a sheet of water cascading over the balcony, enclosing her bedroom in a dark curtain. Hurricane season was at least a month away, but rain of this kind would settle in and stay, suspending over the harbor until a crescendo of light would pierce the clouds. She had felt it coming for days, the oppressive heat and humidity building up like steam in a pressure cooker.

For only a moment, half cognizant in the unusually gray morning light, she could have believed that she was still in Seattle. It took only a moment to realize where she was and, again, how she had gotten there. She allowed herself to think about David long and hard: where he was, if he thought about her, if he felt remorse. She imagined him returning to the empty E. Highland Drive town house, a tinge of pain greeting him when he realized she was gone, his face riddled with repentance for leaving, his knees buckling under the weight of his decisions.

Larken kicked off the covers and made her way to the desk at the edge of the room, overlooking the soggy landscape. She would write David a letter. In hopes of closure, she would even forgive him. She thumbed through her stationery, pulling out cream-colored square cardstock with her initials embossed in chartreuse. Without much forethought, she began writing.

David,

There are so many things that I thought of saying… The truth is though, there are not enough words to say them with or enough paper to write them on so I'll spare us both the misery. I've been waiting for what feels like forever to hear you say that you are sorry, but since you haven't, I don't suppose that you are. I'm actually fine without your apology.

Simply put, I am where I should be. I almost want to thank you, but since that feels unnecessarily kind considering the circumstances in which I returned home, I will instead forgive you. And one day, when it doesn't sting so much to remember the details of your face or the way that you held your fork wrong side up, I will hope you are living a wonderful life. One day, maybe years from now when you finally allow yourself to feel guilty and ask the inevitable question "what if," please know that I didn't waste as much love on you as I did ideas. When we first met, you told me that you didn't deserve me. You were right. For whatever it's worth though, I would have gone on loving you forever, but it would never have been anything like the love that I know I want now.

-Larken

She walked across the room to her nightstand, opening the drawer where she had tossed her engagement ring. She looked at the square, two karat solitaire, realizing it was set too high and void of character. She tried it on her finger one last time before she slipped it into the linen envelope, sealing it closed along with the hopes it had once represented.

The overcast sky had allowed Larken to sleep in an hour later than usual, but it was still quite early. She tugged on the infamous cashmere hoodie and opened her bedroom door, walking quietly down the stairs.

When she walked into the kitchen, she saw Bunny at the breakfast table, uncharacteristically slouched over a cup of coffee, reading through the day's classifieds that Bart had highlighted.

"Everything okay?" Larken asked, stopping in the doorway.

"Yeees," Bunny replied dramatically. "No." She tossed her hands up in the air, letting them fall gently back in her lap. "I don't know."

"Did something actually happen?" Larken asked. "Or are you just depressed 'cause it's raining?" She pouring a cup of coffee and sat down. Bunny hated rain vehemently—another reason she'd never understood Larken's choice in moving to Seattle.

"No, no." Bunny stuck her lips out in a pout. "It's just—are you happy here? I mean, did I do the right thing, bringin' you back home?"

"What makes you think it wasn't the right thing?"

"Oh, I don't know. You won't stop wearin' that post-apocalyptic depression uniform for one thing," Bunny said, waving at Larken's ensemble. "I can smell the stench of heartache on you from here.

Larken pinched at the front of her hoodie, taking a subtle whiff.

"And you and Bart are always laughing and looking for jobs

and it makes me feel like you're gonna spring outta here the first chance you get and... What if next time it's to some foreign land like Iceland or I don't know, New York? You and your sister and Lil, you're all I've got."

"I'm not going anywhere," Larken consoled her. "And New York is actually not a foreign land. And I'd never move to Iceland." Larken waived the envelope addressed to David in the air. "I wrote him a letter. I told him that this is where I'm supposed to be." Larken sighed deeply. "And it's true, you know. This is where I'm supposed to be. If I didn't know it before, I know it now."

Bunny's eyes watered. "Really? So, me draggin' you back here, that was a good thing and I can stop feelin' so guilty?"

Larken laughed. "Didn't exactly have anywhere else to go."

"Oh, stop it." Bunny wiped at her tears. "I can think of worse places than here...like New York."

Bunny took the envelope from Larken, examining the lump from the diamond inside. "Good decision, baby. You only keep the ring if they die. It's tacky otherwise." Bunny smirked, half seriously. "I'll have Bart mail it for you."

Priss knocked and opened up the back door simultaneously, tossing her umbrella to the side. "Good morning, beauty queens." she said with trill enthusiasm. "Have you seen it outside? It's wonderful. All my little plants are gonna just grow, grow, grow." Priss flipped her hair over, colossal with humidity, shaking out the extra moisture.

Rain or shine, Priss walked faithfully every morning. On days that Hank was out of town or already on the water, she would change her route to include a stop at The Ashby House.

Priss poured herself a cup of coffee and plunked down at the table, letting out a satisfied sigh. "Well, if it doesn't smell like gossip in here…" She glanced from Bunny to Larken, eyes twinkling with anticipation. "So tell me! What'd I miss?"

"Well, Larken has written a letter to you-know-who…" Bunny said. "So that's that."

"Ohhh, I see," Priss whispered. "Well…" she reached over and squeezed Larken's arm. "Proud of you, sugar. Hope you gave him what for."

Larken shrugged. "I guess so…"

"Oh. Almost forgot to tell you," Priss interrupted, "Jackson got back last night and he wanted me to tell you that he'll stop by sometime today to see what you're up to." Priss beamed with enthusiasm. "I think we're drivin' him crazy at the house."

Larken felt a knot in her throat. Seeing Jackson again had unearthed ancient feelings of confusion and rejection—leaving her with the unpleasant taste of unforgiveness in her mouth.

Bunny and Priss exchanged a glance when Larken didn't immediately respond. "Lark?" Bunny asked. "Did you hear what Priss said? 'Bout Jackson being back?"

"Yes. Sorry. Great. That sounds great," Larken lied, nodding her head.

"Annnnd," Priss continued, "I *may* have mentioned, just *accidentally*, that it's your birthday next week." Priss conspicuously winked at Bunny. "Whoopsie."

Larken hadn't even thought about her twenty-fifth birthday, let alone made plans for it.

"What's the matter? You used to love your birthday," Bunny

said through a whine.

"Yeah, when I had something to look forward to," Larken said. "Now I don't have anything… A fiancée, a job, a life…" She looked down at the cashmere hoodie laying flat against her chest. "Boobs."

Priss and Bunny laughed. "Well, all of that can be fixed," Bunny said. "'Specially the boobs."

"Speaking of which," Bunny continued, "I have a date tonight, if you can believe it, and I'm due for a dermal-filler tune up at ten."

Larken grimaced. "Like Botox?"

"Oh, honey," Bunny said, "these days it's Botox and Restylane and collagen and butt-fat and anything else they can find to make me look younger. I'm back on the market again, too you know and boy, competition is *stiff* out there." Bunny pushed back from the table, stretching.

"So who is it tonight, Momma?" Priss asked. She glanced at the classifieds, looking confused when she read the highlighted ad for "meat packing plant assembly line worker."

Larken smiled at Bart's joke of the day.

"I have been asked to join a Mr. JD Hart of Boca Raton, Florida for a romantic dinner and night on the town," Bunny said with a hint of flare.

"What's the JD stand for?" Priss asked. "I can't stand initials when I don't know what they mean."

"Well, then. I'll be sure and make that our first topic of conversation," Bunny said sarcastically. "*Anyway*, he's the real estate developer interested in that old lot in the Lowcountry. And wickedly handsome. And single."

"So is this a date or a business opportunity?" Larken asked.

Bunny shrugged. "Same thing... Mrs. Bunny Hart does have a good ring to it though."

*

After everyone dispersed from the kitchen, Larken immediately called Caroline and arranged to spend the day with her. She tried to hide the urgency in her voice as she peeked out the window watching for any surprise-attack visits from Jackson.

Bart drove her to Edgewater Park where Caroline and Aaron lived in a charming stone cottage that had been completely renovated.

Sam ran out of the house and into the rain to greet Larken. He wore Kermit the Frog galoshes and jumped in every puddle along the way, stomping vigorously and shrieking when the water splashed onto his face.

Caroline didn't ask why Larken needed to retreat to their house for the day—she was happy to have the company on a rainy Saturday to off-set the attention of a bored three-year-old.

Hours after Sam had gone to bed and Larken thought it was safe to return home, Caroline drove Larken back to The Ashby House, idling on the street in front of the illuminated house.

"Thanks for driving me," Larken said as they stopped. "Maybe I should get a car."

"Take one of Momma's."

"Nah," Larken declined, "she'll feel like she has the right to know where I am all the time."

"Well, I don't mind picking you up and I'm sure Bart doesn't mind driving you around. It's really no trouble."

"Actually," Larken said, "I'm thinking I'll get a job. A real job. Bart's been helping me look." She looked out of the window at the water drops collecting on the glass. "I always thought I would just fall into whatever it is I want to do, but that hasn't happened yet. And if I don't find something, I think it might get found for me." She pursed her lips together at the thought of Bunny's continued involvement with her day-to-day.

"What a great idea," Caroline answered. "I'll keep an eye out, okay?"

The two hugged goodbye and Larken hopped out of the car, making her way to the wrought iron gate and climbing the marble steps leading to the front porch. It must have been past eleven o'clock. The street noise was padded by the gently falling rain and the harbor was a still, black liquid surface reflecting what little moonlight shone through the bulky cloud cover.

Larken opened the front door, greeted by the stillness of a tranquil house. She steadied herself on the lion head door knocker, removing her damp shoes when she saw a note with her name on it folded in half and propped up on the credenza in front of the banister.

"Bird, sorry I missed you. My timing always seems to be wrong. I'll try again." -Jax.

Larken took in a slow, deep breath and let out a frustrated sigh.

"Hey, love bug," Lil called from the formal living room. She was stretched across the cream suede sofa, taking notes while reading a biography on Julia Child. "You get Jackson's message?"

Larken walked into the room, holding the paper up. "Yep. Have it right here."

"He looked like he'd lost his puppy when I told him you were out for the day. Poor boy."

"Ohhh, too bad I missed him." Larken winced, faking sympathy.

"Not on purpose, I hope…" Lil studied her granddaughter's face. "You know sometimes we don't want what everybody else wants for us. And that's okay. Just don't torture him because of it."

"Oh, it's not like that, I'm sure. Just not sure why he wants to be friends now." Larken felt a pinch in her chest. She'd always been so honest with Lil. Lying even a little bit felt wrong. She knew exactly what Jackson was interested in.

Lil let out a deep, sleepy laugh. "I love that you think you've got everybody fooled. It's kind of adorable. But really, Larken, did you think that all this time, nobody would find out about you and Jackson? This town is too small for that. Or maybe this *family* is too small for that. I do find it *very* interesting that he came back home just a few weeks before you did, though. Maybe it's destiny or fate or….somethin'."

Larken felt light-headed, like the room was suddenly spinning. Her cheeks felt warm, but she couldn't tell if she had turned ghost white or burning red. This complicated everything. The expectation everyone had for her and Jackson was suddenly realized. Bunny, Priss, Lil—they'd known about her and Jackson all along.

"Well, good grief. It's not the end of the world, you know." Lil patted the couch cushion beside her, motioning Larken to sit down.

"It's just *embarrassing*," Larken said, floppily joining Lil. "That was a long, long time ago. We're not even the same people anymore. I mean, he practically fell off the face of the earth and now he just shows up and wants to hang out?"

"Well, now," Lil began in a soothing voice, "from what Priss has said over the years I don't think Jackson has had the easiest of times down in Alabama. It's been a real hardship on him to stay with that girl for so long. Sad situation for everyone really. I think he's just looking for some familiar faces."

"Why does that have to be my problem? Larken asked. "I have plenty of problems of my own without needing Jackson Winslow's problems, too."

Lil arched an eyebrow in consideration. "Know what my problem is? Your mother. I mean, look at me, I'm an old woman sittin' here waiting up for her to come home." She clucked in disapproval. "This has been my problem off and on for decades." Lil craned her neck to look out the window as a car passed by. "I keep hopin' she finds one she likes or doesn't kill so I can finally get some sleep, but here I am, once again, waiting up until the wee hours of the night… Worrying over her is exhausting."

Larken leaned her head on Lil's shoulder. "You can worry about me if you want to."

"Oh, you're the one I *don't* have to worry about, sugar. You already do that enough for God and everybody." Lil planted a kiss in Larken's auburn hair.

A silver sedan turned onto Tradd Street, pulling up in front of The Ashby House. Lil jumped up from the sofa, folding the throw blanket she'd had draped across her lap and grabbing her book and journal.

"Shoo. Shoo!" Lil waived her arms at Larken, motioning her to move. "Your Momma thinks I'm tryin' to spy on her when I wait up." Lil smoothed out the creases on the sofa where she had been sitting. "I'd get up those stairs quick if I was you. See you in the morning."

Lil blew a quick kiss at Larken and grabbed her book. She scooted her feet slyly across the living room, down the hall, through the kitchen and out the back door, back to the carriage house.

Larken followed Lil's forewarning and quickly made her way up the stairs, reaching the top landing just as Bunny and Mr. Boca Raton opened the front door. Larken was relieved when she closed her bedroom door before she had to hear if there was a goodnight kiss involved or not.

After an unsightly encounter with Howard Holland in the west wing piazza during her freshman year of high school, Larken generally avoided the practice of wandering around the house on Bunny's date nights. The image of Howard's rather hairy, rotund body still haunted her thoughts and, since he had been the family's pharmacist, Larken suffered through multiple illnesses for the duration of high school without medicinal intervention.

Larken heard the ignition of Bunny's date's car turn over as she changed in to her pajamas. After the Howard Holland incident, Bunny was always discreet with men in the house, but still, Larken felt at ease knowing there was no one strange in her mother's bedroom for the night. The thought alone gave her goose bumps. She walked out of her bathroom, glancing at the note from Jackson that she'd placed on her desk and stubbing her toe into the doorway.

Shit.

She looked down at her toe, the same ill-fated one she'd dropped the knife on all those weeks ago. She hopped to the bed, leaning closer to inspect the damage. For the first time, she noticed that not even so much as a mark was left from the knife blade and consequent stitches. The skin was pink from hitting the door jam, but the phantom doctor had been right about not leaving any scars—he'd also been careful to not leave any traces of himself.

Larken didn't know why she kept thinking about him. More frustrating than thinking about him was trying to figure out why she couldn't *find* him.

She turned off the lights and wiggled into the covers. The rain outside had amplified again, hitting the windows in confused, varying installments of pelting drops and melodic sheets.

Larken thought about the letter to David, Jackson's note to her, Lil's admission of everyone knowing their secret. And then she thought of Dr. Miles and the scar he had promised not to leave. Then she realized in a strange, hopeless way that he had left one anyway. Men always do.

*

The next day, Larken woke up with a start. She felt guilty for avoiding Jackson and since everyone apparently knew about their past anyway and Lil seemed to think he just needed a familiar face, there was no need to play cat and mouse with him.

Larken went for a morning run, pretending to avoid Priss' house strictly for routing purposes and returned home just as Bart finished highlighting the classifieds. He quietly waited, watching Larken's face as she read over the day's selection. Larken let out a laugh when she got to the ad for "hot tar roofing supervisor" that he had not only highlighted, but also circled and starred with enthusiasm.

"I think that one's perfect for you actually," Bart said coolly, motioning to the ad. "I can picture it now—just what your mother always wanted for you."

"C'mon, Bart. Can't you find something we can *all* be happy with?" Larken pointed to the ceiling, indicating Bunny. "Don't they have any postings for 'socialite' or 'professional debutante' or 'serial bride'?"

Bart shrugged. "I'll see what I can do. Although… you'll be in the perfect place to interview for all of those positions on Wednesday night."

Larken gave Bart a puzzled look. "Which would be…?"

"The Sailor Ball. First Wednesday in May as always." Bart pretended not to know that Larken had completely forgotten about Bunny's favorite event of the year. Bunny would be crushed if she knew of her daughter's oversight.

"Oh *God.* You've got to be kidding me." Larken sat down at the table, deflated. "How bad would it be if I didn't go?" Larken tapped her fingernails on the table, considering her options of escape. She felt hives creeping up her neck at the thought of such a social setting.

Bart sipped at his coffee. "I won't dignify that question with a response."

"You're right… She'd murder me." Larken rolled her eyes. "Actually, that might not be so bad. If there's one thing I don't feel like doing it's going to a ball." Larken released an exasperated groan.

Except for Sylvia, who was so far into her own world that no one else existed, Larken had managed to avoid all of her childhood friends since returning home. She had countless messages from people welcoming her back and throwing in the "we are so, so sorry to hear what happened," but she couldn't bring herself to see any of them.

She was sure that The Sailor Ball would feel much like her Debutante Cotillion where she was the only girl without a father to present her for the formal introduction. And now she would be attending The Sailor Ball as a social pariah without even so much as a date.

"Well, you know," Bart suggested, "you could go all out and just really do it up—show everybody what they've been missing."

Larken wrinkled up her nose and laughed. Promoting anything garish was uncharacteristic of Bart.

"What's missing?" Bunny asked, walking into the kitchen hurriedly as she caught the last of Bart and Larken's conversation. She was fully dressed in a brightly printed tunic dress—the colossal diamond stud earrings that she wore when she was ready to take on the world weighed down her earlobes.

"I was just telling Bart that I'm missing a dress for tomorrow night." Larken plastered a smile on.

"Oh, don't worry—we have an appointment today at noon for you to try a few gowns that Raquel at the shop pulled. I'm more worried about you finding a date for tomorrow night than a dress. Hmmmm. What to do, what to do." Bunny pretended to think long and hard. She snapped her fingers together. "I got it. You could take *Jackson*. I know he doesn't have a date and you've both just come home. Why don't you show yourself friendly and—?"

"Momma. No." Larken cut her off abruptly.

"What? What'd I say?" Bunny looked shocked.

"The last thing I need is you playin' matchmaker."

Bunny shook her head in disbelief, still acting innocent. "I am *just* trying to help you. Can't two friends, two *childhood* friends get together and have a good time?" Bunny threw her hands up in the air. "I guess like everything else I do, it goes without thanks."

Bart silently exited the kitchen.

"That's not what I meant at all. I do appreciate what you do, or try to do, but Lil told me that you know about Jackson and me and… I don't want anybody getting their hopes up that it *means* anything now. Because it sure didn't *mean* anything then."

Bunny nodded in understanding. "I see. Well, nobody expects anything. God forbid. And nobody's judging. But you need to understand where I'm coming from. As your mother, I will always have your best interest in mind and when Jackson told me about you two—"

"Wait," Larken stopped her again, not quite sure she believed her ears. "*Jackson* told you?"

"Yes. Right after you moved to Seattle. He was home for a visit and I don't know, maybe he felt like he could finally fess up. Anyway, he made it sound very real. I have to remember that he was a little bit older than you were, maybe that made him more serious, but he sure didn't wave it off it like you do now." Bunny paused for effect. "I think that maybe there were real feelings there. At least there used to be."

Larken felt a sick, sinking feeling. It was always hard to tell with Jackson if he did things for spite or sincerity. They had sworn to never tell anyone, especially not their families about that winter break, but it seemed apparent yet again that only Larken was capable of keeping promises.

"Don't worry, though." Bunny rolled her eyes. "I'll make sure and mind my own business." She poured coffee into a travel thermos, dialed voicemail on her cell phone and headed toward the back door. "I'll be back just before noon to pick you up."

"Thank you," Larken called as Bunny shut the door. She wasn't sure if she'd heard her or not.

*

After Bunny left, Lil called the main house and asked Larken if she'd like to have breakfast with her. Larken showered quickly and threw on a sundress and flip-flops. The rain from the day before had released the usual humidity, so her hair was semi-cooperative and long, loose curls draped over her tan-lined shoulders.

Larken met Lil at the yellow Cadillac, top down and opera blasting. Lil wore a huge sunhat, large enough to cast shade over all of derby season, and white capri pants with a green silk top and a lightweight zebra print duster. Judging by her outfit, Larken knew exactly where they were going. Lil handed Larken a scarf to tie around her hair and the two were off, bound for a dockside breakfast at Boudreaux's.

The wind whipped at their faces while Lil hummed along with the opera and orchestrated the music with her hand. Larken held on to her scarf-covered hair, staring out contentedly as they ventured from the city and toward the Isle of Palms. Lil turned onto Palmetto Drive, continuing past all of the resorts and beach clubs until they reached the Wild Dunes on the tip of the island overlooking Dewees Inlet where Boudreaux's restaurant sat firmly established in waist-high bog growth.

The restaurant was in an old salt marsh house with open air porches on two separate levels. This close to the water there was a constant symphony of natural sounds and the distinct scent of mud sediments and Spartina grass that was comforting once a fondness for it was acquired.

Lil parked the car and climbed out excitedly, waiting for Larken to finish combing through her windblown hair. Martha, the proprietor of Boudreaux's, was Lil's friend from childhood. After Martha's husband Hester Boudreaux died, she sold their home on Rainbow Row and renovated the upstairs of the restaurant into an apartment. Their son Bobby took over the restaurant and Martha continued doing what she did best—entertaining the guests and making the restaurant feel like a second home. The Boudreaux's had a small fishing fleet and the family prided themselves on having a menu that changed with the daily catch.

"Well aren't you a sight for sore eyes," Martha called from the top deck. "What did you bring me?" She motioned at Lil's guest, squinting to see who it was.

Lil smiled widely. "It's my Larken!" Lil yelled up to her. "Can you believe it?"

Martha clapped her hands together and quickly made her way down the stairs and to the car. She hugged Lil quickly and ran over to Larken, pulling her in for a tight embrace.

Martha was a small, strong woman with boundless energy and short, almost boyishly-styled gray hair. Her skin was the color and texture of tanned leather, more evidence of her life near and on the water, but she was weathered elegantly and entirely charming.

"Do you realize that I have not seen you since your college graduation party?" Martha pulled away from Larken, holding onto her wrists. "You are absolutely stunning."

Larken smiled. "Thanks…it's been a while. Doesn't look like anything has changed out here though."

"Not one bit. Only thing that time has touched is me." Martha laughed. "Y'all come on in." She waved them enthusiastically toward the restaurant. "Bobby and the boys got back not twenty minutes ago with a beautiful catch."

Lil and Larken followed Martha up the stairs to the porch overlooking the marsh. An expansive dock that seemed to go for miles connected the shallow marsh to the deeper waters at the mouth of the estuary where the fishing boats shoved off from and returned to. A couple of small boats bobbed in the water as the fishermen busied themselves with putting away nets and crab cages.

Besides Larken and Lil, only a few other guests were busy drinking coffee, dining on bone china that Martha had collected from estate sales over the years and sitting at the mismatched walnut tables, distressed by constant use and exposure to the elements. Like the Lowcountry itself, Boudreaux's was a perfect mix of wild elegance and raw earth.

Martha made her rounds through the restaurant, greeting the locals by their first names while Larken and Lil sat watching the cranes lurking through the water, gigging the occasional helpless fish.

"When you were very young, no bigger than knee-high to a grasshopper, you said you wanted to live out here." Lil twinkled as she reminisced years past. "You said you were going to be a dolphin that the boats could never catch. You 'member that?"

"Mmm." Larken smiled. "And you told me you thought there was a fin growing on my back."

Lil laughed gently.

Larken thought that being there, soaking in the sounds and breathing in the salty, boggish air, that she knew precisely how Peter Pan must have felt each time he returned to Neverland. She felt so light and carefree there, suspended in time with Lil, transported to a much simpler time when nothing had gone wrong and her whole life was still a mystery. Much of her life was still a mystery, but the almighty firsts that you so look forward to when you are very young were spoiled, ruined by poor choices and bad experiences. None of that mattered now though. Sitting on the porch with Lil looking across the marshland where everything dwelled in harmony, Larken could have believed she was seven and keen to life again.

Martha brought out two shrimp and grits breakfasts, a Lowcountry classic and Lil's absolute favorite. Basketfuls of Boudreaux's home style bacon wrapped biscuits were brought out to the table until Larken and Lil were unfathomably stuffed.

Martha said her goodbyes to them after refusing Lil's money and playfully berating Bobby for bringing her the check in the first place.

Larken felt refreshed and reluctant to leave the bubble of heaven that she and Lil had been enveloped in. Lil didn't turn the opera back on once they were in the car—it paled in comparison to the organic concerto of nature they had been listening to.

Larken breathed in deeply as they crossed back over onto the mainland, exhausted from the sensory overload on Isle of Palms.

Until they pulled through the gate of The Ashby House at 11:59

a.m., Larken had forgotten about her appointment with Bunny and made a quick mental plea that her mood had improved significantly.

*

Bunny walked toward the car purposefully as Lil and Larken parked. She couldn't tell if the look on Bunny's face was out of irritability or from the sun being in her eyes, but Larken sensed that she was going to exhaust any guilt she felt entitled to anyway.

"Oh boy," Lil said as she watched Bunny stride forward. "She looks a little feisty. You ready?"

Larken smiled at Bunny through the windshield as she walked closer to the car. She did not smile back.

"Can you come with us?" Larken asked Lil. "I think I might need protecting." Larken kept the smile plastered on her face, not wanting to agitate Bunny further.

"Uh-uh. No need in us both bein' eatin' alive." Lil opened the door before Larken could plead.

"You were almost late," Bunny said curtly as Larken opened the passenger door.

"Good grief, it's two minutes away."

Lil gave Larken a quick look, reminding her to tread carefully on Bunny's tumultuous soil.

"Don't be difficult," Bunny said curtly. "If you're on time you're late." She pulled a pair of sunglasses from a case in her handbag and turned quickly on her heels, sashaying toward her car.

Larken mouthed the words "help" at Lil as she followed after Bunny.

"Have fun." Lil snickered. "And play nice, Bunny."

Bunny threw an arm up in the air at Lil, resembling an indifferent wave.

*

Bunny drove quickly to Delaney's Boutique—fidgeting with her phone the entire way to avoid conversation.

Larken was determined to not let anything muddle her mostly delightful morning and in true Bunny fashion, Larken knew she would put on a good show for the duration of their shopping trip. Larken people watched out the window as they approached the hustle of King Street, keeping her emotions as flexible as possible for the ensuing drama.

Bunny whipped her Lexus SC into the parking lot behind the shop and grabbed her handbag from the backseat.

"Let's get this show on the road."

Larken resisted the urge to snicker and instead smiled tightly.

Raquel, the store manager, met them at the door with enough enthusiasm to float a boat. She was probably Larken's age with reddish hair in a bob haircut and a curvaceous figure squeezed into a designer pencil skirt and vest. Larken peered to the back of the store where a rolling rack of cocktail dresses hung by the dressing room.

"Oh, just wait until you see what Raquel has pulled for you," Bunny said with flare. "It's all fabulous. Absolutely fabulous." The last of Bunny's words trailed off as she was drawn toward a display of costume jewelry like a moth to the flame.

Raquel stood with her hands clasped in front of her, a smile plastered on her face as she waited for Larken's attention.

"I think we've got just the thing for you," Raquel said, the words a bit rehearsed.

Larken smiled widely at the girl to compensate for the lack of excitement she felt. She knew it wasn't the girl's fault to assume she was as demanding as her mother.

Raquel walked Larken toward the rolling rack draped with luxurious fabrics and lavish embroidery in all cuts and colors.

"I'm guessing…size four?" Raquel asked.

"Oh, please," Bunny yelled from across the room, "most of those twos you pulled will swallow her alive. We have petite bones."

Larken looked at Raquel apologetically. "I think it probably depends on the dress…"

Raquel nodded in agreement and pulled a nude silk Alberta Ferretti and a red chiffon Valentino off the rack and held them up for Larken with an encouraging smile. "Let's start with these."

Larken walked into the dressing room behind Raquel. "Thank you," she said before closing the curtain.

The first dress wasn't off the hanger when Bunny flung the curtain back and handed Larken a glass of champagne and three more dresses—one plain black with spaghetti straps, a practically see-thru white strapless and a canary yellow Greek styled dress with ornate beading.

While Larken tried on the dresses, Bunny riffled through the hangers on the rack, directing Raquel on what would and wouldn't work and occasionally shouting, "Nope!"

Larken listened to Raquel's courteous responses to Bunny and hoped she worked on commission—she would earn every penny.

"Don't you need to find something to wear, too, Momma?"

Larken asked from the dressing room.

"Already got it. I'm wearing the silver Halston that I got for your wedding. I figured I shouldn't punish the dress for what happened." Bunny laughed heartlessly.

Larken stared into the mirror with the red Valentino half on. She felt limp. The reminder of her failure would weigh on forever it seemed, with no escape by distance or time.

"You remember it?" Bunny continued. "The one-shoulder silk number—I think I emailed you a picture of it… It's a stunna!"

Larken didn't want to respond and acknowledge the hurt, but supposed silence did the same thing anyway.

"Lark?" Bunny called.

Raquel excused herself to the back room to top off champagne glasses and avoid the obvious awkwardness.

"I'm sorry, Larken. I should have thought about how that would make you feel before I blurted it out. How awful of me."

Larken pulled the Valentino onto her shoulders before gliding the side zipper up.

"It's fine."

"No." Bunny's voice carried a rare tone of sorry. "No, it's not. It's not fine for me to just say or do whatever I want and expect you to deal with it." She sighed heavily. "I'm done tryin' to make you see everything my way."

Larken waited a moment before peeking her head out of the curtain. "Promise?"

Bunny rolled her eyes. "Swear. It's just hard seeing you, my own daughter, with every opportunity in the world not realize it and continually punish herself for things outta your control… Now get on out here and let me see you."

Larken reluctantly peeled the curtain of the dressing room back and stood stiffly in front of her mother.

"Well…it's something alright," Bunny said blinking hard at the lipstick red Valentino. "Reminds me of something one of the McAwful girls would wear."

Larken's eyes widened at the comparison. Bunny had a long-standing aversion of the "McAwful" girls' mother, Regina McAffrey, since childhood. Larken didn't find them that off-putting, but she knew it wasn't a compliment.

Raquel emerged from the back of the store with a bucket of ice and a freshly corked bottle of champagne. "Have we found any winners yet?" she asked hopefully.

"No, but we will." Bunny winked. "Never thought a Valentino would pale in comparison to anybody, but Lark's got him beat."

Larken looked at Raquel and shook her head in disagreement. "We don't think red is my color." She motioned to Bunny.

Fourteen dresses and four glasses of champagne later, Bunny asked Raquel if she could explore the store.

"I just feel like there's something here that we're missing," Bunny said as she placed her fingertips on her temple, channeling the fashion spirits. She shuffled through racks of clothes, not looking for anything as much as she was waiting for something to reach out and grab her.

After a few minutes, Raquel and Larken jumped at a shrill squeal from the back of the store.

"Larken!" Bunny yelled as she clip-clopped down the hallway towards the dressing room. "You will *never* believe what I found. Just *hangin'* there like a bat in a cave."

Raquel's eyes swelled as she tried to imagine what Bunny could have found that she hadn't seen.

Bunny reached the two girls and drew in a sharp, noisy breath for dramatic effect. "Are you ready for this?" She looked back and forth between Raquel, captivated by the mysterious discovery and Larken, unamused by Bunny's antics.

"I—have—found—a—vintage—Coco—Chanel—Haute Couture—gown. I can tell just by lookin' at it that it's the right size and everything. Look at it!" She held it up and spun it around on the hanger, her eyes twinkling with excitement.

Larken couldn't help but smile. From the strapless, sweetheart neckline all the way down to the stacked, knee-length hemline of the black lace fabric framed delicately into an hourglass shape, the dress was perfect.

"Now, what's the story with this dress, missy?" Bunny asked, turning to Raquel with a scrunched face. "Were you holdin' this back for someone else? Maybe Monroe Ludlow or Regina McAffrey?"

Larken was relieved that Bunny hadn't referred to them as "McAwful" again.

Raquel spat and sputtered before collecting her words. "No, not at all. I pulled everything I could for you. I saw it back there, but—I thought it just looked old."

Bunny scoffed. "Oh, my darling girl. This is the *essence* of vintage haute couture."

Larken took the dress from Bunny and disappeared into the

dressing room one more time. She stepped into the liquid fabric and pulled it up over her hips like it was a second skin of black lace. She turned in the mirror, admiring the definition in her legs that the dress' length complimented and for the first time in a long time, something felt right.

"Well?" Bunny's voice squeaked from outside of the curtain. "You gonna let me see it or what?"

Larken emerged from the dressing room and stood smiling in front of Bunny and Raquel. Even in flip-flops with windblown hair and make-up that had burned off in the sun hours ago, she felt a piece inside of her heal.

"Ohhhhhhh," Bunny hummed. "Ding. Ding. *Big* time winner, baby."

Larken nodded. "I think so, too."

"Well, you won't be dancin' alone long." Bunny winked encouragingly. "That's for sure."

"I won't be dancing alone at all," Larken said, admiring the dress in the mirror again. "I'll be dancing with Jackson Winslow."

CHAPTER SEVEN

Coco & Harry

The phone rang several times before Jackson answered.

"Hello?"

Larken grimaced in disappointment and defeat at the sound of his voice. The prospect of him not answering was enticing.

"Heyyyyyy. It's Larken." She sat on the edge of her bed in a tight ball, her knees pulled up to her chin. If she had waited any longer to call him, it would have been inappropriately late and as Bunny said, "suggestive."

Several seconds went by without any sound coming from the other end of the line.

"Jackson?" she asked. "You there?"

"Yeah—sorry," he responded. "I thought I was dreamin' for a second." Jackson paused again, drawing in a deep breath. I was startin' to think you were avoiding me."

Larken laughed nervously. "Don't know why you'd think that."

"What have you been up to?" Jackson asked.

"Oh. Ya know. This and that. I'm just making plans for the week and I guess The Sailor Ball is tomorrow? So, there's that… Are you going by the way? To The Sailor Ball?" She squeezed her eyes shut tight at the lack of subtlety and the rambling.

"Oh. Yeah," Jackson started slowly. "See, here's the thing—I *would* go, but I have a little problem." He paused, prompting Larken to ask why.

"K," she indulged him, guarded. "Which would be…?"

"Well, you know how it is with moving back to town recently and all and not really having any time to reacquaint myself with old friends, I find myself in a little bit of a situation without a soul to go with."

"Ohhh. Hmph. Well that's too bad," Larken said, faking empathy. She immediately recognized his underhanded tone and clinched her jaw.

"Yeah, well, I mean, I had hoped that an old friend or something would just *happen* to find herself in the same predicament and I could dust off the 'ol tux in time to go, but she hasn't, uh, she hasn't exactly offered." Jackson sighed heavily into the phone, a smile audibly curling his lips.

Larken held the phone out and glared at the receiver. She mentally reprimanded herself for thinking this would be a good idea. In no time in her life had anything having to do with Jackson Winslow been a good idea.

"Since when do you wait for anyone to ask you out?" Larken said curtly. "I thought you had more game than that."

"Guess not." Jackson laughed. "Especially with this particular girl. She's different. And 'sides—I get the feeling she's been avoiding me for one reason or another."

Larken pursed her lips together in defiance of giving into his game. In true Jackson fashion, he had turned something already uncomfortable into his own personal entertainment. She felt no choice but to return the favor, even if it meant she went alone to The Sailor Ball.

"Well, that's just too bad," Larken began. "I'm sure you'll get it all figured out though." Larken took in a deep, satisfied breath. "Hey, listen, I've got to run out and meet someone for drinks, but I just wanted to thank you for stopping by the other day. I got your note and, yes, absolutely, let's try and schedule something soon." She smiled wickedly as she waited for his response.

"Oh. Okay," Jackson said, sounding taken aback. "So. I guess I will—see you around?"

"Sure," Larken chirped. "Maybe tomorrow night. That is, if you can find someone to bring." She felt a tinge of guilt for being so cold, but quickly shrugged it off.

"You bet," Jackson said, trying to regain his position in the conversation.

"Have a good night," Larken said casually, hoping to sound rushed to get off the phone.

"Hey, Bird. Wait." Jackson nearly fumbled his words, scampering to salvage the conversation. "I didn't mean for that to sound so…conceited. I imagined it, you know, smoother when I rehearsed it. I've actually been meaning to ask if you wanted to go, ya know, with me, to The Sailor Ball."

"Oh yeah?" She was caught off-guard by his complete lack of

self-preservation.

"So do you want to?" Jackson asked. "Go with me?"

"Oh. I mean, sure. I could use a ride…" Larken bit her finger to hide a laugh. Jackson Winslow: forced to surrender.

"Okay… It's a date then." Jackson's voice was mischievous again, the shock of Larken's upper-hand wearing off. "I'll pick you up at seven."

"Know how to find the place?" Larken joked, flirtier than she expected. "I'll see you tomorrow."

Larken got off the phone and immediately tugged on a pair of galoshes and a rain slicker over her cashmere hoodie and yoga pants. Now in the midst of intense southern heat, an encounter with the relentless garden sprinklers that seemed purposefully programmed for her nightly entrance into the garden was eminent. As the rubber soles of her galoshes squeaked down the stairs, across the main level and out the back door, Larken smiled with delight as she made her way to Lil's for an irrigated night cap of chilled cucumber vodka and watermelon wedges.

*

The Ashby House was buzzing with activity by the time Larken returned from her morning run at seven thirty. Even for May, the weather was mild and a pleasant, coastal breeze swept through Charleston's cobblestone streets.

Larken was walking through the garden to say good morning to Lil when she spotted Bunny and Priss in extended chair poses with a yoga instructor that she didn't recognize.

"Hey, sugar," Bunny strained. "Be ready for hair and make-up at four o'clock, okay? Four—o'—clock."

Larken nodded once in resigned agreement. Upon waking, she had immediate reservations about going as Jackson's date and regretted their childish charade on the phone the night before.

Bunny and Priss transitioned into half-moon poses, maintaining the even breathing that only years of yoga could make possible. Iris the Havanese slept quietly in the shade on a pooch-sized yoga mat, stretching and opening one eye as the women stirred into another formation.

"Lark," Priss called, her face pointed toward the sky as her hair overwhelmed her shoulders, "Jackson is so excited about tonight. You just don't know how good this will be for him to get outta the house and have some fun. Finally! Poor sugar's been so down. Well, I'm sure you understand."

"Oh, good," Larken said, smiling politely as she continued walking toward the cottage house to check in with Lil.

"It'll be just like old times." Priss winked.

Larken stopped mid-stride and twirled slowly back around. "Did he say that? Did he say that it would be like old times?"

Priss and Bunny came down from their poses and looked at each other, clearly sensing that there was an issue. The yoga instructor remained in perfect pose, taking one look at the distracted women before resuming focus.

"Well, no sugar. I just meant that… it would be nice." Priss shrugged at Bunny implying a lack of explanation.

Larken drew in a quick breath and recomposed herself. "Oh. Okay." She forced a smile at Priss and once again began walking briskly toward the carriage house, shrugging off the embarrassment of overreacting.

Lil opened the front door before Larken could even knock. The heavenly aroma of cinnamon and sugar wafted out into the garden as Lil licked cream cheese icing off her fingers. "If you bake it, they will come," she sang. "Works every time." Lil held the plate out to Larken. "Cinnamon roll?"

"How did you know I was coming?" Larken asked with a smirk.

"Oh, sugar, please. You are in my soul." Lil batted her eyes at Larken. "Plus I saw you out talkin' to the spandex twins."

Larken took a hot cinnamon roll with a smile and caught dripping icing with her tongue.

Lil poured two cups of French press coffee, the only way she would prepare it since her return from Paris—and sat down at the kitchen table contentedly.

"So I'm going to The Sailor Ball with Jackson tonight," Larken blurted out in between bites.

"I heard," Lil said as she pinched off a piece of roll. "What changed your mind? I thought that was a shoe box you were gonna leave under the bed."

"Well, for one thing I thought it would make Momma happy if I listened to her for once and… I don't know. It might be kinda' fun? Plus, Priss said he's been kinda' down lately and—"

Lil held her hand up to interrupt. "No need to convince me. Old flames are the hottest kind."

"I wish you were going."

Lil protested the idea with a groan as she took a long sip of coffee. "Ohhhh, goodness. You and I both know there's already gonna be enough Ashby women there to burn the place down." Lil rolled her eyes as she watched Bunny outside in a bridge pose, cruelly taunting a batch of young landscapers who were helpless but to gawk.

"Who is she taking, anyway?" Larken asked, shaking her head as she watched the men stare drop-jawed at her mother.

"Oh, let's see," Lil replied thoughtfully. "Who's the one who wants to buy that land in the Lowcountry? The one that always smells like suntan lotion?"

Larken raised an eyebrow in recall. "Mr. Boca Raton?" Larken thought briefly about the land in the Lowcountry. She had heard of several different properties they owned over the years, but never any property in the Lowcountry.

"Yes. Yes, that's the one," Lil confirmed. "I guess we should start planning for a fall wedding soon. This will be their second or third date, I believe. You know for Bunny that usually means weddin' bells."

Larken fixed a tight smile across her face. "Are you sure she's related to us?"

"Oh, sugar. Believe you me… I've considered more than once about pulling some of her hair out for the DNA labs. But I know she's mine. She's Ashby through and through. Same as you."

The two women watched as Bunny gracefully stood up from her pose and turned around to bark at the landscapers, telling them to get back to work.

"I'm not sure how genetics work," Larken said as she watched the misled men return to shoveling mulch onto the flower beds, "but I'm pretty sure all of her genes skipped straight over Caroline and me. We're just whatever you are."

Lil laughed deeply and reached to pat the top of Larken's hand in thanks. "If genes skip a generation in this family, we better pray you are never blessed with a daughter."

*

The hours leading up to The Sailor Ball seemed to drip by like molasses in winter that afternoon. Until Caroline's little family arrived for Bunny's excessively unnecessary Sailor Ball pre-party at The Ashby House, Larken prepared mentally for her evening with Jackson by following the champagne from room to room. Bart, usually incapable of casting judgment, gave one solitary look of disapproval as Larken uncharacteristically asked the server pouring champagne to, "Fill 'er up."

As it turned out, Bunny was having one of her rare bad hair days, so Larken, not really caring what her hair looked like anyway, relinquished her scheduled appointment time and accepted Caroline's generous offer to play hair stylist for the evening.

By the time Sylvia Winslow arrived for the pre-party and ventured upstairs to Larken's room to say hello, Caroline was adding the finishing touches to a loosely curled up-do, sending Sam and his babysitter to the garden to pick a white peony for Larken's hair.

Sylvia seemed happier than her usual solemn self and wore a dress instead of the post courtroom attire that Larken had only seen her in since returning to Charleston.

"Talked to Jackson on my way over," Sylvia said as she leaned against the wall, smoothing the dress she was unaccustomed to wearing. "He sounds excited."

"Oh, yeah?" Larken asked, blowing off the comment and audibly gulping her champagne. "Ohhhh, Veuve Clicquot. I love this stuff." Larken tipped her glass up as far as it would go and popped her bottom lip out when she found it empty.

"Okay, Lark," Caroline said as she pulled the glass away. "I think that's probably enough of the bubbly for you then." Caroline's voice automatically adjusted to pre-school tone, something quite natural since Sam's arrival.

"Aww," Larken whined. "I was just starting to not feel nervous." She pulled her bathrobe tighter, sinking her face into the plush white terry fabric.

"Why are you nervous?" Sylvia patronized, her eyes darting at Caroline in disbelief. "First of all, you're going with *Jackson*, who's practically your *brother*."

Larken grimaced, realizing Sylvia must still be in the dark about her past with Jackson.

"And secondly," Sylvia continued dryly in her courtroom deliberation tone, "Not *one* person tonight won't wish they were an Ashby. The Sailor Ball is like y'alls Oscars." There was the slightest hint of envy in her tone.

Sam's raspy laugh distracted all of them as they heard him climbing the last flight of stairs, filling the third floor landing with instant, unbridled joy.

"This is this one wite hewer," Sam said in a failed whisper as he got closer to Larken's door. "This one is Lawk's room."

"Yes it is," Jackson's unmistakable voice said as he entered the doorway with Sam on his shoulders.

Larken snapped her head up in surprise, trying not to look as horrified as she was by Jackson's early arrival.

"I haven't been up here in a long time," Jackson said reminiscently looking around. He reached his arms up to pull Sam down, his white suit shirt pulling tight against his chest. "Hey, Bird."

"Oh," Sam whispered to him from the floor, tugging at his leg. "Hew name is Lawk."

"Hi." Larken nodded at Jackson and plunged a hand into her hair, readjusting a bobby-pin. She wanted to start the evening off right—only the amount of conversation called for, no flattery, no cheap banter. Jackson needed to know this was a companionable arrangement—just two old friends going to an event.

Jackson greeted Caroline with a kiss on the cheek and hugged his sister. He seemed as surprised as Larken was that Sylvia was wearing a dress.

Caroline took the fragrant peony from Sam's chubby fingers and placed it delicately in Larken's auburn curls. "Good job, little man. That's got to be the prettiest flower I've ever seen." She winked at Jackson in thanks for his assistance before turning around to make eyes at Larken.

"Nope," Sam disagreed, his eyebrows arched. "Jatson said that Lawk is the pwettiest flowwa."

Larken's cheeks flushed as she reached for a mirror to see the finished look, pretending to not to hear the conversation.

"Well, hey now," Jackson defended playfully, poking Sam's round belly. "So much for you being a secret keeper, huh brother?"

Sam giggled in rebellion as he ran and jumped onto Larken's bed, face-planting into the pillows with a growl.

Though Larken knew that Jackson was a parent, it was entirely surprising to see him acting paternal. His entire demeanor was different in the presence of this tiny person. Larken thought very quickly again about the daughter he had, wondering if he was the same with Avery as he was with Sam.

"Well, it looks like you girls have everything under control," Jackson said as he backed out of the way. "I like what you did there, Caroline." He pointed to the peony in Larken's hair. "How 'bout Sam-the-man and I wait for y'all outside?"

Sam's eyes got huge as he stood up on Larken's bed and began jumping wildly in agreement.

"Oh, Jackson, you don't have to do that," Caroline fussed. "Why don't you mingle and enjoy the party? We brought a babysitter for Sam and—."

Jackson interrupted her with a headshake. "I think Bunny commandeered the babysitter for an errand with Bart, and, it's not really my kinda' people downstairs anyway."

Caroline rolled her eyes in the reference to the house full of Bunny's hoity-toity friends.

"Well, if you insist," Caroline agreed. "It would just be for a little bit though—we are full steam ahead to bedtime."

She turned to face Sam in one liquid move, her expression changing from polite to stern without notice. "Young man," she started with her chin in the air, capturing all of the attention a three-year old could muster, "you know that I have spies. Everywhere. Spies. You behave for Mr. Jackson, you understand?"

Larken held back a smile as she watched Sam stare slack-jawed at Caroline, inarguably the most powerful woman in the world.

"Yes, ma'am," Sam answered, keeping perfect eye contact.

With his word, Caroline's face melted back to her usual charm and she nodded at Sam with a smile, permitting him to leave.

"We won't get into any trouble," Jackson promised. "Not with spies around anyway." He nodded at Sam seriously.

"Hey, I'll just be a minute, Jax," Larken said without realizing she hadn't called him that for years. "Unless you think bathrobes are the new in thing."

Jackson smiled on one side of his mouth. "Well, if anyone could pull it off, it'd be you."

Larken forced a tight smile. "Ha. Thanks." Her cheeks burned with embarrassment and alcohol.

Sylvia leaned her head back in disgust. "Oh, Jackson. Grow up."

"You're pretty, too, Sylvia," Jackson said, belittling her. He scooped Sam up and headed for the stairs. A shrill giggle ripped through the hallway as Jackson held him upside down with one hand, tickling his exposed belly with the other.

"Jatson," Sam said through a laugh, "pretend I'm invisible and you can't see me, k?"

What a good idea.

*

"Oh. My. Word, Larken. It's amazing." Caroline stood with her hand over her mouth at the black lace Coco Chanel dress that Bunny had found.

"You like it?" Larken asked with her nose scrunched. "It's not too much?"

"Too much? Yes. It's *completely* too much. It's perfect."

Caroline busied herself with the hem, automatically perfecting every detail. "You wearin' some of Momma's pearls or diamond pendant or what?"

"Well, I thought since my hair was up I'd wear those Harry Winston earrings. Ya know, keep it simple." Larken shrugged.

"Perfect," Caroline confirmed. "I'm gonna go tuck Sam into bed while you grab those. I think the combo on the safe is the same."

Larken walked barefooted in the direction of Bunny's bedroom as she heard Lil begin playing a piano rendition of *Night Ride and Sunrise* for the guests downstairs. Even though she pretended to hate the social requirements of being an Ashby, Lil was a natural at it and always enjoyed captivating everyone's attention. She supposed Bunny got that trait from Lil, only Bunny survived off it.

Bunny's suite was down the hallway on the other side of the house. Unsurprisingly, it was a grand place that Bunny renovated as a wedding present to Sailor. Sparing no dramatic detail, she had the roof line elevated on the south wing of the house so that the sleeping quarters overlooked a private living area and veranda, enclosed by a wall of trained ivy trellises.

Larken couldn't remember the last time that she had seen her mother's room. There was no secret as to why she retreated to it regularly with its airy palette of light grays and whites, delicate millwork and billowing curtains of Dupinoi silk framing full-length casement windows. Gold and crystal-framed pictures were placed perfectly near expensive European perfume bottles and monogrammed jewelry boxes. The room reflected Bunny perfectly— beautifully inviting and intimidating at the same time.

Larken moved towards Bunny's massive walk-in closet, the

automatic lights turning on as she opened the French doors. Bunny's safe was medium in size and full of every piece of jewelry anyone could ever wish for.

Larken entered the code, still the digits of Caroline's birthday and her birthday combined, and reached for a tray of earrings. The two-carat Harry Winston emerald-cut studs were placed perfectly between a pair of Canturi chandelier earrings and Graff yellow teardrops that Larken couldn't recall ever seeing Bunny wear before.

She locked the safe again and turned around to see a small portion of the closet dedicated to a few items of men's clothing. Some freshly laundered shirts and a suit hung on the rack, a pair of dress shoes and sneakers on the floor beneath them. On the table in the center of the closet sat a silver tray with a man's watch and ornate silver cuff links.

Bunny was famous for not being sentimental with things, so Larken knew the clothes couldn't have been from anyone in her past. She considered Lil's mention of a fall wedding and rolled her eyes. Mr. Boca Raton had infiltrated the family without anyone noticing.

Larken walked back to her bedroom and saw Caroline tiptoeing out of the playroom where she had put Sam to bed. The babysitter, Lauren, halfway listened as Caroline told her how to work the TV in the study, effectively releasing her from her duties for the evening.

"I'm pretty sure he's playing possum in there right now, but he should be out like a light in no time," Caroline told her.

Larken went back to her room to put the earrings in and grab her shoes. She had missed most of the pre-party, not on accident, and conveniently timed her arrival downstairs as the guests were departing for The Sailor Ball.

Caroline looked radiant in a red silk wrap dress that Aaron admired her in from the bottom of the stairs as she made her descent. A familiar laugh from the top landing broke their gaze and she looked back to see Sam in dinosaur pajamas, sneaking a peak.

Larken nodded at Caroline, agreeing to escort the escapee back to his room with a solitary smile.

"Come on, big guy," Larken said as she made her way back up to him on the second landing. She held her hand out and he jumped up from the floor to take it.

"Lawk," Sam asked yawning, "do I have to go back to bed?"

"Yeah, buddy. You do."

Sam sighed and rubbed his tiny hand on the top of hers. "But I'm all by myself in dewer." Larken squeezed her eyes shut so she wouldn't laugh. Maybe it was the way he couldn't say his R's or the fact that there was such a big person in such a small body, but Larken knew she never wanted to be Sam-less again.

"How about this?" Larken proposed. "When I come home tonight, in just a few hours, I'll check on you. And it'll be like a sleepover."

"Can Jatson come, too?" Sam asked innocently.

"No." Larken smiled at him. "He has his own house."

Larken tucked Sam back into bed and left a lamp on at his request. She wondered if anyone knew she slept with a light on sometimes, too.

After one last goodnight Eskimo kiss from Sam, Larken closed the door and made her way to the staircase, careful to walk on her tip-toes so her stilettos didn't click on the floor. She remembered being little and thinking that the sound of being left alone was so much worse than actually being left alone.

Jackson stood waiting for her on the third landing when she rounded the corner for the staircase. He waited propped with his legs crossed, chic and classic. Most of the house was empty now, only Priss and Bunny running aimlessly around reapplying lipstick and touching up their hair.

"Hey," Larken said with a succinct smile. After witnessing Jackson as a child-whisperer, she had to at least be civil. "Sorry it's taken me so long—been a while since I was Cinderella."

Jackson watched as she walked closer, taking in every inch of her.

"Wow," he said. "You look—stunning. I mean it. Wow." Jackson stood up straight and uncrossed his arms.

"Thank you," Larken said, dipping her face near her shoulder in embarrassment. "You look great, too. I like the suit—looks like you got all the dust off."

Jackson walked down the stairs behind Larken, a triumphant grin on his face.

"Bunny, come quick!" Priss shouted as she watched the pair make their way down. "There is an absolute vision in Chanel on the staircase."

Bunny sashayed over, the silver Halston plunging deeply to reveal perfect, plastic cleavage—its material wrapping around her yoga-toned body like a glove.

She gasped dramatically at the sight of Larken. "Amazing." Bunny smiled proudly. "It almost hurts to look at you. You're *that*

122

pretty."

Priss nodded in agreement. "You two are off the charts beautiful," she said pointing to Jackson and Larken. "Better go into the party one at a time so you don't kill anybody." She threw her head back and laughed, her massive hair waving around her.

Larken's cheeks were fully engulfed in bright pink now. "Thank you," she said looking at everyone individually. "It's the dress. Oh, and the earrings. It's hard to look bad when Coco and Harry are involved." Larken reached up to her ears, the weight of the earrings already pulling at her ear lobes.

Bunny shot Larken a warning look when she realized she had her earrings on. "Anything happens to those and—well, just don't let anything happen to 'em, k?"

Lil walked up with a martini glass, eating olives off the stir-stick. She patted Larken on the hip with her free hand, winking at her in approval then holding up the okay sign with her fingers. "Well, go. Get!" she said, shooing them all away with her hand. "It's already half-past."

Jackson complimented Priss on her classic black dress before excusing himself to fetch the valet. She beamed with pride, her eyes going misty after he walked out the door.

Bunny waved Priss and Hank off, telling them she'd see them there.

"Larken," Bunny said, catching her just before she headed outside. "I need a favor if you don't mind."

Larken nodded, waiting to hear what Bunny wanted before giving verbal acceptance.

"Will you introduce me tonight before I give the annual

speech? It would be such an honor if you did. Everyone likes to know where their money goes for these benefits, you know."

An instant knot formed in Larken's belly. She felt the blood rush from her face, quickly replacing the pink cheeks for pale white ones. "What…what do you want me to say? Like, just your name or— I mean, what do I say?" Larken wrung her hands together in anticipation. She grabbed an almost full glass of champagne from a nearby credenza and drained it.

"Well don't flip out on me," Bunny gawked. "Hopefully you can find a few *entertaining* and *charming* things to say about your own mother." She smiled widely. "Won't you do this for me? Please?"

"Of course," Larken agreed, swallowing hard.

"Jewels on your crown." Bunny clapped her hands together. "It will be great PR for the family, too. No one has seen you in a while and there are just so many questions surrounding…" Bunny leaned in closer, "…the engagement."

Larken let out a deflated sigh.

Of course.

Mr. Boca Raton opened the front door, his white teeth lighting up the room. "I'm ready when you are, madam," he started, winking at Bunny.

"JD," Bunny greeted him, her voice sickly sweet, "I don't believe you've met my baby. This is little Larken."

JD slid across the floor like he was in a Broadway show, reaching for Larken's hand and kissing it. He let his lips linger a fraction of a second too long, giving Larken an immediate chill. "It is truly my pleasure to meet you," he said, his forehead line free and unmoving. "You are the spitting image of your gorgeous mother." Mr.

Boca Raton made big eyes at Bunny like he could devour her. "More like sisters I'd say."

Larken let out an empty laugh and forced a tight smile. "Charmed."

"Isn't he something, Lark?" Bunny patted her hand on his chest and gazed up at him.

"He's something all right," Larken agreed.

Bunny darted her eyes at her in warning.

Larken walked with Bunny and Mr. Boca Raton outside. He had a driver waiting curb side for them by a flashy Bentley. Bunny climbed in the car giggling while Mr. Boca Raton popped open a bottle of champagne for their ride to the yacht club.

Jackson's car was next in line—a freshly washed baltic blue Range Rover with Alabama tags. It wasn't at all what Larken would have pictured him driving, but probably came in handy with a child in the picture.

He got out to open her door and walked informally back to the driver's side. The entire car smelled like him—a mix of musk and mandarin engrained into the sand leather seats.

Jackson opened the driver's side door and took his jacket off, laying it across the back seat on top of a couple of Disney princess movies and a pink bejeweled tiara. Larken smiled when she thought about how different his life had become.

"Ready?" Jackson asked, his brown eyes liquefying as the car's interior light faded off.

"Nope," Larken said matter-of-factly. "But I'm goin' anyway."

"Yeah. Story of my life." Jackson smirked.

"I always thought you loved going to these kinds of things," Larken questioned.

"Me? Naw. I go for the same reason you go." He gave Larken a look, implying their mothers. "Though... I guess we're grown-ups now and could probably say no."

"Hah. Are we grown-ups?" Larken asked with an eyebrow raised, the last glass of champagne suddenly finding its way to her head. "I mean. We both live at home. I don't have a job. Or a prospect of a job. I haven't reconnected with my friends here because I don't want anyone to ask questions." She stopped after that, realizing she had already said too much.

"Okay, then," Jackson humored her. "I'll be the grown-up. I'm *staying*, not living with my mother. And I own my own company— I do pretty damn good actually, and I also have a kid. I'd say that qualifies me as an adult."

"Sure." Larken nodded. "We're both adults. But are you a grown-up? Big difference."

Jackson shrugged. "Well then, I guess that's debatable."

CHAPTER EIGHT

The Sailor Ball

They drove in silence for several miles before Jackson opened the sunroof. The evening was gorgeous and warm, only a kiss of chill from the moving air. As they got closer to the yacht club, the full moon reflected off the Ashley River and created a golden glow even though the sun had been down for over an hour.

It was this time during the evening when all of nature relaxed, releasing fragrances that the daylight absorbed before they could be consumed by the senses. As they drove closer to the river, the typical sounds of a susurrus southern summer embraced them. Bogish and sweet air swirled together as the dark, fresh water of the river flowed resolutely toward Charleston Harbor to weave with the salt in the Atlantic.

The distant glow of the yacht club became a bright beacon once Jackson drove around the last curve in the road. A massive white tent was set-up before the dock began its dark passage to the water.

Larken took in a deep breath as Jackson stopped the car beside the valet station. Bunny arrived just a couple of cars ahead of them and was already walking into the party, Mr. Boca Raton on one hand and a glass of champagne in the other. She glided gracefully into the tent, disappearing in a sea of people as she gave air kisses and waved coolly.

A slight man, probably just a teenager, opened Larken's door as she swung a leg out, readjusting the peony in her hair.

"Wow," the valet said as Larken stood up and smoothed her dress. "Have a wonderful evening."

As Larken took a few steps away from the car, the valet stood still, looking at her. She felt uncomfortable yet flattered at the same time, suddenly aware of how tight the dress was on her body, showing every detail of her subtle curves. She reached again to secure the peony and smiled at him, more out of embarrassment than gratitude.

Jackson walked around the back of the car as it drove away, slipping an arm into his suit jacket and transforming into a striking creation as he joined Larken at the tent's prominent entrance. Jackson never looked like he was trying with his attire—he was just nonchalantly timeless.

The Sailor Ball was well underway as they entered the tent. A big band playing 1940's music filled the air with sophisticated elegance and charm. People lined up around a silent auction to bid on jewelry and wine packages while servers offered appetizers and flowery cocktails. The dance floor was packed with women wearing beautiful dresses and men in tuxedos spinning them around, laughing.

Larken felt overwhelmed as she walked through the crowd. Jackson was two steps behind her as she found their table, front and center of the dance floor. Her place card was beside Mr. Boca Raton's name, a simple oversight that she was certain hadn't been intentional.

She paused for only a second before swapping her card with Aaron's name, apologized to him under her breath with a scowl.

"How about a drink?" Jackson asked.

Larken nodded her head with an emphatic yes. "I'll go with you."

They walked back through the crowd toward one of the bars—Jackson moving in quickly when the line died down enough to walk directly up to order.

"What'll it be?" the bartender asked. His friendly, set smile implied mere toleration for his post.

"Champagne for the pretty lady," Jackson said with confidence. "And bourbon with a splash of mineral water for me. Basil Hayden, if you've got it."

The bartender poured Larken's champagne and placed it on the bar top, its golden bubbles eagerly rushing to the top. Jackson reached for the glass and leaned to hand it to Larken, placing his hand on the low of her back.

Larken took a long sip as Jackson's drink was being mixed. Caroline was across from them, talking to a friend of hers from high school. Caroline pointed out Larken to her and she waved courteously.

"Shall we?" Jackson asked as he gently stirred his drink.

Larken sighed. She knew this was part of it, but mingling in this crowd seemed overwhelming. She felt self-centered for thinking everyone would care so much about her. She tried convincing herself that the people there didn't even know who she was. She took a burning, effervescent gulp of champagne.

As if sensing Larken's uncertainty, Jackson came to her side, walking strongly beside her, seemingly joined at the hip. He placed his hand on the small of her back again, this time escorting her into the crowd.

Larken considered the irony of Jackson Winslow being her only friend in a place like this and let out a muted giggle. She couldn't relax into his touch, but he didn't seem to notice. He kept a steady hand on her, almost as though he was supporting her frame from collapsing.

"Larken?" a high-pitched voice called, its overwhelming southern drawl gaining Larken's full attention. "I cannot believe it."

Larken looked up to find Mitsy Lancaster standing with her arms outstretched and mouth wide open in awe. Mitsy was the single-most annoying person in Charleston. She was a towering figure with a large mouth, flat, mousy hair and had been responsible for spreading more rumors at St. Cecelia Academy than her own mother. Bunny said their family was flamboyant because they were overcompensating for being "new money" and since Mitsy's mother was Canadian, Bunny also blamed their unfortunate lack of finesse on the ill-fated fact that, were they not only void of southern heritage, but they were not even American.

When Larken signed up for Facebook years earlier, the first person that had been suggested to her was Mitsy Lancaster. She deleted her account immediately and swore off social media entirely.

"Sweetie, I thought you died," Mitsy said dramatically as she hugged Larken loosely, patting her back with large, cold fingers. "I swear, it's so good to see you. Heard you were back in town, but I guess we've just missed each other at the spring parties." Mitsy adjusted one of the three gaudy cocktail rings on her martini holding hand. "I thought for sure you'd join us at Junior League once you got back."

Larken laughed apprehensively.

Mitsy's eyes left Larken's face to see Jackson. She unconsciously licked her lips and shifted her glance between Jackson and Larken, begging for an introduction.

"Oh. Mitsy," Larken obliged her, "this is Jackson Winslow. He's an old childhood friend."

Jackson reached out his hand to her in formality and nodded with a tight smile.

"Well, he doesn't look old to me," Mitsy said, batting her eyes at Jackson and laughing so that her big teeth were fully exposed.

Jackson backed up a little.

"Mitsy and I," Larken said to Jackson, a sense of fake sincerity in her voice, "went to school together, K through 12, then to finishing school and finally, our Debutante Cotillion."

Jackson raised his eyebrows, pretending to be intrigued. "Ahhh, very nice."

"So," Mitsy started again loudly, "I heard you...had a little man trouble in Seattle." She gave Larken a sympathetic pat on the hand. "I just want you to know that I'm here for you if need anything."

"Oh, thank you," Larken said. "I'm actually great." Larken cringed at the obvious lie, but quickly reminded herself it was necessary.

Jackson grabbed another champagne glass from a serving tray passing by, fluidly replacing it with the empty one in Larken's hand.

"Hey, Larken, we better get our last bid in," Jackson interrupted them, pretend anxiety woven in his tone. "Ready?"

"Oh, that's right," Larken said, placing her hand on her cheek for emphasis. "So sorry to cut this little reunion short."

"Ohhh," Mitsy whined. "Well maybe we can talk more later?" She waved at them as they hurried off, her mouth gaped open awkwardly. "I'll look for you"

Jackson grabbed Larken's hand and led her toward the silent auction area of the tent. She turned up the champagne glass and stepped quickly to keep up.

Larken wriggled free of Jackson's hand and walked around the table, noticing Bunny's name—in Bart's handwriting—was the first on all of the large item bids: a crystal salad bowl from Tiffany & Co., a coastal scene painted by a local artist, a hideous diamond pendant.

Larken stopped at a Kate Spade clutch, writing her name down as the only bidder. Jackson was across the table adding his name to a picnic package from a local caterer, a group of women standing dangerously close to inspect his offer. One woman, presumably the previous high-bidder, flapped her arms in defeat and stomped off.

Jackson looked up at Larken with a smile on his face and motioned at the woman. "What'd I do?" he asked deviously.

Larken rolled her eyes and walked around to the other side of the table to see that he had broken the unspoken rule of silent-auctions by grossly outbidding everyone else. She turned around to find no one babysitting their precious bids anymore.

"You know that a picnic doesn't cost *that* much, right?" Larken asked, her speech slightly slower than usual.

"I wanted it." Jackson shrugged.

Larken finished her champagne and looked around the room.

"What?" Jackson asked, pretending not to see the virtue missing in his actions. "Is it wrong to make sure you get what you want?"

"If it means you are inconsiderate of the rules, then yes," Larken responded. She wasn't sure why she was surprised. Jackson, after all, had never followed the rules.

"Awww, come on, Bird," Jackson sidled up to her. "Don't make me feel bad. I'm just havin' a little fun. 'Sides, it all goes to a good cause."

Jackson stood so close to her that their hands brushed every time she moved. A tray of champagne floated by as Larken grabbed another glass.

"And I did it for you anyway," Jackson said, his eyes insinuating more than the auction items.

Larken looked up at him, her head floating in champagne. "Hmmm. Picnics with cheaters isn't a habit of mine."

"Oh, but I think it is." Jackson winked at her. "I seem to recall one rather *tasty* picnic with present company some years back."

Larken's face flooded with heat at the recall of their riverbank picnic on New Year's Day before he left for Auburn. She remembered it was cold and overcast that day, the warmth of Jackson's body on hers the only protection from the chilled, brackish air. They had been desperate to be alone—the seclusion of the riverbank a welcome one.

"You alright?" Jackson asked, leaning towards her face to break the daze she had been in for more than a few seconds.

She nodded yes, still starring off into the party as she recalled other details from the day of the picnic.

"I'm thinkin' that's probably enough champagne for you then," Jackson whispered. He took the mostly empty glass from her hand, finally breaking her stare.

Bart appeared like smoke in the crowd, dressed sharply in black and smoothly weaving his way through the sea of people.

"Ah. Just who I was looking for," Bart said as he approached Larken. "Your mother wanted me to let you know that you're on after the next song."

"On for what?" Jackson asked.

Larken took in a nervous drag of air, rubbing her palms together in anticipation.

"Bunny has asked Larken to introduce her prior to her speech this evening," Bart replied with a smile.

Jackson's eyed widened. "Oh, no, no, no. I *really* don't think that's a good idea." He leaned in to Bart. "She's had *quite* a few."

Bart turned to Larken without expression. "Are you prepared to make the introduction or should I make other arrangements?"

Larken paused for a second in consideration. "No need. I'm perfectly capable." Hiccup. "It's just a quick introduction anyway." Hiccup.

Jackson pressed his lips together and nodded once in acknowledgement at Bart. "Well, can't argue with that logic."

"Great, then," Bart confirmed. "No doubt you'll wow them all." He walked away as the cue song started.

Jackson and Larken stood in silence as the song played. Her heart pounded louder with each beat until it turned to ringing in her ears. She didn't ever want the song to end.

"You sure about this?" Jackson asked. He rubbed at his jaw line, obviously sharing in her anxiety as another round of hiccups shook her body.

Larken rolled her eyes, faking confidence. "Of course. Don't be silly." She slapped at his arm. "Why are you being so silly?"

Jackson laughed dryly. "Oh, I'm being *silly* am I?"

Larken felt the bottom of her stomach drop as the bandleader motioned the song's end to the orchestra.

She started walking toward the stage, smoothing her dress and repositioning the peony one more time. The last note of the song held out, dangling in the air as she reached the stairs to the left of the stage. The bandleader nodded at her, inviting her to the podium. She took each stair slowly, trying to steady both her breathing and her spinning head. Another hiccup.

The entire tent fell silent at the lack of music for the first time in two hours. All eyes focused on the girl on stage, many people taking their seats for the first time and giving their full, undivided attention. A tray of food crashed in the back of the tent.

Larken swallowed hard before putting on a gloriously fake smile. She was relieved when she spotted Caroline and Aaron in the back. Caroline was smiling encouragingly, giving a subtle thumbs-up.

Jackson stood with his head tilted and eyebrows furrowed. His arms were crossed as he watched Larken begin.

"Hel—Hello," Larken said into the microphone, feedback squealing out of the speakers. "Hi. I'm Larken Devereaux. I am the, um, proud daughter of Bunny Ashby, whom most of you know, and I have the honor of introducing her this evening." Customary golf claps filled the tent with a dull roar for a few seconds.

Larken cleared her throat and nervously pushed the peony further into her hair. She immediately heard the voice of her cotillion etiquette coach saying, "When speaking in public, speak-up, speak with confidence and under no circumstance are you to use filler words." Larken remembered that she had also mentioned something about taking notes to the podium and not ever drinking alcohol, but maybe the rules had changed now that she was older.

"As many of you know," she continued, "my mother's husband, well, *one* of my mother's husbands..." *Oh shit.* You could have heard a pin drop before the entire tent surged with laughter at Bunny's well known marital history.

"Jesse Vasser," Larken soldiered on, but no one heard her through the roar of laughter. She looked up to see Bunny sitting cross-legged and expressionless, the color draining from her face as the pandemonium continued. Priss sat beside Bunny, her hand covering her mouth in horror.

Larken felt the heat of immortal embarrassment pricking her cheeks. Her head swirled with champagne. *This is salvageable. Get it together. Shit. Fuck. Shit. Get it together.*

Caroline gripped Aaron's hand until both of their knuckles turned white. Larken could see that she was holding her breath, wincing in embarrassment for both her sister and her mother.

Mitsy Lancaster sat front and center, her mouth wide open, her chinless face scrunched in glorious entertainment at Larken's expense.

Larken scanned the room with frantic eyes, looking for a friendly face. She stopped looking when she saw Jackson. He nodded once and mouthed the words, "It's okay." He smiled at her, urging her to continue.

The laughter died down and Larken cleared her throat again. Her mouth was dry.

"Jesse Vasser was—he was a wonderful man whom we lost to cancer a few years ago." Larken looked at Bunny who sat with slit eyes, looking either ready to hide or pounce. "And because of my mother's dedication to cancer research and her ability to bring a remarkable group of well-funded people together, The Sailor Ball is making a marked difference in the fight against cancer for generations to come." Larken watched Bunny's face soften. "So, please join me in welcoming my mother and founder of The Sailor Ball, Bunny Ashby."

Larken looked to see Caroline clutching her chest, relieved it was over.

Bunny stood from her chair and acknowledged everyone with a nod as applause rang out. Priss hastily clapped and rubbed Bunny's back as she walked confidently up to the podium, waving like the Queen of England the whole way.

"Well," Bunny started with a tight smile and almond-shaped eyes. "Thank you all for being here and especially to my *precious* daughter, Larken for that—well, *charming* introduction." She nodded at Larken with her eyebrows raised, excusing her to leave the stage before she could embarrass her further. "Thank you, honey."

Larken didn't hear her mother's address once the relief of leaving the stage hit her. Her head swirled rapidly from the rush of blood and alcohol and she looked for the handrail to support herself. She was comforted to see Jackson waiting at the end of the platform, his hand extended to guide her down the stairs.

"Well, that's one way to do it." He smiled as he helped her off the last stair. "You sure do leave an impression, Larken Devereaux."

Larken was too upset to acknowledge the compliment, if that's what it was. Tears pricked at her eyes.

"Oh, come on." Jackson squeezed her hand. "Nobody's gonna remember this tomorrow. Hell, half of 'em don't remember it now."

Larken hoped he was right, but in the freshness of the moment all she could think about was running away and hiding from herself.

Mitsy stood up from her table and tip-toed away from Bunny's speech as gracefully as a gorilla. She had her eyes focused on Larken, her mouth gaped open in an unsettling smile.

"Come on," Jackson said, tugging at Larken to speed up. "You can thank me later."

"Thank you for what?" Larken asked confused, following him with the composure of a rag doll.

Jackson rounded the corner of the tent and headed through a breezeway connecting the tent to the catering kitchen. Larken looked around apologetically as they passed servers with trays of food, nearly running into one of them before Jackson darted out a side door and into the open air.

Applause filled the distant tent, followed by a murmur of voices.

Larken continued to follow Jackson—over a ramp leading to another walkway that finally became water-side. They seemed miles away from the party now, the band playing mellow dinner music. Lights from the tent reflected off the water, allowing just enough light to see a smaller building with boats docked outside.

Jackson let go of Larken's hand as they walked toward the small boathouse. It was a beautiful structure with a cabana overlooking the water. Larken could tell that it was for the serious boater, not like the main building of the yacht club reserved for soirees and weddings. Jackson sat down on a wicker sofa and stared out at the water, gentle waves licking up on the sides of the well-maintained boats. He leaned back with his hands behind his head and his legs outstretched.

"I used to come here with my dad when I was younger," Jackson said. He smiled at the memory. "Almost forgot it was even here."

Larken plopped down on the seat beside him, sighing in relief to be away from the party. "Well, I'm glad you remembered it tonight. You did everyone a favor by pulling me out of there."

"Nah," Jackson smiled, looking her over. "I did myself a favor."

Larken was quiet as she felt Jackson's eyes on her. She had had too much to drink to remind him that they were only friends, if even that. It was hard with someone like Jackson, always playing defense. Larken couldn't tell when he was being sincere or just flattering her for the sake of admiration.

"Larken," Jackson said as he leaned in closer to her, the sound of him saying her name bringing a wave of sobriety. His cologne had intensified since they'd been outside in the humidity. "I want you to know—."

"Jackson, don't," Larken said, stopping his words before he could say too much. She turned her face away from him.

"God, don't do that," Jackson said, more sincerely than

Larken had ever heard him sound.

"Do what?" Larken turned around to him again, alarmed.

"Look at me like you haven't known me all your life."

"Well what do you want me to do?" Larken asked. "You come chargin' back after seven years—no calls, no letters, no visits, and want me to pretend like we have this unstained history?"

Jackson looked hurt.

"No," Larken continued. "I know what you want. You want what you always want. You want what you can't have."

"I wish you knew how much that was true." Jackson stood up and ran a hand through his hair in angst.

Larken watched him, startled by his uncharacteristically disheveled behavior.

"What in the hell is that supposed to mean?" Larken asked.

"The only thing I've ever wanted and couldn't have was you, Bird."

"You have a funny way of showing it," Larken hissed. "You *had* me. If anybody ever had somebody, you had me. But you didn't *want* me once you had me. Remember?" Larken huffed. "And don't do yourself any favors by pretending you never get your way because you had your way—with me! You know I loved you? And then you left! You said you'd come back after graduation. You said you wanted to be with me. But why? Why did you say all those things when you already had someone else?" A single tear rolled down Larken's face. Until that moment she hadn't admitted to anyone, not even herself how much she had been hurt by him. "No. Don't answer that. It doesn't matter."

Jackson looked at her earnestly, wiping away the tear that gave her resolve away. "It *does* matter, Lark. It matters because you don't know the whole story. That's what I'm trying to tell you... I wanted to tell you so many times, but I had to be fair to you."

"By completely shutting me out of your life."

"I didn't want to," Jackson plead, "but it was the only way I knew how to not make myself crazy. He sat back down beside her. "I was so sure about us. After that Christmas break we spent together—"

"You don't have to do this, Jackson," Larken interrupted him. "Don't dig up something that got buried a long time ago."

"It's not buried for me," Jackson said, his eyes sincere. "And you need to know." He waited for her to acknowledge him before starting again. "I'd been dating Kayla for a few months, and it was okay, but I had planned to break it off with her—even before that Christmas." Larken watched Jackson's face drop as he spoke. "Anyway, when I got back to school, she told me she was pregnant."

Larken nodded, acknowledging that he was talking about Avery and finally interested in hearing what he had to say.

"I knew I couldn't come back here and see you," Jackson continued, "it was just too hard."

"Too hard for who?"

"Too hard for me," Jackson answered her quickly. The recall of it all made him seem frustrated.

"Why are you tellin' me this now?"

"I gave it my best with Kayla," Jackson said absolutely. "And I know it's selfish, but I'm never gonna love her how she wants me to. Not like—," he cut himself short. "I love Avery more than anything, though." He smiled when he thought about his daughter. "And the truth is, Bird… I've held out hope for me and you all this time."

Of all the thoughts she could have had, Larken imagined the betrayal Kayla must be feeling. Her own raw memory of being left by David surged through her again and she suddenly found herself empathizing with the stranger that she was somehow connected to through Jackson.

Jackson looked at Larken with pain in his eyes. "Larken, I'm not asking for the past to be undone or for you to forgive me. I can't tell you how hard it was to stay away… I know I've hurt a lot of people, but it's you I regret hurting the most. You deserved better than that. Still do." Jackson balled his fist up. "I can make it up to you. I *need* to make it up to you."

Larken stared at the water in silence, numbed by champagne and Jackson's admission. A warm breeze blew off the dock, bringing with it the undeniable smell and heaviness of rain. The breeze blew Larken's eyes closed and softly whipped her hair back away from her face. She breathed in and released a sigh.

"Are you gonna say anything?" Jackson asked in a whisper. His cologne radiated off his neck in the warm, humid air. Larken slowly opened her eyes while she breathed it in.

He leaned closer to her until his forehead was pressed against her cheek. The warmth of his breath on her face sent a chill down her core and back up again. "Say you hate me. Say you love me. Say you don't wanna see my face again or ask me to never leave. I've waited so long to tell you how I feel. Just say *somethin'.*"

Larken tried to smile, but tears pricked her eyes instead. "I'm sorry."

"No," Jackson said, shaking his head. "Don't say that. Don't be sorry. I'm the one that's sorry."

Jackson pulled her chin to his face and looked in her tear-filled eyes as if he was struggling with something in his own mind, something he had battled for years without closure.

Then he kissed her, placing his lips so softly to hers that she felt the heat of his mouth before she felt the pressure of them.

Tears rolled down Larken's face as she kissed him back, letting her body almost collapse next to him. Jackson wrapped his arms around her bare shoulders and pulled her close to him.

"I've wanted to do that for a long, long time," he said as he kissed the top of her head, her hair still scented with wilted peony.

Larken sat with her head planted firmly against Jackson's chest—partly so that he wouldn't kiss her again and partly so she wouldn't have to say anything. She listened to his heart beat steadily and, even though it had been years, it was a familiar, comforting sound. It felt good. Too good.

Two hours passed as they sat on the cabana of the boathouse. Larken didn't pull her hand away when Jackson reached for it and in return he didn't make her talk about anything uncomfortable. They watched the storm finally roll through—grumbling with thunder as rain fell in sheets across the water. Jackson kept his arm around Larken's shoulder, leaning down to smell the wilted peony in her hair.

The orchestra had been replaced by contemporary jazz playing over the sound system and the rain died down to a sporadic drizzle—leaving behind the earthy scent of soaked ground. In the distance, lightning illuminated the water outside the harbor, warning of more serious weather to come. Larken stirred under Jackson's arm, sensing the crowd leaving and the late hour.

Jackson squeezed her arm. "You ready, Bird?"

Not at all.

*

The champagne left Larken's head dizzy with its bubbly aftermath. Jackson helped her up and they walked silently back to the main tent, releasing his grip when the danger of her slipping on wet boardwalk had passed.

Larken hid in the shadow of the tent's foyer while Jackson paid for and collected his auction items. She watched as two ambitious women observed him, discreetly straining to look for a wedding band or evidence of a lingering girlfriend. The scene reminded Larken of a last-call at a bar and the frenzy of drunk, lonely people searching for a partner in desperation.

Jackson and Larken emerged to find the crowd obnoxiously loud, laughing and schmoozing as they waited for out of breath valets to bring their cars around.

Jackson gave the valet his ticket along with a ten dollar bill and arranged to fetch his own car. The exhausted boy tossed Jackson his keys before he set off robotically in a liquid sea of dark metal.

Larken stood propped against a tent pole, squinting from the bright glow of the party lights. She thought about the unexpected evening with Jackson, suddenly feeling nervous about the future and what would change with the morning, as all things do. She cringed thinking about the kiss and how much she'd liked it. *So stupid. You never learn.*

Larken tossed a polite wave to the valet who had admired her earlier. He distractedly tripped over the curb before jogging off for another vehicle.

The deep growl of a serious engine came revving up to the tent's entrance. With the high-pitched squeak of the brakes, a valet brought a mud-covered vintage Ford Bronco to a halt and hopped out, proud to have delivered the black beast with such manly gallantry. The truck idled with a rhythmic, throaty purr, exhaust billowing out. Larken noticed the bright-red hydraulics that peaked from under the body of the truck like a garter-belt and the "I'd Rather be Giggin Frogs" bumper sticker that had nearly peeled off, evidence of obvious rough and tumble use.

"That's quite the ride you've got there," the valet admired as he tossed the keys to the owner.

Too many appalled guests blocked Larken's view of the driver. She leaned forward, tilting her head to catch a glimpse of the person so unconcerned with appearances that they would bring a mud-covered Bronco to a society event frequented by Bentleys, Mercedes and Porsches.

"Yeah, ain't she something?" a man's voice boomed. "A '74 Rock Crawler. Been a work in progress since I got her, but we have a good time."

Larken strained, recognizing the profile of the driver's face as the corresponding voice conjured her memory. Dr. Miles stood basking in the party lights, his sun-drenched skin just as luminous as it had been in the artificial fluorescent lighting of the hospital when they first met all those weeks ago.

Larken froze, her heart beating loudly in her ears. She moved forward quickly, not thinking about what she would say once she got to him, only that she must get to him before he vanished again.

The valet opened the passenger door as Dr. Miles helped a

beautiful, petite blonde into the passenger side of the Bronco. She giggled as he sloshed water off her seat—the seemingly singular downfall to owning a topless truck.

Dr. Miles jogged to the driver's side and slid through the door of his truck with what seemed like two liquid movements. With a loud gurgle of acceleration and a high-pitched squeal from the blonde, he was gone.

Tears pricked at Larken's eyes. She stood against the pedestrian flow in a sea of people, watching the spot in the road where Dr. Miles' tail lights last glowed.

"Hey, you ready?" Jackson asked through the open passenger side window. He looked her over, furrowing his eyebrows.

Larken nodded without turning to face his car. "Yeah." She had almost forgotten about him entirely.

Jackson met her at the car door. "Everything okay? You look a little... shocked or something."

"Disheveled" was the accurate adjective for Larken's sudden appearance. She had pulled the peony out of her hair and rubbed mascara all over her face watching Dr. Miles drive away.

"I'm fine," she said when she climbed into his car, lacking just a tad of grace. "I just wanna go home." She squeezed back relentless tears, the kind that cannot be concealed as anything other than heartache and utmost sadness.

"Sure. Sure. I'll get you there ASAP, Ms. Devereaux." Jackson winked at her and wiped mascara away from her face before closing the door.

Larken stared out the window as they departed the lights of the party. She started feeling angry about Dr. Miles. The frustration of being so close to him without him even noticing was more than her alcohol-riddled blood could handle. The sky opened up sending sheets of rain across Jackson's windshield.

She considered the ridiculous blonde girl Dr. Miles was with, their ill-fated timing, her inability to find him after months of searching and, in that moment, decided she was done forcing something that obviously wasn't meant to be. As Lil would say, "If the shoe don't fit, run barefoot the other way."

"No. You know what? Don't take me home." Larken flipped down the vanity mirror, tussled her hair and wiped at the mascara on her face with her thumb. "Take me out. Let's get very, very drunk."

CHAPTER NINE

One Way or Another

"Whyyyyy?" Larken moaned, rolling onto her stomach and shoving her head under the pillows.

Bunny whipped back the curtains, letting the late morning sun shine full force into Larken's eyes like razor blades.

"Oh, shug you're awake," Bunny spoke loudly and sat with a thud beside Larken, making her bounce up and down.

"Shhhh. Momma...please," Larken begged in a weak voice. "I don't feel very good. I think I'm sick."

"Sick? Oh no. I betcha' feel like a little hussy though. 'Cause that's what you are." Bunny rubbed Larken's back so sweetly that Larken thought for sure she had misheard her.

"A hussy?" Larken rolled over to face Bunny, grabbing a handful of covers when she realized she had no pajamas on.

"Yes ma'am," Bunny said through clenched teeth. "And don't pull the too-drunk-to-remember card 'cause I'll just show you the text I got from Jackson at four o'clock this morning and jog that little hungover memory of yours." Bunny knuckle-rubbed Larken's head.

"Oww!" Larken swatted Bunny's hand away. "What are you talkin' about?"

"I am much too busy and important to play games with you right now." Bunny kept her voice loud enough to evoke pain. "I would, however, advise that you call Jackson and apologize profusely. Or maybe you could put that Public Relations degree to some daggum use and issue a public apology to…hmmm... Oh I don't know. Maybe the *entire state* of South Carolina?" Bunny pulled the covers up over Larken's body and walked out of the room, slamming the door shut.

Larken held her head in her hands and moaned. She tried to recall the night before, but could only focus on breathing in and out without moving.

A light knock at the door brought on a new onset of the jackhammering in her head.

"Hey, love bug," Lil whispered from the doorway. "Let's get you better."

Larken opened one eye to see Lil carrying a silver tray with a Bloody Mary, crackers, grapes and an assortment of prescription pills.

"Let me die. I apparently don't deserve to live anyway," Larken said as she struggled to sit up. "There will probably be a back lashing for your kindness."

"Oh, hush. She'll get over it," Lil reassured her. "I seem to remember a time or two when your Momma came home in less than what she left the house in. Last week actually."

Larken froze. "Wait. Are you saying I came home—naked?"

"Oh, goodness, no," Lil swiped at Larken's pale cheek with her hand. "Jackson wrapped you up in his jacket... and don't worry about the dress. He brought that, too."

Larken flung herself back under the covers and let out a wave of sobs and indistinguishable curses.

"Oh, now, sugar. Besides a fast metabolism and skin that defies gravity, don't you know the only real perk to being young? Hmmm?" Lil peeled down the covers to see Larken's face. "It's the excuse of youth." Lil looked off, a small smile creeping across her face. "I'd give anything for just one more night of relentless youth, diminishing my sense of repercussion and responsibility." She sighed. "I should have been much more reckless."

Larken bit down on her bottom lip and let the tears free-flow as she listened to Lil.

"You're a pressure cooker, baby and you let all that steam and frustration just build on up until the top blows off and makes a big 'ol mess." Lil handed Larken a cracker. "Your Momma made it sounds worse than it is anyway, I'm sure. She makes everything sound worse than it is."

Lil made sure that Larken got the Bloody Mary and crackers down and left instructions for the prescription strength Ibuprofen when she felt like she could handle it.

After three more hours of sleep and some lavender, lemon and sandalwood aromatherapy courtesy of Bart, Larken felt semi-human again. When she could stand without feeling light-headed, she took a hot soak and ate homemade chicken noodle soup that Lil brought over.

Despite the vicious hangover, Larken looked relatively normal again. Now that it was mid-afternoon, she threw on a pair of sweats and wandered to the staircase—stopping to listen for signs of Bunny before descending to the main floor.

The house was empty and quiet—not a sign of Bart or even Gloria, the ever present housekeeper, anywhere around. The daily mail had come and sat in a neat pile on top of the kitchen table. Two birthday cards addressed to Larken were on the top of the stack. Larken grabbed a piece of bread from the fridge and poured a glass of Gatorade before sitting down to flip through the newest catalogues and magazines. Under the hydrangea issue of Southern Living, Larken saw the envelope to David, the bulge of the engagement ring inside covered by a "Moved-No Forwarding Address" sticker.

Larken instinctively reached for the phone and dialed David's home number. Disconnected. She shook her head, disgusted by the fact that he had picked up his life and moved on so quickly.

She ran back upstairs to grab her cell phone and noticed three missed calls from Jackson. She scrolled through her contacts, relieved to realize that she didn't remember David's cell number by heart anymore. His old, familiar voicemail message came on immediately. "You've reached David Maddox. Leave a message." Larken pressed "end" and stared at the phone in her hand.

She hadn't talked to any of their Seattle friends since moving back home, but had to know what was going on. Larken took in a deep breath and dialed Suzanna Daly, a mutual friend of theirs during their happy couple days. Suzanna had called several times over the past few months, but Larken hadn't been ready to discuss anything. She realized now that a polite call back would have been appropriate.

"Larken?" Suzanna picked up on the second ring. "Oh my God. Are you okay?"

"Hey. Yeah—I'm fine." Larken tried to sound upbeat. "I'm really sorry I haven't called you back, but I've been in Charleston and—"

"Ugh, you two have had us so worried," Suzanna interrupted. "What happened? I got this engagement cancellation notice and then both you and David are MIA."

Larken stammered. "No, I'm good. I'm home and—I'm actually calling because I wanted to see if you'd heard from him?" Larken heard only silence crackling on the other end. "I take that as a no..."

"Oh this is not good," Suzanna said, panic and confusion flooding her voice. "He left a message for me a couple of weeks ago saying he was laying low, but it sounded like he was on vacation or something." Suzanna moved restlessly through the phone. "His office is running on auto-pilot, his house is empty, he disconnected his numbers."

Larken's head buzzed with confusion and fear. She explained the break-up to Suzanna, her move back to Charleston, the returned package with her engagement ring.

"I'm truly at a loss right now, Larken. I wish I had something to tell you. I'm sure David's just recovering—you know, trying to sort everything out." Suzanna sighed heavily into the phone. "I know he'll come around. He always does."

"Well..." Larken shrugged. "It is what it is. I'm not exactly holding my breath."

"I understand," Suzanna said resolutely. "It's probably best then." As one of David's oldest friends, Larken knew where Suzanna's loyalties had to stay.

"Would you let me know when he turns up, though?" Larken tried to keep her voice calm. "I'm not looking for reconciliation. I just want to make sure he's okay."

"Of course."

"Thanks again, Suzanna. I'm really sorry I didn't call sooner." Larken meant it.

"S'okay. It was really good to hear from you, Larken. Don't be a stranger, okay?"

"I won't. I promise." Larken said somberly. "Oh, and Suzanna? Please don't tell him I asked about him either."

Larken hung up the phone, exhausted from the conversation. Something felt very wrong about David's vanishing act. Larken crawled back under the covers, reminding herself that a healthy concern for another human being doesn't make you weak.

"Knock, knock," Jackson's voice filled the doorway as he peeked his head inside Larken's bedroom door. "You decent?"

"Does it matter?" Larken snapped dryly. She pulled the covers up to her chin and glared at him.

"Hey, don't be mad at me." Jackson laughed. "You took your own clothes off. A guy could lose his man card for stopping a woman from gettin' naked. I was just protecting my reputation."

Larken rolled her eyes. "Whatever. Tell me what happened. What did I do? Oh God. Just—get it over with."

Jackson lay on top of the covers beside her and put his hands behind his head, enjoying the recap. "Let's see… We went out to Wild Willy's where you insisted on doing Patrón shots. I now know that's a no-no… That was followed by dancing—very, very vigorous dancing."

Larken flashed back to the evening before. Her hair was all over the place, sweat and humidity taking control of her once perfect up-do. Jackson had his arms wrapped around her while she shouted the words to Blondie's "One Way or Another." She pushed her body against his and he kissed the top of her bare shoulders and her neck— singing along to the house band when they got to, "I'm gonna getcha, getcha, getcha, getcha."

Larken groaned and buried her face in her arm. "Alright. I remember the dancing."

Jackson laughed. "As will I. Forever."

"Where did the...undressing part come into play?" Larken couldn't make eye contact with him while she waited for his answer. *"Did we do something?"*

"Oh, give me a little credit, Bird. I don't go sloppy. Plus you'd remember if we had." Jackson grinned deviously.

Larken shrugged. That was probably true. "Don't be so sure."

"Anyway," Jackson continued, "you were well past your bedtime, so I sat you on a barstool and went to bring the car around. When I came back, you were dancing on the bar and had ripped the zipper in your dress doing what the bartender explained as a backflip/high-kick/split combo? I'm still kickin' myself for missing that."

Larken had the covers pulled completely over her face now, unable to face the truth.

"I don't think everybody saw everything. The whole place was blackout drunk anyway. I got you outta there pretty quick."

"Thanks." Larken's voice was muffled under the covers. "I guess it could have been worse, right?"

"Ehhh, well," Jackson continued, "you insisted you were too

hot to wear your dress home, so off it went. I didn't argue too much on that one... It was only a problem when I realized you didn't have a key and I'd have to take you home naked. Bunny was less than thrilled apparently, with both of us, based on the glare I got from Priss this morning."

"I don't even care what they think right now," Larken said, throwing the covers off her face. "Momma's the one always telling me to 'Live it up, Larken' and 'Don't be such a bore.'"

Jackson laughed. "She'd be hard-pressed to use either of those lines any time soon. I mean, she was *pissed*." Jackson muted a laugh with his arm. "I felt like I was twelve again."

"Jackson. I'm sorry." Larken sat up and put her hand on his chest. "You must think I'm insane. Actually, I might be insane."

"Nah. I thought it was kind of fun. I hadn't been out like that in a long time. Plus, I got to see your ass when you danced out the top of my sunroof." He made an okay sign with his hand. "Very nice."

"You're hilarious." Larken smacked him on the arm. Hope you enjoyed your one and only view."

"Well, actually, I was kind of thinking that bringing these back might score me enough brownie points to see it again?" Jackson reached into his pocket and held out the emerald-cut Harry Winston earrings to Larken.

"Oh my God," Larken gasped. She lay her head on Jackson's chest. "I didn't even know they were gone..."

Jackson radiated satisfaction. "I found one in my floorboard and spent most of the morning turning Wild Willy's over to find the other one." He shrugged, always the gentleman.

Bonding over their uncivilized night at Wild Willy's, Larken felt hopeful for the first time that she might just be able to return his affections. She felt childish for still judging him based on memories from so long ago. No matter how hard she fought it, little by little he proved to her that he was indeed not the same Jackson Winslow that had pulled her hair and broken her heart.

Jackson looked at Larken like he could absorb everything about her. He pulled her closer to him and kissed her gently. "So are we good, then?" he asked.

"Yeah." Larken smiled. "We're good. But I'll probably be grounded the rest of the summer, so that might put a damper on things."

"I guess that's fair." Jackson shrugged. "I'm sure Bunny gave Priss the long version. Might give me the nudge to move out."

"I'll get a job if you get your own place," Larken bargained.

"Oh, really?" Jackson sat up. "And why's that?"

"Well, I've gotta do something. I have nothing to show for my life except a broken engagement and really bad public speaking skills." Until she said it, she'd forgotten about the tasteless introduction of Bunny she had delivered the night before. In retrospect, Bunny's reaction that morning suddenly made more sense.

Jackson tussled Larken's hair. "Ehh. You're an Ashby. That's a full-time job."

"Sure, if I wanted to be a socialite," Larken corrected, shrugging him off.

"Is your crown of southern royalty suddenly feeling like a crown of thorns?"

"Something like that." Larken sighed. She scratched her head at the thought.

"Speaking of work," Jackson said, segueing out of potentially rough waters, "I've had something come up last minute and am headed outta town for a couple of days."

"Everything okay?" Larken asked.

Jackson nodded without answering her. "Just a glitch with a new investment. When I get back though, I believe you owe me the pleasure of a picnic."

"Yeah, sure," Larken agreed, trying to sound casual. "Just, umm, let me know when you get back." The sudden weight of knowing Jackson would want to label their relationship pressed down on her again.

Jackson got up from the bed and stretched, exhausted from the evening before. "Oh, and happy birthday tomorrow."

Larken smiled. "Thanks. Next year's gotta be better than this year, right?"

"I sure hope so. I'm countin' on it for both of us."

*

Larken let Jackson show himself out. She held the earrings up against the late afternoon sun, replaying the onslaught of old history and new confessions she heard while wearing them the night before.

After reluctantly sitting up, Larken got out of bed and tiptoed down the hall towards Bunny's room, stopping again to listen for her before opening the door. She held the earrings delicately in the palm of her hand and opened the closet. Bunny's dress from The Sailor Ball was carelessly thrown on the floor, a man's suit crumpled beside it.

Her stomach turned thinking of Mr. Boca Raton and her

mother. Together.

Larken quickly made her way to the closet, unlocked the safe and put the earrings back. She closed the closet doors and turned to leave, subconsciously holding her breath to avoid any more sensory evidence of her mother's orange friend. Bunny's bed was still unmade, a tangle of sheets and pillows piled up like a child's fort.

Larken bolted for the door, inhaling dramatically once she exited.

*

Early evening had finally fallen on The Ashby House, bringing with it the comfort of completion. Larken wandered outside for the first time all day, sitting on the swing near the lilies and enjoying the last burst of heat from the setting sun. Larken breathed in the humidity, replacing the cold, air-conditioned air in her lungs with warm, sweet, sticky air.

At the hum of Bart's arriving car, a cicada flew from a tree branch and sang its high pitched shrill. Lil hopped out of the passenger side door and opened the garden gate to see Larken. Bart disappeared immediately into the house, unloading flowers and groceries and what appeared to be a birthday cake.

"Well, we just ran off and left you all day, didn't we, shug?" Lil asked, sitting beside Larken. "You feelin' any better?"

"Much." Larken yawned. "Somehow I'm still tired though."

"Yeah? Well, you better rest up for your big day tomorrow. Twenty-five. I can hardly believe it." Lil patted Larken's leg.

"You and Jackson had fun?" Lil asked, prodding for details.

"Yeah. Apparently too much."

"Uh-huh," Lil nudged her. "And?"

"Annnnnd, he loves me or something." Larken held her hands up.

"I see... Well. No surprises there. And you love him back? Or not yet?"

"Not yet."

"Good girl," Lil said matter-of-factly. "I don't care who it is— good love is earned." Lil's phone buzzed, a text message from Bunny scrolling across the screen. "Except this one better watch it. She's fixin' to get disowned."

Lil adjusted the phone back and forth to read it more clearly in the dusk. "She says she's out for the night... And wants to know if you are feeling better —and did you see the package from David." Lil looked up at Larken for explanation.

After Larken told Lil about the returned engagement ring and her conversation with Suzanna, she couldn't get David off her mind. Lil seemed worried by the news, justifying Larken's initial concern and making her feel upset for having to care so much about someone who obviously cared so little for her.

"You really haven't talked about him much," Lil said. "I didn't 'spect you to, but I sorta' get the feeling your heart was fully aware it had been given a first-class ticket aboard the Titanic."

Larken hadn't thought about it quite like that—certainly not that dramatically. She was disappointed and embarrassed by what had happened, but was she heartbroken on the grandest scale? Maybe Lil was right. Maybe she was relieved more than anything.

"It all seemed to make sense at the time," Larken tried to explain. "David made me feel like I learned so much when I was with him—like I was growing up. He has that West Coast cynicism that seemed so eye-opening to me at the time. He was different and I guess I wanted to be different, too. Now I pity him and his emptiness."

Lil nodded in understanding. "He sounds like all the rest to me. And anybody that *wants* to change you to match them doesn't deserve to know how absolutely wonderful you are in the first place. My girl's the best kind of different there is."

"Thanks, Lil. I guess we are different, aren't we?"

"Mmmhmmm, that's right," Lil agreed. "Your Momma's different, too, but she's been fightin' it for so long the dark side might be taking over."

"You mean the orange side." Larken shuddered, remembering her earlier discovery in Bunny's closet.

"Oh Mylanta." Lil laughed. "Yes. The orange side. Oh shug, what is she thinkin'?"

After neither of them could come up with an answer that resembled anything acceptable about Bunny's uncomfortable relationship with Mr. Boca Raton, the sun set flawlessly over the Battery.

Lil insisted that Larken join her in the carriage house for supper and even Bart uncustomarily agreed to join them. By the time Lil's buttered scallops and asparagus were long gone and a bottle or two of wine was finished, Bart and Lil counted down to midnight, ushering in Larken's twenty-fifth year.

CHAPTER TEN

Twenty-Five

Bunny acted if nothing had ever happened. She and Priss picked fresh flowers from Priss' Asiatic lily garden and woke Larken up in the carriage house to sing their own "Beaches-esque" rendition of the Happy Birthday song. It was sweet, but depressing.

Caroline and Sam were at The Ashby House by mid-morning with original seashell and macaroni artwork glued into misspelled words.

Bunny had brunch catered in from Shrimp & Grits Cafe and invited Sylvia, who surprisingly showed up between hearings—and Hank, toting a wriggling, yappy Iris.

Priss proudly presented Larken with a family reserve jar of Tip's Moonshine, a luxurious gift indeed. Hank licked his lips, eyeing the jar with slight jealousy.

Once she had everyone's full attention, Bunny presented Larken with emerald-cut sapphire and diamond earrings—smaller versions of her own Harry Winstons, squeezing out a tear or two as she retold how her own twenty-fifth birthday seemed like it was only yesterday and that she hoped Larken would treasure her youth "with every sparkle of these stones."

Lil fidgeted throughout the gift giving, giggling with Bart and making it obvious that their gift would be the party favorite.

Careful not to outshine Bunny, Lil waited for just the right moment to signal for Bart to bring it in.

"Well," Lil started with a sneaky grin, "Bart and I have come up with a little plan."

"Oh, boy," Larken joked. "Should I be scared?"

"Yes, of course," Lil laughed heartily. "Very."

Bart rolled something large through the front door as Lil jumped up to meet him to present it to Larken.

"Ta-da!" Lil sang in her best Vanna White voice as she whipped back the cover on a vintage cherry red Vespa scooter.

Larken's mouth fell open. "You've got to be kidding me. This is mine?"

Larken was out of her chair and running her fingers down the shining red scooter before the rest of the cover was even off.

"Well, Bart and I saw it in the classifieds one morning, misplaced in the want ads while we were looking for jobs for you. It read, '1957 Vespa Scooter in mint condition.' I mean we didn't even know what color it was, but we knew it was a sign."

Bart stood in back of the Vespa with his hands clasped by his waist. He grinned proudly, admiring the newly waxed paint and re-upholstered seats.

Bunny twitched nervously at the scooter, busying herself by keeping Sam from climbing on top of it.

Caroline disappeared from the dining room and returned with a basket initialed with Larken's name for the front of the scooter. In classic Caroline fashion, it was filled with practical items like a water bottle, a first-aid kit and scarves for tying back hair.

"I love it." Larken swung a leg over the scooter, feeling the grainy cream leather seat. "I can't believe you found this."

"Well," Bart began to explain, "this scooter found you, really. And it also found something else…"

Larken looked at him from between the handle bars. "Yeah? There's more?"

Bart reached into his jacket pocket and pulled out a folded piece of paper, handing it to Larken. "Well, Lil and I think the Vespa was misplaced in the classifieds for a reason."

Larken wrinkled up her eyebrows and looked around the room as she unfolded the piece of paper. Bunny was not amused, but was faking it well.

Larken read the note out loud. "215 Calhoun Street, Suite 3, Monday, 9:00 am."

"I don't follow." Larken looked back and forth between Lil and Bart. What does this mean?"

"It means we got you a *job*!" Lil exclaimed.

"We got you an *interview*," Bart corrected gently. "It's a public relations position at a clinic offering services to low-income families. The pay is actually impressive considering the type of work they do. Lil and I put your résumé together."

Bunny was fully glazed over.

"I don't know what to say," Larken stammered as she got off

her new scooter to hug Lil and Bart.

"We thought—we *all* thought," Lil paused, looking pointedly at Bunny, "that this would be a wonderful way for you to start this next year."

"And to think I almost applied for the meat-packing plant," Larken laughed.

"Oh, Lord, Larken, don't even joke about that." Bunny rubbed at her temples while Priss patted her on the back.

"Momma, I'm not going to war," Larken said, finally addressing Bunny's unnecessary distress over the new job opportunity. "It's perfectly natural to eventually get a job. And you know I want this. I actually kind of need this."

"My baby sister's all grown up," Caroline said, softening the room with her sentiment. "A real job interview without a favor from Momma. Imagine…"

Bunny shot Caroline a warning look.

"Lawk, you can dwive your bicycle to your new work." Sam jumped up and down, still mesmerized by the shiny scooter.

"Well, I'll have to get the job first, little man." Larken winked.

"I betcha I could fit into dat basket on the fwont, too," Sam discovered, inspecting it closely to make sure.

"Well," Bunny said hesitantly, drawing out every letter and enjoying the suspense. "If you can't beat 'em, join 'em—or whatever it is they say about that." She let a demure smirk grow across her mouth, instantly charming everyone back into her favor. "I suppose you'll need some new work clothes, too." She sighed indignantly.

Larken jumped up and hugged Bunny. "Thanks, Momma. I

promise this is a good thing."

"Well, don't make me cry, Larken." Bunny squeezed her quickly before smoothing down her blouse and fixing her hair. "And you be careful on that... *scooter*. Those are dangerous."

"And you," Bunny said, turning to face Bart with slitted eyes, grabbing the sleeves of his jacket. "You'll teach her how to ride it?"

"Of course." Bart agreed. "It would be my pleasure."

"And me, too?" Sam jumped up and down.

Caroline swooped Sam up and tickled him. "Let's start with your Big Wheel first, buddy."

*

Mid-morning had leaked into late afternoon when Jackson called with a raspy rendition of "Happy Birthday." Larken felt the anticipation of his call all day, signaling the reality that they had seamlessly crossed the treacherous territory of "friends" into the land of "friends plus."

Larken told herself that no birthday phone call would mean she had played the game correctly: Jackson was not advancing. She maintained the position that she would be made uncomfortable if he called, but just the opposite happened when that familiar, southern drawl held out the two syllables of her name.

She went through the detail of her day, but managed to leave out the part about getting a job interview as a present. After all, like Jackson, it was only a possibility.

Jackson sounded tired from his day of what Larken assumed was full of business hustle. He didn't indulge her with details, so Larken kept their conversation celebratory and pleasant.

167

"Are you disappointed that I didn't get you something?" Jackson asked, half joking.

"No. Why would I be?" Larken laughed. "You've never given me a birthday present before."

"Yeah, well that's true. But, it's never been like this before."

Larken drew in a quiet breath and counted to three while she exhaled. Somehow his admission of love after all these years had propelled her back into the same insensibility she'd felt at seventeen.

As if on cue to prevent her from protesting their muddled relationship status, Jackson had another call that he had to take. He quickly wished Larken a lovely birthday evening and promised to call the next day.

*

Monday morning came altogether too soon. Larken woke up at 5 a.m. with butterflies from the impending job interview.

A new version of a reoccurring dream of walking around David's house had left her sleepless and disturbed.

She pulled on a pair of running shorts and threw on a tank-top before descending the stairs on tip-toed feet, careful not to wake Bunny.

The morning air was heavy with humidity, but it brought a calmness and peace with its oppression. Larken cut through the side garden and slipped out the wrought iron gate onto South Battery. Almost overnight the magnolia trees were out in full force with their stoic, theatrical blooms. Smelling them reminded her to breathe in deeply.

She skipped her usual neighborhood route and ran by the

harbor on Murray Boulevard where the water was as still as glass. Several well-worn Charlestonians walked ritually by the water, slow and steady. Larken passed them with a wave and wondered what her life would be like when she was in her twilight years.

She turned around before the busyness of East Bay Street could unsettle her and ran back the way she came toward The Ashby House. When the U.S. Coast Guard base was in view, she dropped to a walk.

A solo cicada sang as the morning warmed up. Larken wiped sweat away from her face and rubbed her eyes. By the time she stretched on the front porch steps and got back into the house, it was a quarter past six. No one seemed to be awake yet, so Larken brewed a pot of coffee and headed upstairs to take a shower.

Her cell phone flashed red from her bed side table, indicating a text message from Jackson. "All done here. Boarding now. Call you when I land." They'd somehow arrived at flight-status relationship terms overnight.

She hopped in the shower, standing under the hot water face first. She began to wonder that, if Jackson felt the need to tell her when he was boarding airplanes, if she was obligated to tell him about job interviews. She shook her head "no" in self-dialogue and remembered what Lil once told her about obligations: "When you trouble yourself to be obligated to someone, they better have already proved their worth to you."

Larken turned the shower off and grabbed a towel. She walked back into her bedroom to find Bunny holding two cups of coffee. "Well, are you havin' any second thoughts?"

"No," Larken said, rolling her eyes and reaching for her cup.

"I am not."

Bunny sighed and took a sip of coffee. "You wearin' that to your interview?" Bunny pointed at a tiny black dress that most mothers would cringe over, a look of approval of it on her face.

Larken sighed. "Nope. It's a clinic for low-income families, remember? Not sure that's the right message to send. Besides, I've got to wear pants so I can drive my *scooter*." Larken raised her eyebrows, antagonizing Bunny.

"Oh, God, Lark," Bunny started, "are you sure that you're ready because I just don't think it's a good idea and where do you *park* that thing and what if you *wreck* it or Lord, if it *rains* and then—"

Larken cut her off with a raised hand. "Momma, we talked about this. Bart showed me how to drive it, I practiced all weekend and I'm going two miles away at twenty miles an hour." Larken set her coffee down and picked up her matching red helmet. "And if I wreck it, though my body may be mangled, my brain will still be protected."

"That's nowhere near funny." Bunny closed her eyes. "Do you think that I ever considered golf carts dangerous before your daddy died in one? No!"

"I know. I'm sorry. If it rains, I give you permission to come rescue me."

Bunny pouted. "Fine. That makes me feel a little bit better."

"Well, good, Momma," Larken said sarcastically. "Today is all about you anyway."

Bunny glared at Larken playfully. "Alright, shug. I'll let you get ready."

"Love ya, Momma," Larken lilted after Bunny as she left the

room.

"Uh-huh, I'm sure."

Larken walked into her closet, still undecided about what to wear to her first real job interview. As promised, Bunny had taken her shopping over the weekend, but none of the clothes were Larken's taste. She scanned her closet, taking inventory of her new interview attire: a sea-foam bodice top with black high-waisted gaucho pants, a red pique dress in silk, a black pant suit with a racy lace bodice built into the blazer and a light-pink houndstooth suit with school girl ruffles at the hem. Larken grabbed a pair of blue wide-leg trouser pants that Bunny hadn't approved of buying and a cream eyelet boatneck top that had survived the great closet-cleaning raid.

Larken put on more makeup than she was used to wearing and decided to dry and curl her hair. She wore the earrings that Bunny had given her for her birthday—the center-stone sapphires matching her pants perfectly.

Larken stood in the mirror for one final approval before heading downstairs. She smoothed down the top, grabbed the attaché that she'd borrowed from Bunny and grabbed her helmet.

Bart and Lil were in the kitchen reading the latest social magazines when Larken made her way into the kitchen at eight-twenty.

"You're hired," Lil joked as she hugged Larken. "No way they can't hire you lookin' like that."

Larken held out her hands. "We'll see."

Bart unveiled a basket of banana muffins on the counter and placed one on a plate for Larken. "Compliments of Lil."

"Oh, thanks, Lil," Larken said excitedly as she inhaled the homemade aroma. "Still warm. You got up early to make these."

Larken closed her eyes and smiled as she nibbled the warm muffin.

"Well, you know," Lil explained with a smile, "I was too excited to sleep."

Larken poured a glass of milk and tapped the counter top anxiously. The kitchen was silent. Bart and Lil watched Larken count every second on the clock until everyone was aware of the anticipation.

"Well, shoo! Go then," Lil motioned to Larken. "You're gonna drive us batty."

Larken gave Lil and Bart a thumbs-up. "Thanks again for the very interesting birthday gift. I hope I don't mess it up."

"Give it your best shot," Bart encouraged as he handed her the keys to the Vespa. "If it's right, it's right. And if it's not…well, you know."

Larken smiled at both of them as she headed out the door to the courtyard. She wondered if all families were this involved in the job-hunting process and decided probably not. "Tell Momma that her absence was noted."

She slung the attaché across her chest like a crossbody bag and pulled the helmet down over her curls. She winced, realizing that helmet hair was just going to be part of the scooter experience. *It's not a beauty contest.*

She pushed the Vespa forward and off its stand and turned the key to the "on" position.

Bart watched from the window as Larken turned the key, twisted the right handlebar and accelerated down the courtyard and out the front gate—smiling as strands of windblown hair stuck to her lip gloss.

*

Larken drove too slowly down Tradd Street, but felt confident enough to almost drive the speed limit once she turned onto Coming Street through the College of Charleston campus.

At five till nine, the humidity had settled firmly into the morning heat and left a shellac of moisture on all exposed skin. Blasts of sweet air wound through porticos and alleys making Larken glad she hadn't worn a dress. She enjoyed the attention that the Vespa garnered—proud to be atop the humming, robust motor.

Larken took a deep breath as she approached the three-story restored white brick building at 215 Calhoun Street. She turned past the building to access the parking lot and stopped her Vespa between a Mercedes and a Bentley. Other cars parked in the lot were all of luxury value, too. She strained to verify the address above the back door entrance to the clinic.

Larken struggled with the kick-stand for just a moment, making sure the scooter had rocked back into a secured position.

She opened the back door entrance that led into a hallway lobby with small offices on both sides and an elevator to the upper floors in the middle of the building. The lobby was well-lit and painted dove gray with white chair railing and bead board. Gray and white swirled marble floors reflected the morning sun that shined through old, wavy glass.

Larken hit the elevator button and heard the engine crank over as the elevator descended. The doors opened with an unsettling loud chime and Larken walked in, smoothing her helmet hair in the reflection of the mirrored walls.

From inside the elevator, Larken heard the front door to the building open and the rapid clicking of heels coming down the hall. The door had just begun to shut when a tall girl with overflowing black curls wormed her way through. She giggled at Larken as she straightened her skin-tight pink mini skirt and adjusted a low-cut button down revealing what were obviously new fake breasts with the skin pulled so tight they were shiny.

Larken rolled her eyes to the ceiling, trying to avoid the unavoidable. "Which floor?" she asked the girl.

"Oh, the top one," she said in a breathy voice. The girl applied another layer of red lipstick and smiled absentmindedly at Larken.

"Are you going there, too?" she asked in forced baby talk, blinking slowly. She looked Larken up and down, staring for a moment at her chest.

Larken pressed the three and pursed her lips together. "Seems I am," she said coolly. If this was her fellow candidate, she might as well leave now.

"Oh, good," the girl fake-clapped. "A friend for the journey."

Larken looked back at her blankly, eyebrows raised in confusion.

The elevator doors opened on the third floor to face a large reception area. Light blue crystal chandeliers hung from a cathedral ceiling, catching light from beautiful sky lights that flooded the office with sun. The receptionist's desk was a large oak work table with only a MacBook and a Euro office phone and notepad. Light blue chaise lounges, elaborate arm chairs and farm-styled coffee tables were grouped in areas throughout the waiting area. Raffia rugs warmed up white high-gloss concrete floors.

The Betty Boop character from the elevator had skipped childishly, albeit awkwardly, to the receptionist's desk as Larken took in what she assumed to be a very nice doctor's office.

The receptionist paged someone to come collect the bouncing, busty girl and in a matter of moments she was whisked away, chit-chattering all the way to the back of the office with more giggles and over exaggerated hand gestures.

Larken walked slowly to the receptionist's table, the office suddenly feeling smarter with the recent departure. The faint sounds of classical music danced in the cathedral ceiling.

"Hey, there, how can I help you?" The receptionist asked with a warm smile and rosy cheeks as she typed blindly, straining to look at Larken as she finished typing. Her blonde, corkscrew curls bounced with each small movement.

"Hello." Larken smiled unsure. "I…have an interview. I think."

"Well, then you must be Larken," the receptionist smiled. "Nice to meet you."

"Oh, good. So I am at the right place," Larken said out loud to reassure herself.

"Oh, you're at the right place alright," the receptionist answered her. "I'm Hazel. Hazel Anson." She stood up from the table and held out her hand to Larken. "Vice President of First Impressions."

Larken shook her hand and smiled. "So, I don't really know much about the job." Larken looked at Hazel, prodding for information.

"Ahh. Well," Hazel started. "Let's see… Dr. Beckway does a

lot of community service, if you will, and has a lot of side projects and philanthropic endeavors and what not. So it would be helping him with benevolence, per se."

Hazel downplayed a backwoods accent. Larken thought she probably grew up somewhere in the area, just not Charleston proper.

"Okay…" Larken shook her head pretending to understand. "So—"

Hazel cut her short. "What it *is* is a great job with good benefits and some pretty—nice—perks." Hazel pointed to her nose and then her lips with a wink and a smile.

"What?" Larken asked, not following the insinuation.

"You should have seen me before," Hazel continued. "I looked as country as I sound. For Christmas next year I'm asking for lipo."

"Plastic surgery," Larken said. "Dr. Beck—something is a plastic surgeon?" She looked around again, not needing Hazel's confirmation now that she figured it out. "So, Jessica Rabbit is a patient, then. Not a candidate for the job?"

"Oh, Krissy?" Hazel laughed. "Yeah, she's in for her pre-op. Guess *the girls* ain't quite big enough…again." Hazel muffled a laugh and slapped her own hand in self-discipline. "Jessica Rabbit's a good name for her though... I might just change her chart."

Larken couldn't help by laugh with relief. She felt suddenly less self-conscious knowing that Krissy and her insurmountable breasts weren't competing for the same position.

"So let's get you back there then," Hazel said as she motioned for Larken to follow her to the back of the office. "Doc isn't in yet, but should be soon. I'll have you fill out our background check until he gets here. Ya know, just a precaution since we work with such *delicate* matters." Hazel winked sarcastically.

Hazel walked with heavy feet down the hallway, swinging doors open quickly and with force. She led Larken past several exam rooms, all of them very bright and inviting. Only one exam room door was closed and a still giggling Krissy could be faintly heard from the other side. A nurse in scrubs sat at a small station going over charts. She smiled at Larken before going back to her work.

Larken followed Hazel into a large office down a short hallway away from the exam rooms and, at Hazel's suggestion, sat in one of two leather wingback chairs across from a large mahogany desk.

"Doc had a facelift at six this morning," Hazel explained, "so all the surgical staff is at the ambulatory center. It's not normally this quiet."

Larken nodded her head in understanding and took a seat in the chair closest to the door.

Hazel searched for something in a cabinet across from the large desk, coughing and waving dramatically at the displaced dust. She pulled out a form of some sort and handed it to Larken along with a pen.

"You start on this do-hicky and just…leave it blank if you don't feel like answerin'. You look pretty straight up anyways." Hazel looked Larken up and down again before clearing a space on the cluttered desk for her to write. "I'm runnin' an errand 'cross town for Doc, but I have the feeling I'll be seein' you again. Good luck." She winked as she closed the door, leaving Larken in complete silence.

Larken didn't bother reading the background check form that

Hazel had handed her. She filled in her name, social security number and Caroline's address then sat looking around the interesting yet messy office.

A bronze statue of a cowboy riding a bucking horse took up too much space on the right corner of the desk. Dust had dulled the shine. Wooden statues and South American influenced figurines dotted the bookshelves and brought about a feeling of global awareness. There were accolades and framed medical school certificates hanging on the walls just out of reading distance. Larken knew that if she stood up to get closer, the door would surely open. She sat with her leg jiggling as five and then ten minutes passed.

She considered what Lil and Bart had told her about the job at her birthday party and wondered if they'd somehow misunderstood. There seemed to be little philanthropy happening in this office.

Larken smoothed her pants, cleared her throat and sat up straight as two voices descended the hallway behind her.

It fell quiet again before the door opened with a rat-tat-tat and then swung fully open.

Larken turned around and stood up with her hand outstretched before looking at the doctor's face. "Hi, I'm Lar—." She stopped as she looked up to meet the eyes of Dr. Miles, liquid and smiling, just as they had been under very different circumstances.

"You," she said, forgetting herself and allowing all emotion to show on her face. After months of searching and wondering, here he was again, standing in front of her.

"And you," the doctor said happily. "Kindred Hospital pinkie toe, right? A fainter, too, if I remember correctly." He smiled as he made his way to his desk chair, sitting down with a thud. "Good to see you again."

Larken nodded her head up and down, speechless. She shook it off, trying to collect herself. "I'm sorry," she said. "I'm confused..." Larken moved to the accolades on the wall for verification. Plaques from the University of North Carolina at Chapel Hill, the American Society for Aesthetic Plastic Surgery and American Medical Association all read *Dr. Miles Beckway, M.D., F.A.C.S. Plastic Surgeon.*

"*You* are Doctor *Beckway*? You're *Miles* Beckway? That's your name?" Larken trailed off, finally understanding. "I had it wrong," she said under her breath, feeling a rush of exhilaration and confusion as she sat back down in shock.

"Were you looking for somebody else?" Miles smiled, interrupting her realization. He watched her carefully, intrigued by her questions.

"No. No, not at all," Larken assured him. "I'm just surprised to see you here. Like this."

"Well, I'm surprised to see you here, like this, too." Miles rocked back in his chair, hands clasped behind his head.

"Can I get you anything to drink?" he asked, opening a mini-fridge hidden under his desk, pulling out a bottled water.

Larken declined with a subtle head shake, realizing that she must seem so strange to him.

"It's alright to be nervous," Miles comforted her. "Most people are." He took a generous swig of water.

Larken swallowed hard and nodded.

"Well," he started, opening a folder in front of him, "let's see what we have here." He skimmed through the papers, flipping pages and furrowing his brows. Larken immediately felt self-conscious.

She watched him carefully, his hair a little longer than she had remembered it being at The Sailor Ball. His tan was darker now, too—his brown hair now lighter with more sun-kissed highlights. As if feeling her eyes on him, he ran a hand quickly through it and brought the back of his hand to his lips.

"So..." Miles started with one eye squinting and pointed toward her, "do you have a size in mind?"

Larken wrinkled her brows in confusion at his question.

"If you don't mind me making a suggestion," Miles started as he rose from his chair and walked around to face Larken. He sat on the desk, casually swinging a leg below him. "I really wouldn't advise anything above a C-cup on a frame your size unless...you just really want to prove a point. If you are absolutely set on undergoing the procedure though, a full "B" is more than plenty."

He turned around and shuffled through a pile of papers on the desk behind him. "Here," he began again, "I find that 'before and after' pictures seem to help a lot in the decision making process." He flipped through a collection of photo pages. "Yeah, here we go. These are a good representation—" he stopped as he looked up to see Larken's face, sheet-white and full of horror.

She stared blankly at him out of confusion and utter embarrassment. He held out pre-and post-op photos of naked torsos, breasts of all shapes and sizes exposed.

"I'm so sorry, but I think there's been a misunderstanding," Larken said, feeling like there were a dozen cotton balls in her mouth. "I'm not here for a boob job. I'm here for a... *job* job."

Several dead seconds passed before he said anything. "Oh,"

Miles finally broke the silence, leaving his mouth in an o-shape. He stood up from his make-shift seat on the desk and walked around to his chair.

"I'm Larken Devereaux. My… résumé was sent over last week for the public relations position?" Larken's ears were hot and ringing with anxiety. She took note of how insecure she sounded, ending every statement in the tone of a question.

"Right, right," Miles said dryly, caught off-guard by the exchange. He nodded. "No, I remember now. I mean, I didn't know it would be *you* that was coming in, but…I feel really…really bad about this. I grabbed a chart outside and—assumed you—well…" He began tapping his fingers on the desk and a steady smile grew on his face. "I mean, I'm relieved actually. Embarrassed, but relieved."

"Relieved?" Larken asked, an eyebrow perked.

"Well, yeah," Miles explained. "I thought 'here's this pretty girl, thinkin' that somethin' is wrong with her and wanting to fix things that aren't broken.'" He let out a solitary laugh. "I was trying to figure out how I would tell you no."

"Oh," Larken said, trying to appear unfazed. "That's very flattering."

"Anyway…*yes*—about the job." He waved his hand, moving on. "Hazel thought you sounded like a good candidate." He looked at Larken and started laughing again, shaking his head. She could tell he was trying desperately to act professionally.

"I'm sorry, but what if I had asked you to take your shirt off?" Miles eyes twinkled. "I mean…that was coming next, but—oh, thank God."

Larken couldn't help but smile at his reaction. "Well, every employer has different qualifications…" She pushed away the thought that she would have gladly taken her shirt off for him, given different circumstances.

Miles composed himself again, rustling his hair back into place and releasing a sigh. "So, in addition to what I do here, I do community service…*stuff*, for lack of a better term."

"*Cosmetic* community service?" Larken asked. She imagined vouchers for face lifts and tummy tucks for the underprivileged offered up like food stamps.

"Hah, not quite," he explained politely. "More like basic medical care. I've done it for years, but now that the practice is growing and my insurance has changed, I need to set it up legally and have it run as a non-profit." Miles shrugged. "Something about liability and taxes and something else bureaucratic that my lawyer told me I had to do, so…anyway. Here I am. And here you are." He stretched his arms out, muscles defined through the sleeve of his button down.

Larken sat up straight, remembering for the first time since being in Miles' presence that she was there for a job. "That sounds wonderful," she said with a smile. "I've worked with a non-profit before—fundraisers, galas, committees, that sort of thing?"

Miles bit his lip at the thought. "Well, those kinds of things may come into play at some point. Not my cup of tea, really, but I'm happy to hear you can razzle and dazzle should the need arise."

Larken smiled with pride. "I do what I can."

"I never really intended on doin' boob jobs and face lifts for a living," Miles explained as he looked around his office. "I started out in plastics for reconstructive purposes only—did a lot of third world tenures. For years I wouldn't even think about taking on a cosmetic procedure."

"What changed?" Larken asked, intrigued.

"Everything." Miles smiled quickly, something hidden underneath his tone.

"I don't have a lot of time to devote to the day-to-day side of the charity work anymore," Miles continued, "but there's a certain donor-base here that I haven't tapped into." He shrugged. "A lot of the funds we have now come from outside of Charleston. People I've met over the years. Hobnobbin' really ain't my thing."

Larken nodded. "So you need a face?"

"Exactly." Miles squinted his eyes at her, hopeful she was willing to consider it. "It's really just rubbin' elbows with Charleston's finest and asking them to give you money. They're good people—very generous. Some need some babysitting from time to time, but if you can coddle the high-maintenance, take 'em to lunch, remember their grand-kids names, that sorta' thing, you should be good to go."

Larken almost laughed out loud. Her entire life had been practice for coddling the high maintenance. And her name was Bunny.

"Interested?" Miles tilted his head in anticipation of her response.

"Absolutely," Larken answered in her most professional tone. "It sounds like very rewarding work and I'd really like to be involved with something meaningful."

Miles gave her a solitary nod. "That sounds like a yes."

Larken's eyes grew large in surprise. "Was that an official, *official* offer?"

"I mean," Miles said, motioning to the chaotic sea of papers around his desk, "nothing is that official around here, but yes. That was an official, *official* offer." He winked, mocking her.

Larken took a quick breath. "When should I start?"

CHAPTER ELEVEN

Molasses Creek

Larken rode the Vespa to The Ashby House with a smile plastered on her face. She hadn't decided if she was more excited about the job or the fact that she'd found the phantom doctor, but either way, she felt the happiest she'd been in months.

By the time she returned home, everyone had fluttered off to go about their days and the house was quiet and still. Larken sat restlessly at the kitchen table, leaning toward the window to look out at the street for signs of anyone returning home.

She rewound the interview back in her mind and replayed it, being critical of herself and desperately trying to remember details that may or may not have happened.

Restless with excitement over her news and having no one to share it with, Larken changed into running shorts and a tank top before grabbing a half-read copy of *The Years*, Virginia Woolf being one of the few authors able to pull Larken out of her own mind. Despite the late morning heat, Larken wanted to escape the house and set out to read in the garden.

Somewhere in the novel between the Pargiters' estate being sold in the picturesque January snow and Kitty taking a motorcar to her husband's castle, Larken fell asleep on the outdoor chaise lounge, sprawled gloriously out in the sun, *The Years* covering her face.

A familiar voice woke her up as she felt the weight of someone sitting down beside her.

"Hey, pretty girl," Jackson whispered as best he could through the gravel in his voice. He lifted the book up off her face. "I see you're wastin' the day away in Margaritaville."

Larken sat up, peeling away sweaty hair stuck to her face. "You're back," she said sleepily. "Did you have a good trip?"

"I'm just glad it's over. I kinda missed you, you know…" Jackson raised his eyebrows and smiled. "It's good to be home."

Larken yawned and stretched, rubbing smudged mascara away from her eyes.

"You know some people get up and do stuff during the daytime," Jackson teased. "The last time I saw you you were sleepin' one off."

Larken sat up hastily, glaring at Jackson. "Well, aren't you charming. I'm not hungover. I had an interview this morning. And I got the job."

Jackson drew back with a smirk. "Well, how about that," he said encouragingly. "And what might this job be?" He raised one eyebrow skeptically.

"You are looking at the new Public Relations Coordinator for a very well-to-do doctor's office," Larken said with an air of sophistication in her voice.

"Mmmm." Jackson nodded. "Sounds sexy." He leaned forward, dangerously close enough to kiss her.

Larken pulled her head back. "It's a real job, too. And I interviewed like a champ. They offered it to me on the spot." Larken realized her intentional omission of Dr. Beckway's name.

"Well, I don't doubt it," Jackson nodded. "Alright, so what does this very real job entail?"

"Well," Larken smiled proudly, "I'll be procuring funds for a non-profit arm that they run. Maybe oversee some events, throw a gala here or there." Larken was already imagining Dr. Beckway in his tuxedo, toasting to Larken from side stage for a job well-done.

"Ah. So…kind of like what Bunny does then," Jackson said smugly, interrupted her daydream.

"Ugh, no," Larken growled, smacking Jackson in the knee. "Why on earth would you say that?"

"I'm kiddin', I'm kiddin'," he said, rubbing the sting off his leg. "I wanna hear all about it, every detail." Jackson reached up to push the hair out of her face.

Larken shrugged him off. "I don't start 'till next week. *Maybe* I'll tell you about then."

"Alright. Then we'll talk about me tonight."

"Tonight?"

"You said I could take you to dinner when I got back," Jackson reminded her. "And here I am…"

"Hmmm," Larken said, looking out distractedly across the garden. "I'm clearly pretty busy."

She hadn't anticipated feeling so normal with him, but

Jackson's energy was electric—drawing her into him whether she wanted to be drawn or not, like the tide with the apogee of the moon.

"Yoo-hoo, y'all," Lil chirped as she opened the garden gate with some difficulty, surprising both Larken and Jackson. She wore rolled up jeans, still damp at the cuffs, a safari hat and an open linen shirt over a mud-streaked tank top. A five gallon bucket full of brackish water slung precariously as she held a quart of fresh blackberries under one arm and carried sand crusted rubber boots in her free hand.

Jackson rose gentlemanly to greet Lil with a hug. "Prettier and prettier every time I see you," he said politely.

"And you're still an *awful* liar," Lil argued, smacking him with her elbow, sloshing the water inside the bucket.

"Where did you come from?" Larken asked, snatching a small handful of the berries and catching a whiff of pluff mud.

"Bart dropped me off," Lil replied with an adventurous smile. She tossed her boots in the grass and set the bucket down. "We checked on the beach house, then we went down to Chechessee Creek in South Edisto for the last day of clamming season." She smiled ear to ear as she tipped the bucket forward for Larken to see her recreational limit of one-half bushel of clams and three shrimp inside. Lil stuck her hand in the bucket, a diamond tennis bracelet shining as she waved the contents and unsettled the sand that hid her generous collection of Littleneck clams.

Jackson peeked in the bucket and whistled. "Quite the catch you got there."

Lil raised an eyebrow in thanks and picked up a huge, juicy blackberry before passing them around. "So," she said, "how was your morning?" Lil chewed a berry deliberately as she impatiently waited for Larken to offer up news of her interview, but not wanting to give her away if she hadn't told Jackson.

"He knows," Larken answered her, jerking a thumb in Jackson's direction. She took the bushel of blackberries from Lil and combed through them.

"He knows…what?" Lil asked, playing dumb.

"He knows—," Larken held the words out for dramatic effect, "that I got the job."

Lil jumped up out of her chair with the energy of a teenager. "Oh, I just knew it," she said, gleaming. "I knew you'd get it."

"Well, you and Bart made it happen." Larken smiled.

"No, ma'am we did not," Lil corrected her. "Cain't never could. Me and Bart just gave you a little nudge."

Larken lowered her eyes at the sentiment.

"This one's a little self-deprecating," Lil said behind her hand to Jackson.

"I noticed that," he agreed, swatting at a June bug.

Lil's eyes squinted into slits as she sat back down. "Bunny knows?"

Larken shook her head. "Not yet, but I'm sure she'll be thrilled…"

"Oh, she'll come around," Lil encouraged with a wink and a pat on Larken's arm. "Your first real job." Lil shook her head sentimentally.

"Well, my first *paying* job," Larken reminded her, suddenly self-conscious of sounding as juvenile as she felt.

Jackson shook his head in validation of her input.

The quiet of the garden was disturbed with the torque of Bunny's Lexus pulling into the drive. She parked the car dangerously close to the Vespa and opened the door slowly, taking her time as she got out.

"Hey, everybody," she said indifferently, throwing her hand up in a lethargic wave.

She walked up the path to the garden slowly in an Armani power suit and her lucky Christian Loubitons.

"When did you get back, Jackson?" she asked, significantly more animated with him in her view. She removed her sunglasses, her eyes glowing with approval of his presence.

"Just now," Jackson said, rising again from his place on Larken's chaise to greet Bunny. "Came straight from the airport."

Bunny made eyes at Larken before responding to him. "Well, how 'bout that. Straight from the airport…jewels on your crown." She shrugged her shoulder approvingly.

Jackson laughed uneasily. "Ahh, well, that's debatable."

"And goodness, Larken," Bunny started, giving her daughter's sweat-flattened hair and mis-matched clothes a once over. "Looks like Jackson caught you by surprise." She pursed her lips in disapproval.

The mood was as thick and heavy as the afternoon humidity.

"Well, y'all, what do you say we all have a toast in my honor this evening?" Bunny said, waving her fingers in the air.

"What's the occasion?" Lil asked.

Bunny ran a hand through her hair. "I've spent all day slaving over negotiations with JD to broker the sale of that land in the

Lowcountry. And let me just say… I've still got it." She snapped her fingers together.

Larken cringed at the thought of them "negotiating."

"So." Bunny shrugged. "What do you say? Reservations at seven o'clock?" She pouted her lips out.

"Ahh, Bunny," Jackson said, knitting his eyebrows together in disappointment. "I've already agreed to celebrate with your daughter tonight."

Bunny tilted her head. "Ohhh? Is that right?" She smiled wildly. "And what are we celebrating?"

"Larken," Jackson said, redirecting the question. He nodded at Larken, giving her the floor.

Bunny's eyes opened in curiosity, shifting to look at Larken. "Well?"

"I got the job," Larken confirmed. She nervously tucked her hands in between her knees.

Bunny held a smile in place, it growing tighter the longer she stood. She coughed, forcing herself to speak. "Oh. Your interview. I almost forgot."

Lil cleared her throat audibly, taking rare advantage of her matriarchal role.

"Well, goodness," Bunny answered. "I suppose congratulations are in order." She forced her face into an uneasy smile.

"Thank you," Larken said cheerfully, as if Bunny had meant it. "I'm finally part of the good 'ol American work force."

"Well," Bunny snickered, rubbing at her neck in agitation. "I don't know that it's exactly something you want to go around *braggin'* about." She looked at Jackson for support, but he had conveniently busied himself with the blackberries.

Larken nodded, not in agreement, but in understanding of Bunny's intention. "Well, I'm excited about it." Larken brushed hair out of her face.

"And that's all that matters," Lil said, slapping her knee and settling the matter. "She just knew how proud you'd be, Bunny." Lil's addition of a glaring smile made Bunny's composure suddenly come to a halt.

She pointed at Lil's bucket of clams and shook her finger. "Don't let those stink up the garden. It ruins my yoga."

Bunny turned to Larken. "Congratulations again. I'm sure you'll do great. And Jackson," she said, painting a smile back on, "so glad you're home." She turned on her heels with a nod and set-off briskly for the house.

"Well, I think that went well," Jackson said sarcastically once Bunny was out of earshot.

Lil stood up from her chair and patted Jackson on the shoulder. "Nicely done. Now I'm off to my little corner of the garden," she explained, inspecting the bucket of clams with a jiggle. "I better shuck these before they smell up the Battery and ruin Bunny's life." She waved spritely as she set for the carriage house, leaving Larken and Jackson alone again.

"You're kind of a hypocrite," Larken told him, smiling at Jackson as they watched Lil tramp victoriously through the garden, picking out a solitary clam from the bucket and tossing it into a rose bush out of spite. "I thought you were on Momma's side with the whole job thing." She fanned at flushed cheeks with her humid copy of *The Years.*

Jackson moved to Lil's empty chair and stretched his legs out with a sigh. "Yeah, well. I guess I'm learning to be flexible. I figured you'd have it your way anyway and Bunny's a control freak enough for everybody, so I figure this makes me the hero." He raised an eyebrow in question. "Plus now you are locked into having dinner with me tonight."

Larken eyed him skeptically. "Always a motive."

"It is a little bizarre how upset she is about it, though," Jackson said, settling into his chair and ignoring her comment.

"I know…I love it." Larken laughed.

Jackson closed his eyes in the afternoon sun. "So that's why you did it then? To piss her off?"

Larken hadn't really thought about it before, but felt a shade of acquaintance with the notion when Jackson mentioned it.

"Of course not," Larken defended. "I want to be independent, women's liberation, self-sustainability, that whole thing." She waved her hand carelessly in the air.

"Mmmmhmmm," Jackson said, his eyes still closed. "So I guess you're on your way out of this hell hole then."

Larken looked around the perfectly manicured garden, the soothing swoosh of water from the marble fountain bubbling behind her.

"I'm not ungrateful, you know," Larken explained. "I could easily live here and just float. But it isn't fulfilling."

Jackson lifted his head in interest. "Well, if you're bored, I have a treatment for that."

"No, not bored," Larken said swatting at him again, "just not significant."

Jackson shook his head. "Well, hell, Lark. Nobody feels *significant.*"

"Well, I wanna feel something close to it at least." She knotted up her hair, pulling it off her neck. "I realize self-discovery is an overused expression, but I want to know who I am, not just what I am."

They were interrupted by a new housemaid carrying a tray of mint lemonade. Her English was broken but she smiled happily. "Miss Larken, some drink for you and friend?"

Jackson took both glasses from the tray, nodding in thanks to the small woman before handing one to Larken. "So, I guess there's not much hope for me then."

"Why's that?" Larken asked, plucking a mint leaf from the tip of her tongue.

"I was counting on you being the one who knew what both of us are." Jackson laughed into his glass of lemonade, but something told Larken he had meant it.

When the sun melted even the ice from their drinks, the mid-afternoon heat forced Larken back into the house, excusing Jackson home to unpack from his trip.

After Bart had cleaned himself up from his clamming expedition with Lil and returned to The Ashby House, Larken told him about the interview, not mentioning the part about finding the phantom doctor. In customary Bart behavior, he nodded resolutely and responded with one word expressions of encouragement.

Larken detailed Bunny's despondency over her new job,

recalling her comments from the garden verbatim. Bart's mouth turned up into a suppressed smile.

"What?" Larken asked him. He shook his head in dismissal, the smile growing larger.

Larken didn't press him for feedback. Bart's loyalty to Bunny was impenetrable.

Larken showered again after her outdoor nap and tidied up her room to pass the time. She planned the first week's worth of outfits for her new job, entertaining thoughts of which ones Miles Beckway might like to see her in best. She remembered Jane Austen's words from *Pride & Prejudice* about a lady's imagination being very rapid and jumping from admiration to love and from love to matrimony in only a moment. She didn't know why that passage always stayed with her.

She audibly sneered the notion away, making a conscious effort to not allow Miles Beckway's sun-kissed face and sideways smile to spoil what would be a perfectly enjoyable evening celebrating a new chapter.

Larken thought about Jackson, smiling at his valiant display in the garden earlier. Forcing Bunny to face something she wasn't fond of was not for the faint of heart and whatever reservations she had been feeling before towards Jackson were starting to melt away like a popsicle in August.

She slipped on a strapless red silk dress. The material felt vibrant against her skin, the subtle pleats of the skirt moving like graceful ribbons as she turned to view the low back.

Decidedly reveling in her triumphs of the day and the welcome attention from Jackson, Larken held nothing back when she curled her hair into large, loose waves and stepped into four-inch stilettos.

"Well, now he certainly doesn't stand a chance," Bunny said mellifluously from the doorway, watching Larken give the dress a final once-over in the mirror. She walked in holding out a necklace like a sacrifice to an angry deity. Larken smiled, accepting the accessory by turning around so that Bunny could clasp it on.

"I'm glad you're givin' Jackson a shot," Bunny said, straightening the necklace and turning Larken to face the mirror. A delicate strand of pearls held a diamond-crusted bow that hit just below her clavicle.

"It's beautiful," Larken said, touching the necklace. "How come I haven't seen this one before?" She eyed Bunny in question, running her index finger across the pearls.

"Well, I just want you to know how proud I am of you." Bunny waved a hand in dismissal.

"I thought you were mad, not proud," Larken said surprised, realizing the necklace was a consolation gift and not a piece on-loan from Bunny's own collection.

"You're just difficult for me to understand, Lark," Bunny confessed. "I thought all mothers were supposed to know what their children want, but I just don't know what you want. Frustrates me to no end."

"That's because I want something very different from what you want." Larken shrugged, downplaying the seriousness of her admittance. "And I haven't been a child for a long time."

"I'm realizing that." Bunny sighed. She walked to the curtains, fanning them out so that they draped properly. "Well, just be mindful of other people that might want something very different from what *you* want. Whatever that is."

Larken understood her reference to Jackson, but made a face pretending that she didn't know what she was alluding to.

"He's downstairs, by the way." Bunny smiled, hoping to alleviate any heaviness in the room. "And quite frankly, he's never looked better."

Larken walked downstairs to find that, for maybe the first time, Bunny hadn't exaggerated in the slightest. Jackson looked illegally handsome wearing stone-colored Italian chinos and a gray and white striped sweater. His thin, muscular frame was detailed by the clothes precisely, every inch of him groomed to perfection.

"Now that is a dress," Jackson said, greeting her with a friendly kiss on the cheek. Larken's face flushed warm where his lips touched.

"Eh, you look pretty good too, I guess," she said surrounded by Jackson's aftershave and musk like a heavenly toxin.

"Never make it easy, do you?" Jackson joked. "C'mon. I'm starvin'."

Even though they'd been to The Sailor Ball together under similar terms, the evening felt very different. Larken was relieved to be in Jackson's presence, mentally noting that she hadn't suffered any pre-date jitters.

Jackson's Range Rover was freshly washed and practically evidence-free of Avery's existence if not for a Cinderella-esque slipper in the floorboard. Larken took the liberty of opening the sunroof, enjoying the relief that the sunset had brought to the unseasonably warm day. Now in mid-May, the daylight hours had extended dramatically, leaving a warm, fading orange glow until finally setting a quarter after eight.

"Is it a surprise?" Larken asked as they drove North on East Bay Street.

"Mmm, not really." Jackson shrugged, turning onto the Ravenel Bridge. "At least, it won't be a surprise when we get there."

Larken was content with not knowing. She lay her head back on the headrest and looked out across the Cooper River, the green of the marsh ahead accentuated by the beaming orange light from Charleston in the rear view mirror.

Jackson reached across the seat and squeezed Larken's hand. She squeezed him back and held on, interlacing her fingers into his.

Larken sat up straight when a Beauty and the Beast instrumental ring-tone suddenly filling the car with whimsy.

"That'll be Avery," Jackson said with a smile as he reached for his phone. "It's bedtime in Alabama."

Larken smiled and relaxed against the headrest again. It was strange to think of Jackson as a father, but he so naturally fit the description at the mention of his daughter.

"Hey, Little A," Jackson's voice beamed when he answered. "Whatcha' doin'?"

Larken felt like an intruder as she overheard their conversation. Jackson spoke deliberately and softly to his daughter, laughing and asking her for details about her day.

"Well, I'm gonna see you soon," he said sweetly. "I promise."

Larken could hear her tiny, squeaky voice lilting from the phone with animation.

"Be good for your Momma," Jackson instructed her before a

final goodbye. He ended the call and held the phone to his chest. "Man, I hate bein' away from her," he said, shaking his head.

"I bet." Larken grimaced. She thought about Sam and how more than a week without his bulldozer noises and chubby hugs was unbearable.

"She's coming to visit," Jackson told her, looking hopeful at Larken. "School's out now so Kayla doesn't have that as an excuse."

Larken smiled. He'd only mentioned Avery's mother a few times, neither times making it sound like they ended their relationship amicably.

They came to the end of the bridge, crossing into Mount Pleasant. Jackson finally released his grip on the phone, dropping it into the cup holder and concentrating on their destination.

"Let's see here," he said, turning onto a back road that Larken wasn't familiar with. "Molasses Creek is this way, I believe."

Larken looked back across the bridge to see The Pink City looking like a distant memory. After ten short minutes, she felt completely removed from everything that had become familiar again in the past two months—a security blanket of home. She sighed deeply, enjoying the unknown.

"Hey, you alright?" Jackson asked, placing a warm hand on her leg.

"I'm more than alright," Larken answered him, meaning it. "I haven't been to Molasses Creek since Molly Andover's twelfth birthday party at the Hobcaw Yacht Club."

Jackson turned into a residential neighborhood with plantation trees lining a one-lane road, black horse fencing running the length of the lane. The homes were set way back from the road, creating an impressive grand entrance. Expansive yards led to enormous brick and stucco homes boasting deep porches, arched dormers and coastal accents. What the newer homes lacked in patina, they more than made up for in classic southern architecture.

"Molly Andover, huh?" Jackson mused.

"Did you know, Molly?" Larken raised an eyebrow at him suspiciously.

"No, no. I can't say that I knew Molly." Jackson bit his lip. "But I sure knew her big sister Kate pretty good."

"Oh, is that so?" Larken asked, feeling a tinge of jealousy. She eyed him playfully. "Wasn't Kate Andover older than you?"

"By two years," Jackson confirmed proudly. "Do you know what kind of power a nineteen-year-old girl holds over a seventeen-year-old boy?" Jackson shook his head. "You women."

"Me?" Larken scoffed. "I had no part in this." She began to laugh, imagining Jackson in a daze of youthful lust.

"We spent an entire summer following the Dave Matthews Band on tour," Jackson continued. "I didn't even like Dave Matthews."

"Sounds pretty serious," Larken said, looking out the window as the evening fog began to settle over the marshy shallows of Molasses Creek.

Jackson shrugged. "It was alright, I guess."

The car approached the end of the lane as Jackson turned again onto a white sand access road used for slipping boats destined for the Cooper River into the deep, gentle Hobcaw Creek.

"This is pretty untraditional for you," Larken said as Jackson brought the vehicle to a stop beside a dune.

"Yeah, well, you're not just anybody." Jackson winked. "Stay here for a sec." He hopped out of the car quickly and opened up the back hatch, disappearing momentarily before returning—telling her to not peek as he rummaged for more items in the back of the SUV.

Larken covered a broad smile with her hand. She took a deep breath, composing herself as her chest fluttered with nervous excitement for the first time all evening. She wrung her hands together, rubbing the wet, clammy feeling away.

After several more minutes of waiting, Jackson opened the passenger door and extended a hand to help Larken out. She tiptoed carefully in her heels until a boardwalk descended to a small set of stairs. A man-made beach lined the creek bank, lights from private docks on the other side illuminating the water of Hobcaw Creek.

A small wooden table and chairs had been set up on a flat area of sand, the sweet marsh of Molasses Creek concentrated as it meandered into the Hobcaw.

Several large bell jar lanterns lit up the sand around the table and tiki torches smelling strong of citronella marked a pathway to the humble spot.

"You did all this?" Larken asked in amazement.

"Sure did." Jackson shook his head proudly. "Well. I might of had a little help…" He walked over to the table, pulling out a chair for Larken. "It's rustic, but I wanted to make an impression."

Larken smiled, genuinely impressed. "Well, you've done that."

Jackson took his seat across from her and uncorked a bottle of white wine, pouring two generous plastic glasses. A large covered dish sat between two Chinet plates, fancy paper napkins folded carefully beside them.

Jackson took the lid off the dish, revealing heaps of Littleneck Clams in Lil's classic lemon butter and garlic sauce.

Larken pinched her lips in a smile. "You did have a little help."

Jackson brought out more culinary surprises: Russet potato wedges with rosemary and olive oil, Priss' mini-biscuits and even Bart had contributed to the evening with his grilled asparagus tips.

Jackson and Larken ate and drank until the sun did finally set, uneventfully lost in their fluid conversation. Cricket frogs united in a symphony of marbles, chirping together on the creek bank, accompanying a whippoorwill's haunting solo when the mood struck it.

Full of aphrodisiac clams and wine, Larken listened intently to Jackson tell story after story of Avery, his face lit subtly in the candlelight.

"Oh, I'm sorry," Jackson said, shaking his head. "I've been talking about my kid all night."

"I don't mind," Larken reassured him. "I really don't."

The stories about Avery showed a side of Jackson so nurturing and masculine, Larken couldn't distract herself from the increasing urge to kiss him.

"Well, I'm more than a little rusty at this." Jackson ran his fingers through his hair.

Larken smiled, amused at his frankness. "I guess that's what happens when you become a father so young."

Jackson sighed and picked up an asparagus tip with his

fingers. "Yeah, but it all fell into place somehow. I mean, I lost a lot of ground in my dating skills, but, man, can I play dress up." He laughed at the reality of it.

"What was it like when she was born?" Larken asked, not wanting to conjure the emotional details of Jackson's turbulent relationship with Kayla.

Jackson leaned back in his chair and smiled. "Scary as hell. I kept thinking maybe nobody would notice if I just disappeared somewhere. Started over, ya know? But then I saw her. And that was it. Little tiny fingers—little toes. So helpless, but the most powerful force of nature I've ever felt." Jackson smiled broadly. "She's the best thing I ever did."

A breeze blew from the water, quieting the frogs until only the wisp of cordgrass swooshed helplessly in the wake. Larken rubbed at her bare arms, cooled by the night air.

"Oh," Jackson said, remembering something as he rose from his chair. "I thought that might happen." He pulled out a shirt from a wooden picnic basket engraved with Priss' initials and draped it across Larken's shoulders, lingering for a moment while she shrugged it on.

The musky fragrance of his cologne was heavy in the soft fabric, enhanced by the humidity in the air. His hands felt warm on her shoulders and she leaned back against him for warmth as she became aware of just how chilled she had been.

She felt his chest move up and down with a laugh. "Still a lightweight, Larken Devereaux."

"Am not," she responded, looking up at him innocently, her head still resting on him.

He leaned down quickly and kissed her, his thumb rubbing

the side of her face, tugging at her ear lobe, tracing the length of her collar bone under the silky weight of the pearl necklace Bunny had given her. Goose-bumps covered her body, anticipating the movement of Jackson's hand.

Her pulse beat audibly in her ears, her head swirling from looking backwards. Jackson released her from the kiss and wrapped his arms around her, crouching behind her chair. She breathed in quietly, trying to still her heart from the conflict of wanting.

"What are you thinkin' right now?" Larken asked, not able to see his face. She tugged at his arms then wrapped her hands around them, relieved and disappointed at the same time that they had stopped their exploration.

"I'm thinking about how I hope you don't break my heart," Jackson said, smiling into her hair. "Even if I do deserve it."

Larken laughed nervously. "Why do you say it like that?"

"Well, the way I see it," Jackson said, standing up to pour another glass of wine for each of them, "I'm makin' it pretty clear how I feel about you."

Larken nodded, going along with his explanation, but showing no partiality.

"And I don't think you'd mean to, but," he nodded at Larken, "you're a wild card. And I've put it all out there." Jackson held his hands out, his smile showcasing his chiseled face. "At the risk of being vulnerable, whatever we are…" he motioned between the two of them, "…is pretty much all up to you. I'm all in."

Jackson handed Larken's wine to her, crouching beside her in the sand. She felt his warmth again as his body blocked the breeze from the creek.

She took a generous drink of wine and leaned her face close to his, tilting her chair precariously onto two legs as she propped her elbows on her knees. "Well, if we're gonna be honest," she said, holding her words for a time, "I have a whole lot of reservations about you. For good reason, too."

Jackson looked down, a sense of guilt washing over his face. He nodded in understanding.

"Except right now," she said, leaning even closer to him, "none of my reasons seem to matter…and this," she said kissing him, "this feels strangely natural."

Jackson rose to his knees and wrapped his arms around Larken's waist, laying his head against her chest. His breath was hot against her silk dress, sending another surge of turmoil through her body. "Hey," he said in a husky, wine drenched voice, "you're the boss." His hands moved from her waist and firmly across her hips, his breathing increasing the closer he moved to her thighs.

"…then there's gonna need to be some ground rules," Larken said, stopping his hands at the wrist and pulling back to look at him.

Jackson knit his eyebrows together before he hung his head. "Oh boy," he said, grumbling. "Here it comes." He let out an understanding, disappointed sigh.

"I'm just human," Larken pleaded. She set her cup down, rubbing the chill away from her arms again. She knew the wine was responsible for the honesty, but she couldn't help herself now. The truth was she had missed being pursued by someone, being touched and wanted by someone. And Jackson Winslow wasn't just someone. He was alluring and absorbing—crushing logic and instinct in his wake of beauty.

"I just think that it would...complicate things," Larken said, blushing. "It's not like I don't want to." She sighed. "That's *definitely* not the issue."

Jackson held back for a second, his eyes flashing with a moment of restraint before grabbing her and kissing her. "Why do we have to be reasonable about this?" he asked.

"Because," Larken said, wiping at her lips. She left the rest of her reason open for question, but Jackson nodded in acceptance.

"I'm way ahead of you," Jackson admitted. "I forget that you need time to catch up." He bit his lip in consideration. "I've spent years hoping for these moments."

"Well, I did think about you, you know," Larken offered.

Jackson laughed. "I probably don't wanna know what you were thinkin' though, huh?" He squinted at her in question.

"Nuh-uh."

Larken decidedly didn't finish her wine, realizing it had already impaired her decisions enough for one night. She did her best to not think about all of the kissing and the touching and how she wished she could let it continue. Still, a small shroud of triumph in the matter empowered her. She remembered the seventeen-year-old version of herself that would have given anything to have Jackson Winslow begging her for more.

"Do you wanna talk about him?" Jackson asked, making reference to David.

Larken shifted uncomfortably. "There's really nothing to say." She smoothed her dress and wiped sand off her feet. "I'm not hung up on him though if that's what you're asking."

"Well, I would understand it if you were." Jackson shrugged. "You wanted to marry the guy after all." He spoke tightly, as if the thought alone was more than he could stand.

"Feels like a lifetime ago now though."

A wave of recall washed over her. She did her best to not think about David and for the most part it worked. Only the pressure that she woke up with in her chest reminded her of the something lost.

Jackson watched her face intently, reading into the façade of strength that she'd learned to wear.

"I've been in his position," Jackson said sadly. "It's not a good feeling—crushing somebody that you care for."

Larken listened intently.

"I'm not defending him," Jackson explained, holding his hands up. "I just think you should know that it probably isn't cut and dry for him either."

"You obviously don't know David," Larken said bluntly. "Besides, he's not the one that's alone right now." Larken brushed crumbs off the tablecloth. "It's always easier to leave when you have someone to leave with."

"I just think you'd be surprised," Jackson offered diplomatically. "Sometimes the only way is the hard way."

Larken understood what Jackson was talking about now. He had alluded to it before, but the guilt he felt towards Avery's mother obviously still affected him. Larken felt another tinge of sympathy for the woman that had loved Jackson and probably still wanted him to love her back.

"Well, as hard as it is for me to say this, maybe you aren't like most men." Larken smiled, hoping to comfort him somehow.

Jackson tipped up the last bottle of wine, letting the final few drops drain out slowly.

"You do realize you're sayin' this to the guy who just tried to get some on a first date..." Jackson smiled wickedly. "Pretty sure I'm just like all the rest of 'em."

Larken slapped at a mosquito that landed on her leg before wrapping the shirt that Jackson loaned her around tighter. Jackson covered the food, placed it all back into the basket and disassembled the table in record time as the tiki torches flickered frantically in the breeze.

Upon Jackson's insistence, Larken waited in the car while he packed-up and loaded the rest of the picnic supplies. She was glad to be sheltered from the watery breeze and thought about how she had just been in this new place of possibility with David—wrapped in a cocoon of impossible expectation that blinds reality with hope and desire. Larken shook the thought away, reminding herself to stay positive. It wouldn't be fair to hold Jackson in comparison with David as if they were the same person.

Jackson closed the back of the SUV with a controlled thud and hopped in the driver's seat, rubbing his hands together. "We must have a storm comin' in," he said, leaning forward to check the sky through the windshield as he started the car. "Got dark fast, too," he added, sliding his arm around Larken's neck, rubbing gently down her spine.

The warmth from his palm radiated through Larken's back like rays from the sun. "I'm glad we did this," she said, looking at Jackson with her head propped against the head rest. "I think it's the best date I've ever been on." Her cheeks flushed with the admission.

Jackson smiled ear-to-ear. "'Course it was. You were with me." He turned around carefully in the sand and accelerated once the road was in the headlights.

Larken laughed, somehow endeared by his lack of humility and boasting of confidence. "You never did need much assurance, did you, Jackson Winslow?"

"Only with you, Bird." Jackson smirked. "As long as you tell me I'm doing somethin' right, that's good enough for me."

Larken liked how empowering that sounded. "And what if I *don't* like something?"

Jackson shrugged. "Well, if Momma ain't happy…ain't nobody happy. That was always the rule in our house. Still is."

"Yeah. I hear ya." Larken laughed, thinking of their mothers. "Who do you think would win in a Bunny vs. Priss showdown?"

"Oh easy," Jackson said. "Priss. By a long shot."

Larken squinted her eyes in doubt.

"You never got paddled by the woman," Jackson argued. "She's something fierce when she wants to be."

"Well, if we're basing her ability to overcome the forces of Bunny based on her so-called spanking skills, I'd say don't put too much money on her."

Jackson cocked his head waiting for an explanation.

"You are obviously still rotten, so it's safe to assume that she did not have a successful campaign delivering whoop-ass to you as a child."

Jackson laughed heartily and reached to hold Larken's hand.

"Yeah, but imagine what I would have been without her though."

Larken shook her head slowly. "I don't even wanna think about it."

Larken squinted at the brightness of the lights as they crossed back over the cable-stayed bridge, heading back into Charleston.

"It is beautiful, isn't it?" Larken said rhetorically. Sometimes she missed the larger-scale living that she'd easily become acclimated to in Seattle, but what Charleston lacked in size, it made up for in charm.

"Beautiful enough to bring us both back," Jackson answered. "I never planned on being gone as long as I was anyway."

Larken paused for a moment, considering the peculiar coincidences that found them both back in Charleston at the same time. "Yeah, about that," she started curiously, "when did you decide to come back?"

Jackson blew out a puff of air. "Well, it all kind of just fell into place, really. I mean one day I was in Alabama and the next day I was back here." He shrugged. "I saw an opportunity. And I took it."

"So sudden?" Larken asked, still blurry on the details.

"Well, I'd wanted to for years, but I always found an excuse to stay," Jackson said, "but you of all people know that life doesn't always go the way you planned it."

Larken recoiled at Jackson's reluctance to discuss his return to Charleston and the added personal attack. "Okay then…."

"No, I'm sorry," Jackson said, trying to recover. "That came out wrong, but you know what I mean. The truth is I made a brash decision in coming back and I probably didn't do it the right way.

Every day I wonder if I did the right thing. For everyone involved."

"That's about as clear as mud."

"Just know that I want to be better than I am." Jackson rolled to a stop at a red light, his blue eyes lit up in the glow of the amber that filled the car. He accelerated toward the Battery when the light turned green again, shrugging off the heaviness of the conversation.

Jackson was quiet as he pulled up to The Ashby House. "Man, I hate ending it on a low note." He clicked through his teeth and tightened his jaw.

"I don't think we'll end it on a low note," Larken said, perking his interest. She leaned across the seat, hesitating for just a moment near his lips before finally kissing him.

Jackson shook his head as if he'd been hit by a soft pillow, a satisfied smile creeping across his face. "Well, I guess not then."

CHAPTER TWELVE

The Doctor Is In

Larken had considerable time during the remainder of the
week and through the weekend to practice riding her Vespa. At her
grandmother's insistence, Larken embarked on a lengthy trip to
Dewees Inlet for brunch at Boudreaux's—Lil perched resplendently
on the back and channeling Dame Montserrat Caballé singing *Arabella*
the whole way.

Larken met Caroline for coffee in the French Quarter,
enduring the ride over rough cobblestone streets and evading a fly-
away scarf without incident.

And after meeting Jackson for drinks Saturday night and
enjoying more than her fair share of sweet tea vodka, the Vespa, as it
turned out, found a convenient spot in the back of Jackson's Range
Rover. Also convenient was the precarious position in which Larken
found herself in the back seat of Jackson's Range Rover, the sweet tea
vodka allowing for more leniencies than she had permitted just days
before.

Now motoring the short distance to Beckway Cosmetic and Reconstructive Surgery to report for her first day at a real job, she smiled confidently, enjoying a slightly overcast and breezy drive.

Larken parked the Vespa near the back door entrance under an awning and smoothed down her mint green capri pants. Bunny had kept her distance most of the previous week, but had insisted on helping Larken pick out her outfit. Considering the pandemonium created in Bunny's universe due to Larken's first real-world job, Larken welcomed the white flag flown via wardrobe recommendations and was pleased with Bunny's pairing of a black and white polka dot summer sweater and ballet flats to go with the pants.

Larken tried not to focus on Dr. Beckway, remembering what he had said about them not working together much anyway. Still, she practiced her most professional-yet-demure smile in the mirror while waiting for the elevator.

After the short three-story ride to the top, the elevator doors opened to reveal Hazel sitting on top of her desk holding a tiny mirror and applying mascara, mouth gaped in concentration. Her pile of blonde curls was wadded up in a messy bun, her button-down shirt untucked and half-buttoned.

"Damn," Hazel started from behind her mascara wand. "You're a mornin' person, ain't you?" The gravel in her voice insinuated exhaustion.

"A little bit," Larken apologized. "I mean, I don't mind them much."

"Well I do," Hazel growled. "I'm what they call a night owl." She smiled wickedly, a twinkle from the night before shining in her eyes.

She snapped her mirror shut and hopped off the desk. "I'm always the first one here—I like it that way 'cause I need my peace and quiet to be personable with all these highfalutin Barbie dolls." Hazel set off hurriedly down the hallway, motioning for Larken to follow her rapid, hard footsteps. "Don't switch on the lights until 8:59 am or whenever Miles gets here—and here we are." Hazel gave Larken's office a nonchalant wave, sweeping herself out of the doorframe so Larken could see inside.

The pale blue office was cozy with unique wall angles and plenty of natural light. A white farmhouse table served as the desk and a white tufted settee donning brand-new sales tags created a small sitting area.

Hazel quickly studied Larken's face to see if she liked it. "Picked it all out myself," she said, glowing.

"It's perfect. Really." Larken tried to hide her surprise at Hazel's eye for design and walked through the doorway into her new office. She set her bag down, touching the fabric of the settee and admiring the small decorator touches of vintage fashion magazines and an hourglass that Hazel had thoughtfully placed on the seagrass coffee table.

"Well, it sure as hell beats the card table and kitchen stool you woulda got." Hazel scoffed. "I told him if he expected you to put up with *this* job *and* him, he better put in some effort." Hazel arranged some of the dainty desk accessories with pride, wiping at invisible dust.

"He doesn't seem too difficult to work for," Larken said, more question than observation.

"Why? 'Cause he's good lookin'?" Hazel straightened a mirror hanging on the wall, paying no mind to Larken's startled reaction.

"Hmmph. Don't let him fool you."

"No, I just mean—" Larken tried to correct the direction of Hazel's understanding.

"A po' cat and a coon dog have better chances of hookin' up, so you'll have to kiss that little daydream goodbye." She fluttered her fingers through the air.

The ding of the elevator redirected Hazel's attention. "But just in case you *were* wonderin'," she said before walking out of the doorway, "Dr. Beckway never dates patients or employees." She winked at Larken, a corkscrew curl bouncing loose and swinging up and down as she walked.

Larken sat down at her new desk and turned the computer on. She was surprised to see that an email address had already been set-up for her—one solitary email from Miles Beckway occupying the inbox.

Howdy and welcome. We are glad you are part of the team. Have Hazel give you the grand tour if you have not seen it already. She will get you anything you need and has a project I would like for you to look over, too.

See you soon! Miles

Larken smiled at his extremely proper punctuation and lack of conjunctions. His careful, warm dialect bled through the words like spilled ink. She pulled the paper backing off a variety box of pens and highlighters before plopping them into a pen holder with a sigh.

Hazel giggled and flirted from the front of the office, her voice carrying like a kite in the wind. Larken poked her head out of her office to watch as Hazel, perched on the front of her desk, signed for a collection of packages. The deliveryman didn't seem to mind the interaction in the least. He slowly took the pen back from Hazel, sharing a knowing glance before promising to see her the same time next week.

The man winked and then turned to walk away, whistling while the elevator doors closed.

Hazel slouched on the front of her desk once he was gone, her short legs dangling lifelessly. Larken walked towards her, not wanting to disrupt the longing she seemed to be so enjoying.

"Why don't he ever ask me out?" Hazel demanded, slapping her knees.

Larken sputtered. "Oh. I don't know. Maybe he doesn't know you like him?"

Hazel swiveled around to look at her, raising her eyebrows in amazement. "Doesn't know I *like* him? Do I *seem* like the hard-to-get kind?"

Larken stood like a schoolgirl in the principal's office.

"Trust me," Hazel said, hopping off the desk, "he knows."

"Oh, then… Maybe he doesn't think that a girl like you would be interested in him."

Hazel's eyes glimmered. "Well if he's that dumb then he's definitely my type."

Hazel's attention shifted with the hum of the arriving elevator—something only she was so finely tuned to hearing that Larken didn't even notice it. Hazel slipped into her heels and applied fresh lipstick before sitting busily in her chair.

Minus a few medical assistants that had been busy filing charts and prepping exam rooms for the day, the entire surgical team arrived all at once, creating an instant buzz of energy with their entrance. Larken's presence seemed to go unnoticed as they engulfed the office in a post-surgical high, cheerily joking and laughing with one another. As they dissipated into the break room, the front of the office was quiet once again, Hazel's old-time country music playing softly over the sound system.

Larken adjusted her posture and looked at the elevator expectantly.

"He takes the stairs," Hazel said without looking up from a small pile of mail that she was meticulously opening with a long fingernail. "Oh," she remembered, opening a drawer. "This is for you." She handed a disheveled folder to Larken with a thud. "Your first project."

Larken muttered something indistinguishable and quickly retreated to her office to review the folder, anxious and excited at the same time to see what her first assignment from Dr. Beckway could be.

She took a deep breath of mental fortitude before pulling the contents of the folder out. An air of achievement and adulthood filled her chest—feelings of self-worth overwhelming her.

Her manicured fingers pinched at torn magazine clippings, dog-eared editorial columns and folded photos of Charleston's most prominent people and events. Her once eager smile melted into furrowed brows as she fanned the contents of the folder out across her desk, the papers resembled a serial stalkers scrapbook.

Larken thumbed through the clippings, mumbling the highlighted names of people that she had known her whole life, circled and underlined. Pictures of Pelham Overby, a write-up on Dr. Lamar and Sula Richards, an article on Sammianne Swan's estate, a full spread on Miller Worth's political career and countless other personal connections jumped out at her from the papers.

Larken shook her head and started from the beginning of the stack, carefully reviewing each page. A few business cards with dates and events written on them were tossed loosely in with the pages, some of them falling out carelessly as she scrutinized the pages. Clippings from the Junior League of Charleston's newsletter were torn out—more names highlighted and circled.

The startling horse-tooth smile of one Mitsy Lancaster bounded from the pages of *Charleston Magazine*, forcing Larken to quickly flip to the next page.

And then there she was. Larken's thumb and index finger gripped tightly to the gloss coating of a society clipping with a photo of Elizabeth "Bunny" Ashby and Lil at a garden party fundraiser for the Historic Charleston Foundation. The word "linchpin" was scribbled in red ink by Bunny's picture—radiantly smiling as her champagne glass was being topped-off.

Larken rubbed at her temples as she stared at her mother's picture, unsure of what Dr. Beckway had meant by "linchpin."

She brought a hand to her cheek as she felt her face flush hot with embarrassment or confusion, she wasn't sure which. Larken neatly folded the picture of her mother and Lil and plunged her hand deep into the bottom of her purse, holding it there as if drowning evidence.

"Hard at work already, I see," Dr. Beckway's voice boomed from the doorway. Larken tossed her purse on the floor, spinning around in her chair to find him smiling through deep brown, engaging eyes.

"Yes. Hi," she said, jumping up from her chair and extending a hand professionally.

He reached out to greet her, his warm hands wrapping around her small, cold fingers.

"Sorry I couldn't be here first thing," he started as he plopped down in the settee with a sigh. "We had back-to-back FTBs. I'm not doing that again. Took forever." He grumbled as he rubbed his face with his hands.

"FTBs?" Larken asked, sitting back down in her chair politely.

"Facelift, Tummy Tuck, Boob Job," Dr. Beckway said with a wink. "Don't worry. You'll be speakin' our language before you know it."

Larken laughed nervously and she watched as Dr. Beckway immediately picked-up on it. Being in the business of self-conscious people must allow one the ability to sense uneasiness.

"And the office is okay?" he said, elevating his voice in encouragement.

"It's perfect," Larken said, anxiously jiggling a pen between her fingers. "I wouldn't change anything about it."

Dr. Beckway smiled and ran his hands across the faux sheepskin pillow, flicking at the tag it still had dangling. "Yeah. Haze is good at this stuff."

He gestured to the file on her desk. "I suppose we should talk about that?"

Larken nodded yes, heat flooding into her face again.

"Well *those* people," he said pointing to the file, "are Charleston's royalty."

Larken tried to engage him, but her ears were ringing. She

suddenly remembered why it was she left Charleston in the first place.

"You're from here, right? Like born and raised?" Dr. Beckway asked. He waited for Larken's confirmation before continuing. "That's what I thought... So you've probably heard of some of these people then—and may even know some of them." He rose from the settee and moved to Larken's desk. He hovered over the pictures, tossing them around one by one. "I'll tell you right now that I've done work on *most* of them." He laughed light-heartedly as Larken breathed in the woodsy, clean-cotton scent radiating from his shirt. "Now there's a nose I recognize," he said proudly, thumping a photo of Lexie Leverette, another prominent member of Lowcountry society and close frenemy of Bunny. "That one's all me."

He continued to flick through the contents of the file, as if looking for one photo in particular. Larken winced with each flip of paper, anticipating the empty click of the chamber in this bizarre game of Russian roulette.

"So as the face of the non-profit arm of the practice," Dr. Beckway said as he finished rifling through the papers, "you're basically just going to be meeting these people, getting to know them, being your pretty, charming self and earning their trust." He clapped his hands together, the muscle in his biceps flexing.

Larken somehow felt like she was deceiving him by not telling him she already knew most of these people and more than five of them owed her mother a favor and a cup of sugar.

Dr. Beckway smiled crookedly. "So I've got quite a few donors that give regularly to Kindred Hospital to help cover medical costs for Charleston's low income that get admitted. And I of course volunteer there once a month—like the day we met. There's more I want to do though. Right now it's a self-funded project so I'm limited, both with time and money."

Larken thought back to that fateful day at the hospital, understanding more of the puzzle now—the pieces falling in place.

The doctor smiled. "We'll talk about that project another time... For now, these are your targets." Larken glanced down at the folder of clippings, swallowing hard at the photographs of familiar faces. Miles flipped through the pages again, no doubt looking for the picture of her mother and Lil.

"I have contact information for some of them, but not a lot. Sorry." Miles shrugged.

"No worries." Larken smiled tightly. Most of their phone numbers were on Bunny's speed dial.

"Hazel ordered a credit card for you," Miles added. "Once that's in, you can start setting up lunches. Get the ball rollin'."

"Sounds good, Dr. Beckway." Larken smiled.

"Please. Call me Miles."

Hazel knocked at the door before popping her head into Larken's office. "Hate to interrupt, Doc but you got a 'leven o'clock consultation waitin'."

"Right," Miles said, shaking his head to jog his memory. He followed Hazel toward the door and turned around to face Larken. "Oh, one more thing."

"Yes?"

"Do you know Bunny Ashby?"

"No." Larken said without hesitation. "Never heard of her. Sorry." The lie stung the back of her throat like nettles.

"Oh that's okay." Miles smiled warmly. "Ahh, getting ahead of myself again anyway."

Larken felt hives creeping up the front of her chest and onto her throat.

Miles left the room, taking Larken's breath with him.

She inhaled sharply once he was gone and held onto the edge of her desk in disbelief of what had just transpired. As her knuckles turned white and her face became engulfed in the flames of what she imaged hell to feel like, she reached for her purse.

Her fingers trembled as she dialed Caroline's number.

"Hello?" Caroline's voice answered.

"Oh, Care. I did something baaaaad."

*

The open-air ride home intensified the realization of her lie. Larken imagined sweating out the sin in the unrelenting afternoon sun like it was poison.

After speaking with Caroline and being soothed by her birds-eye perspective, Hazel had kept her busy for the remainder of the day. The diversion of work as demonstrated by Hazel was welcome entertainment. As far as Larken could tell, all delivery men were fair-game for the gettin' according to Hazel.

Larken's limited interaction with Miles went without any more mention of Charleston's so-called royalty. He spent most of his day in consultations with new clients and stopped by her office only a couple of times to make sure she was settling in well. With the most subtle of mentions, he had army-crawled underneath her desk to connect her computer to the printer. Larken pretended to be completely unaware of his scrubs playing a dangerous game of peek-a-boo with sun tan lines and *very* firm skin.

At the end of the day, Hazel had organized a small birthday celebration for Carol, a middle-aged woman who, as far as Larken could gather, had something to do with insurance filing. Larken was thankful for the distraction of cake during her introduction to the entire office. While dessert was present, all other things seemed admissible.

When she wasn't doing her best at explaining her job description, Larken was trying desperately to memorize the names and faces of her new co-workers. From what she gathered, the day-to-day office staff consisted of ten people and everyone seemed relaxed and amicable—most of them sharing a long work history. With the exception of Miles Beckway, the office was all women. "An unfortunate disbursement of estrogen to testosterone levels," according to Bunny's theory on hormones.

Miles hugged Carol, wishing her a happy birthday and making the woman blush with a short speech on how none of them would get paid if it weren't for Carol's diligence with paperwork. Miles politely excused himself mid-way through the celebration, making sure to gush over Hazel's baking skills and asking for a piece of cake to-go if Carol would be so kind to share it with him.

Larken watched as Hazel beamed with pride at the compliment from Miles. She slapped at the air, playing it off coolly, but her ear lobes, glowing red, gave her humility away. Larken realized that though Hazel's years of discernible life experience separated them drastically, they must be about the same age. She was fascinated by her candor and self-sufficiency—again made aware of her own immaturity in comparison.

Five o'clock came with much relief. Larken followed Hazel around as she closed down the office, turning off lamps and equipment. She knocked on Miles' office door, but did not open it.

"I'm outta here, Doc," Hazel called through the wooden door as she reached into her purse, recovering a loaded keychain that had a Medusa-like quality about it.

"Okay. See you tomorrow," he said muffled from behind the door.

"Thanks again, Dr. Beck—I mean, Miles," Larken chimed in from behind Hazel. Larken realized how tinny her voice sounded after hearing Hazel's indifferent, gravelly voice.

There was a clamoring from within the office before Miles swiftly opened the door.

"Hey, yeah, we are so happy to have you here," he said, smiling at Larken, paying no notice to Hazel. He tapped at the doorjamb excitedly. "See you in the morning then?" he asked hopefully.

"Of course," Larken answered, careful to not squeal this time.

Hazel turned to leave, rolling her eyes as the door shut again. "Not once has he opened that door to tell me goodnight," she said.

Larken swallowed hard. "I'm sure it's just because it was my first day."

"Humph." Hazel shrugged. "It's not like I care either way. Just remember what I told you."

The Vespa was shining like a ruby in the sun when Larken walked out the back door. The leather had soaked up all of the heat from the day and sitting down took several attempts before Larken could stand continuous contact with it for the short ride home.

Larken coasted into the driveway, her head vibrating from the cobblestones. Miss Anne's Catering van was backed up to the door as two middle-aged uniformed women emerged from the house carrying empty lug-racks. One of the women waved to Larken before lifting the racks into the back of the van and wiping sweaty bangs off her face.

"Don't even think about it," Lil called from the back door. "I know exactly what you're plannin' to do and it's no good. I already tried runnin' and she caught me."

"Lil," Larken whined. "Please. Hide me. I can't do one of Momma's parties tonight. I just can't."

Lil laughed, roping her arm around Larken's waist and pulling her in for a hug. "Oh, mercy you're hot as August. Listen, you only wish this was one of your Momma's froo-froo parties." She sucked in air through her teeth. "I'm afraid this is much, much worse." She paused. "The Middletwins are visitin'."

Larken let out an exasperated sigh of indignation.

"Hush now," Lil continued, "it's been ages since they've seen you and don't worry, they're just as pleasant as ever." Lil winked sarcastically.

Even in the heat and humidity of the sun, goose-bumps shimmered across Larken's skin. "The Middletwins" were actually Larken and Caroline's second cousins, Madison and Addison Middleton. Lil's younger brother Ansel and his "gold-digging Yankee wife" Beatrice were responsible for the pair. Lil had never gotten along with Beatrice, for obvious reasons, but had done her best to welcome and guide her nieces every chance she got. When Ansel carelessly sold the Middleton family house on Rainbow Row and moved to Washington D.C. to pursue a political career, it greatly decreased interactions with the twins.

Larken immediately understood why Bunny had failed to mention their arrival.

"It won't be that bad," Lil patted. "Bart made Planter's Punch. Chug it fast and just...don't stare. They're as gaudy as ever."

Larken composed herself before walking up the stairs through the back kitchen door. Bart stood in the far corner of the kitchen, busying himself unnecessarily with pistachio shells impossibly hard to open.

"Did they run you out already?" Lil asked him in a whisper.

"My sinuses seem to be in disagreement with their copious amounts of perfume." Bart wiped at stinging, watery eyes.

A shrill, unison laugh broke through from the sitting room. Larken reached for a highball to ladle the Planter's Punch into. She drank half of it quickly, choking on the rum before refilling it and topping Lil's glass off, too. Bart stood in rare dismissal of Larken's lack of delicacy.

"You comin'?" Larken asked Lil, facing her body toward the doorway.

Lil shook her head adamantly. "Nope. Already did my time. I've got a slew of benne wafers to make for the women's luncheon at St. Philip's."

Larken nodded in acceptance of Lil's holy excuse and walked out of the kitchen, pushing the hair out of her face. As she approached the sitting room, she heard the non-stop chattering from Madison and Addison. Bunny's fake laugh was used intermittently between exaggerated "Mmmm's" and "Uh-huh, is that right?"

"Oh. My. God," the twins cooed as Larken entered the room. They stood up simultaneously, revealing skin-tight bandage dresses in neon colors. Larken had remembered them with auburn hair, but orange-red shoulder length bobs framed their nymph-like faces now. Just as she had imagined them when she was younger, the twins seemed to operate as one monster in two separate bodies—Addison as the brain and Madison as the hype-man.

Bunny sat with her legs crossed. She held a delicate hand under her chin, the dazed look of social fatigue tugging on her eyelids.

"Oh, you are *finally* here," Bunny greeted Larken with a nod. She looked relieved to share in the burden of the weighty visit.

The Middletwins were several inches shorter than Larken— both small, but built up-hill like bulldogs. They carefully navigated around the furniture in enormous high-heels, dripping in perfume as Bart had mentioned. Each of them wore a solitary gold letter around their necks—"A" for Addison and "M" for Madison. Addison wore an orange sherbet colored dress that was the antithesis of complimentary to her hair color. Madison, who Larken seemed to remember as disliking the least, wore a lime green dress. The rest of their accessories matched exactly.

"My goodness," Larken said with a forced smile as each of the women took turns air kissing both cheeks. "What a surprise."

"Well, hon, you were still in Seattle when we came through last time," Addison said as the twins took their seats on the sofa again. Larken sat near Bunny in a very uncomfortable wooden chair.

"We were so looking forward to your wedding," Madison chimed in, breathy and diffident. "You would have been a beautiful bride." Both twins stared at Larken with blank faces.

"Oh." Larken politely dismissed them with a wave of her hand. "Thank you, but it really is for the best." She had gotten so used to hearing and saying those words that she had stopped even considering the truth in them.

"It really is," Bunny interjected, reaching for her glass of Planter's Punch on the sofa table beside her. "Larken's doing so well now. And you can't imagine how excited everyone is to have her back home for good." She pursed her lips proudly, sitting back in her chair.

"I always say you can't stay away from Charleston very long," Addison added. "At least I know we can't... The people here are just so...cute and simple." She sighed.

Larken glared into her highball as she took a long swig of punch.

"I heard that Jackson Winslow has come back, too," Addison said demurely, looking at Bunny for confirmation.

Bunny tilted her head like a bird of prey. "I didn't know you knew the Winslows."

"Oh of course," Addison said in a sultry voice. "We stay up on our Charleston gossip. The whole Eastern seaboard, really."

Madison enthusiastically shook her head up and down in agreement.

"We see Taylor in New York from time to time and Jackson, too when he's up visiting from Alabama," Addison continued. "You know how we southerners are drawn to each other." Addison snickered self-indulgently.

Bunny breathed an ironic laugh. They were as southern as

they were alluring.

"Anyway, Taylor's quite the eligible bachelor in New York," Addison explained. "We're at *all* the same parties and we know *all* the same people."

"Naturally," Bunny said coolly.

Larken could feel Bunny's intolerance of the twins' self-appointed socialite status radiating off of her.

"Addison and I have always joked about ending up with the Winslow twins and how funny that would be," Madison finally interjected. She smiled widely at Larken. "Because we're twins and they're twins and we're all southern. The Twinslows and the Middletwins. Wouldn't that be funny?"

"That *would* be funny," Larken responded through a forced smile.

"It's not ideal that he has a child, but at least he finally left that trailer trash of a girl he was with forever." Addison scoffed. "Such a gold-digger, too."

Larken shifted uncomfortably in her chair and opened her mouth to protest.

"Yes. Well," Bunny spoke tightly, beating Larken to a response. "I think we've all had more than our fair share of gold-digging trailer trash inconvenience our lives from time to time, don't you?" Bunny swung her crossed ankle like a perturbed cat's tail.

Addison blushed pink, sensitive to the insinuation Bunny had made about their mother. She giggled uneasily.

"I hardly doubt she's trailer trash," Larken corrected. "I would guess I probably have a lot in common with her actually."

Addison laughed shrilly in protest. "Oh, I doubt that *very* much. She's a stage five clinger if you ask me." She raised an eyebrow for emphasis. "I've met her you know. In the Stella Artois tent at the Kentucky Derby. She was like a fish out of water with all of us society people. It was cruel of him to bring her really... She's pretty enough, but you just never want to see one of our *own*, especially someone like Jackson Winslow, with someone so...opportunistic. I don't even know who her connections are."

Larken felt the familiar sting of empathy for Kayla zing through her. Avery would be her constant reminder of Jackson and the life that she could not have with him. She didn't deserve women like Madison and Addison belittling her on top of that.

The newest housemaid, Amara, providentially redirected everyone's attention as she carried in a beautiful platter of tomato tarts and explained in broken English that the shrimp in the ceviche was fresh-caught on James Island. Bart and Gloria watched her presentation carefully from the hallway and nodded at each other with approval when she walked by. Larken noticed Bart had changed into a nautical themed outfit, complete with Sperry's and a black and white striped pullover.

"I do hope we get to see Caroline and the baby," Addison asked as she hastily bit into a tomato tart, the juice running down her chin. "Will her family be joining us on the boat tonight?"

Larken realized Bunny's plan of removing the girls from the house and out of her hair. The ultimate compliment of her hospitality had been extended to them on a very long stick.

Bunny threw on a quick smile, avoiding looking at Addison's mouthful of food. "Oh, yes. And just wait until you see Sam with his

Auntie. The two are practically inseparable." She winked at Larken and reached over to squeeze her leg.

Larken nodded in defeat. Bunny had secured her participation for the evening with the lure of Sam, knowing she wouldn't happily go along with the company of the Middletwins otherwise.

"And Larken…make sure Jackson comes along, too." Bunny batted her eyes. "It sounds like the girls would love to see him."

Addison squirmed, the hint of alarm across her face. "Well, don't do anything on our account."

Madison was still two sentences behind in conversation and hadn't caught the plot, a wispy smile still fixed on her face.

"Oh, it's no bother at all," Bunny said deviously. "He and Larken are a couple now. Childhood sweethearts, really…" She beamed triumphantly. "But you probably already knew that—being society people and all."

The twins were silent, their mouths agape.

Larken was amazed at the intricate way her mother could wind an insult around a compliment. In any other setting she would have contested the label of coupledom, but just to see the twins twitch, she carried the title of Jackson Winslow's girlfriend with honor.

"I bet you have lots to catch up on," Larken said, torturing the twins with the reality of coming face-to-face with the object of their gossip. "He'll be *so* thrilled to see you."

Bunny hid a smile behind a fork full of ceviche.

*

Jackson could not recall ever meeting the Middletwins in New York or any other place for that matter, so he agreed naively to a night of their inescapable company. Larken saved him the trepidation of a warning and convinced her conscious this was only fair as gossiping was a sin anyway.

The orange glow of a lazily burning sun and the sweet swell of humidity-drenched flowers ushered in late-afternoon energy. Larken had just enough time to throw on a navy and white striped racerback dress and grab a sweater by the time Jackson pulled up to the curb. Before he could knock, Larken swung the front door open and squeezed out through a cat-sized opening.

"C'mon," she said, kissing him breathlessly before twirling around and pulling him down the stairs.

"Where's the fire?" Jackson asked, following her.

"Oh, no fire. I just wanna get there." Larken shrugged as she opened the passenger side door and hopped in hastily. She closed the door quickly behind her, refusing Jackson's chivalry.

Jackson walked slowly to the other side of the car and leaned in to look at her. He recoiled from the rum on her breath. "Alright. Let's hear it."

"Fine, but can you drive at the same time?" Larken winced.

Jackson shook his head as he buckled up. "Never mind. I don't even wanna know how bad it's gonna be. Nobody ever has second cousins from anywhere that are normal, but the kind you don't even wanna ride in a car with?"

Larken bit her bottom lip. "Thank you for coming. I owe you—big time."

Jackson smirked. "Well, strictly speaking from an investment perspective, it never hurts to have a pretty girl in your debt... Don't think I won't collect."

*

The City Marina was a very short drive from The Ashby House. Still, Larken had enough time to finally decompress from not only the waylay of the twins' arrival, but also from her first day of work.

Larken told Jackson about her new office and some of the office staff, casually leaving out all mention of Dr. Beckway. She stopped herself before describing the birthday party for Carol, remembering that Bunny had always said, "Men find the tedious details of a woman's day boring."

Jackson pulled into the marina and parked beside a familiar Mercedes.

"Is that Bart's car?" Jackson asked as he reached for a thermos in the back seat.

"That would be *Captain* Bart tonight," Larken said. She thought back to when Jesse Vasser, Bunny's fourth and most popular husband to date, had insisted that Bart learn the ropes of seafaring. Bart had taken to the nautical life like a fish to water and seemed to be the only one in the house that used the yacht on a regular basis. On Jesse's worst days during his battle with cancer, Bart had taken him out on the water to enjoy the ocean air and feel the sun on his face.

Jackson carried a thermos with him as he and Larken walked down the long, undulating dock. Bunny's inherited boat slip was on the outer side of the Ashley River with a straight shot to the Charleston Harbor that meandered to the Atlantic.

Larken hadn't seen or been on the yacht since Jesse's ashes were spread six years earlier. Now among the tranquility of the marina and the grand vessels that ebbed at the docks, Larken tried to remember why she hadn't spent more time on the water, counting the years wasted on dry land.

They approached the vessel, a ninety-eight foot pristine white yacht called "Lady Elizabeth"—the name painted proudly in navy blue on the starboard side. Jesse had designed the entire craft with Bunny's every luxury in mind. It was an elegant, commanding vessel and the only one of Jesse's impressive, handcrafted collection that Bunny had kept following his death.

Bart was standing on the flybridge, dark hair blowing in the wind, a pewter mug of rum, water and nutmeg grog in his hand when Larken and Jackson approached.

"Permission to come aboard?" Jackson called out with a smile.

"Ahoy," Bart projected in his best skipper voice, nodding once with a stoic smile. "Permission granted."

Jackson boarded first, turning around to help Larken aboard. She quickly removed her flip-flops and stowed them in storage bench.

Jackson climbed up to Bart's perch and they surveyed the water together. Larken watched Jackson as the wind flapped at his navy linen pants and pressed his white T-shirt against his chest. He reached up to roll the bill of his ball-cap tighter, nodding with a smile at something Bart was explaining to him. A feeling of delight surged through her at the sight of him.

The same ladies from the catering van that Larken had seen at the house a couple of hours earlier emerged from below deck. They smiled and quietly took their stacks of food trays with them.

Bart came down from the flybridge to thank them again for the delivery and set-up.

"Any chance we could make this a party of three?" Larken

asked as she heard the twins' shrill voices travel down the docks, unsettling the tranquility of the marina like a siren.

Bart smiled. "I'm afraid not."

Priss and Lil lead the way, scarves and hats in tow. Hank happily escorted the twins, one on each arm as they oohed and ahhed over the boats in their slips.

Larken pursed her lips to stifle a laugh when she saw that they hadn't changed out of their dresses or high-heels, both inappropriate items for a cool night at sea.

Bart evaluated their outfits, too. "They'll be spending most of the evening below deck it seems," he whispered to Larken with a straight face. He looked as if he could sneeze at the thought alone, his sinuses still recovering from the earlier encounter with their perfume.

Larken bumped into him with her hip and laughed.

Bunny was nowhere in sight, but Larken supposed that a fashionably late entrance, even on her own boat, was in order.

"Now girls," Lil called to the twins as Bart extended a hand to her and then Priss. "You'll have to take those high-heels off before you climb aboard the Lady Elizabeth. Bart would have your hides if you scratched her." She winked at him proudly.

Madison and Addison shared an agitated glance from the dock before obeying their Aunt's instruction.

"I don't care if they are thirty-eight years old," Lil said quietly to Larken as she leaned in for a hug, "they ain't clompin' around in those hooker heels on this baby."

Jackson descended to the main deck, hands in his pockets. He held an intrigued smile at the side of his face.

Madison and Addison climbed aboard awkwardly, each of them holding their shoes and struggling to keep their dresses from riding up.

Madison immediately regained her composure when she saw Jackson. She elbowed Addison to get her attention.

"Oh, Jackson," Addison said loudly, "it's so good to see you again."

Jackson politely moved forward to shake her outstretched hand. He glanced at Larken for any sign of an explanation, clearly not remembering ever seeing her before.

"We heard you were back home," Madison continued casually. "We saw your brother at David and Phillipe Blond's party in New York last week in fact."

"Uh-huh," Jackson responded, still trying to place their whereabouts. "I'm sorry…tell me your names again?" Jackson motioned toward the twins, noticing for the first time their coordinated ensembles.

"Oh I know," Madison said, batting her eyes, "even being a twin yourself it's hard to tell other twins apart, isn't it? No offense taken at all."

Whether she was playing it cool or legitimately thought Jackson knew who they were, she didn't show it.

Jackson laughed uncomfortably.

"I'm Addison," she explained. "And this is Madison." Madison pathetically held up her letter "M" necklace as proof.

"Okay then," Jackson grinned. "Good to see you…again." He turned around to Larken, who was stifling a laugh.

After a half hour of drinks and appetizers, Bunny ambled down the dock with Mr. Boca Raton on her arm. The entire group, minus the twins, released a collective sigh at the sight of him.

Bunny took deliberately wide strides in her flowing coral gauchos. She had a black wrap thrown across her right shoulder and a silk scarf tied over her head into a turban. She smiled at a few of the other boat owners, occasionally adding a nod here and there. Mr. Boca Raton kept a hand at her lower back, his shockingly white teeth revealed through the same smile he kept plastered on his leathery face at all times.

"Oh goodie," Larken whispered to Lil. "Why did Bunny have to invite him?"

"She didn't. It was my idea." Lil winked. "I'd just as soon go overboard, but look here… JD Hart prides himself on being a society man."

Larken had to think for a second before remembering Mr. Boca Raton's real name.

Lil motioned toward the twins who were posing suggestively for pictures on the side of the boat and making duck lips. "I suspect they'll take to each other like pigs to mud."

*

Once Bunny boarded the boat and a fresh round of cocktails was served, Bart and Jackson untied from the dock with the help of the marina crew and the Lady Elizabeth embarked out to sea.

Caroline had grown wise to Bunny's scheme and she regretfully declined the invitation, citing Sam's bedtime as the reason for their absence.

After accelerating past the no-wake zone, the sea breeze

blowing melodiously across the vessel, the twins dove for the cabin—begging their new best friend Mr. Boca Raton to come with them.

"Aren't they just *fabulous*?" JD said with a goofy smirk as he pranced behind the twins. He draped an arm around each of them.

Larken watched Bunny who, surprisingly, didn't seem jealous. Bunny climbed up to visit with Bart, discussions of dinner being served and a run-down of the yachts operations as part of their conversation.

The boat moved toward the mouth of the Ashley River, the remaining glow of the setting sun kissing the peaks of gentle waves as Lil announced dinner. Larken drew in a deep breath of the boggish, floral scented river air as it mixed with the brine of the open sea.

"It's a shame to go inside and miss all this," Jackson said.

Larken hadn't felt Jackson standing beside her until he spoke—the alcohol partly to blame. She reached for his hand and they went below deck to join the rest of the party for dinner.

It was a raucous affair in the dining room. Despite the twins as poor family connections, they did prove to be entertaining in a crowd. Still, Larken agreed with Bunny's fortuitous decision to not take them out in Charleston proper. Hank and JD hung on their every word, mesmerized by their loudness and contrasting neon colors like moths to a flame.

Bunny and Lil served up seafood stew as a starter and then left the rest of the food out buffet style.

French chicken in vinegar sauce, mashed potatoes, roasted broccoli and sourdough rolls steamed in chafing dishes—the fragrance filling the dining room completely. One-by-one, everyone served their own plates, the Middletwins careful to only take a tablespoon of everything.

After a little while of steadily cruising, Bart shut the engine off and anchored down in order to join the party. The smooth jazz playing over the sound system could finally be heard—a thoughtfully compiled playlist from Bart's own collection. He quietly served himself a plate and took a seat near Jackson. They discussed the latest investment news, Jackson giving Bart a few pointers on trends in stocks and bonds. Bart nodded politely, always careful to not speak too much of money at the dinner table.

Priss left the table momentarily to return with an unmarked jar of her famous moonshine. She pursed her lips together, proud to share her latest batch.

"Now we're talkin'," Hank said as he clapped his hands together excitedly. "Ever had moonshine, girls?" He stared at the twins, hoping to introduce them to something new and exciting.

Madison and Addison shook their heads no. "I can't say that we have." Madison laughed uncomfortably.

"Well, you won't find any of *this* in New York City, I can tell you that right now," Priss squealed.

Lil stood quietly, biting her tongue. She winked at Larken from across the table and hid a giggle with her hand.

Bunny watched with perked eyebrows as Priss served them each a double dose of her secret sauce.

"Now this has just a hint of apple pie, girls," Priss explained as they took their first sips. "Careful not to let it fool you because—"

The whole table watched in astonishment as the twins downed their full servings of moonshine.

"—it's about a hundred and ninety proof," Priss finished, a little stunned.

"They'll be out like a light in ten minutes," Lil said from behind her napkin to Larken.

Larken excused herself from the table politely. It was too warm and already too noisy to endure the twins' chemical reaction to Priss' moonshine.

A gust of fresh, cool air greeted her when she made her way onto the deck. Larken had peeled her sweater off at dinner and while the temperature difference on the deck sent a chill through her, she couldn't will herself to go back below and get it.

She walked to the back of the boat where the deck was sparsely lit and the moon made reflections on the water as it weaved and bobbed through cloud cover.

The sound of the water hitting the boat almost muted the laughter from the dining room. She pressed her waist against the railing and inhaled the fresh air deeply, goose bumps running across her bare arms.

Jackson came up behind her, wrapping his arms around her and clamping his hands together by her waist. The seawater air mixed with his cologne and the warmth of his body against hers sent a shiver down her spine.

"I didn't realize how cold I was," Larken said, explaining the shudder that ran through her body.

Jackson moved the hair off her shoulder and kissed her neck.

"Jax," Larken warned, "your mother is on this boat."

"So is yours," he contested between kisses. "Besides...they're all below deck eating dessert anyway." He traced her belly with his fingertips. "And three sheets to the wind."

"Well, the captain can see us right here," Larken argued, turning around to hide a shiver. She nodded toward Bart's dark figure above them, oblivious to their nearness.

In one swift movement, Jackson moved Larken to the shadow of the overhang where they were safe from view of the captain's perch.

Larken stood breathless, her back against the ship's wall. Jackson pushed against her body as he kissed her, moving his lips to her neck as he ran a hand down her thigh, pulling her dress up.

She inhaled sharply when she felt the warmth of his hand under her dress.

"Tell me to stop or I won't," Jackson whispered, his breath tickling her neck. "I can't quit on my own." He hovered over her with intense eyes, waiting for a response.

The undeniably controlling part of Jackson is what Larken both loved and hated about him. The selfless offer to tell him no was always met with the guilt of refusing him.

"If I don't tell you to stop," Larken explained, her breath quickening, "it's only because I'm being selfish."

Jackson nodded, a little stung by the realization of what she meant.

"It won't mean anything," Larken clarified, leaning her head back against the wall and closing her eyes. Jackson dove to kiss her exposed neck and opened her legs with his knee.

"Not here." Larken grabbed his hand and pulled him toward a

set of six stairs leading down to the back deck.

White chaise lounges for sunbathing on warm, sunny days were set up under the overhang of the top deck. The occasional splash of water hit the deck when the boat surged, but it was as quiet and private a spot as they could find.

Larken walked under the dark of the overhang, leaving Jackson standing on the deck, waiting. She slipped out of her dress and walked out to meet him.

The evening had brought with it partial cloud cover—even still, enough light shone through the clouds to steal Jackson's breath when he saw her standing there nearly naked, her body illuminated by the reflection of the moon on the water.

He wrapped his arms around her, touching her as if he was trying to memorize every curve. They walked slowly toward the cover of the overhang to the chaise where her dress lay. Larken sat down, unbuttoning his pants while he cupped her breasts, gently tugging at her nipples.

He met her on the chaise, the heat from his body covering her like a blanket. He reached underneath her, her back arching as he pulled her thong off. Jackson smiled and tossed them overboard before losing himself in kissing her lips, her neck, her breasts.

It had been seven years, but the feeling Larken experienced all those years ago was still the same, only more experienced.

Jackson moved deep inside of her with gentle, rhythmic pressure. He required less concentration now, seemingly enjoying every second of her pleasure before losing himself in his own.

*

By the time Jackson and Larken redressed and stood

243

innocently on the back deck, hand in hand, Bart had returned to his post. The stuffy air below deck had finally driven the loud, drunk party to the upper deck for fresh air.

Bart brought up the anchor and the quiet of the water was drowned out again by the large engine churning over as they headed back toward the marina.

Larken and Jackson walked up the stairs to the main deck, Larken self-consciously smoothing her hair down.

"Well there they are," Priss waved. "Y'all been up to no good?"

"No," Larken whined, trying to hide her embarrassment. "We were lookin' at the stars." She looked up to see thick cloud cover moving lazily across the sky—not a star in sight. "…tryin' to at least." She noticed Jackson's hair, tussled and pulled.

"Hmph." Priss took another drink and set her attention on Hank, roping her arm through his and leaning her head on his shoulder.

Everyone had switched to beer except for the twins who were reportedly passed out below deck in the dining room. An untroubled atmosphere settled over the party in their absence.

Now that dark had made its stay for a couple of hours, the chill of the water had resigned confidently in the air. Bunny pulled out several throw blankets from one of the storage benches and distributed them by couple. Priss and Hank, Bunny and JD and Larken and Jackson took seats beside each other, throwing the blankets over their legs. Lil grabbed her blanket and headed up to the captain's roost to stand with Bart. She threw the blanket over their shoulders, the smile of perfect happiness beaming across her face at the helm with her best friend.

Larken watched as Bunny sat perfectly unamused. Mr. Boca Raton sat beside her with the blanket tucked around his legs, keeping his hands outside of the blanket—a symbol of complete lack of interest.

"So what exactly are you doing in Charleston, JD?" Larken asked pointedly. Jackson pinched her under the blanket.

JD squirmed before setting his face with a forced smile. "Well, I came for just a quick business trip—to talk your *dear* mother into selling me that hideous swampland in the Lowcountry. But of course one thing lead to another and now I feel so...at home here."

Bunny threw a quick, tight smile at him, completely void of any fondness. Larken thought again about this property in the Lowcountry, certain she'd never heard Bunny mention it before Mr. Boca Raton entered the picture.

"I find it *most* invigorating here," JD continued with a smirk. He reached for Bunny's hand, kissing the top of it before placing it back on her side of the blanket with a sterile pat.

Larken yawned, the day's events finally catching up to her. Jackson pulled her close, her head falling naturally onto his shoulder. She felt his chest rise with a deep, contented breath.

It felt nice to be somebody's again. The lull of the boat and the warmth of Jackson felt practical. She stiffened at the thought. Her relationship with David had felt practical, too. No doubt she had loved David, but she also loved their functionalism as an obvious match. Jackson stared out across the water, rubbing her arm and unknowingly soothing her back to a state of ease.

Bart brought the engine down to a rumble as they ambled

back into the marina. They idled for several minutes while the marina crew readied for their return. Two of the men looked as if they'd been sleeping in the boathouse, waiting for the last vessel of the evening to return.

Jackson helped the women off the boat—Hank swaying as he helped them back into their shoes once off-board and laughing heartily at his own inebriation. Waking the twins had been a gruesome task that Lil volunteered for. With smeared lipstick on their mouths and fake eyelashes dangling off their eyelids, Lil pulled them from below deck with military-like orders to "get a move on." Their drunken stupor showing their age and crease marks from near constant frowning.

Once the Middletwins had sauntered off, Larken's feet hit the boardwalk with a wobble, another reminder of how long it'd been since she'd gone out on the water.

"Lost your sea legs there, Larken?" Bart called down from the balcony as he oversaw the safe departure of his passengers.

"Just a little bit."

"I try to take her out a couple of times a week now," Bart told her. He nodded, turning to look out across the harbor. "Too pretty not to. You know, I could use a couple of deck hands when I make a run down to Southport next month. We could make a weekend of it." He smiled at Jackson, confirming the invitation to them as a couple.

"I appreciate that, Bart," Jackson said, rubbing Larken's back. "Maybe you could teach me a thing or two."

Bart saluted them before turning and finishing his captain's duties. Larken watched the rest of their party climb into two separate Escalades and be driven away.

"Looks like I need a ride home." Larken gestured at the taillights disappearing into the darkness.

"Good," Jackson said, wrapping his arms around her and kissing her.

Larken played with the hair at the base of his neck while they swayed side to side under a street light, the dock creaking and moaning with each lap of water. She moved her hands to his neck, her wrist brushing something at the back of his shirt.

Jackson kissed her forehead. "I hope you don't regret tonight."

"Me too."

Jackson laughed nervously. "I only wanna do right by you, you know." He smoothed her hair down. "You make me try harder. I need that. I'm innately selfish, you know."

"Well, I'm having my own season of selfishness right now," Larken admitted, stopping his self-deprecation. "I'm close to falling into this, but I want to walk into it with my eyes open. I owe myself that." Larken choked back the notion that a deeper resistance kept her from total surrender.

"I know." Jackson nodded. "And I'm fine with it. I've waited this long already." He kissed her forehead again. "And I ain't goin' nowhere, Birdy girl."

Larken yawned, her eyes watering from sleepiness.

Jackson jostled her playfully. "Let's get you home."

They walked towards Jackson's car, holding hands more as friends than as lovers.

"By the way," Larken said, knocking into him with her hip,

"your shirt's on inside out."

"Oh yeah?" Jackson smiled, bringing Larken's hand to his lips and kissing it. "Well your underwear are floatin' somewhere in Charleston Harbor."

CHAPTER THIRTEEN

Unexpected

The start of Larken's second week at Dr. Beckway's office was met with much more understanding of her job description.

Larken arrived at the office early enough most mornings to brew a pot of coffee for Hazel before any negativity could be propagated. For a typically mild mid to late May, spring felt more like summer on the Vespa and Larken found herself timing everything around the hottest parts of the day.

She fell easily into the routine of a work schedule again, enjoying the majority of her time being doled out in increments and the sense of organization it brought. It gave her time to sort her thoughts, too.

During her first week, Miles left a pendaflex folder stuffed with miscellaneous papers on her desk with a sticky note saying, "Charitable Giving Database." From business cards with amounts written on the back to even movie ticket stubs with contact information jotted down hurriedly, Larken spent an entire work week compiling the information and inputting it into an electronic database.

Miles stopped by her office several times, apologizing for such a mundane task and letting her know that she was over-qualified for data entry.

"As you can see," he said standing in her doorway with a sideways smile, "I've needed you for a long time."

Miles had made contacts over the years in almost every state and an assortment of other countries, too—some she'd heard of and some she hadn't. There were pictures of him in the field with fellow doctors, at discussion panels with low to high level political figures, pictures of him with people of various ethnicities, smiling and embracing them. All evidence of his well-traveled life.

"Hazel," Larken asked from her office as she walked briskly by her door one day. "One time Dr. Beckway mentioned another project of his. Do you know anything about it?"

Hazel shrugged, obviously satisfied to keep her in the dark. "Yeah. You'll see." Hazel tapped her fingernails on the doorjamb of Larken's office and kept walking.

She knew it wasn't her business, but if Miles wasn't meeting with new patients or doing post-op checkups, he was scarcely visible in the office. The presence, or lack thereof, of the surgical team indicated when surgery was the reason for his absence. As soon as he could wrap-up clinic business and change into shorts and a T-shirt, he was gone again.

Despite her best attempts to not think about it, Larken could almost count the minutes he'd been in the office during her nearly two week tenure. And she could recall all of their interactions word for word, all of them briefly spoken from under an ancient Mossy Oak ball cap as he hurried off to whatever tee-time or fishing hole she imagined he escaped to. The weight of most day-to-day decisions fell on Hazel—not that she seemed to mind ruling the roost. No one else in the office gave away any inkling of concern with his lack of involvement in the office either—though it was hard to question someone as charismatic as Miles Beckway.

Larken was relieved to not have any more mention of Bunny—though she could feel the lie she told Miles on her first day festering inside of her like a septic splinter.

*

The Friday before Memorial Day weekend, Larken woke to the roll of thunder and a cascade of rain falling outside her bedroom window.

She lay in bed and watched the clock tick through her usual morning run time. She'd gotten used to running in the rain while she lived in Seattle. She hadn't particularly cared for it at first, but David promised she wouldn't even notice the rain after a while. He had been right.

The spring rain in South Carolina was different though. It felt heavier—wetter. The drops fell with purpose and had an objective, each one leaving a residue that sunk in slowly to the skin like sweet oil.

Larken figured that running was the only thing she'd really kept of David's. When she first came back home, each mile of pavement felt like she had borrowed something of his. It had been as bittersweet as wearing a lamented ex-boyfriend's sweatshirt—a self-inflicted pain that brings healing through the opening of old wounds. Now she ran because she was disciplined to it. And only every now and then did she feel like she had loaned it from him without asking.

Larken finally crawled out of bed with twenty minutes to get ready for work. She skipped the shower and headed straight for the closet, pulling on the first pair of jeans she could find. Without checking the weather, she could tell it would be soupy from start to finish.

She reached for a brown canvas bag full of outerwear in the back of the closet and pulled out a purple North Face rain jacket that she'd ordered before leaving for Seattle. She skipped the rubber wellies and slipped into some more work appropriate boat shoes that nearly tied her jeans and slouchy button-down together in some form or fashion.

Larken looked in the mirror and shrugged, hoping that casual Friday was implemented by office staff this drastically. She ran frizz serum through her hair and wiped her face with a washcloth before applying a quick coat of mascara and dusting her cheeks with bronzer.

Larken peeked out her window to gauge the likelihood of driving the Vespa to work. It was doable in a life-threatening situation, but certainly not ideal. As if on cue, Jackson pulled up in front of The Ashby House. Larken smiled, momentarily considering driving the Vespa out of spite for his presumptuous gesture. She threw on her rain jacket and grabbed her purse before setting off down the stairs.

Bart and Lil were already in the foyer to meet Jackson by the time she got to the bottom of the stairs.

"Well, aren't you just the sweetest?" Lil complimented him, patting Jackson's rained-on back.

Bart shook his head approvingly at Jackson's chivalry. Larken noticed that he was dressed in a rain slicker with keys in hand ready to offer her a ride.

"You ready?" Jackson nodded at Larken with a smile. She

knew he was proud of himself. "Coffee's in the car."

Lil zipped up Larken's rain jacket and kissed her cheek like she was sending her off to school.

"Bye-bye, Jackson." Lil waved. "Thanks again for pickin' my girl up."

"Naw, my pleasure." Jackson winked at her.

"Oh and Jackson," Lil called as they walked out onto the porch, "will we see you on Edisto this weekend?"

Larken's face flushed hot with embarrassment. She had completely forgotten to mention anything to Jackson about the beach house. He of course knew the Ashby family went for almost every occasion, the ritual pilgrimage to Edisto for holidays both observed and Bunny-made engrained in both of their childhoods, but it had slipped her mind to invite him. She knew he wouldn't think it was unintentional.

"Oh." Jackson scowled. "That's right—Edisto." He smiled warmly at Lil as he and Larken made a dash for his car. "We'll see."

Larken climbed into the passenger side door as a sheet of rain blew directly in. Lil and Bart ducked back into the house quickly, Lil throwing Larken a wave before closing the door, the lion head door knocker bouncing with a metallic clang.

Jackson started the car and handed Larken an insulated cup of coffee that read *JCW Investment Group*.

"Your own coffee tumblers, huh?" Larken mocked. "I'm very impressed with you, *Jackson Carter Winslow*."

"Oh, don't be," Jackson dismissed. "Save it for the beer koozies—they've got dollar bills on 'em."

After several sips of coffee and some navigating from Larken, Jackson pulled up in front of the office building.

"I really appreciate you driving me, Jax." Larken smiled. She casually glanced outside to look for anyone that may be watching before leaning over and kissing him lightly on the lips.

"That's just what boyfriends that aren't *really* boyfriends do for girlfriends that aren't *really* girlfriends." Jackson winked, playing off the explorative statement.

"At least all the benefits are still there," Larken reminded him suggestively as she opened the door. "Bart said he'll be close by around five, so he'll drive me home."

"Hey," Jackson said, stopping her, "we should probably talk about this weekend, too. Call me after work?"

"Sure." Larken took one final drink of coffee before hopping out of the car, avoiding puddles as she ran to the front door.

The rain had thrown off her usual schedule and Larken walked out of the elevator a couple minutes past nine o'clock.

Hazel was in a happy, unusually perky mood. Her casual Friday look of sweatpants and an off-the shoulder T-shirt caught Larken off guard—Larken's own outfit choice seeming more than acceptable in comparison.

"We don't see patients on half-day Fridays," Hazel said, defending her attire.

"Oh. I didn't know it was a half day today." Larken shrugged. She ran a hand through her hair, tangled from wind and rain. Hazel turned a country station up louder than usual and started organizing paperwork in her bare feet.

"Yep," Hazel said over the music, "Fridays before holiday weekends are always half days. We just do administrative stuff and basically no real work. Doc never comes in, so usually it's just me and the medical records and insurance staff."

Larken shrugged her rain coat off and held it over the entry rug to drip.

"You know, you probably didn't even need to come in today," Hazel said with a twisted mouth. "Sorry. Didn't think about it."

"Well, you're here." Larken smiled.

"Yeah, but I'm office staff. You're more like Doc's little pet." She winked at Larken before spinning on her heels and grabbing another pile of papers to sort.

"Um, no," Larken said through a failed attempt at hiding a smile at the notion of being something special to him. "I'm—I'm just like anybody else here."

Hazel lowered her nose. "Oh right, 'cause you're *just* like the rest of us." She laughed dryly.

"I'm not really sure what that means, Hazel. Am I doin' something wrong?"

"Oh Lord, no, girl," Hazel chirped. "You're obviously doin' everything right. It's just you got your own sort of humble high-brow thing goin' on. You're Target and we're Wal-Mart, ya know? Doc can't help but treat you different. You *are* different."

Larken's shook out her rain coat again. "I'm Target?"

"Oh, sorry," Hazel said. "Target's this store where you buy like *almost*-designer labels and they've got home goods that are too fancy for us trailer types where as Wal-Mart is like—"

"I hope you're kidding," Larken interrupted her with a glare. "I know what Target is. I just don't know why you think I'm Target."

"Well, don't let it ruffle your feathers," Hazel soothed condescendingly. "I'm more a K-Mart and Piggly-Wiggly girl myself, but I really think it's all determined by where you're Momma shops. I'm sure there's fancier stores than Target, but it's all I could think of.

"So you're saying I don't fit in here?"

"That's the thing, see," Hazel said, going on about her paperwork, "you fit in real good. That's how come we can't tell if you come from money or you just have a stolen credit card you buy those fancy handbags with."

Larken swallowed hard at the thought of the office staff discussing her background. She tucked her Chloe purse behind her.

"But then," Hazel said, her voice escalating, "I figured it all out." She thumped a large stack of files down.

Larken stopped breathing for a second—quickly replaying her last two weeks and the denial of her own mother.

"You've got yourself a sugar daddy." Hazel's eyes flickered with the hypothesis.

"Hazel—"

Larken was cut short by the sudden arrival of Miles Beckway. His insistence on using the stairs created a constant element of surprise.

"I didn't think we'd be seein' you in the office today," Hazel said, hand on her hip. "Need somethin'?"

"No, no," Miles answered without breaking his stride or looking up. "It looks like it's clearing up though, so I thought I'd head south."

Larken looked at the skylights and saw a steady stream of rain distorting the view.

"I figured you'd be runnin' off down there today." Hazel shook her head in disapproval.

"I'd already be there if I could find my journal," Miles grumbled. "You didn't move it again did you?" He opened a cabinet behind Hazel's desk filled with office supplies and scoured it, knocking over a box of pens in the process.

"Would you cut it out?" Hazel barked, pushing Miles out of the way and setting the mess he made straight. "I did not move your journal this time or last time or any of the other times you lost it. I bet if you cleaned your office once in a blue moon or let me have at it, this wouldn't keep happenin'." Hazel started opening drawers in an attempt to appease him, pushing them closed with force when they came up empty.

Miles ran a hand through his hair in frustration and finally looked up to see Larken, clutching her jacket and purse. "Oh, Larken. Hi. Good morning."

"Hmph," Hazel grunted.

"Hello," Larken said quietly, suddenly aware of the special treatment Hazel had recently made her aware of.

"Where was the last place you know you had it?" Hazel asked, trying to redirect his attention.

"Smoaks—I think," Miles said. "But I always bring it back with me." He looked at Larken confidently and smiled.

"Smoaks," Hazel repeated disdainfully. "Ten bucks says it's in the floorboard of the mud truck."

Miles chewed on the side of his mouth in consideration. "Hmmmm."

"I'm right, ain't I?" Hazel smirked. She sat down with a thud and released a huff of air. They spoke to each with a level of fluency far above that of mere colleagues.

"Maybe," Miles said, turning and walking back toward his office, mumbling something else along the way.

Larken quickly moved to her office, tossing her jacket and purse on the settee carelessly. The file of Dr. Beckway's financial donors sat neatly put back together with a print-out of all previous contributors fastened on top with a paperclip.

She stared at the file for a moment, the anticipation to find out his interest in Bunny Ashby nearly eroding her from the inside out.

Larken picked the file up and headed toward Dr. Beckway's office, the sound of shuffling papers greeting her from the hallway.

"Dr. Beckway—um, Miles," Larken said meekly as she knocked.

He stood over his messy desk, smiling briefly at her arrival.

"Come in. Please." Miles pointed to the chairs across from his desk and continued his search in the desk drawers.

"Ah-ha," he said excitedly, finally pulling out a bag of Dum-Dums from the second drawer he searched. He tossed them in a beaten brown leather bag and sat down in his chair with a sigh.

"What can I do for you?" He asked, running a hand through his hair. He made a quick pile out of his paper-filled desk in an attempt to straighten up.

"Well, I finished the database yesterday," Larken explained, tapping on the folder. "And I reached out to about half of the targets you gave me...some have already contributed."

"I know. It's very impressive."

Larken felt guilty for how easy it had been to ask her mother's friends for money.

"So I thought...maybe there's a time that we can talk about the other project you mentioned."

"Oh, right." Miles nodded thoughtfully. He chewed on the side of his mouth for a moment, studying her carefully. He stood up from behind the desk and grabbed his leather bag. "How's today work?"

*

Within a matter of minutes, Larken had grabbed her rain jacket, purse, given a vague explanation to Hazel for her sudden departure and met Miles in the parking lot.

He waved her over to an old, white half-ton Ford pickup truck that was a far cry from the Bronco she'd seen him in at The Sailor Ball. She climbed in and closed the passenger side door, its hinges creaking and rubbing before closing with a rusty bang.

Miles coaxed and sweet-talked the engine, twisting the key again and again before finally getting it to turn over with a magnificent, sputtering roar. They rumbled out of the parking lot, the axels and springs in the seats working against each other with each bump and pothole.

The truck smelled like WD-40 and sycamore—part old truck and part Miles Beckway. A Randy Travis tape stuck out from the dash, discolored from years of sun exposure and age.

Miles politely excused himself from conversation and made a quick phone call. The person on the other line seemed to know him well as he confirmed an order of gauze, surgical tape, sutures and an assortment of other surgical supplies that Larken had never heard of before.

Larken felt the same excited nerves she had felt as a sophomore in high school when Nathan Anderson offered her a ride home from a party. After a year of pining for him from a distance, she sat across from him in his dad's Toyota Camry, her heart beating so fast that she was too winded to say more than, "Thanks."

Nathan Anderson moved to Colorado that summer, but she'd never forgotten the feeling of sharing an experience with someone who by only speaking your name brought you into existence—from nothingness to somethingness.

The rain held a steady drizzle as Miles turned onto Savannah Highway heading south out of Charleston. He positioned himself in his seat, seemingly accustomed to the familiar drive. He ended the call and tossed his phone into the brown leather bag that sat between them.

"Sorry 'bout that," he said, looking at her from the driver's seat and re-gripping the steering wheel. "I usually make a lot of my business calls on these drives. Makes 'em go by faster." He smiled and leaned back against the dusty fabric seat. "It'll be nice to have some company instead."

"So, how long are these drives?" Larken asked through a squinted eye.

"Oh, just down the road an hour or so today." Miles shrugged, dropping a hand from the steering wheel. "I mean, sometimes, depending on where I'm going in the Lowcountry, it can be two or three hours just to get to whatever swamp or bog I'm headed for. I wouldn't do that to you though. Unless you really wanted to…" He raised an eyebrow in question and laughed.

"Let's see how today goes," Larken joked, realizing she was on the verge of flirting.

"You know how sometimes you just have to see something for yourself before you can begin to understand it?" Miles asked.

"I do." Larken nodded, admitting to herself that she didn't have the faintest clue what he was referring to.

"This is kind of one of those things," Miles said seriously. He looked at her with a smile and held his eyes on her face before glancing back to the road. "I 'precciate you being willing to come."

"Sure," Larken said with a shrug.

Forty minutes into their drive, they crossed over Edisto River, reminding Larken immediately of Jackson and the real reason she hadn't thought to invite him to the beach house for the holiday.

"Big plans for the weekend?" Miles asked, bringing Larken back from her thoughts of Jackson.

"Not really." Larken smiled. "My family does the same thing for every holiday."

"The backyard cookout, game of corn-hole, slip-n-slide kind of thing?" Miles asked. He laughed under his breath like he remembered something.

"Yeah, sorta' like that." *Nothing like that.*

The rain picked-up as they crossed into the Ace Basin, an acronym for the Ashepoo, Combahee and Edisto rivers. The roomy, four lane Savannah Highway became the Ace Basin Parkway where the road narrowed—funneling travelers into the Lowcountry with large, encroaching trees.

Logging trucks ambled slowly by, splashing waves of water across the truck's windshield. Old white churches, small houses with yards full of broken down cars and road-side stands speckled the parkway.

There was an empty beauty in the drive as the trees gave way to farmland. The trees stood back from the road now, growing taller to sit above the sandy soil. Marsh mud had begun dotting the land, uniting a convergence of rain runoff and river water. The smell was like that of Dewees Inlet, an eruption of sensory overload.

Miles watched Larken take in every piece of changing scenery. "You don't come this way much, I take it," he said breaking the silence.

"Not since I was little," Larken answered from a daze. "Which feels like a shame." Larken thought back to the time she rode to Savannah with Lil when she was twelve. This trip with Miles already far different than the tea social she had attended then.

"Well, I'm from here," Miles offered. "A little bit north of here in Colleton County, actually. In Ruffin. Right on the Lowcountry Highway." He pointed with his thumb towards Larken's window.

"Never been there." Larken strained out the window in the direction he'd pointed.

"Oh, no." Miles shook his head with a smile. "A girl like you wouldn't have any need to go there." He repositioned in his seat again, the springs in the seat pinging and popping under him.

"My family grew Virginia peanuts," he said with a raised

262

eyebrow. "Three generations of peanut farmers. My mother was a nurse—Miss Annie." He smiled thinking about her, the same smile of someone who is remembering a lost loved one.

Larken watched his face, trying to guess his age. *Thirty-seven, thirty-eight maybe?*

"You didn't want to be a peanut farmer?" Larken asked.

"Nah," Miles replied. He chewed the side of his lip like he had the day she'd met him in the hospital. "Wasn't an easy decision though." He shrugged in acceptance. "My brother Duke tried it for a while, but he's got a black thumb and a short temper."

"You're not what I would expect," Larken blurted out. "I mean that, ya know, in a good way." She felt her face flush hot.

Miles smiled. "I appreciate that."

"I haven't figured you out yet," he said with a squinted eye. "But when I do, I figure you won't be what I expect either."

Larken laughed nervously—the reminder of her lie ever present.

"Hey, speakin' of peanuts," Miles said as he slowed down and pulled into a gravel outlet. "How 'bout some of the best boiled peanuts you ever had?"

He hopped out of the truck quickly and walked to a road-side stand fashioned with mismatched pieces of wood and plastic tarp for rain-proofing. A sign reading "Grunnuts" and "Reezy Peezy" advertised the Gullah word for peanuts and the slow-cooked Lowcountry dish of red peas and rice.

A smiling, middle-aged black woman with a floral head wrap stood up from a camping chair and opened an aluminum pot sitting on a charcoal grill. She stirred the contents of the steaming pot before ladling several large portions into a strainer. She shook the strainer vigorously, excess liquid dribbling out, before dumping the contents into a brown paper bag.

"T'engky," Miles said as he handed the woman a five dollar bill. She smiled at him widely—the exchange seemed routine for them.

"T'engky" was one of the few Gullah words that Larken remembered learning from Hawa, a Gullah house-keeper that was much too self-respecting and outspoken to work for the likes of Bunny for more than one grueling season of the annual Festival of Houses and Gardens.

The rain was only a drizzle now, sometimes bits of sun peeked through the clouds, ricocheting light on drops of water for a nearly blinding spectacle. Lil always said that when you could see sunlight through the rain it meant the devil was beating his wife and like so many sayings Larken had grown up with, no one really knew the origin.

Miles took a handful of peanuts and gave the warm brown paper bag to Larken. Larken's stomach growled, reminding her she'd skipped breakfast. Boiled peanuts were a welcome meal, the aroma of salt and steam making her mouth water.

"Do you know about the bunny?" Miles asked, biting a peanut in half and giving it a quick glance as he drove.

Larken's pulse quickened. She felt the color draining from her face.

"In the peanut," Miles explained, passing it to Larken. "There's a bunny in every peanut. See?"

Larken looked and saw the outline of a rabbit—a body and

two large tell-tale ears. She laughed, relived that he wasn't referring to her mother. "I've never seen that before."

"Sneaky little critter, huh?" Miles smiled.

Larken cracked a peanut and popped it into her mouth. *You have no idea.*

Miles put the truck in reverse, swinging his right arm around the bench and extending it, lightly brushing Larken's hair. He wore a T-shirt like the one he had the first time she'd met him—tanned and toned arms tugging gently at the stitching.

"You do something different to your hair?" Miles asked as he threw a peanut shell out the window.

Larken tussled her hair in awareness, smoothing down the rain and wind styled strands. "I didn't do it at all."

"Hmph." Miles raised his eyebrows, reaching for another handful of peanuts. "I like it."

The scenery changed yet again as they wound farther south. Live Oaks wearing sheets of Spanish moss hovered lazily over the roadway, trapping in the humidity from the rain.

Their destination was certainly a rural one as they passed fewer cars and saw fewer signs of civilization. Cicadas calling in the trees created a hum as loud as the engine, reminding all visitors of the wildness that would never be tamed from this place.

Larken was comfortably adjusted to the bouncing truck bench as Miles turned onto an unmarked red dirt road. He rolled the window down and drove slowly across potholes that the rain had weakened and washed away.

"We'll see how far she gets us," Miles said with his arm out the window, holding onto the frame of the truck.

Larken could have asked him exactly where they were going, but there was something about being with Miles that didn't need explaining.

Several miles back and before the bend in the road, Larken had seen a sign for Yemasee—yet another place in the vast Lowcountry that she'd never ventured to. This area felt more secluded though—unchartered enough for a name to be unnecessary.

Tall pines rose out of sandy soil, woodpeckers briefly interrupting the constant drone of cicada songs. The front tire hit a large hole in the road sending both of them bouncing violently.

"Whoohoo," Miles yipped. "That's what I'm talkin' about."

Larken laughed nervously, her heart racing from the cajoling truck. They rolled to a bog of mud and stopped. Miles put his index finger to his mouth and surveyed their chances of crossing.

"I tell you what," he said to himself as he forced the truck into reverse. He swung his arm behind Larken again, carefully watching for potholes and trees as the truck retraced its path.

He rolled to a stop about forty-feet from the mud bog and put the truck back into drive.

"Hang on a sec," Miles said as he stomped on the gas, dirt and pebbles noisily spraying out from under the truck.

Larken squealed as they lurched forward, Miles swerving quickly here and there to miss gaps in the road. He reached across the truck bench with his right arm, hovering just above Larken's shoulders as if he could keep her from going through the windshield should the seatbelt fail. She wanted to reach out and hold onto him, but kept a tight grip on the peanuts instead, some of them popping out of the bag.

Mud sprayed everywhere as the truck tore through the bog, leaving the left side of Miles' face splattered with the stuff.

"Hot damn!" he shouted out of the window as he wiped at mud with his forearm. "That's my favorite part!"

Miles reached for Larken's cheek and gently wiped a small splattering of mud away. "Guess I coulda' rolled my window up," he said through an apologetic smile.

"Oh, no, it's fine." Larken wiped her whole face with a napkin from the peanut stand. "I go muddin' all the time."

Miles roared with laughter. "Yeah, I bet you do."

At the speed they traveled across the rugged terrain, it was the longest five mile road Larken had ever gone down.

"What would have happened if we couldn't pass that mud bog?" Larken asked.

"What, back there?" Miles shrugged like it was nothing. "You trek in with mud boots. I'm usually just a couple miles out if I get stuck."

"Oh," Larken said as she looked down at her pristine boat shoes. "I'll bring my wellies next time. Just in case."

"Next time?" Miles looked shocked. "So I guess it's goin' pretty well then…"

"Does it… not normally go well?"

"I dunno. Never brought a girl out here before."

"Not even Hazel?" Larken asked surprised. It felt like a natural question.

"Nah." Miles shook his head. "You kiddin'? She'd be hot as a two dollar pistol on this drive."

The rain started falling lightly as the road widened into a dirt-packed flat. The pungent smell of creek water and clay poured in through Miles' open window.

He rolled the truck to a stop by a fallen tree, the engine shuddering out with exhaustion. Larken opened the passenger door, the hinges creaking loudly as they had earlier.

Miles grabbed his leather bag from the middle seat and set off down a well-walked path.

"I'm supposed to follow you, right?" Larken asked, unsure.

"Yeah, c'mon." Miles waved. "Just right over here."

An expanse of bright green plants poked up surprisingly in perfect rows. Larken looked around to realize they were surrounded by a sea of paddy fields—beautifully serene chartreuse rice plants reflected in standing water creating a vivid color contrast against the red clay beneath them.

Larken followed Miles around a bend of tung oil trees to a collection of shacks elevated three or four feet above bare earth on cinder blocks.

The shacks were situated in all directions—almost as if they were built wherever the wood that had been used to build them washed up from the creek. Screen doors hung precariously on worn hinges, mismatched rags served as curtains in the windows, the porches littered with everything from buckets to rusty appliances.

Larken walked slowly behind Miles, carefully stepping over pieces of trash and debris. A scrawny cat scurried from its curled-up position on the stair railing of one of the homes to take refuge under the porch, bright yellow eyes watching every move from the safety of shelter.

"Do people...live here?" Larken asked in a whisper.

"Oh yeah," Miles answered back in full-voice, seemingly unfazed by the poverty around them. "It's a whole tribe. Some Gullah people mixed in, too. There's at least twenty different families up and down the creek that live in these parts and work the rice."

He repositioned the bag on his shoulder, setting his jaw as they approached a house close to the tree line.

"I'm familiar with Gullah people, but what do you mean by tribe?" Larken asked, confused. "Like Indians?"

"Hey, Mītta Mile," a husky voice boomed from behind them.

Larken turned to see a small, light-skinned black man with a bright white smile standing behind them—rod, reel and bucket of fish in tow. He wore too-big navy khakis and a white T-shirt stained with red dirt, sweat and creek water.

"What's up, Roland?" Miles smiled. He changed his course and turned back to meet the man. Larken followed cautiously, suddenly feeling like a trespasser.

The two men shared a firm handshake—Roland glancing at Larken curiously.

"Catch anything?" Miles asked, peeking into the bucket.

"Did I catch anythin'...?" Roland repeated mockingly, slapping at his leg. "Who you thinkin' I am?" Roland laughed heartily, his raspy voice traveling throughout the flat. "I thnagged me up thum a dem trout and theepshead, ya know. Gotta put thum thuppa' on the table thumhow. And a fat, juthy bull frog duth thittin' on the bank, so I grabbed 'em up quick ath a thwamp cat. I be the only one care fer frog legths though."

"Roland, I want you to meet my friend Larken," Miles said nodding in Larken's direction. "Larken, this is Roland Oxendine."

"Oh, oh," Roland nodded. "I thee, I thee." Roland wiped his hands on his pants before extending a handshake to Larken. "Any friend of the docta a friend a mine."

Larken could see his face more clearly now—high cheek bones and almond shaped eyes.

"So how's Momma doin'?" Miles asked as they set back towards the shack near the tree line.

Roland shook his head. "Dith baby thtill give her the worth time, you know. Thumtime it theem dat baby comin' early, but I know ith too thoon."

"Yeah, it's still too soon." Miles nodded, understanding the man perfectly. Larken struggled to follow.

"Your Momma bring about her firth one," Roland continued. "Tha wuth thickthteen yearth ago now. Maybe you bring about her lath one." He laughed hopefully.

"Well, we've talked about what's makin' all these babies, Don Juan." Miles elbowed him with a grin.

"I know it." Roland shook his head. "Don't matter no way. We ain't got nothin' elth ta do." He laughed again, quieter this time as they approached the stairs of the porch. "We too old for more chirren now anyhow."

"You go let her know I'm here and tell me when she's ready." Miles smiled.

Roland hurried up the stairs, dropping his fresh catch off

before pulling at the screen door, the frame wobbling from the disturbance.

"Are you an O.B., too?" Larken asked Miles with wide eyes.

"I'm a little bit of everything out here." Miles chased a mosquito away. "I've only assisted a couple of births—the midwives are usually here for that. Roland and Miss Ellery have ten, almost eleven kids, so he's pretty good at delivery now, too, but they've had some complications with the last two."

Roland came back to the screen door and waved Miles up.

"Do I come with you?" Larken asked, still unsure of her role in their visit. She felt lightheaded with anxiety.

"Yeah, c'mon." Miles nodded. "Miss Ellery will love you."

Larken followed Miles up the four stairs leading to the house, each one creaking underneath them, but sturdy enough.

The house smelled of freshly fried food and the musk of creek living. The shack was really one large living area with a curtain separating what Larken thought must be a bedroom.

Several small children played quietly in the front of the house, all of them stopping and staring when Miles and Larken walked inside.

Larken noticed that all of the children had the same facial features as Roland—high cheek bones and smiling, almond eyes.

Larken smiled at a little girl who looked to be no more than five, her flower dress passed down from years of use by much older sisters. Her small, light brown face showed deep dimples when she smiled and she quickly appreciated having an audience, picking up her baby brother and twirling him around. The baby squealed with delight with each rotation, his eyes growing big at the speed.

Larken followed Roland and Miles through the curtained room. A full-size mattress was pressed against one wall, multiple other pallets on the floor nearby littered with stuffed animals and old quilts.

"Hey, Doctor Beckway," a weak, sweet voice greeted from her position on the bed. The woman turned over and sat up with some difficulty, her pregnant belly exposed beneath a stretched-out shirt. She regained her breath, winded from the minor movement.

Ellery was a very small woman with smiling, kind eyes. She had strong Native American features with silky black hair and the same light brown skin as the children. It was hard to tell since her belly seemed to be the majority of her mass, but she stood no more than five feet tall, thin limbs extending gracefully out from her body.

"Roland tells me you're still havin' some trouble," Miles said as he approached the bed. "Let's take a look here." Miles sat his bag on the floor and reached inside for a stethoscope.

Larken noticed that Miles talked out of the side of his mouth—the perfect complement to the side-smirk he held most of the time. She hadn't noticed it before, but this was the longest she'd spent with him.

Ellery looked at Larken briefly, a tired smile serving in place of a greeting before her eyes went back to the floor. Larken suspected that Roland had informed her of the new visitor.

"I just know somethin' not right," Ellery told Miles as she rubbed her belly. "Sometime I feel birthin' pains in the front. And I got a ache awful bad in my back—don't 'member havin' before. I'm not but twenty-six weeks."

Miles dropped to the floor on his knees, leaning forward with the stethoscope to Ellery's belly. He placed his left hand against her back as he pressed the metal receiver to her abdomen.

"Well, everything sounds good," Miles said as he removed the stethoscope and stood up. "But I think you feel different because this is your first set of twins." Miles smiled at Ellery, her face set with shock.

"Twins," Ellery repeated. "How you know?" She watched him intently.

Miles clapped Roland on the back. "I heard three sets of heartbeats—yours and two fast, little heartbeats."

Roland kissed Ellery on the forehead, pride washing over his face.

"Now there's a couple other things I need to check out today," Miles continued, unfazed. "Show me where your back's hurtin'."

Ellery rotated on the bed to show Miles the pain, lightly touching both the left and right side of her mid to low back.

"Tell Mitta Mile 'bout the blood, too," Roland chimed in.

Ellery winced. "When the pain real bad I get blood in my urine...and sometime I wet the bed."

Miles touched Ellery's back gently, carefully examining the tender areas.

"You have fever?" Miles asked, reaching into his bag again.

"Sometime." Ellery nodded.

"Sounds like you've got a kidney infection," Miles said, straightening back up. "That would explain why your back's hurtin', and your other symptoms."

"I tell her thee just be too lazy ta go to da outhouth." Roland laughed loudly. His face looked lighter with the explanation of her symptoms.

Ellery glared at Roland playfully, too tired to be embarrassed.

"Now, Ellery," Miles said as he pulled out a bottle of antibiotics from his bag, "because baby Luke was born just a couple months before you got pregnant again and because this is your eleventh pregnancy, these babies are comin' early. Twins don't always go full term anyway, but I don't think your body is gonna go all the way this time."

Ellery nodded slowly while she listed to Miles, her brows furrowed with concern.

"Unless you want to come to the hospital in town, which I know you don't, I'd like the midwives here for weekly checks for the next three weeks. And then I want them here for daily checks after that. If something happens, they'll let me know and I'll be here fast as I can."

Larken swelled with worry for the woman despite the reassurance and authority in Miles' voice. Their everyday conditions were not fit for a complicated pregnancy.

Miles handed the bottle of antibiotics to Roland. "She needs one of these pills twice a day, in the morning and at supper, for ten days. These will get rid of the kidney infection. Even if she feels better, keep giving them to her 'till they're gone, okay?"

Roland nodded at Miles, taking the pills gingerly.

Ellery laid back down, Roland covering her up with their worn bedspread, chills covering her arms even in the damp humidity of the room.

Miles and Larken emerged into the main part of the house,

the children still quietly sitting and playing. Miles pulled out two Dum-Dums from his leather bag and handed one to each of the kids old enough to have them, the baby watching closely and drooling.

Larken noticed the oldest child, a boy, with a faint scar from a cleft-pallet on his upper lip. He was beautiful—his Native American heritage obvious in his features.

"Hey, Levi," Miles said bending over to stand face-to-face with the child. "Are you ears still hurtin' sometimes or are you all better?"

"All better," Levi said quietly. He smiled.

"Good boy," Miles said, rubbing his head. "Glad to hear it."

"Everybody else doin' okay out here?" Miles asked Roland once they'd reached the porch.

"Oh, yeah, you know." Roland shook his head. "I tell errabody to thtay outta trouble till they Momma better. The little oneth no trouble yet, but the big oneth now," he whistled, "the big oneth like to kill me. I try to keep 'em busy out in the rith paddy wit me though. They do alright when they plantin' rith plugths and ain't bickerin'."

"Well, tell them all hello from me." Miles smiled. "You're doin' a real good job, Roland. I know it's not easy with Ellery bein' down."

Roland shook his head. "It be alright. Long ath I can keep my land I be thankful."

"We're gonna get to the bottom of that," Miles told him reassuringly. "You've got plenty of people willing to fight on your behalf. Me included."

Larken listened to their conversation as she looked around to see some of the other residents outside of their houses—curiously watching the Oxendine's shack and the activity there. Miles offered a friendly wave to one of the men a few doors down.

Roland followed them to the truck, holding a medium-sized sheepshead fish that he insisted Miles take for his trouble. Miles pulled a canvas tart back in the bed of his truck and handed Roland a sack of everything from bar soap to powdered milk. He threw the fish, gutted and cleaned, in a small cooler saved for such an occasion, covering the bed of the truck back up with the canvas.

The exchange was anything but charity. Miles offered up the basket as a friend would and Roland accepted it as such. Miles agreed to be back in ten days once Ellery had completed her round of antibiotics. Roland closed Larken's passenger door, smiling at both of them as they drove away from the creek flat.

Larken sat in stunned silence as they turned back down the five mile dirt road full of potholes and rain run outs. The bumps in the road and the shaking cab didn't seem to faze her this time—she looked down at her hands, filthy from nothing except exposure to the ways of creek living.

"I don't know about you, but I'm starvin'," Miles said, breaking the silence.

Larken scoffed. "It's hard to think about eating after...all of that."

"Why?" Miles asked.

"Well, because, I've never seen anything like that before."

"You can't pity them, Larken," Miles told her. "That's not what I come out here to do."

"I'm sorry. I can't help it." Larken shrugged. "I didn't know...people lived like that. If you can even call it living." Her eyes burned with dirt and the prick of tears.

"You *can* call it living," Miles said seriously. "Not the kind you and me are used to, but living all the same."

Larken felt the sting of correction, her pulse quickening. Maybe she was her mother's daughter after all—judging and entitled.

"Roland Oxendine is one of the smartest, most capable men I know. He fishes, farms rice and harvests tung oil. There's pride in that. He and Ellery love each other and have done one hell of a job raising some of the most polite and well-behaved kids I've ever met. He has nothing and yet everything because he's free." Miles tapped the steering wheel. "I envy him."

"But if it weren't for you, how could they get by?" Larken asked earnestly.

"I'd be foolin' myself if I thought my small contribution to their lives made the difference between them makin' it or not." Miles scratched his head. "If anything, I get more out of it than they do. These people have been livin' out here for at least three generations. There lots to learn from them."

"I'm sorry," Larken apologized. "I don't mean to be offensive it's just—"

"No, not at all," Miles interrupted her. "First time I went on a Lowcountry house call I felt the same way. Your instinct of empathy is good—it's vital. But they aren't suffering. They're thriving out here."

"What did he mean about being able to keep his land?" Larken felt like she was talking to a friend now, suddenly pushed past the threshold of strict professional interaction.

"Ahh," Miles grimaced. "There's a developer trying to buy the three hundred acres that they're on." He had already anticipated the mud bog ahead of them and floored the truck, extending his right arm again to keep Larken secure in her seat.

"A developer?" Larken asked.

Miles nodded his head. "And the thing is, the Oxendines don't actually own the land—apparently not legally anyway. Roland said somebody from Charleston suddenly says they own it even though they've been living on it and farming rice on it since his great-granddaddy's time. I have a hunch as to who it is…"

Larken's stomach knotted up. She had a hunch, too.

"Old money is hard to fight," Miles continued. "And that's exactly what this smells like to me." Miles held the gas pedal down until the truck popped over a log. "They're black indians, but the state doesn't really see them as indigenous. Their tribe is Lumbee—they're mostly in North Carolina, but some of them broke off and came down here."

Larken's mouth was dry. She looked out the passenger window and squeezed her eyes shut tight.

"My main goal right now is getting a clinic in place down here," Miles explained. "For visits like the one we made today, I don't need my whole surgical suite, but when I'm trying to treat a staph infection or perform an appendectomy, I need something more permanent that these people can access and feel like is theirs."

"Surely there are other doctors that are willing to come and help you."

"You would think so, huh?" Miles smirked. "You hear about doctors and nurses in the medical community that selflessly spend a week or two every year in a third world country offering their services, and that's noble, but nobody wants to come out here. I should know because I used to be one of them." Miles looked out of his window as they reached the main road, the transition from rough dirt road to smooth asphalt creating a sound void in the truck. "It's beautiful land. Sounds like it's gonna be a fight to keep it wild though."

Larken's stomach bottomed out thinking about the Oxendines and the other families and what they would do if Bunny got her way.

"Why do they stay here?" Larken asked.

"Because it's home," Miles answered simply. "And it's all they know."

Miles turned the truck the opposite direction from where they'd come and headed for Yemassee. The town was quiet and quaint, twelve miles and a far cry from the creek flat living that the Oxendines and other families did. The sun burned through cloud cover and steam from the asphalt rippled across the road.

The truck self-guided to a service station, Miles pulling around back to a small building with a smoker out front and a sign for Cherry Cider dangling haphazardly on a post.

The aroma of food, salty and fried, awakened Larken's senses once again.

"C'mon," Miles said as he climbed out of the truck, "you're gonna love this place."

Larken walked onto the porch of the little building skeptically and followed Miles to the ordering window. A chalk board spattered with age and grease hung out of reach above a silvery-haired woman ready to take their order.

"Always good to see you," she said, greeting Miles with a

maternal wink. "The usual?"

"Oh yeah." Miles smiled, rubbing his stomach. "But let's make it a double today for my friend here."

Miles turned around to Larken. "Trust me on this one."

"Sure," Larken said enthusiastically. She didn't tell him she would have eaten a tire.

"You got it," the woman said. "Be right out."

"So you know everybody in these parts?" Larken joked.

Miles thought about it for a second. "Mainly the ones that cook good food or need medical care." He grabbed two Styrofoam cups and filled each of them with tea from a sweaty, orange beverage cooler.

"And this is what you do? I mean, when you leave the practice?"

"Well, not all the time." Miles shrugged. "Sometimes I fish and work on my truck and fix stuff on my property, too." He handed one of the cups to Larken.

"Mmmm. You're not the social soiree, type?" Larken laughed.

"Not like you are." Miles tipped his tea up and chewed a piece of ice. "I'm no good at that stuff."

"What makes you think I am?" Larken asked defensively.

"I saw you at that..." Miles snapped his fingers together in recall. "... The Sailor Ball. Looked like you fit right in."

"Oh," Larken said, taken aback. Her cheeks flushed with warmth, remembering the speech she gave for Bunny and wondering if he'd heard it.

"Yeah, you were at the auction table." Miles scratched his

head like he was embarrassed. "I wanted to say hi—see about your toe, but I got pulled away. Like I said, I'm no good at that stuff. I put my name on some tacky auction items, left for a while, then came back to see if I'd won."

Larken breathed again, realizing he had missed her botched introductory speech for Bunny—her secret still safe. "I'm surprised you remembered me..."

Miles softened his eyes and fastened them onto Larken. "You're impossible to forget."

"Food's up," the woman shouted from the window, plopping down a tray of food.

Miles rubbed his hands together in excitement and picked-up the tray.

"Mind if we eat here?" He asked walking to his truck.

Larken didn't respond. She followed him in agreement, wishing their moment hadn't been interrupted yet not knowing what else there was to say.

He released the tailgate with an ear numbing squeak and put the tray in the center. He sloshed left over rain water out of the grooves with his hand, laying a pile of napkins down for Larken to sit on.

Larken hopped up onto the tailgate, curious as to what Miles had ordered for them.

A huge tray of steaming Frogmore Stew piled high with shrimp, sausage, halved corn ears and red potatoes anchored the back of the truck down. Larken breathed in the billowing aroma of garlic and allspice.

"Do you want me to get us plates?" Larken asked.

"Naw," Miles protested with his mouth full. "You kiddin'? Plates are for sissies."

Larken watched in amazement as he devoured an ear of corn.

"Get in here." Miles nudged the tray towards Larken.

Larken tipped some tea out of her cup and rubbed it on her hands, shaking the excess over the side of the truck. She grabbed a shrimp and popped it in her mouth, flicking the tail into the gravel parking lot following Miles' example.

Every bite grew more flavorful than the last. Larken delicately sampled everything on the tray until she didn't care about appearances anymore and followed Miles' "take no prisoners" dining style.

The feeding frenzy lasted until each of them were stuffed beyond belief, a pile of discarded shrimp tales and corn cob skeletons littered the gravel around them.

Miles grabbed a stash of wadded up napkins and wiped his face and forearms down, splashed with corn juice and broth. "When I was oversees, this is what I missed the most," he said leaning back into the truck bed on his elbows, the silver skin of an old gash on his chin glimmering.

"You always knew you wanted to be a doctor?"

"Not really," Miles answered, wiping his mouth with a napkin. "Just knew it wasn't peanuts." Miles sat back up and brushed stray corn kernels off his pants. "Miss Annie, my mom, told me I was a healer. I guess she's the one who kinda' planted the idea in my head."

Larken understood that, much like everything else about him, there was more to the story.

"You got time for one more stop?" Miles asked as he hopped off the tailgate. "Just need to pick somethin' up real quick."

"Sure." Larken jumped off the tailgate and brushed her hands on her jeans. Between the unusual events of the day and the unexpected, pleasant company of Miles Beckway, the urge to go back hadn't hit her yet.

Miles coaxed the engine into turning over once again and they ambled out of the parking lot of the service station, stray gravel dinging underneath the carriage of the truck as they accelerated on the asphalt.

After ten minutes of driving through winding back roads the opposite way of Charleston, Miles turned into a shaded driveway. A small, well-kept house with a screened in front porch was at the end of a dirt road.

Several beagles happily bayed at the arriving visitors and busily sniffed at the tires as soon as Miles rolled to a stop. A cleanly dressed man in his early seventies opened the door leading to the porch and whistled at the dogs, their tails wagging their entire bodies at his call.

"Hey there, Mr. Honeycut," Miles called as he climbed out of the car. "I was hoping you might have some good news for me…"

Larken stayed buckled in the passenger seat, watching the exchange.

The man lowered and shook his head as the screen door slammed and wobbled behind him.

"You ain't gonna like what I got to tell you then, son," the man said. His eyes briefly moved to the stranger in the passenger seat from under a John Deere hat. "I ain't got a lick of the stuff in two weeks nearly."

"Oh man." Miles clicked at the side of his mouth. "Any idea when more's comin'?" He kneeled down to rub the belly of one of the dogs, its ears flopping back happily.

"Can't never tell." The man shrugged. "Hope you didn't go to too much trouble comin' out."

"Ah, naw," Miles said standing back up, the dog jumping onto his leg for more attention. "We were already this way."

Miles shook hands with the man and gave one last head rub to the friendly beagle before jogging around to the driver's side.

"Well that's a bummer." Miles sighed as he started the truck up, this time starting right away.

"Is it...something you can get somewhere else?" Larken asked, trying to be helpful.

"I guess so, but Mr. Honeycut's the only one I know around here that sells the *really* good stuff."

"What kind of *really* good stuff?" Larken asked suspiciously. She laughed nervously awaiting his answer. Mr. Honeycut didn't look like a drug dealer, but you could never tell.

"Tip's Moonshine." Miles laughed at her insinuation. "Best I've ever had—and that's sayin' somethin'. Ever heard of it?"

Larken looked back to the road and nodded. "Yep. I've heard of it." What Larken didn't say was that she had access to an unlimited supply of it from one Priss Winslow, distiller of her late husband Tip's famous moonshine.

"Oh well," Miles said, brushing the disappointment off, "hopefully next time."

Larken's phone rang, muted at the bottom of her purse. She

dug for it furiously, unable to answer it before it stopped. The screen read three missed called from Jackson, a text message from Bunny that she didn't bother to open and showed the time as 2:50PM. She turned the ringer off and threw it back in her purse, leaning back into the seat.

"I really appreciate you coming today," Miles said again. "Hopefully it didn't affect your weekend plans." He winced, hoping she didn't resent the trip.

"Not at all," Larken reassured him. "I needed to get out of my own skin for a while."

"Ha. That's a great way to put it."

The drive back to Charleston went by quickly, conversation defrosted by the events of the day and an air of relaxation from the familiarity shared by a day trip.

Forty minutes out of town, Larken unknowingly tapped her toes anxiously on the floor board, full of sweet tea and not having access to a bathroom all day.

"Are you really not going to ask me to stop?" Miles laughed. "Could you be that polite?"

"Stop?" Larken acted surprised. "For what?"

Miles shook his head and laughed. Two miles up the road, they pulled into an Amoco station for a pit stop.

"Well, only since we're already here…" Larken said playfully. She grabbed her bag and set off for the bathroom, digging inside for her cell phone.

Jackson had called a fourth time since she turned the ringer of her phone off. He left a message sounding half distressed that he couldn't get in touch with her and half annoyed that she hadn't called him back.

The details of the message revolved around a last minute trip to see Avery in Alabama for the holiday weekend—Kayla still dragging her feet about driving all the way up. He apologized for missing the weekend at Edisto and asked her to call him after work.

Bunny's text message was the length of a novel.

"Hey, sugar we all left for Edisto early. Figured you'd ride out with Jackson after work anyway. Had Bart drop your scooter off at the office. Hope it doesn't rain again—wish you'd get a car. Doing all white family beach pictures Sunday so pack accordingly. The Marc Jacobs dress would be perfect. Jewels on your crown if you can bring my Chanel diamond studs. The big ones. Love, Momma."

Larken finished up in the bathroom and bought two Cokes and a pack of strawberry Twizzlers on her way out.

Miles topped the gas off on the truck and threw a thumbs-up when he saw the Coke in Larken's hand.

The closer they got to town, the less it had looked like it had ever rained. The heat was sweltering—humidity trapped between asphalt and oppressive cloud cover.

Miles rolled all of the windows down, hot air whipping around them as they finished the drive back to the office. "Sorry there's no A/C," he yelled over the noise.

Larken ran a Twizzler between her fingers before taking a bite. "I'm used to it with the Vespa."

Miles laughed. "Well, next time I'll take a vehicle suitable for guests."

Larken's heart jumped, not wanting to have to wait for more

time with Miles Beckway. A stab of guilt flashed through her, suddenly thinking of Jackson.

"Now that it's cleared up," Miles said, craning to see out of the top of the windshield, "the cook-out at my place is back on."

"Fun." Larken nodded, not sure if it was an invitation.

"Are you comin'?"

"Tonight?" Larken asked.

"Yeah. Didn't Hazel…" Miles trailed off. "Hazel didn't tell you."

Larken squinted one eye at him. "I'm sure I just missed it somehow."

"Damn it, Hazel," Miles said to the air. "I should have figured as much."

"No, it's really fine," Larken said, laughing it off. "I'm sure it was an honest mistake."

Miles bit the side of his mouth. "Well now you have to come just so I can see the look on her face when you show up."

"I don't want to cause any trouble," Larken protested. "I kinda' had the feeling she liked me."

"Oh, she does." Miles reached his hand toward her in encouragement. "She just has a funny way of showing it."

Larken thought back again to her conversation with Hazel earlier in the day and felt the uneasy disturbance of betrayal. Hazel had every right to want to keep Miles to herself. Still, the obviousness of the intentional act was hurtful and disappointing.

The parking lot of the office building was empty except for the bright red pop of Larken's Vespa. The old white truck sputtered to a stand-still in the spot beside it, shuddering in a wake of exhaust.

Miles reached across Larken's legs and opened the glove box of the truck. His hair smelled faintly of shampoo despite the dust and humidity they'd been surrounded by for hours.

Miles pulled out a scrap piece of paper and wrote down his address—27 Wampler Drive, James Island—and phone number.

"Here you go," he said, handing her the paper. "We'll get things cookin' about 7:30?"

"Okay," Larken agreed. "Should I bring anything?"

"Nah. Just come hungry. It's real low-key."

Larken grabbed her purse and waved one last time at Miles. He waited until she was safely on the Vespa and out of the parking lot before starting the truck again.

She turned the opposite way of the Battery, winding down side streets until she could safely head back toward home without the risk of Miles seeing her.

She thought about the web of lies she had spun herself into starting with the denial of knowing Bunny Ashby—let alone the fact that she was her mother.

The Ashby House was tranquil without its usual inhabitants buzzing around hurriedly. Larken entered the code into the privacy gate and pulled up the drive. At half past five, the heat of the day was relentlessly heavy. Larken pulled her helmet off and wiped at the hair sticking to her face.

Gloria the housekeeper opened the door for Larken. Bunny preferred that the deep cleaning be done when the house was empty so she and Amara had been busily wiping down baseboards and steam cleaning drapes.

"Almost done here," Gloria explained. "Do you need anything?" She smiled, but Larken could tell that she was tired and hoping to not be bothered by any unexpected tasks.

"Oh, no thank you," Larken declined. She kicked her shoes off and hit them against the stairs to remove sand and Lowcountry dirt, her toes suddenly feeling grimy and hot.

Within the relief of the air-conditioned house, exhaustion washed over her. She wished Gloria and Amara a nice weekend and walked heavy-footed up the stairs to her room.

After a lukewarm shower and nominal effort shampooing her hair, Larken crawled into bed wearing her robe. She called Jackson, but it went straight to voicemail—more than likely a sign of his rural locale.

Larken texted Bunny to let her know she'd be at Edisto tomorrow and explained what she was sure Priss had already learned and told everyone about Jackson's last minute trip to be with Avery.

"*NO WAY YOU'RE DRIVING THAT DAMN SCOOTER TO THE ISLAND*," Bunny texted back immediately. "*Car service will come in the AM.*"

Larken sighed and buried her head in the coolness of the pillows.

*

It was ten after seven when Larken woke up from her nap. She checked her phone to see if Jackson had called, but saw he hadn't. She stared at the ceiling, wondering if going to Miles' cook-out was a good idea.

After some self-deliberation, Larken decided it would be rude, professionally, to not accept her new boss' invitation, especially now that she had no good excuse to refuse him.

She hopped out of bed and dried her hair, though the helmet and fifteen minute ride to James Island would surely undo all effort to maintain any sort of style.

A pair of cut-off shorts, a gray racer-back tank-top and some pink flip-flops later, Larken moved the contents of her purse into a small cross body bag and set off down the stairs.

Bunny's liquor closet off from the kitchen was stocked with more than its fair share of Tip's Moonshine. Larken grabbed the jar of the precious family reserve that Priss had given her on her birthday and secured it snugly in her bag, carefully positioning it back across her body.

Here's some moonshine made by the mother of the guy I'm sleeping with, Larken thought as she imagined giving the jar to Miles. *I do hope you enjoy it.*

Within several minutes of snail-speed motoring, Larken hit the open-aired James Island Expressway, the evening warmth feeling good against her skin as she crossed over the bridge, the strong smell of the marsh below surrounding her.

Wampler Drive on James Island could easily be seen from Larken's bedroom window of The Ashby House. She wondered if she'd seen Miles' house before without knowing it—her eyes glancing in his direction inadvertently across the harbor.

Larken took the Harbor View Road exit, snaking her way back toward Wampler Drive.

The houses were modest, traditional structures evoking a

feeling of life lived simply. The farther back toward the water that Larken drove, the more sparse the homes grew. Wild vegetation and marsh on this side of the island suited the type of place Larken imagined Miles living—wild, lush, uncultivated landscape. And smelling of Sycamore. A chill ran down her spine.

The evening wind picked up quickly, forcing Larken to squint. The smell of more rain filled the atmosphere. Larken thought briefly about turning back, the Vespa decidedly a dry-weather vehicle.

The mailbox at the mouth of the last possible driveway on Wampler Drive was numbered twenty-seven. Larken pulled the piece of paper out again to double check Miles' directions before turning down the shaded drive.

She drove slowly around potholes and sticks, squinting to see in the dim twilight of the tree-covered property.

Once down the secluded driveway, a graciously sized two-story brown shingle and stone cottage erupted ruggedly in front of a circular driveway, perfectly situated within trees and shrubs. Soft landscaping lights warmed a path to the house as well as around to what Larken presumed was a prime water-front view of Charleston Harbor.

Larken parked the Vespa out of the way of other vehicles and tussled her helmet hair. A handful of other cars, none of which were Hazel's, were parked around the driveway.

A lanky, splotchy colored dog with blue eyes came around the side of the house wagging his tail and sniffing Larken's legs. The dog whimpered when Larken rubbed the top of his head, leaning into her for more affection when she took her hand away.

She pulled the cross-body from around her chest and walked

toward the porch, laughter and music floating through the screen door the closer she got. The dog jumped onto the porch in one movement and sat beside her like a statue, tail perfectly still and ears perked in anticipation of the door being answered.

Larken rang the doorbell, her heart anxiously beating in her ears.

"Hey!" Miles' voice resonated happily a few moments later as he opened the door to welcome her. "You came."

The dog took the open door as an invitation, bolting through the entryway and disappearing into the house.

"I see you met, Uly," Miles said motioning to the dog who had disappeared into the house.

Miles wore long linen shorts and a famously tight v-neck. He hugged her in welcome, smelling like wine and woodsy masculinity—his hair slightly damp from a shower. Seeing him in his home element added depth to Miles. He was no longer only a concept, but a living, breathing man.

"Oh, I brought you this," Larken said nervously, pulling out of their hug and reaching into her cross-body. She struggled to remove the large bottle of moonshine—suddenly feeling uncoordinated and mentally reminding herself to take a deep breath.

"Here." Larken extended her arm quickly, nearly thrusting the jar into Miles' chest.

Miles looked wryly at Larken, his eyes squinting as he smiled. He unscrewed the top of the jar to verify the contents and quickly put the top back on when he realized it was Tip's Moonshine. "How?"

Larken bit her bottom lip. "There was an extra at the house."

"It's practically prohibition and you have *extras?*"

"Hey, Miles," a woman's voice called as she approached. A rosy-cheeked brunette with short hair pulled back with a silk scarf rounded a set of bookshelves. "Oh, there you are," she said sweetly once she'd found him. "Sorry to interrupt, but Ulysses is back at the grill again…"

"Ah, okay, I'll get 'em." Miles shook his head. "Emily, this is Larken, she heads up the PR side at the practice now."

"Oh, fantastic." Emily smiled, offering an outstretched hand to Larken after wiping her hands on her apron.

"Emily is my childhood buddy Ernie's wife," Miles explained.

"And tonight, I'm sous chef," Emily added, curtsying in the apron. "But I let the boys play with the grill."

Miles gave an enthusiastic thumbs up. "That's 'cause it's man work."

"Well, right now your dog has assigned himself to the task, so… " Emily reminded him.

"Do you need help with anything?" Larken offered, relieved to learn that Emily was only a friend.

"Oh, sure," Emily said. "Would love some."

"Just…something that doesn't involve a knife, okay?" Miles warned. "I've had too much wine to stitch you up worth anything tonight." Miles nudged Larken with his elbow playfully before leaving the room to tend to the grill.

"Ah. So you're the knife girl…" Emily winked, already familiar with the story.

"Guess so," Larken mumbled, her cheeks flushing pink. "You

can trust me with sharp objects though. Swear."

Larken followed Emily into Miles' kitchen where five other people congregated around the island eating an assortment of appetizers and drinking wine and beer. The conversation was light hearted and in good nature—everyone smiling and laughing as only old friends can.

"Everybody," Emily said, instantly capturing the attention of the kitchen, "this is Larken. She works with Miles."

Emily's bohemian style brought a surge of informal friendliness. The room threw their hands and drinks up in greeting.

Max and Lana, who both knew Miles in high school, and Rudy and Jessica, who owned a chop shop where Miles took his trucks, congregated to Larken with hellos and unpretentious introductions.

A middle-aged man with scholarly looking glasses and a quiet demeanor introduced himself as Christopher, Miles' attorney and friend. He made several unsuccessful attempts at being humorous, but Larken laughed anyway.

"Christopher," Emily chided, coming to Larken's rescue, "let the girl settle in before you run her off with your stand-up comedy."

Once the whirl of meeting new people had subsided, Larken saw open French doors leading to a large patio. A gentle breeze carried the charred smell of smoke from the grill and the earthy aroma of creek water through the kitchen. Miles' laughter and the company of several other people with him suffused through the door creating a buzz of life.

Emily set Larken up with a cutting board for chopping lettuce, tomatoes and onions as she busily put the finishing touches on banana pudding, dancing involuntarily to seventies rock that played on the sound system.

Larken felt completely at ease in the unfamiliar environment surrounded by strangers, but she was happy to have something to occupy her.

Miles' kitchen was well stocked with gourmet appliances that looked unused, but well placed. Outdated wedding invitations and Christmas cards from years passed were affixed to the fridge with colorful pizza company and tire brand magnets—tell-tell signs of bachelorhood.

Larken looked through the kitchen to the living room. Decorator paint colors, designer furniture, tastefully placed throw pillows and lamps. All undisputed evidence of a home that a woman had made.

Larken arranged the sliced burger accoutrements on the cutting board and washed her hands before helping Emily top the banana pudding with the last layer of vanilla wafers.

Miles interrupted the individual conversations in the kitchen with the arrival of a platter of hamburgers, Uly walking carefully beside his master. Miles marched triumphantly to the kitchen island, setting the platter down with a thud beside the toppings that Larken had neatly arranged.

"*Those*, my friends, are burgers," Miles boasted.

"*Those*," a voice said from behind him, "are hopefully beef burgers." Laughter erupted in the kitchen.

"You serve wild boar burgers *one time* and no one can get over it." Miles moaned. "Cow. Pig. What's the difference?"

Larken realized he was being completely serious and inspected the burgers closely.

Miles opened a cabinet and grabbed several handfuls of mismatched shot glasses. He had carefully stowed the moonshine Larken brought above the refrigerator, safe out of reach from anyone of average height.

Larken watched as he lifted his right arm to reach for Tip's Moonshine, displaying the length of his six foot three frame.

Miles noisily clanged the shot glasses together on the kitchen island as everyone stood with paper plates in hand, ready to serve up the burgers.

Emily swatted at Ernie's hand as it hovered over a bowl of potato salad. He forked a bite when she turned around to reach for pickles, smiling at Larken when he realized he'd been caught.

"So I think everybody met Larken, right?" Miles said, clapping his hands together and taking a wide stance in front of the kitchen island like a coach to his football team. "Anyway…after I made several unsuccessful attempts at acquiring some hillbilly pop today, Larken came through and made our traditional toast possible this evening, so—everybody give our very own moonshine rustler a hand."

Larken's face felt like it was melting from the attention. She smiled shyly and moved back towards the sink, away from the whoops and hollers of applause.

Miles poured a shot glass full of moonshine for everybody and walked Larken's portion over to her.

"Oh. No," Larken declined. "I quit shinin' a long time ago." An ancient memory of drinking moonshine with Jackson flashed across her mind.

"C'mon," Miles encouraged. "If nothin' else it keeps the

skeeters off ya." His sideways smile was very convincing. "Plus it's a tradition around here."

"Well, if tradition is on the line," Larken mocked.

Miles clinked his glass to hers and they both turned the moonshine up.

The room swarmed with gasps and coughs. Ernie and Max beat their fists on the kitchen island while Emily and Christopher cautiously sipped the potent liquid, Emily rolling her eyes at her husband's reaction.

Larken covered her mouth as she coughed and sputtered, the taste of Tip's Moonshine familiar yet still overwhelming on her lips.

"That'll put hair on your chest," Miles managed to choke out between coughs.

"Just what I always wanted," Larken said with a laugh, her eyes watering from the pungent heat filling her throat.

"I don't remember it ever being this strong," Miles said as he grabbed a couple of beers out of a cooler on the floor, laughing between coughs.

"Oh." Larken squinted, "This isn't street 'shine. It's a special family reserve."

Miles pulled the top off a beer for Larken and handed it to her, his eyebrows perked.

"Alright." Miles shook his head. "Street 'shine? I'm fascinated."

She threw the longneck back, guzzling until the burning in her throat had been extinguished. "With what?"

"With you."

Larken dropped her gaze to the floor shyly and chased a drip of condensation down her beer bottle. "Then you are easily fascinated."

"That's the thing," Miles said, leaning in closer, the moonshine on his breath strong and warm. "I'm not."

"It's true," Ernie interrupted them, throwing an arm over Miles' shoulder. "Nothing fascinates him but trucks and mud bogs. Nothing." Ernie swayed side to side, long taken by alcohol before the moonshine was ever opened.

Miles laughed and shoved at Ernie like they had probably done since they were both small boys.

"Alright everybody," Miles announced, pulling the group back to attention. "Let's do this." He handed out paper plates and an organized onslaught of hungry party-goers made their way to the burgers.

Larken waited for the rush to die down before building her burger. As the kitchen emptied out onto the patio, Emily hung her apron up and joined Larken at the island.

"That's about as civilized as it gets with this group," Emily said, rolling her eyes. She speared a pickle and put one on Larken's plate. "You look like a pickle eater."

Larken followed Emily out onto the patio, seeing the back of Miles' property for the first time. The setting felt isolated and craggy— a private retreat with an uninterrupted river view and tidal creek frontage.

Different levels of stone patios descended from the house until it met the bank of the tidal creek. A large outdoor fireplace and stacked stone grill looked more lived in than the other indoor areas of the house. Larken assumed Miles had built the patios himself. It seemed like the type of thing he would take pride in doing himself.

The water glowed pink from the position of the tiring sun, dusting everyone's complexions with a peach filter. The group was happily eating their burgers around the fireplace, small puffs of smoke rolling out of the top and into a hand painted sky.

Emily took a seat beside Ernie and Christopher on the circular stone wall where built-in seating had been thoughtfully placed. Christopher scooted over, making room for Larken to sit down, too.

"You don't mind the smell of pipe tobacco, do you?" Christopher asked, patting at the pipe in his pocket. "Just a bad little habit of mine."

Larken said no, catching a glimpse of Emily rolling her eyes at Christopher's attempt at impressing her.

Miles was standing up on the other side of the patio, his foot propped on the fireplace, half eaten burger in hand. He chewed fervently in between sentences, laughing at old stories, completely content. Uly stood beside him, eyes fixed on the burger that his master held.

"Oh, Ulysses," Miles said, reaching for the dog's ears after his burger was finished. "C'mon, buddy. You get one, too."

Larken watched Miles jog back into the kitchen, Uly staying on his heels to secure the promise of food. The two emerged moments later, Miles pinching pieces of burger off and handing them to Uly.

"You must be a vegetarian," Christopher stated hopefully.

Larken looked down at her untouched burger. "Oh, no." She smiled, wondering how long he, or anyone else, had seen her watching

Miles. "I had a huge lunch."

"Oh," Christopher said. "Looks like I'm the odd man out again then." He poked at his plate benignly.

Larken looked at his serving of potato salad and grilled tofu and laughed. Somehow being vegetarian suited the mild-mannered man.

"He tryin' to get you to eat that?" Miles said as he walked over and took a seat across from Larken. He pointed at the tofu on Christopher's plate. "Uly wouldn't even eat that. And he eats everything." The dog lay down on the patio, exhausted by the tactics it took to get a burger.

"I just noticed," Christopher explained diplomatically, "that she wasn't inhaling the animal protein that you had prepared. I thought she was, perhaps, too polite to decline."

"Oh no," Miles waved his hand in the air. "This girl can throw down some Frogmore Stew. Sausage and all. Witnessed it today when we were down south." He looked Larken up and down. "She is pretty polite though."

"Oh," Emily interjected, seeming surprised. "You went to the Lowcountry?" Her focus shifted to Larken.

"Yes," Larken said. "Today. For work. With Miles." The moonshine had left her foggy—the feeling of slight detachment from reality setting in. Their day in the Lowcountry already seemed like a lifetime ago.

Emily's face softened into a smile and Larken noticed her subtlety elbow Ernie to make sure he was listening.

"Well, that's great," Emily said, her voice soft and powdery. "That's really, really great."

With Ernie and Emily now looking at her, Larken got the distinct impression that her trip with Miles somehow meant something to them.

"Yeah, it was a good day." Miles shrugged, dismissing the unwelcome attention.

"By the way," Christopher remembered, "I looked into the deed on the Oxendine's property like you asked me to."

"And?" Miles tilted his head, interested to hear more.

"It seems they don't have much of a case to go off." Christopher shook his head pessimistically. "This other side has some major clout. Old family land and even older family money... Like you thought. A coal energy company out of New Jersey seems to be the buyer though. They just built an electric power plant near Boca Raton." He sucked in his bottom lip at the situation. "Doesn't look good, but I'd be happy to help pro-bono."

"I appreciate that, Chris." Miles smiled, but his face was worried. "So would Roland."

Larken took in a gasp of air, realizing she'd been holding her breath listening to them discuss the property.

Uly scrambled up from his place on the patio, running tail-wagging to a new arrival. Larken looked up to see Hazel holding a casserole dish of banana pudding in front of her—the contrast of her Betty Crocker presentation creating a stark contrast to the skin-tight white mini skirt and midriff bearing tank top she wore.

Hazel cocked her head to the side when she saw Larken, the look of disappointment wearing heavily on her face. She smiled, but Larken could see the line of tension in her cheeks.

Carol and two members of the surgical team walked in behind

Hazel, two six packs of beer in tow between the three of them.

Miles stood up to greet them, embracing them more like friends than colleagues. He unloaded the beer into a cooler and ushered them inside like a good host to serve up burgers.

Hazel seemed familiar with the layout of Miles' house and his friends. She greeted the people at the other end of the patio, showcasing her banana pudding before setting off inside the house.

"She knew I was making banana pudding," Emily whispered to Ernie.

"Oh, you know how she is," Ernie soothed. "And nobody beats your banana pudding anyway, baby."

"Larken," Emily said, refocusing her attention off Hazel's overreaching banana pudding. "You look like you're ready for another beer."

Christopher jumped up from his seat and set off for the cooler. "I'm on it." He returned with two longnecks, caps removed and served with a napkin.

"Very classy." Larken laughed as she accepted the beer.

"Hey, y'all," Hazel said, sashaying to the middle of the group for maximum attention. "Larken…I thought you'd be with your boyfriend this weekend." She paused, making sure everyone heard her. "But I'm so glad you were able to join us."

"Oh, no." Larken shook her head. "No boyfriend to speak of." She glanced at Emily who was listening to every word she said with curious eyes.

Larken immediately regretted the lie, but in comparison to the other lies she was currently keeping from Miles Beckway it didn't even rate.

"Oh," Hazel cut her eyes sharply. "My mistake."

"No worries," Larken said through a tight smile. She hoped it looked more genuine than it felt.

There were many things that Bunny had taught Larken in regard to social etiquette and dealing with other women—among the most useful being to never make them feel threatened while you prove them wrong.

Miles walked back out onto the patio, refilling bowls of potato chips and making sure that everyone had a drink.

"Oh, Miles," Hazel said hurriedly, trying to catch his attention before he started another conversation.

He looked up at her, unamused. "Yep?"

"I brought you something." Hazel gestured for him to follow her inside the house with her index finger. "You're gonna love it," she sang. Miles hesitated before following, his face showing no sign of emotion.

Larken liked Hazel. She didn't want to feel bitter toward her for the hurtful and very intentional act of not inviting her to the cook out, but the emotion of jealousy was one she hadn't anticipated dealing with.

"Emily," Larken said, "do you mind showing me where the bathroom is?"

Emily hopped up from her seat beside Ernie. "Not at all. I need to set dessert up anyway."

Larken followed Emily back to the house, Uly treading lightly behind them to see if the offer of more food was still good.

"Now I know it's not your favorite kind," Larken heard Hazel's voice carry from the kitchen, "but I checked everywhere and nobody, and I mean *nobody* has it." Hazel giggled excitedly. "This is 'sposed to be *almost* just as good."

Larken and Emily walked into the kitchen to see Hazel presenting Miles with a small bottle of what looked to be moonshine.

"Awesome." Miles nodded, accepting it graciously. "Very thoughtful of you, Haze."

Hazel beamed with self-satisfaction and shrugged proudly at Emily. "You know he can't have his Memorial Day cookout without a moonshine toast."

Emily clucked in approval as she eyed the bottle, its label reading *Gooder Than Snuff.* "Is this different than the moonshine you brought?" Emily asked, turning to Larken. She was pleased as punch to one-up Hazel.

Hazel's jaw set firmly, stewing with resentment toward Larken.

"Um, I don't know." Larken shrugged, trying to keep the peace. "Moonshine is kind of all the same, I think."

Hazel glared a hole through Larken.

"Well, thanks again," Miles said to Hazel, seemingly immune to the mounting tension around him. "We'll have to open this up in a little while."

Hazel smiled indignantly. "Yeah. Uh-huh. Whenever."

"The bathroom!" Emily said in a eureka moment, snapping her fingers together as she remembered the purpose for their coming inside. "Right this way."

Larken nearly ran behind her to escape the stress of the kitchen.

Once inside the bathroom, Larken ran cold water over her wrists until her head stopped swirling. Any hope she had of friendship with Hazel was all but dead now. Though her intention in bringing Miles moonshine hadn't had anything to do with Hazel, Larken realized now that, while the reason was still unclear, anything having to do with Miles would undoubtedly have something to do with Hazel.

She found herself wanting to run away and never come back. A knock at the door startled her out of her daydream of escape.

"Be right out," she said, drying her hands and running a hand through her hair.

Larken opened the door to find Hazel propped against the wall.

"Can I talk to you?" Hazel said as she entered the bathroom with Larken, closing the door behind her.

"Sure," Larken said hesitantly, anxiety filling the bathroom like smoke.

"Don't you think I had a very good reason for not inviting you to this party?" Hazel asked, pursing her lips together with a snap.

"Um." Larken shook her head, taken aback. "Well, I kind of was hoping it was just an oversight."

"It wasn't," Hazel confirmed. "I seen the way he looks at you." Hazel let out a puff of air. "You not being here was for his own good."

Larken mumbled, searching for words.

"And when he finds out about the boyfriend or whatever it is you're hidin'… Well. That'll be real good, won't it?" Hazel bit her lip. "He's not ready for that kind of disappointment."

"I'm sorry," Larken said, trying to make sense of Hazel's outburst. "I didn't know you…liked him."

"You didn't know I liked him?" Hazel mocked. "I *love* Miles Beckway. I love him like a *brother*. And I can't stand to see him get hurt. Not by you or nobody. He ain't ready."

"Hazel," Larken started, more confused by her response.

"You ain't our kind of people anyway, remember?" Hazel placed her right hand on her hip defensively. "I've got your number, you know. I know you get exactly what you want, when you want it. You play this sweet and innocent doe-eyed girl real good, but I ain't buyin' it."

"Now wait a minute," Larken said, raising her voice slightly. "You're assuming a whole lot about me and that's not fair. I don't know what you think I'm here for, but I'm only here because Miles asked me to be."

Hazel raised an eyebrow in disbelief.

"You know I hoped you and I could be friends," Larken continued, the second beer in her bloodstream giving her courage. "But seeing as how your opinion of me is so low as to exclude me, and you've completely misjudged me, I was obviously very wrong. You don't know the first thing about me. You wouldn't know that I moved back to Charleston because my fiancé left me. That I feel completely lost in my own hometown and I'm less afraid of living life alone than learning to trust someone again. That for the first time in my life I feel like I'm doing something worthwhile and that I won't turn into my mother. And as a matter-of-fact I've never gotten what I want because

I don't know what that is."

Hazel took a shallow breath, refusing to make eye contact with Larken.

"I obviously *ain't* your kind of people," Larken finished, mocking Hazel's drunken overuse of the word. She brushed past Hazel and opened the bathroom door quietly. She immediately regretted justifying Hazel's accusations with her brief life history.

Larken made her way back to the kitchen where Emily had served up bowls of banana pudding.

"She does this to everybody, you know," Emily whispered to Larken as she leaned across her to reach for more spoons.

"Does what?" Larken pressed the backs of her hands to her flushed cheeks.

"The 'don't you dare mess with Miles Beckway' song and dance that I'm guessing you just got," Emily said knowingly. "I mean, for the love, it's been three years. He has to move on. Someone new validates that you-know-who is gone though…"

"Right." Larken pretended to know what Emily was talking about. She felt cold and hollow.

"Help me pass these out?" Emily gestured as she picked up as many bowls as she could carry and headed for the patio. Hazel's banana pudding sat untouched on the counter.

Larken situated the remaining bowls in her hands and on her wrists and followed behind Emily, the mild relief that the setting sun brought to the evening greeting her on the patio. Uly sniffed at the air above him as he ambled over to investigate the arriving food.

"Whoa, whoa, whoa," Miles said, rushing to help Larken with

the bowls of pudding as one of them started to slip from her grasp.

"Thanks," Larken thanked him quickly, not making eye contact. She didn't want anything Hazel said to affect her, but she couldn't help but feel a sudden distance. A whip of wind blew napkins across the patio, sending Miles scurrying to catch them.

Larken handed banana pudding out to Christopher and the three other ladies from the office before taking a seat near Emily. Ernie volunteered to trade Larken a beer for her banana pudding when he saw she wasn't planning on eating it.

Hazel stayed on the other side of the patio from Larken for the rest of the evening. She carried on loudly, flirting with all of Miles' friends who she seemed to know exceptionally well.

"Guess I'll be driving her butt home again," Carol said resentfully to the two ladies on Miles' surgical team as they watched Hazel shotgun a Bud Light.

"I guess I'm gettin' old," Miles joked as he walked up from the lower level of the patio to stand near Larken. "'Cause that does not look fun to me anymore." He laughed, shaking his head at Hazel.

Uly ran up behind Miles, soaking wet with a stick in his mouth.

"Uh-oh," Miles said before quickly leaning over Larken's back, shielding her from a wave of water that Uly violently shook off.

"Ulysses!" Christopher gasped at the surprise of being soaked by the dog. He reached to touch the back of his dress shirt. "And pluff mud, too no less."

"Man," Miles laughed, "he got you good." Miles looked over his shoulder to see that his shirt hadn't been spared either. "Me too."

"C'mon, Christopher." Emily muffled a snicker. "Let's get you cleaned up."

The wet, muddy dog was enough to disband the small group.

"Ah, he's too stuffy for his own good anyway." Miles nodded toward Christopher. "Uly knows he's a cat person."

Christopher turned around before entering the house, "I heard that."

"Still true, brother." Miles shrugged.

Miles swiped the back of Larken's tank top. "He didn't get you, did he?"

"Oh, no. I don't think so." Larken reached her arm back to feel her shirt, brushing Miles hand.

Hazel watched the exchange through a glare. Larken repositioned, pulling herself away from Miles' hand.

Uly walked around to Larken, stick lodged firmly in his mouth. He lay his head on her leg, wagging his tail in an obvious attempt to entice her in play.

"I always wanted a dog," Larken admitted, tugging at the exposed end of the stick.

"Uly here's a ladies' man," Miles said, taking a seat beside Larken. He mussed the dog's ears. "Aren't you, boy?"

Uly spit the stick out by Larken's feet, maintaining constant eye contact.

"Well, unfortunately," Miles said with a smirk, "he's not gonna stop until you throw that stick in the water for him."

Larken snatched the stick up playfully. "Show me the way, Uly boy."

The dog took off down the darkened patio in an energetic leap, disappearing behind a line of water reeds.

Miles stood up laughing. "Oh, you've done it now. C'mon."

Uly waited with piercing eyes and a lowered head as Miles and Larken approached the tidal creek—the sound of frogs and crickets drowning out the laughter from the patio above them.

Larken chucked the stick into the water, Uly flying through the air and splashing gloriously into the darkness. He paddled back smoothly, head and stick above the water.

Larken looked across the harbor to the distant lights of the Battery—the silhouette of The Ashby House impressively dominant.

"Pretty, huh?" Miles said, standing behind her. "I come out here almost every night and look across the harbor at those houses." He swept his hand across the landscape. "I like thinkin' about what's going inside of 'em."

Goosebumps shimmered across Larken's shoulders at the likelihood of thinking of Miles at the same time he was watching the Battery.

A green plastic patio chair sat precariously on the water's edge, half sunk into the marsh of the tidal creek. It was lonely to see it there, as solitary as Miles life seemed to be. Larken imagined him sitting here every night, beer in his hand, throwing the stick again and again for a tireless Uly until the moon was high.

"Your place is really nice," Larken said looking back up to the illuminated house, its glow casting ambient light around the property through the branches of a live oak. "Your friends are great, too. Emily and Ernie...Christopher."

"Ah, yeah," Miles agreed, squatting down to pry the stick

from Uly's mouth. "They're like family."

"Seems like it."

"What about your family?" Miles asked.

"Oh." Larken shrugged. "I've got my mom and older sister, Caroline. Caroline's got a son—Sam. He's pretty much the greatest kid ever. And my grandmother lives...near us. Me and her are really close."

"Yeah I wish my brothers were closer," Miles said. "Got one in Texas and one in North Carolina. With both of our parents gone now and everybody busy though, it's hard. They've got wives and kids and ya know, I'm here."

Larken nodded in understanding. "I didn't know how much I missed my family until I moved back from Seattle. Just the little things that you take for granted."

"Is that what brought you back?" Miles tilted his head, interested to hear.

"Oh, um," Larken messed with her hair.

"You don't have to tell me." Miles put his hands up, sensing he'd asked more than he should.

"No, no, it's okay." Larken grimaced. "I actually got sort of dumped." She hadn't had to explain the situation before to someone who had no clue, but it wasn't as hard as she thought it would be.

"Really?" Miles asked, leaning towards her to see her face in the dim light.

"Yup. We were supposed to get married in—two months?" She pretended like she hadn't counted the weeks and the days to July 18th like a ticking bomb.

"Gosh." Miles blew out a puff of air. "That's too bad."

Larken shook her head, dismissing the need for empathy. "It's really okay actually. I didn't think it would be, but somehow it just is." She didn't know why tears pricked her eyes, blurring her vision momentarily.

"Still," Miles started, "you're too young and sweet to have something like that happen to you."

"I'm twenty-five," Larken reminded him. "And I mean, I'm not that sweet." She set her jaw, not sure she liked being thought of by him as childlike.

Miles nodded sarcastically. "Yeah, you're a real bad ass on your little scooter, aren't you? Does that thing have a basket and everything?"

Larken laughed. "Yeah I guess scooters aren't very sexy."

"Oh, well I wouldn't say that," Miles replied quickly. He shrugged. "You're cute as hell on that thing."

"No, it's fine. I'm actually okay with it." Larken reminded herself who she was talking to and tried to steer their conversation back to safety.

"Well, I'm sure it was hard to go through all that," Miles said. "But I think you're better off here anyway."

"You do?"

"Well, at least selfishly," Miles admitted with a shrug. "I mean, you've already brought in almost seventy-five thousand dollars, Larken. I'm blown away. I'm not sure how you're doing it, but...you are."

"Oh, just lucky I guess," Larken said nervously. Her stomach knotted up thinking about him finding out the truth of who she was,

312

who her mother was and how she'd lied about it all. She made a mental note to slow down on the meetings with Bunny's friends before he became suspicious.

"Been meaning to ask you," Miles snapped his fingers together, "everything okay with your paychecks?"

"I think so." Larken blinked. "Why?"

"It's just that you haven't deposited any of 'em." Miles watched her curiously.

"Oh." Larken exhaled. She wasn't even sure where she'd put the paychecks she had been getting every two weeks since she started working.

"It's none of my business. It's just most people work for the money…"

Larken forced a laugh. "I'm still getting everything in order since moving back." She felt trapped in her lie at every turn in their conversation, the holes in her story resembling a poorly played game of Jenga.

Another gust of air blew through, this time sprinkles of rain falling and dimpling the water. She couldn't help but wonder what cruel joke of fate had made her an Ashby.

"Hey, you need another beer?" Miles asked, scratching his head.

"I actually better be gettin' back home," Larken declined, following close behind him on the uneven ground. She eyed the angry clouds hovering in the distance and knew she was already in trouble.

"You sure?" Miles held out a hand to help her up onto the first flagstone step leading back to the patio.

"Yeah." Larken winced in apology. "But I'm really glad you invited me."

"Well I'm really glad you came." Miles squeezed her hand before letting it go.

They walked back toward the house silently, the glow of the outdoor fireplace lighting up everyone's faces. Miles immediately went back into host mode, grabbing beers and slapping friends on the back as he walked by. As much as something inside of her wanted to be favored by him, Larken realized that Miles' was able to make everyone feel special.

Hazel was in her own world talking to two of Miles' friends—enjoying every morsel of male attention.

Larken found Emily cleaning up the kitchen and hugged her goodbye like they were old friends.

"We have to do this again," Emily insisted. "Maybe the four of us can grab dinner or something. You know, when Miles isn't muddin' or giggin' or whatever it is he does." She laughed.

"Yeah, or maybe just you and me can grab lunch one day," Larken suggested, redirecting Emily's ideas of she and Miles as a couple.

"Sure." Emily bit her lip and leaned in to whisper. "Don't take Hazel too seriously though, okay? Her bark is much worse than her bite."

Larken agreed with a nod and gave Emily her phone number and grabbed her cross-body bag.

"And, just so you know," Emily said, catching Larken before she left the kitchen, "Christopher asked Miles what your 'situation' was…"

"My situation?"

"Yeah, like, if you're *with* anybody."

"Oh." Larken laughed nervously.

"I know," Emily said, folding a kitchen towel. "He's not your type at all. You don't even have to say it. I mean, I love him to death, but no."

"He seems very nice."

"Oh, he's the best," Emily agreed. "So anyway, Miles told him he wished he knew what your situation was, too."

Larken stared blankly at Emily.

"Ernie heard all of this and told me," Emily continued. "I swear men are worse than women when it comes to gossip. He sounded like a high school girl telling me about it."

"Hah," Larken laughed. "Just add a little alcohol, right?"

"I know you work for him and everything," Emily continued, "but it's not exactly normal for him to take interest in anybody. Not since…ya know."

Larken again pretended that she knew what Emily was talking about, but all she could piece together was that something tragic had happened in Miles' past.

"Well, I'm sure he didn't mean it like that," Larken said, denying any sort of feelings that Miles may have expressed. She felt inexplicably sick. "Everyone was really, really great tonight."

Emily smiled at the denial. "Okay. So lunch soon for sure."

"Can't wait."

Larken leaned out of the kitchen and onto the patio to wave goodbye to everyone.

315

Christopher sprinted over from his seat by the fire, readjusting his glasses. "Leaving so soon?"

"I am," Larken said sweetly, fidgeting with the strap from her cross-body bag. "Trying to beat this rain home." She felt a strange sort of guilt knowing he liked her.

Christopher gave her an awkward hug, ending it with a very timid pat on the back.

The group had dwindled under the threat of rain. A handful of Miles' closest friends gathered around the fire, the flames flickering madly in the strengthening winds. Larken looked around quickly for Hazel, but realized that she and the other ladies from the office must have left while she was in the kitchen with Emily.

"C'mon, I'll walk you out," Miles said, showing Larken a way around the patio to the front of the house. She followed him down a stone path slightly overgrown with bushes, Uly rushing past them both to lead the way.

Larken had a knot in her stomach as they walked out onto his driveway. She patted the cross-body bag down across her chest as she walked toward the Vespa.

"You drove your scooter here?" Miles asked as he spotted it parked in the corner. "Across the connector?"

"It's fine, really," Larken defended. "I do it all the time." She smiled through the lie, remembering how exposed she felt as other cars passed her on the bridge and knowing that if she didn't leave immediately she would be caught in the rain on her way home.

"I'll drive you. Where do you live?"

"Oh, no," Larken said quickly, panicking. "I don't live far. You can't leave the party. You're the host."

Larken walked hastily to the Vespa before he could stop her
again, sprinkles of rain discoloring her gray tank top with dark
splotches.

"No." Miles turned around and walked briskly into the front
of the house.

Larken scoffed, not sure what he had meant by "no."

Within seconds, Miles emerged from the front door, jumping
off the front porch and back onto the drive. He held up a set of keys
and dangled them in front of her.

"You'll be driving one of mine home tonight," Miles said
matter-of-factly. He didn't break his stride as he walked determinedly
to the detached four car garage set off from the driveway. The old
truck they'd taken to the Lowcountry sat outside of the garage, too
seasoned for the luxury of shelter.

"Miles," Larken called, trailing behind him, "this really isn't
necessary."

"Yeah it is." Miles turned to look at her through squinted
eyes. "I wouldn't exactly classify a storm with a name as scooter
weather. And it's at least seven miles." He shook his head, seemingly
frustrated. "Since you won't let me drive you, this is your other
option."

Larken didn't know if she should be flattered by his concern
or embarrassed. She nodded in consent.

He entered a code into the garage and the door opened
smoothly, revealing a black Audi coupe in the presence of the large
Bronco from The Sailor Ball and a gray Land Cruiser that Larken
remembered seeing in the parking lot of the office before. The fourth
spot in the garage had a half assembled dirt bike and miscellaneous

auto parts scattered on the floor amidst tool boxes and machinery.

Miles started up the Audi and let it idle while he brought her Vespa into the garage, parking it beside the dirt bike. He took the helmet from under her arm and propped it on the seat of the Vespa for safe-keeping.

"Come by tomorrow and we'll swap 'em back out." A small smile crept onto his face. "You're the most dangerous kind of brave, you know that?"

Larken shifted her eyes. "Me?"

"Yeah...you," Miles sneered. "Because you don't know you're brave."

Larken shrugged. "Well, thanks for the car… I think."

"Nah, don't think anything of it." Miles opened the driver's side door and waived her inside.

She carefully backed out of the garage and nodded at Miles. She watched him squat down to rub Uly's ears in the rear view mirror, almost as if he was stalling until she had disappeared.

Larken pulled the coup onto Wampler Drive and accelerated quickly, spraying a few pebbles of gravel. She rolled the windows down, the night air chilling her skin as she drove away. She exhaled, relieved she remembered how to drive a car and enjoying the sensation at the same time.

The car wasn't a brand new model, but it only had a few thousand miles on it and still had that new car smell. Larken opened the glove box at a red light and found it empty except for the registration papers.

Larken imagined the drive across the James Island

Expressway would have lasted an eternity on the Vespa—evening air and darkness whipping up around her. She was thankful for the loaner car after all. As she exited off the bridge, she sighed at the emptiness of the Battery—strong enough to be felt from the street.

Larken entered the code to the gate and was immediately greeted by the motion sensor lights as she pulled through the driveway.

She turned the Audi off and sat inside the cabin until the lights dimmed off, tree frogs singing from the garden. She grabbed her cell phone out of her cross body and dialed Jackson's number. She didn't know why she wanted to hear his voice.

"Birdy," Jackson answered sleepily on the fifth ring. "Everything okay?"

"Oh, yeah," Larken said. "I hope I didn't wake you up. I just…wanted to say goodnight." Hearing his voice was comforting after all.

"Don't worry about it." She could hear Jackson shuffling to sit up in his bed. "I'm glad to hear from you. Always. I tried you a few times today."

"I know." Larken grimaced. "I had kind of interesting work day."

"Oh yeah?"

"Yeah, it was just…unexpected."

"Well, I'm sorry my plans changed before we could talk about it," Jackson said, more alert now.

"You have to do what you have to do." She reprimanded herself for being glad to have had the opportunity to go to Miles' party alone.

"How's everything on Edisto?"

"Actually," Larken said through a yawn, "I'm meeting up with everybody in the morning."

"Ahhh," Jackson groveled. "You mean to tell me we would have had the house to ourselves?"

"Yep," Larken said, finally climbing out of the coupe. She couldn't deny that it would have been nice not to be alone for the night. "How's Avery?"

"Oh, she's good." Jackson smiled through the receiver. "Picked her up from ballet this afternoon and got a big day of Barbie weddings and tea parties planned for tomorrow."

It occurred to Larken that she didn't know the details of Jackson's accommodations in Alabama.

"Where do you stay when you're there?" Larken asked as she searched for the spare key hiding beside the garden gate, quickly brushing the flowers with her hand to knock off any bugs.

"Oh." Jackson hesitated. "Well, I'm at the house."

"The house?" Larken asked, finally feeling the metal case housing the spare key. "I didn't know you still had a house there."

"Well, yeah. I mean it was, uh, it was mine and Kayla's." Jackson's voice was quiet.

"But does Kayla still live there?" Larken asked alarmed.

"Well, yeah, Lark," Jackson said as if the situation was anything but unacceptable.

"You're staying with Kayla." Larken stood up straight, her voice startling the quiet of the garden. "You are sleeping in the same house as your ex-girlfriend."

"Well, not *sleeping* sleeping with Kayla," Jackson corrected. His voice was quiet still. "It's just...easier on Avery if I'm here."

"Right. Of course." Larken felt a swirl of emotions. She was in no position to say anything to Jackson about the arrangements he had made with the mother of his child, but somehow she felt put-off by it. "I just think maybe that's a detail you tell your girlfriend."

"Oh you mean my girlfriend who isn't really my girlfriend?" Jackson laughed at Larken's sudden change of heart, lightening the mood. "C'mon, Bird," he pleaded, "please don't be mad. I swear it's not like it sounds. I drove six hours, I'm tired, I miss you, I just... I have to figure something out with Kayla so I'm not always the one drivin' down here."

"I know." Larken sighed, trying to sound understanding. "I'm sure it's...a hardship."

"More like punishment," Jackson added through a yawn. "But yeah, her not cooperating is getting old. It's like she thinks makin' it hard on me will make me come back."

Larken once again felt nothing but empathy for Kayla and the betrayal she must feel. For the first time, Larken realized she was somehow the other woman in an already complicated state of affairs and she wondered what Kayla must feel toward her.

An unexpected gust of air blew off the harbor and into the garden, creating static in the phone.

"Is that storm finally blowin' in?" Jackson asked, conveniently changing the subject.

"Feels like it," Larken answered as she unlocked the door and turned on lights inside of the kitchen.

The wind creaked at the windows as Larken relocked the door. She said a hurried, unresolved goodbye to Jackson and walked through the house turning on extra lamps until she'd made her way upstairs.

The solitude of her room was comforting. The harbor churned out white capped waves in the sudden fury of wind, tiny beads of rain spitting against her window.

Larken drew a hot bath and sunk into the bubbles, washing away the pluff mud that Uly's tail had whipped across her legs. She felt vividly awake, but her eyes were heavy with exhaustion.

After her bath, Larken pulled on her yoga pants and cashmere hoodie. She wondered if Miles was watching the Battery from across the Ashley River and through the rain in that same moment in time and if he would see the light in her room go out, not knowing it was hers.

CHAPTER FOURTEEN

Namesake

Larken had a sleepless night enduring the tireless beatings of Tropical Storm Ferdinand against her windows. She'd slept through countless tropical storms throughout her life, Ferdinand not being out of the ordinary or unusually intense except for the fact that she'd ridden it out alone.

She'd made a middle of the night call to Jackson for comfort, but when he didn't answer she immediately assumed he was in bed with Kayla and created an entire scenario of betrayal spurred on by frustration and sleepless delirium.

She laid in bed, her gray room casting a timelessness on the morning. The winds had subsided considerably, but the rain continued to fall in rhythmic sheets. Larken thought of The Ashby House as one of the great protectors of the Battery—obstructing the wind from tattering the smaller houses behind it.

Once she coaxed herself into getting out of bed, Larken wound her way to the kitchen, her stomach growling from the previous day of little to no food from travel and nerves.

Lil had made lemon poppy seed bread for a Historic Charleston Foundation champagne brunch at Hampton Park and left an extra loaf under a cake dome. A note was beside it reading, "Put on some coffee. This cake's a choker!"

Larken brewed a small pot of coffee on Lil's advice and looked out of the windows at the garden, restlessly waiting for it to finish percolating. The rain fell in sheets across the back property, the sprinklers pointlessly watering the already saturated lawn.

The coffee pot sputtered out the last few drops of dark liquid. Larken poured a large mug and grabbed two slices of lemon poppy seed bread from under the glass cake dome. She sat cross-legged at the kitchen table and dunked the dry bread while she looked through the social section of *The Post & Courier.*

Bunny and Mr. Boca Raton were in more than their fair share of photographs—Mr. Boca Raton's skin somehow still glowing orange through the grayscale images.

The house phone rang as Larken finished the last of her coffee. "Hi, Momma," she answered without any doubt of it being Bunny.

"Well, thank God. I have tried your cell three times already, Larken," Bunny fussed. "I got a hold of her, y'all," Bunny yelled over the receiver.

"Nope—not dead yet," Larken said in cheery sarcasm. "The house is completely obliterated though. In fact, I'm floating somewhere out in the harbor as we speak."

"Oh, stop it," Bunny whined. "That was quite a storm we had last night. Even lost a couple shingles off Will-o'-the-Wisp."

"Tell Lark I was worried sick about her," Lil's voice called in the distance through the phone.

"I heard that." Larken smiled. "All is well over here."

"Listen, the car service can't get you until late this afternoon," Bunny continued. "Maybe even tomorrow. Roads are washed out terrible."

"Okay." Larken sighed. "Keep me posted I guess."

She hung up the phone with Bunny, slouching in her chair.

She dialed Miles' number and waited three rings before he answered, pleasant, but out of breath.

"Hey, it's Larken," she said, "hope it's not too early to call."

"Aww naw," he huffed. "Uly and I already been for a run and everything."

"So I guess you didn't party too long last night."

"Oh no. That storm was brutal," Miles answered through sips of water. "It ran everybody off."

"Well, I thought I'd bring your car back," Larken continued, rushing into her point. "Whenever it's convenient for you."

"Anytime," Miles said warmly. "I'm here all day."

*

A steady dose of wind and rain accompanied Larken on the short drive to Miles' house. Miles and Uly were in the garage when she pulled up, Miles halfway underneath the Bronco and Uly lying with his back against one of the massive tires.

"You've always got to be doing surgery, don't you?" Larken smiled.

"People and trucks really aren't that different." Miles grimaced as he stood up from his crouched position, rubbing his knees. "Both

325

need an overhaul from time to time."

Larken looked at the Vespa, buffed to a high-gloss and more bright red than ever before.

"I just spit shined it," Miles explained before she could ask. "It's actually a pretty nice little machine for what it is."

"Thank you—if that was a compliment." Larken smiled, feeling silly for taking any credit for the Vespa's stature.

"Maybe one day you'll let me put big tires on it and make a decent scooter out of her." Miles playfully wound up a hand towel from his back pocket and slapped the air with it.

Larken held the Audi keys out to Miles. "Thanks again for making me... I mean *letting* me, borrow your car."

"I can't remember the last time I drove it, so I'm glad you got some use out of it."

The rain picked up again, falling over the side of the open garage door like a wet curtain and creating a dull roar on the roof. Larken somehow felt comfortable surrounded by Miles' machines, breathing in the gasoline and grease. It was strangely peaceful to feel at ease somewhere so foreign.

Miles' cell phone rang from its post on a work bench. "Hey, Roland," he answered, his eyebrows furrowed to hear from the man so soon after their visit the day before. "What's up?"

Miles' eyes lifted up to meet Larken's, alarm surging through his face. "Keep her in the bed, okay, Roland? I'm on my way."

Miles hung up the phone and immediately set off for the house. "Ellery's in labor," he called over his shoulder to Larken. "Creek flooded during last night's storm and the midwives can't get to them."

Larken thought of the sweet Oxendine family she'd met the day before and was overcome with worry for them. "I'm coming with you."

*

Miles raided a cabinet of supplies in his home office and dumped everything he could find into a duffle bag. Larken filled containers with tap water like she'd seen in the movies, not sure if it would be helpful or not in real life.

Within minutes of receiving Roland's call, Miles and Larken were loaded up into the Bronco. Larken's heart was racing, still in shock that she'd offered to go and even more surprised that Miles was letting her. At least she wore rain boots and a good jacket this time.

"Do you normally have a nurse go with you to these kinds of things?" Larken asked as they turned onto Savannah Highway.

"At least one." Miles nodded. "But there's no time now. Sounds like these babies are coming."

Larken swallowed hard.

Miles reached over and squeezed her shoulder. "Don't worry. I won't make you do anything yucky." He smiled tightly.

"You're nervous?" Larken asked.

"It's not ideal." Miles nodded clinically. "But we'll make do with what we've got."

The Bronco hit a lake of standing water and sprayed a glorious wave of rain across the windows on both sides. Larken recognized the grove of Live Oaks from the day before, the Spanish moss clinging together, damp from the rain and swinging in clumps with each gust of wind. Their beauty was ominous in the storm-swept setting—somber figures against a gray, angry backdrop.

Miles had been quiet for the past twenty minute, no doubt running through procedures and protocol in his mind. He had his jaw set funny—worry lines showing in his forehead as they turned onto the infamous dirt road.

Larken took a deep breath and repositioned herself in her seat, bracing for the ride as they dipped down into the gully. The road was all but washed out. Parts of the red dirt road weren't even visible as the Bronco soldiered through several feet of standing water in the lowest parts. The big wheels ambled over logs and through thick mud.

Miles kept his jaw set and his eyes focused. Larken knew he was enjoying the driving conditions. Some sort of bliss in the chaos.

"Ahhh, come on," Miles grunted. "Big bump, Lark."

The Bronco surged down into a ditch, its tires slinging and flinging red clay and sticks every which way before rocketing back up onto solid ground.

Larken had her eyes shut so tight in those few seconds that she hadn't noticed her fingers dug into Miles' leg until he reached down to squeeze her hand.

You wishin' you hadn't come yet?" Miles smiled sideways.

"No," Larken said weakly, removing her hand.

Larken looked at the scenery differently now, desperately trying to find something that would disprove it from being Ashby land. She studied Miles' face, determined as he drove, knowing that it would be the end of their friendship if he were to find out who she is. Or when he finds out who she is. A shiver ran down her spine.

The rain changed its pattern—falling in sheets across the windshield. Miles leaned forward to see the way, or what was left of it, in front of them.

He breathed in deeply, his eyes surveying all around them before turning the Bronco sharply to the right.

"What's wrong?" Larken asked as they mudded in between trees and over tangled branches.

"The river's gonna rise quick with this much rain coming down," Miles shook his head. "The bank can only hold for so long. And I'm not gonna risk it with you here. We're makin' a new way."

Larken was almost used to the bumps and dips from the drive. The Bronco was a beast built specifically by Miles for scenarios just like this one. His hands held the steering wheel tightly, his arms flexed to control it when the ground all but floated away from under them.

The outline of the shacks appeared before them like a beacon. Water lapped several feet below them. Larken understood now the importance of them being built on stilts.

Miles pulled the Bronco up on a small embankment beside Roland and Ellery's house. "That should keep her from floatin' away," he said as he put it in park.

He jumped out of truck with a splash and went to the back to grab his supplies.

Larken licked her lips and opened the door, stepping into the rain. She followed Miles into the house, unsure of both her role and what they would find inside.

One of the older boys opened the screen door. He had jet black, shoulder length hair and had the strongest resemblance to

Ellery.

"Hey, Trey," Miles greeted him.

The boy gave Larken a quick glance as he held the door open for them.

"Daddy told us to go next door," Trey explained, "but me and Lulu is stayin' 'case you need somethin'."

"You're an old pro at this by now anyway." Miles smiled reassuringly. "You've probably helped deliver more babies than I have."

"Oh naw." Trey laughed quietly. "That's nasty."

An older girl sat in the floor folding laundry. She looked fifteen or sixteen. Larken quickly thought about what a typical Saturday afternoon activity would have been when she was her age and felt inadequate in comparison.

"What's up, Lulu?" Miles nodded. "Good to see you again."

The girl smiled at Miles. "Hey."

"This is Larken from my office," Miles said, introducing her to both of them.

"You a nurse?" Lulu asked.

"Umm, no," Larken admitted, tilting her head. "But I'll try to help if I can."

Lulu stacked a pile of laundry on the floor and waved them to follow her back to the bedroom.

"She been real quiet," Lulu said as they got to the doorway. "Hey, Momma, doc's here, okay?"

Roland was sitting in a rocking chair beside her. He was glazed over, operating on instinct alone.

Ellery sat up in bed, her knuckles white from pulling at the sheets.

"Here comth anotha' one," Roland said. "You gosta breathe, Ellery. Gosta breathe it out."

Ellery moaned and rolled her head back up at the ceiling. Larken watched in horror as the pain overtook her body, her whole being shaking during the contraction.

Miles checked the second hand on his watch and rolled up his sleeves. He dumped out some of the water that Larken had packed to wash his hands with and laid out some of his tools on a gauze cloth.

Ellery let out a gasp when the contraction finished and sat down from her hovered position on the bed.

"How far apart are her contractions, Roland?" Miles asked as he put on a pair of gloves.

"Hafta be about theven minuth now," Roland replied, his eyes wide with worry. "Ith too thoon."

"I need to check your progress, Ellery," Miles said.

Ellery nodded back at him, acknowledging his presence for the first time.

Miles pushed on her belly and listened with his stethoscope to the babies' heartbeats. Several seconds went by without anyone breathing or moving.

"They sound strong," Miles offered reassuringly. "You're doing a beautiful job, Ellery."

Larken got cold chills at the news. She'd never been around someone in active labor, even in the best of conditions.

Roland gave Ellery small sips of water before she lay down in the bed for Miles to check her.

One of the younger children whined from outside the curtained doorway, wanting to see his mother, but knowing better than to go inside. Ellery held up her hand and waved him away.

"Larken do you mind checking on him?" Miles asked as he helped Ellery get into a better position.

Larken was relieved to be useful and also have an excuse to leave the room. She felt horribly unprepared for such an intimate occasion and welcomed the child's need for attention.

A boy that looked about seven waited patiently against the wall outside of the bedroom, his hands behind him.

Larken kneeled down and smiled at him. "I'm Larken. What's your name?"

The boy wiped at his eyes, fighting tears or fighting sleep, she didn't know. "Marcus."

"Nice to meet you, Marcus." Larken nodded. "You wanna hang out with me?"

The boy shook his head yes and pushed his body away from the wall. "I'm hungry."

"Okay," Larken said. "That's easy enough."

Marcus was the huskier of the children—his shorts pulled up too high on his round belly.

"I like peanut butter," Marcus said, his eyes growing large as he opened a small, crooked cabinet door.

He pulled out a glass jar of homemade peanut butter and ran flat-footed to get a spoon.

"You want a sandwich?" Larken asked him, looking around

for bread.

"Nope." Marcus smiled, delighted as Pooh in a jar of honey. "Just the peanut butter."

The child smacked and licked the spoon, his eyes closing in pure satisfaction.

Ellery let out rhythmic, slow moans from the bedroom as another contraction started. Marcus' eyes flittered to Larken's face, reading her for signs of worry.

"She's okay," Larken assured him, not completely sure that was true.

Marcus bobbed his head in agreement. "I don't remember being born," Marcus said. "Do you?"

"Nope," Larken answered him. "Don't remember a thing."

"I hope these babies are good babies." Marcus shook his head like an old man.

Lulu opened the screen door and helped it close with the palm of her hand.

"Marcus," she hissed, snapping her fingers. "What I tell you about sneakin' over here?" She looked at Larken quickly. "Sorry he bothered you."

"Oh he's no bother." Larken smiled. "He just needed a snack."

Lulu screwed up her lips and pushed Marcus' head. "He always need a snack."

Lulu shooed Marcus back out the door, telling him he was disturbing Ellery. He turned back and smiled big at Larken. "I love peanut butter. And I love you."

Miles ambled out of the bedroom, leaning backwards to stretch his back.

Larken grimaced. "How much longer?"

"Hard to say," Miles said. "She's progressing well though. Couple hours until transition I think."

"So no hope of keeping the babies in longer?" Larken asked.

Miles shook his head no. "Definitely not. Her water broke. And twins typically come earlier anyway. Plus I really think she's further along than we thought." He took a deep breath. "It'd be great to have an ultrasound machine out here one day."

Miles unwrapped a package of tin-foil by the stove, his eyebrows raising up in delight. "Black-eyed pea cakes," he said, rubbing his hands together. "And if I'm lucky," he continued as he opened the stove, "Fish!"

Miles devoured two pea-cakes and a filet of fried fish, savoring every morsel. "I bet she went into labor making this food," Miles joked, offering a piece to Larken.

She couldn't help but be amazed by how comfortable he seemed in this place. Nothing had ever felt more foreign to her.

"Relax a little." Miles reached out to shake her shoulder.

"Are you a mind reader?" Larken fidgeted, suddenly self-aware of the body language she was projecting.

"Oh man, I wish." Miles rubbed his hands together, greasy from the food. "I'd love to read your mind." He laughed and made big eyes at her.

"I mean, you can just ask me what I'm thinking if you're ever wondering." Larken shrugged.

"You're too careful with your words," Miles said, shaking his finger at her playfully. "Like a politician."

"Like a politician…" Larken scowled. "Like I'm not honest?"

"Oh, no, you're plenty honest." Miles assured her, "But….filtered." He moved closer, a surge of body heat and humidity enclosing them. "I want the raw version of Larken Devereaux."

Larken swallowed hard, her heart racing. "K."

"K," Miles repeated. He reached out and squeezed her hand, his touch almost medicinal.

Ellery breathed heavily through the start of another contraction, a steady, low moan carrying into the next room.

"Five minutes apart," Miles said clinically, releasing Larken's hand to check his watch.

Larken shook her head, coming back to reality. "What can I do? Boil some water?"

"Sure." Miles nodded. "There's a water pump outside. Wouldn't be a bad idea to get some pots on the stove if you think you can handle it."

"Sounds like a pretty easy job to me." Larken winked.

Miles returned to Ellery's side as the contraction was subsiding. "Doin' great," he soothed. "They're comin' at about five minutes apart now."

Larken found two large aluminum pots in the kitchen and headed for the water pump, the excitement of what was happening finally setting in.

Several of the Oxendine children sat quietly on the porch of the shack next door, looking up quickly when they heard the screen door squeak open.

Larken held the pots up. "I'm gonna just get some water," she explained.

Lulu reached over from her spot on the railing and tapped Luke on the head. "Go help her get the water."

Luke hopped down immediately and motioned for Larken to follow him. He walked barefoot through the red mud and standing water, a drizzle of rain falling steadily.

Luke showed Larken to a fifty-gallon drum propped up on cinder blocks with a series of mis-matched buckets and PVC piping below it.

"After it rains the water comes out real fast," Luke warned. The boy opened a spout on one of the lower buckets and clean, clear water flowed out.

"Thank you," Larken smiled at him while the pots filled up. He smiled back, unrestricted by the cleft-pallet scar on his lip.

"I got this one," Luke said as he picked up the larger pot, his small frame hoisting it up the stairs of the porch with ease.

Luke reached up with his foot and somehow opened the screen door.

"That's a handy trick," Larken commented.

Luke smiled shyly, proud of himself. "Momma said it's bad manners, but I seen Daddy do it, too."

Luke placed his pot on the stove and helped Larken lower hers down beside it.

"Hmmmm." Larken sighed, looking at the stove curiously.

"There's still coals going," Luke assured her, opening the

front door. "See?"

"Wow." Larken nodded once. "I do see."

Luke fetched a bucket in the corner and brought over several small pieces of kindling and three stove-sized pieces of wood.

"And so," Larken asked, feeling like she should know the answer as the adult, "you get the fire going and then it just…heats up the stove top?"

Luke giggled under his breath. "You never boil water before or somethin'?" he asked.

"Sure I have," Larken said chewing at the side of her mouth. "I've just never used a stove like this before."

Luke's eyes got wide. "You never used a stove before?"

The truth was, whether it was a wood-burning stove or an electric range, Larken couldn't say with absolute confidence that she had correctly used any kitchen appliance.

"Not really." Larken shrugged.

Luke whistled in amazement and paused. "You go to McDonald's?"

"Sometimes."

The boy stoked at the coals in the stove and blew carefully at the growing flames before placing the larger pieces of wood on top. He closed the door carefully and dusted his hands off.

"You know how to tell when the water boils?" Luke asked sweetly.

"Yes." Larken pursed her lips. "That part I do know."

"Okay, good." Luke nodded. "But don't watch it or it won't boil." He walked back toward the screen door and ran down the stairs once it had closed.

Ellery had three more contractions in the time that it took the water to boil. Larken waited patiently on a folding chair, but was careful to not watch the water like Luke had said.

Roland ambled out of the room to stretch his legs, his face tired and worried.

"Wuth that Luke I heard?" Roland asked, unwrapping the tin foil of pea-cakes.

"It sure was." Larken smiled. "He helped me get water and start the stove."

"Good boy, that one," Roland said with his mouth full. He walked to a cupboard on the far side of the room and pulled out a small white, cotton bag tied with twine.

"Hereth thum rith fa you." Roland smiled, presenting the bag to Larken. "Thith what we grow." His face beamed with pride. "Nobody grow rith like thith—seed come from my great-great-great granddaddy."

Larken had nearly forgotten about Bunny selling the land until she saw the glow of self-worth on Roland's face as he spoke about his crop. Her chest felt swollen with guilt.

Larken took the bag graciously. "Thank you so much, Roland."

"You welcome, you welcome." Roland held his hand up. "Cook it up, put thum thalt and butta on 'em and mmmmm mmmmm." He closed his eyes. "Good eatin'."

"How's that water comin'?" Miles asked as he walked into the room. Roland disappeared again to be by Ellery's side.

"It's done." Larken pointed to the steaming pots on the stove, proud of the small accomplishment.

"A little more involved than you thought, huh?" Miles asked.

"Piece of cake." Larken batted her eyes. "What should I do with it?"

Miles shrugged. "Nothin' for now. Might need it later though."

"Hmph," Larken grumbled. "You didn't by chance ask me to boil water just to keep me busy, did you?"

"Nawww," Miles said, winking playfully.

An onslaught of intense contractions began again in the next room, Roland and Miles taking turns rubbing Ellery's back and soothing her with encouragement.

Larken was nervous again, listening to the waves of suffering and seemingly endless pain that transition brings. Ellery went from belligerent and telling Roland not to touch her to begging him not to leave her side.

Hey, Lark," Miles called as he stuck his head out from behind the curtain, "mind helping with something?"

Larken hopped up from the folding chair quickly, deciding that helping would be better than just worrying. "Sure."

"Come around on this side." Miles waved, motioning for her to stand on the far side of the bed. Ellery was rocking back and forth on all fours, beads of sweat dripping down her forehead. Her eyes were glazed over, deeply entranced in determination—her body overtaken and running on instinct alone.

Miles showed Larken how to press her palms into Ellery's

lower back to counteract the press caused by the descending babies. Miles made his hands into a vice and pressed them on Ellery's hips while Roland held her hands and stayed pressed against her face.

Her body shook in waves as the contractions crescendoed onto each other, the babies' progress a near constant attack on her small body.

Larken watched Miles' face—calm, yet serious. He was in a trance of his own with his arms flexed, the veins in his forearms and hands surging. Larken watched as sweat ran down his face, the room swimming with hot breath and humidity.

Roland and Ellery looked like an Olympic pair having performed this routine so many times over the course of their marriage. Larken envied the trust and naturalness that they exemplified. They were in perfect harmony even in the turbulence of labor—without exception or question.

"You're doing a great job," Miles voice soothed softly.

Larken looked up to see that he was talking to her.

"Thanks," she whispered. "I hope I'm helping."

Miles smiled. "You are."

Larken felt a renewed sense of purpose and gained strength from Miles' encouragement. Ellery's transition went on for another twenty minutes, her need to change positions at the very end unsettling as she sought comfort that wasn't there.

And then at last, her body relaxed and she slowly became aware again, settling down onto her side. Roland climbed into the bed beside her and they closed their eyes together.

"Calm before the storm," Miles explained to Larken.

They left the room to let Roland and Ellery rest and to stretch their own muscles from being tense for so long.

Miles reached for Larken's hands and rubbed her palms, releasing muscles she didn't even know she had. He rubbed up and down her forearms, too, his hands comforting and electric at the same time.

"It's hard work," Miles explained, "caring for a laboring woman."

"I had no idea," Larken agreed. "Everything I knew of labor I learned from movies." She covered her mouth from a yawn. "One sharp pain, a few deep breaths, a couple of screams and then the baby comes out."

Miles smirked and shook his head. "Nope."

Larken's stomach growled as the late afternoon light poured through the screen door, its glow lensed by the cloud cover still lingering over the Lowcountry.

They washed up using some of the now warm water on the stove and quickly ate one pea-cake each.

They heard Ellery breathe through another contraction—this one more tolerable and further apart than the others.

Miles returned to the room to evaluate Ellery. The mood was elevated now, Ellery finding such relief from the intense contractions during transition that she seemed blissful.

"First baby still needs to descend a little bit," Miles explained to her. "We have a little longer to go I think. Just keep doin' what you're doin', Momma."

Roland kissed Ellery on the forehead and went next door to

check on their children at Ellery's request. Miles followed behind him, promising to return after a quick bathroom break, which Larken decided must mean the woods.

"I'm gettin' nervous with them chirren bein' so quiet," Ellery told Larken while she repositioned in the bed, holding on to her belly. "When they makin' too much noise is when I know everything okay." She smiled.

"They are very good kids," Larken complimented her.

"I'm glad you came today," Ellery said. She watched Larken's face intently. "It's nice to see him happy again."

Larken smiled at her, not sure what to say.

"You know we call him 'Gentle Being.'" Ellery smiled. "He get that from his Momma." She shifted again, stiffly. "We all get somethin' from our Momma and that's what he got."

Larken thought quickly about Bunny and sighed.

"Ohhh," Ellery moaned, a look of surprise on her face as she reached out for Larken's hand.

Larken began guide-breathing like she'd seen Roland and Miles do. She squeezed Ellery's hand, feeling entirely incapable of being the only support person in the room.

"Oh, they comin' now," Ellery moaned, writhing into a better position.

"Ellery," Larken said, taking her hand firmly, "try not to push yet, okay?"

Ellery was far away again, a distant look in her eyes. She bore down on Larken's hand and pushed, screaming.

"No, no, no," Larken whispered. "Ellery, please don't push

until Miles gets back." Larken looked toward the doorway, praying Miles would walk through it.

"These babies ain't waitin' for Miles or Jesus or nobody," Ellery cried. "They comin' right now."

Ellery's body relaxed for a second, but she didn't let Larken's hand go.

"I have to go find Roland and Miles," Larken insisted, her eyes filled with panic. "Can I leave you for a minute? Just one minute Ellery."

Ellery's body tensed up again before she could answer her. "Don't leave me," she said. "Don't leave."

"Oh, God," Larken resigned. "Oh God, oh God, oh God." She squeezed her eyes shut for a split-second. *Miles, where are you?*

Ellery used the contraction to push with all of her might. Her intuition was perfect, having done this so many times before.

The contraction subsided enough for Ellery to take in a deep breath, her body shaking from adrenaline and exhaustion.

"This next push is gon' be it," Ellery instructed Larken like she was one of her children. "And you gon' have to get the baby." Ellery nodded at Larken, her eyes searching for affirmation. "It'll be alright."

The blood left Larken's face. "Okay. I can do it."

Ellery was silent, breathing in and out until her body signaled go-time. Her state became trance like again just before a contraction, something Larken had learned to pick up on.

Larken found a muslin blanket that Miles had set out for delivery and draped it across her shoulder. She listened intently for the sound of Miles' footsteps, walking through the door in just enough time, but there was complete silence in the tiny shack. No one else was coming in time. She was all the help Ellery had.

"Get ready," Ellery warned her, pulling her legs back against the pressure.

Larken had no choice but to see the chaos happening now, a surge of horror and euphoric excitement at the sight of a tiny head crowning.

Ellery breathed in deeply and pushed with all of her might, small squeaks of pain slipping out through her breath. The baby's head came out the rest of the way, one shoulder almost coming, too.

"Just another push and I think you've got it, Ellery," Larken encouraged, some sort of strange genetic instinct guiding her to help the woman.

Ellery bit down on her bottom lip and curled her body up. The second shoulder came free and Larken reached out for the baby as its tiny body came following determinedly after it.

A raspy, delicate cry broke the silence of the room, arms outstretched and quivering, eyes shut tight and face scowling. It was the most beautiful thing Larken had ever seen. "It's a girl!" Larken squealed. "And she's beautiful. And so, so, so tiny."

Ellery laughed, leaning forward to reach for her daughter and gasping for air at the same time. Larken laid the muslin across Ellery's chest, quickly covering the baby once Ellery had embraced her.

The baby's cry turned into small whines as she tried opening her eyes, seeing her mother's face for the first time and moving her mouth slowly.

Larken's resolve finally melted in the presence of the new life.

Miles walked into the room to find both women crying and a healthy, tiny baby girl nuzzling into her mother.

"Well, you leave for ten minutes and look what happens," he said calmly, smiling ear-to-ear. "What do we have here?"

Miles inspected the baby as she lay on Ellery's chest, tiny grunts signaling her disapproval of the invasion. "Another looker, Ellery," Miles smiled. "You and Roland have the beautiful baby makin' formula down alright."

Miles listened to the baby's heart, checked reflexes, cleared her airways and cut the umbilical cord. Roland ambled into the room moments later, nearly speechless to find the sudden arrival of his daughter.

Ellery wasn't willing to share her quite yet, but Roland seemed more than adept to the routine.

After checking the second baby's heart rate, Miles left the threesome and came to stand by Larken. "You okay?" he asked, rubbing her arm. He hid a smile, half amused and half amazed at what she'd done.

Larken looked at him, still teary eyed from the experience. "Yeah," she answered. "It was incredible."

Miles raised his eyebrows at her response. "And you didn't even pass out. Amazing."

Larken sniffled at the joke, dabbing at her eyes with her shoulders, her hands still messy from the delivery.

"C'mon," Miles motioned, "let's get you cleaned up."

Miles poured warm water over Larken's hands on the porch while she rubbed a bar of soap between them.

"It wasn't as bad as I thought it would be," Larken thought out loud, replaying the birth in her mind.

"Does that mean you want to help me with the second one?" Miles winked.

"Oh my gosh." Larken leaned her head back. "I forgot about the second one."

Twenty minutes after the first twin's arrival, Ellery's contractions began again. Larken was blessed with the task of holding the tiny baby girl while Miles and Roland took over delivery duties. She studied her impossibly tiny fingers and the quick, shallow breaths that were so new to her.

The second baby put up more of a fight. Miles helped coax the twin into a better position—Ellery crying out with pain. Larken didn't think she'd be able to watch, but she couldn't take her eyes off Miles. He was strong, yet gentle, his eyes soft while he monitored mother and baby. She thought about how Ellery had called him "gentle being." It fit.

"I need one more good try," Miles encouraged her. "You're doing a fantastic job—I know you're tired, but you're almost done."

Ellery was tired—her body fatigued from months of a complicated pregnancy and the relentless pain of laboring for hours on end.

"Elle," Roland said, intervening from his place by his wife's side. "I luth you."

That was all she needed. Ellery took in one more deep breath at the top of the contraction and pushed, Miles guiding the baby boy out in one smooth motion.

The twin didn't cry, his body somehow even smaller than his

sister's. Miles turned the baby upside down and gave him a good smack, holding his entire body with one hand.

"Come on, baby," Miles commanded. "Breathe."

Larken waited for his arms to spring to life like his sister's had, his face to scowl up and a cry to break out, but his eyes were closed and his body still.

Ellery and Roland watched helplessly as Miles tried to bring some life into their tiny son. Miles turned him over in his hand and pressed on his chest then flipped him quickly on his stomach again for another smack on the back.

The baby girl that Larken held let out a heartbreaking, lip-quivering cry as she watched frozen in the doorway, begging God for a miracle.

It was just enough to rouse her brother from his near lifeless state, her cry calling him to join her in the present.

Ellery gasped and cried out, reaching for her son and holding and kissing his wet body.

Larken was overcome again—her fear releasing in body-shuddering waves of tears. She handed the tiny baby girl to Roland to unite the family at last, smiling and kissing and crying with each other.

Larken walked out of the room so she could compose herself, but the emotions only released more in the void of company. She sat in the folding chair, burying her face in her hands and sobbing.

She felt Miles warm hand on her back, comforting her steadily. She kept her face buried in her hands, her feet fidgeting underneath her.

"Hey, hey, hey," he comforted, kneeling beside her now,

pressing his forehead against her shoulder. "It's okay, Larken. The babies are gonna be okay."

"I know." Larken nodded into her palms, tears falling onto the floor. "I was just so—so scared for them."

She felt Miles nod in understanding. He stood up again, stroking Larken's hair smooth.

Miles walked back into the Oxendine's bedroom, Larken relieved to hear Roland and Ellery cooing at the babies' grunts.

Larken got up, flipping her hair around and wiping at the mascara she was sure was streaking down her face. She splashed some of the now lukewarm water on her face and breathed in deeply, pulling herself together.

Her mind flashed quickly to her family on Edisto Island and the comparison of their day's events was a stark contrast. The caterers would be delivering supper about now, no doubt lobster and more cases of champagne. Bunny would be beside herself that the weather hadn't cooperated for a veranda dinner overlooking the marsh. And Jackson. Larken had a shiver run down her spine. She couldn't account for Jackson's day.

Roland walked out of the bedroom, a smile plastered on his face as he held both babies in his arms.

"Oh, Mith Lahken," he said sweetly, seeing her tear-stained face, "don't need ta be thad now, thee?" He held up the babies. "They perfec."

Larken sighed. "They are perfect, Roland. Congratulations."

Roland handed the sleeping baby girl off to Larken. "We callin' her Rainy," he said proudly.

Roland held his son close with both hands, wide awake and making squeak noises. "We callin' him Beckway—after the docta."

Larken knew Roland couldn't say Miles' name properly. And Beckway was a fitting name to grow into anyway.

"I think that's perfect." Larken smiled, her eyes feeling less puffy now.

"I catch baby trout bigga' da dem." Roland laughed as he lifted the tiny babies up and down.

Larken stayed clear of the bedroom until the afterbirth was delivered and Ellery was put back together. She knew she had limits as to what she could handle seeing in one day.

The rain had quit and the air was filled with early evening tree frogs and a lingering humidity.

Rainy and Beckway's brothers and sisters came all at once to meet them before being escorted back to the neighbor's house to let Ellery and the babies rest.

An older woman named Esther came over to be the night nurse, her hands nearly disfigured from arthritis. She held both babies, rocking them forcefully to sleep when they would cry, humming with her eyes closed and patting the bundled twins. Larken wondered how many babies she had done this for.

Miles spoke to one of the midwives and was confident that the waters would recede enough by morning to allow them access to the Oxendine's. He left a bottle of Tylenol by the bedside and some basic care instructions. The babies, despite their small stature, had already nursed well and their vitals checked out, too.

Larken kissed the babies goodbye, sad to leave them, but relieved things had ended as they had.

Miles and Larken left the Oxendine family in the quiet gulley, the sweetness of new life almost glowing from inside the shack.

CHAPTER FIFTEEN

The Bridge

Miles was exhausted, but excited to mud through the treacherous road again, this time without babies on the other side of the bog waiting to be born.

"Perfect conditions," he said, smiling at Larken as he rammed up and over a bank of thick mud.

She wasn't scared this time. The jumps and jolts from the landscape beneath them didn't unsettle her. She felt safe with Miles. Even when they hit something unexpected, she knew he'd make the right correction and set them straight.

"Hey," Miles said as they approached the main road again. "Can I show you something?"

"Yeah. I'd like that." Larken laughed. "At least I think I would."

The Bronco eased onto the pavement and Miles turned left, the opposite way that they'd come. Larken felt herself sigh, comforted by the role of caretaker for the day. It was only when she thought of Jackson that she felt anxious. *Self-sabotage.*

"So it's nothing fancy." Miles shrugged as he turned into a narrow driveway. "But that's kind of the point."

There was just enough light filtering through the trees to make out a structure ahead, only the frame work was complete—bundles of wood stacked around it, vines overgrowing unused building materials.

Miles brought the Bronco to a stop in front of a Bobcat. Larken took Miles lead and climbed out, walking on squishy ground behind him.

Miles crossed his arms in front of his chest and took in a wide stance at the building, looking at it like it was already finished.

"What is it?" Larken asked, trying to see the potential through the overgrown progress.

"It's my version of a Lowcountry clinic." Miles scanned the building, pride and potential covering his face. "Well, it will be anyway."

Larken walked closer and up a set of cement stairs that looked freshly poured. "This is the entrance?"

Miles nodded again.

"How long has this been here?"

"Oh well, my family's had the land for forever," Miles explained, joining her on the stairs. "It's been our fishin' hole since my Paw-Paw was a boy."

Larken scanned the property, imagining generations of the Beckway family and trying to picture a young Miles.

"And this," Miles said, kicking at the stairs, "this has been here a little over three years." He looked around at the structure, scratching at a five o'clock shadow.

"It's just been sitting here?" Larken asked, wrinkling her nose. "Why didn't you finish it?"

"Oh, you know." He sighed. "Life."

Miles' voice was vacant, Larken couldn't read why though.

"I think I'm ready to start building again now though," Miles offered.

Larken stood beside him, quiet.

"I—uh," Miles stammered, "I lost my motivation there for a while." He scratched his head, remembering something unpleasant. "My wife..." his voice trailed off.

Larken bit her bottom lip, vice-like pressure weighing on her chest. "Your wife..."

"She's been gone three years now." Miles shifted, clearing his throat. "She wasn't well," Miles explained delicately. "That's the simplest way to put it."

Larken knew she wasn't expected to say anything. So she just listened.

"There towards the end she wouldn't even leave the house," he continued. "I thought it'd do her some good to have a place out here. Someplace quiet. We grew up together in these parts." He smiled briefly as if remembering something from his childhood. "So I started building." Miles put his hands on his waist. "And then one day she woke up and she seemed happy—the happiest she'd been in a while— and she said she wanted to walk to the bridge." He exhaled sharply, taken back to that day.

Larken's eyes filled with tears. She thought about an article in the paper that she'd read before she left for Seattle. A woman named Hallie jumped off the James Island Expressway Bridge—the search for her body going on for weeks until at last they gave up hope of recovery. Larken remembered her name because she thought it wasn't the name of someone suicidal. She felt such sadness for her, the beautiful brunette with a history of mental illness that had taken all of her clothes off before jumping into the water below, leaving a note in the pocket of her jeans.

"She never even saw all this," Miles said, nodding toward the structure. "We'd moved around for years with Doctors Without Borders, going from crisis to crisis while I did reconstructive plastic surgery. She just got worse and worse. At first I thought it was just homesickness, but then she started showing signs of actual mental illness. That's when I decided to bring us back to South Carolina and got into cosmetics." He plunged his hands into his pockets, looking at the building. "Only thing I can think to do with it is make it into the clinic."

"I think that's a really good idea," Larken said, trying to sound like she wasn't choked by tears.

"Her name was Hallie," Miles said, confirming the name Larken had thought it might be. "I thought I'd call it the Hallie Anson Clinic."

Larken's head swirled. Hazel Anson. Hallie Anson. They were sisters. Had to be.

Miles watched Larken connect the dots. "Yep." He nodded. "Believe it or not, Hazel's my sister-in-law."

"Wow," Larken said, truly astonished.

"She's a pain in the ass, but I think we needed each other." Miles smiled thinking about Hazel. "Well, she at least needed me for the job."

Larken laughed, almost relieved that Hazel's antics were for good reason. What Emily said about someone new validating what had happened now made sense. Larken thought about Caroline, trying to picture being in Hazel's shoes had the roles been reversed.

"Anyway," Miles said, positioning his body toward Larken and taking his hands out of his pockets. "You told me something about you last night, about why you moved back, and I wanted to tell you this about me. I know it's kinda' heavy."

"Oh, Miles." Larken shook her head. "My story was nothing compared to yours." Larken added up all of the things about herself she hadn't told him and lost count—another wave of guilt overcoming her.

"Heartache is heartache," Miles said astutely. "I know you didn't tell me everything. But it was a start. I think for both of us."

He reached out for her hand, his warmth seemingly able to make anything better. Larken thought of his wife, Hallie, and couldn't understand what in this life could be beyond repair from his touch.

"Having you around has been good for me," Miles said quietly, the gravel in his voice bringing weight to the statement. "Just thought you should know that." He moved closer, his face hovering above hers, worry lines in his forehead showing. Larken knew he wanted more. She knew that she wanted more, too.

The sun had leaked out of the sky, leaving them in a cloud of gray dusk.

"It got dark on us," Larken observed, waving the air at a mosquito and finding a reason to step away. She regretted the distance immediately, wishing she'd let Miles kiss her.

"C'mon," Miles said, releasing her hand.

They climbed back into the Bronco and set back toward Charleston, the first illuminations of fireflies visible as they passed old-growth forests.

Miles pulled into a McDonald's just inside the Charleston city limits—Larken retelling the story of Marcus and his peanut butter infatuation and Luke asking if she'd boiled water before.

They drove through town and crossed over the James Island Expressway bridge, its presence suddenly connecting Miles to a sadness that Larken couldn't fully understand.

"Thanks for telling me," she said, breaking the silence. "And for showing me."

Miles nodded. "Life's weird."

Larken couldn't agree more.

*

Uly happily greeted them with a stick back at Miles' house. His body was half way in the driver's side by the time Miles could open the door.

"Ah, Pal," Miles greeted him. "Good job guardin' the house." He took one of the dog's ears in each hand and kissed the top of his head.

Larken covered her face to hide a yawn and dug in the back of the Bronco for her rain jacket. It was only eight o'clock, but the emotions of the day, both high and low, had worn her down to nearly nothing.

"Looks like you're taking the car again," Miles teased.

Larken didn't object.

"Just drive it to the office on Tuesday," Miles offered. "We'll figure it out later."

Larken rushed their goodbye—less afraid of saying the wrong thing than Miles saying the right thing.

Her drive home was helplessly lonely. The clouds had scattered allowing the sky to breathe and a bright, crisp moon to reflect on the water.

The weight of expectation pressed against her like a wall. When she was with Miles, she barely thought of Jackson. And when she wasn't with Miles, she wanted Jackson—or some version of him.

Hazel's warning to not hurt Miles rang in her ears as she crossed over the bridge. *"He's not ready for that kind of disappointment."* She felt a twisting in her gut and for a split second almost turned around to tell him everything she had been keeping from him.

Larken grabbed her phone and dialed Lil. She hoped she was already tucked away in her room at the Edisto house so that Bunny wouldn't ask to speak with her.

Lil answered on the third ring, her voice raspy and warm. "My darling," she said. "I hoped I would hear from you."

Larken told Lil everything—the doubts she had about Jackson, the feelings she was fighting for Miles, the lie about Bunny, the warning from Hazel—all of it. It was a relief just to say it out loud, the inner turmoil of confessing to someone wiser and older bringing temporary comfort.

Lil drew in a deep breath when Larken had finally unwound.

"You don't owe anybody anything," Lil said soothingly. "You've always felt like you do, but you don't."

Larken listened, hot tears blurring her eyes

"Hey, now," Lil chirped, "you've got Miles' car, right?"

"Yeah." Larken sniffled. "His dead wife's car."

"So drive out to Edisto," Lil insisted. "The roads ought to be clear by now anyway. And it's not that late. I just can't stand the thought of you in that big 'ol house alone in this state."

Larken sat in the driveway of The Ashby House, the engine of the car turned off and the interior lights dimming.

Larken tapped the steering wheel in deliberation. "I'll be there in an hour."

*

Larken drove like she was driving away from her problems. The marshes lit her way along the sides of the Savannah Highway, countless creeks snaking and glimmering in the moonlight—pausing their course only between fields of soybeans.

It had been at least two years since Larken had been to Will-o'-the-Wisp, but she was almost certain she could find her way blindfolded.

Once she crossed over Whooping Island Creek on Toogoodoo Road, Larken rolled the windows down in the Audi and let the smell of mud, marsh and rainwater saturate her.

She turned left onto Highway 174, a narrow seventeen-mile grand entry to Edisto. It was too dark to fully appreciate the cathedral of Live Oaks that arched over, touching one another in solidarity, but Larken could make out the dark ceiling that they created.

The setting felt like home, but reminded her of Miles—wild and enigmatic. Before she knew it, her mind had wandered like the undulating waterways of the Lowcountry, imagining what it would be like to have him touch her.

The last leg of the drive was cathartic. The wind seemed to blow any thoughts at all out of Larken's mind—a welcome reprieve.

Larken followed the highway around Big Bay Creek until it melted into to the South Edisto River. She turned onto Docksite Road and followed it to a dead ended, sandy lane.

Will-o'-the-Wisp sat proudly hidden down a quarter mile drive at the hook of the island where the South Edisto River and entrance of the Atlantic Ocean met. Lil still ran the management of the house, leaving it sand blown and slightly more natural than Bunny cared for.

Larken pulled into a makeshift spot in the sand, making mental note to have Miles' car detailed before returning it to him.

The buzzing life inside of the house spilled out onto the lawn, greeting her warmly. Larken sighed in relief to be around the familiar of family and in a place that had always been an escape.

Lil sat on the wrap-around porch holding a glass of champagne. She stood up to greet Larken, an empathetic smile on her face.

"Oh I'm so glad to see you," Lil said as she hugged Larken, stroking her hair. "You won't believe how drunk your Momma is."

Larken rolled her eyes and laughed. "Did you tell her I was coming?"

"I did." Lil nodded, sitting back down. "But she won't remember it."

Larken sat down in a rocking chair beside Lil. "Good. I can sit out here a minute then."

Lil passed her champagne flute to Larken and waved her away when she took a sip and tried to hand it back. "All I've done is drink today, honey. When in Rome..."

"Sam's asleep?" Larken asked. It had been two weeks since she'd seen his little face, curious and sweet.

"Oh yeah. Caroline snuck away too," Lil answered.

An eruption of laughter leaked out from inside the house.

"And Mr. Boca Raton?" Larken asked, her face showing that she already knew the answer.

"Unfortunately." Lil sighed. "I thought maybe he'd grow on me. And honey has he ever—like choke weed."

"Lil?" Larken asked. "You know the land in the Lowcountry? That Momma's selling?"

"Yeah," Lil confirmed, rocking back in her chair. "At least I think so. We've got loads of it. Why?"

Larken added more information to the already thickening plot. Lil listened intently as Larken told her about the Oxendines land really being Ashby land and how Miles was fighting for them to keep it.

"Well, shit, sugar," Lil said, the impact of the story bringing her rocking chair to a halt. "I'm sorry, but I don't know what else to say."

"Me either." Larken bit at a hangnail.

"You know," Lil said after thinking for a few moments, "we could just ask her to *not* sell the land."

Larken loved that Lil took all of her efforts on as her own. She was her greatest ally.

"Do you think we need the money or something?" Larken asked. The idea had never crossed her mind.

Lil gave her a look assuring her that they didn't.

"So if she's not selling it for money, she's selling it *because* of JD." Larken rolled her head back in thought.

"Sounds about right, doesn't it?" Lil leaned in to whisper. "Let's get rid of JD."

"Like...kill him?" Larken asked, her eyes wide with intrigue.

"Good Lord." Lil threw her head back and laughed. "Not unless we have to."

Larken reached to squeeze Lil's hand. "You had me worried for a second."

"Well, if he does go missin', don't look at me. And don't check the crab traps." Lil set her jaw.

Larken inhaled a cleansing breath of salty marsh water and let the night breeze kiss her face before going inside with Lil.

"You look awful," Bunny whined, her lips pouting out in disapproval as Larken walked through the door. Iris let out a single, shrill howl and jumped off the couch to greet her.

"Oh, Bunny," Priss chided, picking the dog up, "don't be ugly."

Larken shrugged the comment off, too tired to care. It was comforting to be in the surroundings of the beach house—its decor remaining mostly the same as it had been for her entire life. The great room was nautical themed with bold navy and white striped sofas, captains chairs and artwork boasting ancient sea vessels. A massive ship wheel chandelier suspended down from the vaulted ceiling, drawing your eye up to the grandeur of the building. Lil always said it was a waste that the old house didn't have more life in it year round.

Priss walked over and hugged Larken, the thick aroma of alcohol wafting with her. She slung her arm around Larken's waist, using her as a prop.

"Well, well. Look what the cat dragged in," Mr. Boca Raton's voice rang out as he entered the living room, some dark liquid in a high-ball glass swirling precariously around. "Welcome, welcome." He wrapped an arm around Bunny's shoulders awkwardly. The action reminded Larken of a dog marking its territory.

Lil tip-toed away to the direction of the kitchen, no doubt in search of Bart's company and a quick escape.

"So good of you to join us," Mr. Boca Raton continued haughtily, a sense of entitlement wearing on him heavily. He rolled his eyes back like a shark when he spoke, alcohol no doubt making him less tolerable than usual.

"No, JD," Larken smiled tightly. "I'm glad *you* could join *us*… I hope this weather won't affect your tan. It'd be a *shame* if you lost your glow."

"Larken," Bunny scoffed. "What's got into you?"

"Oh, leave her be," Mr. Boca Raton said with a wave of his wrist. "The poor girl has obviously had a long, harrowing day." He looked her up and down in disapproval before taking a sip of his drink.

"I'm goin' to bed," Larken said, unfazed. She removed herself quickly, leaving the room before anyone could protest.

She climbed the stairs, the buzz of chatter from the first floor growing more distant. She let her duffle bag drop loudly on the floor of her room and turned on a lamp.

The room smelled like a mixture of clean linens and childhood memories. Some of the best nights of her life were spent within these walls—memorable, dead sleep induced by the exhaustion of playing in the sand for hours.

"Knock, knock," Caroline's voice whispered as she poked her head inside the door. She held out a mug of hot liquid. "Bart thought you might need this…"

"Thanks." Larken smiled, reaching for the mug and breathing in the rich smell of Irish coffee. "Hope I didn't wake you when I came up."

"Oh, no," Caroline assured her, sitting on the end of the bed. "I was just reading." She stretched. "Rained in with Momma for two days makes eighteenth-century poetry a welcome reprieve."

Larken laughed. "Glad I missed that."

"What is that smell?" Caroline asked, taking a whiff of Larken. She wrinkled her nose in disapproval.

Larken gave Caroline an abbreviated version of her trip to the Lowcountry and the twins' delivery. She tried her best to not blush every time she said Miles' name. If Caroline suspected anything, she hadn't asked.

Caroline had question after question about the Oxendine family and the river people. Her initial reaction to their life was much like Larken's had been days earlier—skeptical, but slightly less judgmental.

"So that's your job?" Caroline asked, confused. "To make off-roading house calls?"

"Not really." Larken sipped at her Irish coffee. "I do fundraising for the non-profit arm of the clinic. You know, hobnobbing with old money. Society people."

Caroline nodded. "Oh. Society people, huh? So...like us."

"Yeah." Larken shrugged. "I guess."

Caroline stood up and rearranged her hair. "And I'm guessing this Dr. Beckway still has no idea who you are then?"

Larken shifted uncomfortably. "No."

"And you haven't told him because..." Caroline waited for an answer.

"Just 'cause." Larken bit her bottom lip. "It was a stupid lie. And I really don't think he'd care who I am."

"Hmm." Caroline twisted her mouth up in consideration. "You know he did Lauren McNally's boobs?" She didn't wait for a response. "She said that he's *quite* the eligible bachelor."

"Widower," Larken corrected. "Eligible widower."

Caroline headed for the doorway. "You know, Lark, the longer you keep this secret of who you are from this Dr. Beckway, the worse it will be when he finds out." Caroline clucked from the side of her mouth. "Just tell him, okay?"

*

Larken had showered quickly and slipped into a T-shirt before almost literally passing out on her bed. She slept like the dead, just like she had always done in the old place—this time waking up to find that she was not alone.

"Hey, sleepyhead," Jackson's voice soothed as she stirred under the covers. He reached and patted at her voluminous mountain of bed head.

Larken sat up, disoriented and confused. "What time is it?" Her eyes tried to focus on his face.

"A little after ten o'clock," Jackson told her quietly. He propped himself up on the pillow beside her.

Larken smiled. She was happy to see Jackson, his presence unexpectedly comforting. "I didn't think you could make it." She yawned, covering her face with the covers.

"I wanted to surprise you."

"Well that you did." Larken leaned up and kissed him. "You know, last time we were in this room…" Larken ran her fingers around the buttons on his shirt.

"Ohhhh, yes." Jackson laughed, stopping her hand by holding it. "I remember well."

"And what?" Larken teased, fueled by his attempt to disarm her advances. "You didn't like it?" She snuck another kiss.

"Bird," Jackson pleaded, pulling away. "Avery's here."

"Oh." Larken recoiled, surprised and suddenly anxious at the same time. "I thought Kayla wouldn't let her visit."

"Yeah, well," Jackson nodded, "we came to some sort of an agreement."

"What sort of an agreement?" Larken sensed he was holding something back.

"Well, if Kayla moves here, I'll pay for her living expenses," Jackson explained, fidgeting uncharacteristically.

"And if she doesn't?" Larken asked.

"Then I won't," Jackson said bluntly.

Larken's stomach turned. The empathy she felt for Kayla always superseded all other emotions.

"And, so," Jackson stalled, cautiously, "we sort of agreed that it would be best if she moved here." Jackson shrugged as if he'd delivered news that he had nothing to do with.

"Well, it doesn't sound like you gave her very many options," Larken said pointedly.

"I've given her everything for seven years, Larken."

Larken exhaled, pushing the covers off her. "So when does she

365

come?"

"Soon as she's packed." Jackson twisted his mouth up. "I got an offer on the house in Alabama yesterday."

Larken got out of bed and threw on a sundress behind the cover of the closet door.

"Not like I haven't seen you naked before," Jackson called from the bed.

She combed her fingers through her hair, trying to make peace with the wild strands. Part of her wanted to punish Jackson for not warning her about his plans to move Kayla here—the other part felt like an anchor had been released, freeing her to make her own brash decisions.

Larken painted on some mascara and dabbed at her lips with pink lip gloss. She wondered if it was normal to be nervous to meet a seven-year-old.

"Alright," Larken said, smoothing the hem of her dress. "Let's do this."

Larken followed Jackson down the stairs, the buzz of post-breakfast conversation swarming as they approached the dining room.

The room lit up with hellos and good mornings, everyone but Mr. Boca Raton happy to see that Jackson had successfully fetched Larken.

Late morning light flooded into the dining room, brightening everyone's mood and countenance. Hank read a day-old paper with Iris in his lap while Bunny and Priss told Mr. Boca Raton varying accounts of a trip they'd taken to Paris decades earlier, the specifics apparently muddled after twenty years of martinis.

Larken strained to see Avery and Sam at the far end of the table, lost in child-size conversation and giggling at what appeared to be nothing but each other's company. Caroline supervised silently, handing Sam pinches of breakfast that he'd refused to eat with the distraction of a new friend.

Avery was a petite little girl with straight, shoulder-length blonde hair and country tan skin. She was beautiful—swaying in an eyelet dress with tie-straps. She had a charming smile and one recently lost front tooth.

Larken looked beside her to see Jackson completely smitten by his daughter. He radiated pride as he watched her play, nothing else in the room distracting him but the tiny beauty.

"Let's fix you a plate," Bart said, emerging from the kitchen motioning for Larken to follow him.

The kitchen was the best room in the house with floor to ceiling windows showcasing a spectacular water view of the estuary. Cord grass swayed in the wind, the salty wind whipping it furiously and then gently pushing it back and forth like a game of tug-of-war.

Larken looked out to see Lil leaning over the dock, extended long across the marsh waters, soaking in the warmth of the sea island sun.

Bart pulled tin foil off a dish of shrimp and grits—Larken's stomach nearly roaring with hunger at the aroma.

"I moved Dr. Beckway's car to the Cunningham's house early this morning," Bart said, handing Larken a mug of coffee. "They are out of the country until next month."

"Oh," Larken said, a feeling of guilt flooding her. "Thanks." Bart's foresight was always timely.

Bart nodded. "Sometimes it's better to eliminate objects of question."

"Bart?" Larken asked, spooning the shrimp and grits into a bowl. "Why is Momma selling the land in the Lowcountry?"

Bart pursed his lips. "Well, I suppose it comes down to supply and demand. She has no use for it and Mr. Hart seems to."

"So," Larken asked through a mouthful of breakfast, "it was already for sale?"

Bart raised an eyebrow at Larken. "Taking a sudden interest in Ashby Family Estate affairs, are we?"

"I'm just wondering." Larken shrugged casually and hid her mouth behind the coffee mug.

Bart paused a moment before answering. "Not exactly."

"Hmm. Mr. Boca Raton… JD… approached Momma about selling it then?" She took a bite of grits.

"At first she was reluctant," Bart continued, "but Mr. Hart seems to be…persuasive." Larken picked up on a subtle annoyance in his voice.

Larken didn't have any other questions for Bart. She didn't know what answers she was looking for anyway. She got a second helping of shrimp and grits and a warm-up of coffee before returning to the dining room.

"Avery," Jackson called to his daughter as Larken entered the room, "I want you to meet my friend Larken."

Avery walked over slowly to her father, tucking a piece of blonde hair behind her ear. "Hi, Miss. Larken." The girl smiled, extending her hand. "Nice to meet you."

The subtle difference between Avery's accent and Jackson's accent was no doubt the result of being raised in Alabama. Larken hoped that she'd keep it even after she moved here, but knew that it was impossible.

"Are you having fun playing with Sam?" Larken asked. She looked at Jackson for guidance as to what to say.

The little girl leaned into her daddy, fighting the urge to be shy. "Uh-huh."

"Miss. Larken is a friend of mine from when I was a boy," Jackson explained to her, nudging Avery into conversation.

"Like a sister?" Avery asked, her eyes getting big.

Jackson laughed. "Uhhh, kind of." He looked at Larken and shrugged.

"I like your dress." Larken smiled, pointing at the eyelet material.

Avery looked down, feeling the fabric. "Thanks. My Momma made it."

"Wow," Larken said, impressed. She felt a tinge of inadequacy. "Well, it's very beautiful on you."

Avery whispered something to Jackson and he excused her to go play with Sam again. The little girl walked away slowly, turning around to wave at Larken.

"She has your mannerisms," Larken told him, recognizing the little girl shared Jackson's subtle smile and cool confidence.

Jackson propped himself against the wall. "Yeah, that's about all of me she has though. Well, maybe that and some stubbornness."

"So she looks like her mother?" Larken asked. They both

watched as Avery and Sam played, Priss walking by to tickle them both.

"Spittin' image."

Larken observed Avery closely again, trying to see the adult version that would be Kayla and finding a beautiful, delicate woman. The sickening feeling of empathy invaded her again.

"Listen up, listen up," Bunny's voice rang. "We are doing family beach portraits at one o'clock. Caroline, tell Aaron to be here by then and Prissy make sure Sylvia's on her way—in her whites and ready to go." She clapped one solitary time as her grand finish.

Caroline turned to Priss and mockingly saluted Bunny.

"Larken," Bunny called loudly, "let's do something with that hair, sugar. I wanna use these pictures for our family Christmas cards." She winked and clucked her lips.

Jackson elbowed Larken and gave her the okay sign. He wanted to move closer to her, but looked at Avery and stopped. "By the way, Momma offered to babysit tonight so we can go out."

"What do you have in mind?"

"I was thinking Shell Island if that's okay with you." Jackson looked at her hopefully. He fought the urge to lean in again, his eyes glancing over at a watchful Avery. "Lil said we could use the boat."

"I haven't been there in years." Larken smiled. "Let's do it."

"Yes, please." Jackson winked suggestively. "Let's."

Larken shooed him away and retreated to her room upstairs. She pulled out the white strapless dress that Bunny had instructed she bring and hung it on the doorjamb. She thought quickly about Miles— wondering if he was by the river bank at his home on Wampler Drive, throwing the stick for Uly again and again. She shook her head, erasing the thought like an Etch-a-sketch.

By twelve fifteen she was dressed, had make-up on and tight curls sprayed with shellacked hairspray until they had turned into hard coils. Between ocean surf and humidity, she'd be lucky if the curls resembled waves by the time the photographer showed up.

Larken found Lil on the front porch, swinging back and forth with a glass of iced tea.

"Well, there you are!" Lil exclaimed, smacking her leg in approval. "I've been dying to catch you alone."

"Why?" Larken asked, quickly sitting in the rocking chair beside her. "What is it?"

"I heard Agent Orange on the phone this morning," Lil whispered, rolling her eyes at the mere mention of Mr. Boca Raton. "He walked all the way down to the water just to make a phone call. I was out early watching for dolphins when I saw him coming." Lil flared her nostrils at the thought of him. "I hid in the cord grass just so I didn't have to make conversation."

"Uh-huh." Larken encouraged her to continue, imagining her graceful grandmother crouched at dawn in a sand dune.

Lil continued. "Their legal council, Miles' attorney friend I presume, contacted Mr. Boca Raton's camp and let them know that he plans to move for an injunction citing the land as pertinent to indigenous people. Bart told me they contacted our Estate Attorney as well."

"Oh, wow," Larken said, wrinkling her nose. "That's brilliant."

"I thought so, too," Lil said leaning in girlishly. "But here's the thing…" She paused for effect. "He knows the tribe lives on the land

371

and that Bunny is not aware of it—he plans to rush the sale through so that they can start clearing it and run the so-called squatters off."

"When?" Larken asked, alarm flooding her face.

"He said A.S.A.P." Lil shook her head in disapproval. "Something's got to be done quick."

Larken was relieved that Bunny hadn't moved forward with the sale of the land intentionally knowing it would displace the tribe, but she thought of the rice fields and the Oxendines. Clearing the land would clear their lives. The thought made her sick yet at the same time she wondered how she could keep her involvement and connection to Bunny from Miles.

"But an injunction would put a stop to all of it, right?" Larken asked, hopeful that Christopher's legal skills could put it all to rest without her participation.

"Yes, I think so," Lil agreed. "But these legal things can take time. And baby I wouldn't put it past this joker to not wait for the sale before taking matters into his own hands if you know what I'm sayin'. I mean he's gone through Bunny like Sherman went through Atlanta as it is. She's let her guard down in her age."

Larken rubbed at her forehead in worry.

"I'm keepin' a close watch on him," Lil promised, her eyes sharp enough to cut glass at the thought of JD Hart.

The entire household, minus Bart, descended onto the beach like a great white plague, Bunny in her ideal element of both hostess and pack leader.

Sylvia was jovial and relaxed, reminding Larken of the friend she'd known as a child. They walked arm in arm to the beach, Sylvia, Larken and Caroline reminiscing about summers spent together. In the midst of the lightheartedness, Larken felt a sadness at the realization of just how far apart they'd grown.

Lil eyed Mr. Boca Raton more skeptically than usual, scanning his face for more evidence of his scheming.

The photographer was soft-spoken and emo—managing to convey to everyone through his square framed glasses and vintage vest that family beach portraits were well below his skill set as a photographer.

Bunny set the tone as orchestrator of the shoot almost immediately—completely overwhelming the photographer with her finger snapping and strongly-minded arrangement of each set of pictures. He quickly fell in line with everyone else though, obeying her every command with mild annoyance.

After she was satisfied with the first round with the immediate family, Bunny invited Mr. Boca Raton to join them. Lil, Larken, Aaron, Caroline and Sam immediately disbanded as he pranced into the frame, tilting Bunny back for an awkward kiss. She paraded for the camera, tousling her hair and throwing her arms around his neck.

After Priss, Hank, Sylvia, Jackson and Avery did a family portrait, Caroline, Aaron and Sam posed as well—Sam giggling hysterically at the seriousness of it all.

"Get over there with Jackson," Bunny insisted, pushing Larken toward him. She'd been so preoccupied with what she and Lil had discussed earlier that she had barely noticed Jackson—white linen pants, paper-thin v-neck T-shirt. Larken didn't object.

Jackson wrapped his arms around Larken for a rare public display of affection. She leaned her head on his chest, breathing in a mixture of fresh ocean air and body soap.

"What about Avery?" Larken asked, straining to locate the girl for a reaction.

"Oh she's gonna find out about us sooner or later," Jackson soothed, brushing Larken's hair. "Plus, can't I hug my childhood friend?" He winked.

The little girl was busily being chased by Sam, seaweed in hand as a means of propellant.

"I wonder if we'll do this one day," Jackson thought out loud. "Beach portraits with our own family."

Larken looked up at him to see he was lost in the dream of their future together.

"I'm sorry," Jackson said, kissing the top of her head. "I know how you feel about me making plans."

Larken's throat tightened. Being with Jackson was like being caught in an undertow. Part of her loved it, wanting to be swept away and drowned in him. The other part of her wanted to fight for her life, struggle from the deep and swim to safety. She didn't know why. And she didn't know why she always thought of Miles when she thought of feeling safe—especially when the most precarious moments she'd ever had in her life were with him.

The rest of the day was spent on the porch of the beach house, eating crab sandwiches and drinking Planter's Punch strong enough to tranquilize a horse.

Avery and Sam fell asleep watching cartoons, coloring books and Legos scattered on the floor around them.

The evening rolled in with pink skies and a perfect, warm breeze. Larken changed into shorts and a tank-top for the boat ride to Shell Island. She made two peanut butter and jelly sandwiches, Bart shaking his head in disapproval of her cooking skills while he and Lil prepared a simple yet elegant dish of marsh hen and hoppin' Johns for the rest of the house.

"What?" Larken said to Bart, defending the food. "He said he likes peanut butter." She put two Coke's in a plastic bag and wrapped the sandwiches in paper towels.

"Here," Bart said, extending a small container. "Coconut cream pie."

The boat was a small white fourteen foot Catamaran used for getting around Edisto and the nearby sandbars like Shell Island. Lil's cast nets for shrimp and miscellaneous fishing supplies were piled up on one side, still wet from her most recent expedition.

Jackson hopped in the water and pushed them out before starting up the little engine and heading for Shell Island.

The boat dipped and surged through the water, salty spray whipping Larken's hair around wildly. She watched Jackson steer her steady, one hand on the side of the boat and the other on the motor, his shirt pressed tight against him in the blast of wind.

Jackson brought the boat up to the beach of the sandbar, hopping out again and dragging them onto shore. Larken grabbed the hand that he extended, throwing the plastic bag of dinner over her shoulder.

The island was untouched. Millions of seashells—whelkes, cockles, shoe crab shells and shark teeth littered the beach, bleached white from the sun. Larken watched a hermit crab maneuver carefully over a piece of driftwood, dragging with him a too-big shell that looked recently acquired.

The sun hung precariously above the horizon, shedding a pink glow across the shells. Other beachcombers perused through the sandbar's offerings, some carrying heavy buckets of collected souvenirs.

Larken and Jackson walked along the beach like an old couple, pointing out interesting shells and crunching through broken debris. They sat on a washed up log to have their PB&J dinner, the coconut cream pie undoubtedly the highlight.

"Avery would love this," Jackson said, overlooking the shells and savoring the last bite of pie.

"I loved it when I was a kid," Larken remembered. "Lil always helped me find perfect sand dollars."

"I remember you gave me one once." Jackson nodded at the memory. "I think I smashed it so I could find the seagulls inside."

"That sounds about right." Larken laughed, wrinkling her nose.

"Even then I loved you, you know," Jackson said, a sweetness on his face at the notion. He pushed hair away from her face.

Larken sat silently with her arms hugged around her legs.

"Hey, listen to me," Jackson said, taking in a breath. "I love you."

"Jackson."

"Ah," Jackson said under his breath. "But that's the thing. I don't think that's a normal reaction to an admission of 'I Love You.'" He kicked his legs out in front of him, leaning back on his palms. "I think we're good together," he continued. "It feels right to me to be with you. Does it not feel that way to you, too?" The sun hit his face while he was talking, his eyes sparkling in the light.

"No—it does," Larken answered quickly, realizing she meant it.

"I want this."

"What's keeping you from me then, Bird? Two steps forward, four steps back."

She reached for his hand and squeezed it. "I'm sorry. I don't do it on purpose."

Jackson kissed her hand, accepting the apology. "I'd like it if you came with me and Avery to look for houses." Jackson set his jaw, waiting for her reaction.

"Sure." Larken smiled. The invitation was flattering and exciting. "Love to."

"Good," Jackson said, standing up. "'Cause I'm hopin' you'll wanna live there, too one day."

Larken felt the familiar anxiety in her stomach at the mention of official coupledom.

They left Shell Island at low-tide, the little Catamaran fully on the sand at the receded ocean. Jackson pushed it back into the water and they set back for the beach house, Larken feeling strangely content with her place in Jackson's life.

Darkness had just set in by the time Jackson docked the boat. The house lit up ahead of them like a beacon, guiding them back to the chaos of their families. They walked up the long dock hand in hand, the old wood creaking and giving gently where the posts joined the boards.

Larken stopped halfway back to the house and turned to look at Jackson. She grabbed his face and kissed him, standing up on her toes so that they were eye to eye. Jackson took full advantage of the affection, wrapping his arms around her and pressing her against the rail.

It was easy for her to be lost in Jackson. Everything about him boasting confidence and charm. Larken kissed him without any other thought entering her mind, enjoying every caress and touch.

"Can I come to your room later?" Jackson asked, tugging at the lobe of her ear with his teeth.

"Yes, yes, yes," Larken agreed, laughing. "A hundred times yes."

Jackson ran a hand through his hair, taking in a deep breath and forcing himself away from Larken.

They came in through the kitchen, the smell of Bart and Lil's meal still strong and intoxicating.

"I fixed you up a plate," Lil said cheerfully, walking into the kitchen. Larken could tell she had been waiting for them. "Unless you're still stuffed from that PB&J." She cackled.

"Ah, Lil," Jackson said, kissing her on the cheek, "you're literally the best."

Lil volunteered to stay back with the sleeping Sam and Avery while the rest of the house went down to the ocean for a beach bonfire. With Jackson and Larken back, she left to meet everyone else, wine glass in hand, silk cover-up flowing in the night breeze as she trotted girlishly out of view, her voice carrying the melody of Puccini's "Un Bel Di, Vedremo" like a siren in the sea.

Jackson peaked in on Avery, sleeping sprawled out across the downstairs guest room. He winked at Larken and motioned her upstairs.

"How long do you think we have?" Jackson asked, closing the bedroom door behind them. He pulled Larken to him, pausing from kissing her to pull her T-shirt off.

"Twenty minutes?" Larken said breathlessly, pulling Jackson's shirt off in return. "They'll be loud and drunk walking back to the house. We should be able to hear them."

"Ah, hell," Jackson said, walking Larken to the bed and laying her down. "I really don't give a damn."

*

Larken woke up with the sun the next morning, the house still and quiet. She remembered Jackson sneaking out of the bed, careful not to wake her.

Larken threw on her running shorts and the tank top she'd worn the night before and set out for a run on the beach. It was still peaceful out, the morning air surrounding her with a gentle sweetness, the sun glowing pink and new.

She ran barefoot, the sand firm and cool underneath her— turning around to see her tracks on the beach before a lazy tide rolled in to erase them.

The clarity she felt in the solitude of the morning brought conclusions she couldn't otherwise make during the weight of the day. Her mind harbored on thoughts of Miles Beckway and the great disservice she had done to herself by lying to him. She took in a ragged breath when she realized what would become of her time with him once he knew who she was. A shiver ran across her body.

Lil was busy in the kitchen when Larken returned from her run. She offered her hot coffee and a peach scone, which Larken declined.

"So it's settled then," Lil said, realizing Larken had come to some sort of a decision on the beach.

Larken answered only with a nod for fear of falling apart from saying the words.

"Well, baby," Lil soothed, "tell the truth and shame the devil."

Everyone was up by nine—Bunny having a little hair of the dog for breakfast to counteract the long weekend of drinking.

"I don't know about y'all," Bunny said through a raspy voice, "but I need a vacation and a liver transplant." Mr. Boca Raton lifted his index finger in agreement.

Larken fought back the urge to remind her mother that her life was a vacation, but instead drew in a cleansing breath and looked at Lil, who was thinking the same thing.

Jackson found Larken in the kitchen and grazed her butt with his hand as he walked to the coffee pot.

"Last night was fun," he said quietly, looking around to make sure everyone else was engaged in conversation, especially Avery who was being smothered in kisses by Priss.

Larken nodded, blushing at the reminder of her night with Jackson—his hands on her body, his skin smelling of sea spray and sunblock.

"So," Jackson said, speaking at regular volume, "I hate to do this, but I've got to get back to Charleston."

"Oh." Larken twisted her mouth up in disappointment. "So soon?"

"Well," Jackson braced, "Kayla's coming today." He lowered his voice with Avery in mind. "A little sooner than I thought," he continued, "but she's nervous about Avery being here without her." He shook his head in annoyance. "That's just Kayla."

Larken couldn't help but think back to the last time Jackson had left her for Kayla and realized he would always be at her disposal because of Avery.

"Totally understand," Larken said, forcing a convincing smile.

"Bartholomew," Mr. Boca Raton's voice rang out as he entered the kitchen. Iris dashed at his feet, barking and growling. "I need a car back to Charleston if you don't mind," he continued, toeing the dog away from his loafers.

Bart turned around slowly from his conversation with Lil, poised despite the man's sudden demand.

"Here you go," Larken said, walking to the side of the fridge and pulling a taxi magnet off before Bart could respond. "Help yourself." She handed the magnet to Mr. Boca Raton and stood in front of him, arms crossed.

"Oh for the love, Larken," Bunny chided. "Act like you got some raisin'!"

Mr. Boca Raton laughed nervously, an air of superiority in his tone. "My goodness. So much for southern hospitality then." He forced a strong, southern drawl.

"You wouldn't know southern hospitality if it bit you in the ass," Larken quipped. "Boca Raton by way of New Jersey is it?"

Somehow, even underneath all of the orange, Mr. Boca Raton's face turned red. Larken knew she'd hit the hammer on the nail. She quickly glanced to see Lil's reaction, her eyes wide in surprise at her granddaughter.

"I'll give you a ride," Jackson offered, breaking the tension. "I'm headed that way anyway."

"How kind of you, Jackson." Mr. Boca Raton nodded. "I'll fetch my things." He turned and walked briskly out of the kitchen.

"Larken," Bunny hissed, stomping her foot. "A word?" She walked outside, waiting for Larken to follow her.

Larken looked around the kitchen to see her witnesses, Priss, Caroline and Hank, standing mouths agape. Sylvia hid a satisfied smile in her cup of coffee, the courtroom attorney in her element and completely amused with the discord.

Larken walked outside, Bunny's face unreadable.

"Why?" Bunny asked. "Why do you want to destroy my every happiness?"

Larken laughed. "Him? *That*—is your every happiness?"

"Good Lord no, but we are a match," Bunny said through her teeth. "At my age and with what I've been through in my life, you know a good thing on paper when you see it. And I've learned that paper means a whole hell of a lot. If you want to dissect a perfectly good relationship, why don't you start with your own?"

"Oh, this isn't about me and Jackson, Momma," Larken warned. "I'm pretty sure he's at least not a con-artist."

Bunny inhaled sharply. "Well. That's a new one."

"And why are you selling him that land in the Lowcountry?" Larken questioned, her skin flushed from the sun and the exchange with Bunny. "Am I the only one who can see how convenient this all is for him? How convenient *you* are for him?"

"Ok, Larken, really. Why don't you leave the business to the grown-ups?" Bunny laughed cynically.

Larken realized that Bunny knew exactly why JD Hart was hanging around. She felt a strange sadness for her, the revelation of her diminished self-worth evident.

"Do you know what he's planning to do with the land?" Larken asked.

"Of course I do. He's gonna develop it into condos." Bunny waived her hand and raked it through her humidity-drenched hair. "Good business is good business. You think I don't know when I'm bein' taken for a ride? Ha! I invented it." Bunny smiled tightly. "He's payin' *four* times more than what that backwoods land is worth anyway."

"There are people that live on that land," Larken blurted out. "A tribe. They farm rice and they've been there for forever. Granddaddy deeded it to them—unofficially." Larken wasn't sure if that was true or not, but thought it sounded like something he would have done.

Bunny pursed her lips and looked at the sky. Larken knew without her having to say it that she would surely blame the liberal west coast for polluting her ideology.

"And JD isn't building condos on that land," Larken continued, "he's a contractor for a power plant. He needs the river access to dump coal ash into for a new facility. It will *ruin* the Lowcountry—just like you will ruin our family's good name and reputation."

"How do you know this?" Bunny demanded.

"I've been there," Larken said, her tone sharp, "with Miles."

"Oh with Miles," Bunny repeated contemptuously. "First name basis are we?" Bunny went quiet for a moment, her eyes calculating. Dishonesty was the second highest sin to her. The first being a smudge on the family name.

"Well we don't need the money," Bunny admitted, breaking the silence. "And I sure as hell don't need the man."

Larken nodded, urging her to continue.

"How 'bout I make you a deal we can both sleep with?"

CHAPTER SIXTEEN

Visit From A Ghost

"Thanks for comin' with me," Larken told Lil as they drove back to Charleston that afternoon.

"You kiddin' me?" Lil said, her hand out the window of Miles' Audi. "I feel like I'm escaping Alcatraz. One more minute and I'd use my own legs as crab bait."

Larken couldn't bring herself to tell Lil about the deal that she'd struck with Bunny. She felt cheap enough as it was to agree to Bunny's proposal that she stop seeing Miles. She also knew that Lil was the only person that could talk her out of it.

"Well, what's it gonna be?" Bunny asked Larken after proposing her plan.

"What does quitting working for Miles have anything to do with you not selling the land?" Larken asked, her mind racing to figure out Bunny's motive.

"Not just quitting the job," Bunny corrected. "You have to quit the *man*. That's the deal."

Larken sputtered nonsensical words.

"You let him go," Bunny said matter-of-factly, interrupting her with a wave of the hand, "and I'll drop the sale. Simple as that. It will be jewels on your crown."

"This is ridiculous, Momma."

"No, my darling girl," Bunny scoffed, "what is ridiculous is your rampant disregard for your future with Jackson. You think I don't see it? Because oh, do I ever see it. And I've seen it before, too. With David. He was wrong for you just like Miles Beckway is wrong for you." Bunny traced a bead of sweat down her nose. "This is *me* doing *you* a favor. One day you'll thank me."

Bunny's words stung, sticking in Larken's ears like pins. Panic fluttered in her chest, ushering in fear and deep agony for something not yet lost, but slipping effortlessly out of her grasp.

"My, my, you're awful quiet," Lil said, startling Larken back to the present.

Larken squeezed back a tear and kept her eyes on the road.

"Don't let fear make your heart up," Lil said intuitively. "They are not compatible, you know...fear and love."

They drove quietly back to Charleston, the city draining its visitors at the close of a long holiday weekend. Larken packed a bag of clothes and, anticipating a hostile main house environment, planned to stay with Lil in the carriage house.

"Well, get it on over with then," Lil said, snapping Larken out of a daze. "I'm afraid you'll make yourself sick if you have to keep this overnight."

Larken took in a deep breath and rubbed at her right temple. "I know." Tears pricked at her eyes again, but she shook them away.

It was late afternoon by the time Larken made something of her hair and pulled on a pair of dress shorts and a blouse. It felt futile to try and look decent knowing what Miles would think of her after she told him the truth, but she welcomed the procrastination.

Lil brushed at Larken's hair. "I don't know your reasons. But I'm on your side always."

Larken drove away, her pulse vibrating in her chest as she drove up the ramp to the bridge. The drive to James Island felt like it was one breath away, Larken gripping the steering wheel tightly as she recited her words to Miles.

She paused before starting down the drive, offering herself one last chance to turn around. The garage was open, all of Miles' trucks accounted for. She pulled the Audi into its spot, purring to a stop and climbing out.

It's a sign. A wave of relief flooding her when Miles and Uly were nowhere in sight. She walked to the Vespa, pushing at the kickstand and rolling it to the driveway.

"Sneaking off?" Miles voice called from behind her. She turned around to find him finishing a sandwich. Uly ambled over, his tail wagging his entire body.

"No. Sorry. I didn't think you were home," Larken said, her cheeks flushing. She pushed the kickstand back down and reached to pet Uly.

"What's going on?" Miles asked. He turned his head sideways as if trying to read Larken's mind.

Larken stood quietly, thinking about how to answer him. Now face-to-face, she had forgotten everything she had promised herself she would say.

"Everything alright?"

"Miles," Larken started. She shrugged her shoulders up and closed her eyes. "I have to quit."

Miles repositioned, wiping his mouth with a balled up paper towel that he'd held his sandwich with. "Why?"

"Remember when you asked me if I knew Bunny Ashby and I said I didn't?" Larken asked, a tear already falling down her face. "Well, the truth is, I do. She's my mother."

Miles nodded as he listened. His face was composed, but braced, his jaw tight and square.

"And that land that the Oxendines live on?" Larken sniffled.

Miles nodded.

"My family owns it."

Miles shuffled his feet in the gravel driveway, chewing on the side of his mouth.

Larken told him what she knew of the deal with JD Hart and his plans to clear the land.

"I'm so sorry, Miles." Larken rung her hands together like they were a wet washcloth. "I don't know why I didn't just tell you before." She swallowed hard. "It just felt good to be somebody else I guess."

Uly lay between them, thumping his tail on the gravel at the stark silence.

"So I have to quit," Larken said, taking in a ragged breath at the half truth.

Miles looked off in the distance, squinting his eyes like he was trying to solve a puzzle. "You don't *have* to," he said after a few moments of consideration. His face was kind and understanding. "I mean, if you don't wanna' work for me anymore that's one thing, but I think we're good together."

Larken's chest tightened. She needed him to make it easy for her to leave—to be mad as hell at her deceit and tell her to go. But he didn't.

"We can't be good together, Miles. There's…someone else." Larken rolled her eyes at her own admission, wiping at more tears. Bunny's instruction to "make him believe it" echoed in her mind. "I'm so sorry," she managed to say through a ragged breath. She'd never meant anything more in her life.

"Damn it, girl," Miles yelled. He took one long stride and grabbed her face, kissing her. Larken pulled herself closer to him, his arms falling to her waist and drawing her in. It was chaos and order at the same time, everything about them a perfect mess.

Miles pulled away as quickly as he'd kissed her, his face showing equal parts angst and passion.

"I know why you didn't want me to know who you are," Miles said, pacing in the driveway, his arms flailing with each word. "I can't blame you for that. And what Bunny's doing to the Oxendines—that's not somethin' you can do much about now, is it?"

Larken listened through a buzzing in her ears, her head still swirling from his kiss.

"But the way I feel about you," Miles continued, his voice elevated, "that's my fault. I did that. *We* did that." He ran a hand through his hair, a frustrated groan breaking his stream of consciousness. "I know there's something between us, Larken."

Larken's chest felt like it would cave in on itself. Part of her had believed that she had merely imagined Miles' feelings for her. Hearing him say it out loud was punishment in and of itself—a temptation of what could not be for more reasons than were her own.

Miles turned and looked at her. "Do you want me to fight for you?"

"What?" Larken blinked, tears spilling out of her eyes.

"Do you want me to fight for you?" He asked again. "Because I will. I will if I have any kind of chance."

Larken's stomach sank and a wave of heat ran through her body. She thought of the Oxendines and of the land they would be removed from without her end of the deal with Bunny being fulfilled. She thought of Jackson and the chance they had together—the life he wanted to make with her. She thought of everything that would be ruined if she did not take the path laid out for her.

"There isn't anything to fight for," Larken said dryly. The words stuck in her throat like cotton, bottled up in a million tears. She watched the lie hit Miles like a brick.

"I'm sorry I kissed you," Miles said, his eyebrows furrowed. "That wasn't right." He turned and walked back toward the house. "C'mon, Uly."

Uly leapt up from his spot in the driveway and bounded after Miles, blissfully unaware.

Larken wanted to run after him, to kiss him again and tell him to fight, for everything to go back to the way it was before, but she knew there was nothing she could say. She had no choice but to leave all doors for Miles Beckway closed and padlocked.

Larken pushed the kickstand out from under the Vespa again, her eyes so full of tears that everything was underwater.

She turned onto the main road from Miles' driveway and lost any and all composure that she had left. She sobbed deeply for her own pain and for Miles', drowning in confusion between choosing Jackson and being strong armed by her own mother.

Bunny's words rang in her head again. *Jewels on your crown.*

*

The deep sadness that Larken felt when David left her returned again, this time accompanied by guilt and remorse. She wondered if David had felt the way she felt now when he left her, nearly unbearable pain. She tried sifting through the rubble of her emotions, distinguishing between what was disappointment in herself and what was truly heartache for Miles. She thought of Jackson, looking for solace in a future with him, but could not find any just yet.

Larken returned to the carriage house, the sunset starting to dip into the harbor and a sweet evening breeze stirring up. Her tears had dried to her face in the night air. She tried to pull herself together for Lil's sake, the turmoil she felt as evident as if it had a spotlight on it.

She pulled through the gate and brought the Vespa to a stop—wiping at her cheeks and running her pinkie fingers under her eyes to remove cried-off mascara.

"Larken," Lil's voice called from the back door of the main house. "Come on in this way, sugar. We have a visitor." There was a seriousness in her voice that Lil did not usually project.

Larken knew that Bunny would be returning soon, Bart more than likely coming with her, but no one else was expected.

Larken walked into the kitchen, Lil's face giving little more than somberness away.

"Who is it?" Larken asked quietly. She heard a rustling from the sitting room.

"It's David," Lil whispered, her hand on her heart. "Oh, baby when it rains it just pours."

"David?" Larken asked, her mind racing. "David Maddox?"

Lil shushed her. "Yes. *That* David Maddox. Your ex-fiancé." Lil fidgeted uneasily. "I tried to send him on, but he says he has to talk to you. Said it couldn't wait."

A cold sweat dampened Larken's temples.

"Lil, I can't," Larken pleaded, taking a step back toward the door. Fear had washed her face white.

"You have to," Lil insisted diplomatically. "I don't see another way around it. He's come all this way."

"Fine. But I'm not doing this the southern way," Larken said. She took one great breath and stormed off into the sitting room.

"Why are you here?" She yelled as she flung herself into the room, her rage fueled by more than just David's presence.

David was standing by Lil's Bosendorfer Grand Piano looking at family pictures in the bookshelves. He turned around quickly, his face scruffy and unshaved. He looked thinner than Larken remembered him, nothing about him feeling familiar in this setting.

"You have every right to be upset," David defended, "I'm sorry to just show up like this." He looked happy to see her despite her coolness, his eyes pleading for her to not hate him.

"This isn't okay," Larken said, flustered.

"I know. None of it has been okay."

"Well, I don't need an apology from you," Larken barked. "So if that's why you're here, then we're a little past—"

"That's not why I'm here," David interrupted her. "Not the only reason, anyway." David took a seat in the settee across from where Larken was standing. He motioned for her to sit down across from him, but she refused, crossing her arms in defiance.

"I'm here because you deserve more than what you've been given. You need to know something." David's voice was steady and pleading, but she could tell he was uneasy. "I know that I can't undo what I've done, but what I put you through, what I did..."

"You fell in love with someone else," Larken interrupted him. She shrugged, faking indifference.

"No."

"Oh, so you didn't fall in love with someone else?" Larken mocked. "I must have imagined it all up—you know, for fun." Her tone was sarcastic while she spoke through her teeth.

"There was never anyone else for me. Ever." David seemed as though he had expected Larken's reaction to be of this scale, his tone remaining unwavering and well-thought-out.

Larken looked at him, confusion washing over her face. "What are you talking about, David?"

"I don't want you living your life thinking that there was ever anyone I wanted more than you."

Larken shook her head. "No. You need to stop."

"I never really saw myself settling down," David continued, interlocking his fingers in distraction. "If I had, it would have been with you, Lark. It would have been an honor to marry you."

Larken finally sat down in the settee across from him, her legs feeling like they might give out from under her.

"But," David continued, "there was *something* I wanted more than marriage and a family. Something that I wanted more than you." David stopped and looked at Larken, making sure she was following him. "For me," he continued, his eyes soft, "it's always been my work. You know that. My identity is in what I do. It's just how I'm made."

Larken nodded in agreement, remembering how his happiest times were neck deep in proposals and campaigns, eighty hour work weeks, running on no sleep and caffeine.

"I was about to lose my company," David admitted, the humility of the truth wearing heavily on him. "I had debt I couldn't pay back from loans I'd gotten when the economy fell apart. I stood to lose it all." He sighed at the memory of it, still fresh enough to feel the fear. "Then I got an offer that I couldn't refuse." He ran his hand down his face, the prickling sound of his beard the only noise between them.

"I traded you, Larken," David said. "I traded you for my company."

Larken's face withdrew. She would have cried if there were any tears left. In light of David's confession, the feeling of rejection she had felt from his leaving her should have been replaced by anger, but it was not. It was replaced with vast emptiness.

"I thought it would be easy," David continued, "to cut you loose and forget it ever happened. I knew you'd have your family to come back to. But that's not how it went down at all. I couldn't stop thinking about you—I've never done anything so wrong in my life." David rubbed at his face again, guilt washing over him. "I went away after you left. To Costa Rica. Totally off the grid. I didn't tell anybody—that was part of the deal. When I did come back, Suzanna said you called her and sounded pretty bad."

Larken thought back to the morning she called Suzanne, hungover from The Sailor Ball.

"So I flew to New York," David continued, his voice scratchy from all of the talking. "And I went to the investor, for lack of a better term," he scoffed. "I tried to pay him back, tell him it was a mistake and that I needed to come clean."

Larken hadn't breathed in what felt like an eternity. She finally drew in air.

"But he said it was too late and threw hush money at me," David said, shaking his head. "The deal I cut with him made him the controlling partner in my firm. My hands were tied."

For all of her faults and errors, Larken knew that not even Bunny was cruel enough to be so calculated. There was only one name that came to mind when Larken thought of selfishness that would not stop until it had been satisfied. Only one that could see such misfortune as opportunity. The boy from childhood that had not, despite his greatest efforts, been able to move beyond anyone other than himself even in his pursuit of her.

"Jackson," Larken whispered. "Jackson Winslow."

*

Larken would have collapsed if David hadn't caught her. She clung on to him, finding some sort of ironic comfort in his embrace. When she composed herself enough, she excused herself from the sitting room and fetched the engagement ring she'd kept stowed in the same envelope it was returned in.

"I tried to mail it back," she explained as she handed the package to him, her hand still trembling. She had taken the letter she'd written to him out, seeing no use in forgiving him now for something completely fabricated.

"Larken," David said as he put the ring in his pocket, "there's still a place for you with me. It's not marriage or anything conventional, but it's something still." He rubbed at his face. "We could try to start over."

Larken smiled through puffy eyes. The thought of running back to Seattle, away from Bunny, away from Jackson, away from Miles, was appealing. "I need more than something, David."

David didn't say anything more. He kissed her on the lips like an old friend and it hit her like medicine—bittersweet and familiar.

*

Larken found more tears that night and they came in waves and surges—overwhelming her body and mind until she thought she'd drown in profound sorrow.

Lil kept her hidden away in the carriage house, swearing like a sailor and baking batch after batch of snicker doodles.

"Well, how did Jackson even find out David's company was in trouble?" Lil asked, her eyes wide in wonder while Larken retold the story that David had told her.

"David's college roommate works with Taylor Winslow." Larken recited the facts David had given her in shock. "It's all so bizarre."

Then Larken told Lil about the deal she'd cut with Bunny, ending any chance she had with Miles to keep the Oxendines on the land.

"And Miles said he wanted to fight for you?" Lil asked after

Larken told her the story. "Even after you told him everything about everything?" She sat on the edge of her seat, fascination taking over.

Larken nodded, unable to answer her with words.

"But you told him not to?"

"Uh huh."

Lil sighed. "Well, what do we do now?"

Larken knew it wasn't a question.

*

As he said he would, David confronted Jackson after he left The Ashby House. Two months after accepting Jackson's vulturous offer, David inherited enough money to repay Jackson's loan in full.

"It won't make it any better," David explained to Larken, "but I have the money to pay him back now and that's exactly what I need to do. I have to clear my conscious."

Larken hadn't heard from Jackson since he'd left Edisto, so she knew that he knew that David had told her. She couldn't explain it, but somewhere inside of her she wanted to comfort Jackson. She supposed it was love that still allowed empathy to surge after betrayal.

Bunny stormed the carriage house the next morning after an upset phone call from Priss. "My *God*," she said hysterically, running to Larken. "I don't even know where to begin. This whole thing makes me feel so cheap and used."

"Makes *you* feel cheap and used?" Lil asked rhetorically. "Imagine that."

"My daughters are a reflection on me!" Bunny snapped.

"Well in that case," Lil said sarcastically, "I'd like to have a little chat with *my* daughter."

"Don't start with me, Momma," Bunny warned, exasperated.

"Larken told me about your little arrangement with the land," Lil continued, pursing her lips in disapproval. "You seem to have taken one out of Jackson's play book."

Larken sat up from her place on Lil's sofa, interested to hear Bunny's rebuttal. She had taken great solace in knowing that the Oxendines would benefit from her sacrifice.

"I got a call from Bart this morning," Lil said. "He had some interesting news." She looked at Larken, her eyes telling her the news wasn't good.

"I'm sorry!" Bunny shouted, throwing her hands up in the air. She turned to Larken. "Baby, I did what I could to make it right, I swear, but it was too late."

"What was too late?" Larken asked.

"I'd already signed the papers," Bunny cried. "I signed 'em before you even left Edisto." She was hysterical as she admitted her lie. "I thought it was the only way! I thought you were gonna ruin your life, baby. Don't you see?"

Lil closed her eyes in disgrace at Bunny's wrong.

"And you were right about JD," Bunny continued, still crying. "You were right about everything. He only ever wanted the land."

"I did it all—for nothing?" Larken finally asked, breathless at the reality of her futile surrender.

Bunny turned to Larken. "I'll make it up to you. I swear. Anything you want. Just say it." She clasped her hands in front of her face, begging for forgiveness.

Larken stared at the wall blankly. "There isn't anything I want anymore," she said, no emotion in her voice.

Bunny looked at Lil for guidance, but she had no response.

*

Bunny made every attempt at winning Larken's forgiveness the week after David's visit. She cleared her calendar, risking social suicide for bowing out of the garden committee for the parade of roses, stayed close to the house and made an extravagant dinner every night, which Larken ate little of.

Jackson sent flowers, which Bunny refused on Larken's behalf, along with a letter stating every reason but a good one for why he'd done what he had. "*I know you won't see me right now,*" he wrote, "*but I hope that you understand the drastic measures I took only reflect the amount of love I feel for you. I'm not giving up.*"

Larken returned to her post break-up yoga pants and cashmere sweater, leaving the house only to run in the mornings before the light of day could shine on her, distinguishing the stark contrast between contentment and despair.

Larken thought mostly of Miles, replaying over and over their last conversation, pointlessly wondering what it would be like now if the outcome had been different and she hadn't been swayed by Bunny. She mourned happiness she cheated herself out of by not asking him to fight for her. It was a vat of what-ifs and impossible hypothesis that consumed her.

She thought of Jackson, too, a part of her wishing that she would never have known of his deal with David—wishing they could have gone on and had everything play out just as he'd planned.

Larken waited for some sort of clarity in the ten days following her return from Edisto, but she sank further and further into that quiet, dark place where loneliness winters.

Jackson must have been feeling the quiet, dark place, too. He showed up at The Ashby House unannounced, his face hollow and his voice empty.

Larken sat at the kitchen table when she heard Gloria open the front door and welcome him in. Larken stayed seated as Jackson's footfalls approached, Lil exiting through the back door like a vapor.

Jackson sat down in the chair across from her at the pedestal table, his presence alien.

"How are you?" he asked. He kept his gaze on the table top.

"I'm okay." Larken shrugged. She thought back to the last time she'd seen him, such a different chemistry then, fresh on the heels of the love and plans they'd made.

"Listen," Jackson said, his voice catching in his throat, "what I did was wrong." He swallowed hard before continuing. "When you first came back from Seattle and you were so wrecked, I thought I'd never forgive myself. I knew I didn't deserve you, but then—you started comin' around. It seemed like you could be happy here again—with me. It made me feel like maybe I'd done the right thing." He combed his fingers through his hair nervously.

Larken pressed her back against the chair and listened.

"I have to have you, Bird," Jackson pleaded. "I need you. You are my Estella, remember?"

Larken felt her resolve begin to melt, her strength wavering. She looked at Jackson, the object of so much desire and turmoil in her life suddenly revealed for what it was.

"Do I need *you*?" Larken heard herself ask, the strength

returning. "You always say that you need me, but do you know what I need, Jackson?"

Jackson fidgeted his thumbs. "You need someone who's willing to fight for you."

Larken's ears rang at the words, her mind and heart racing back to Miles Beckway. In that moment she knew the difference between the fight for love, selfless and humble, and the fight for pride, damaging and blind. Jackson had somehow delivered his own death blow.

"I've made a terrible mistake," Larken said in a small voice. She stared through Jackson, her thoughts supernaturally clear. And only of Miles Beckway.

Larken stood up from the table in one swift movement. "Jackson," she said, turning her attention back to him diplomatically. "This sickness between us. It was never for me what it is for you." She felt the truth in her words as she said them. "And I am finally healed."

Larken walked swiftly out of the kitchen, tugging her cashmere sweater off before hitting the first landing of stairs.

Larken rifled through her dresser before throwing on a tank top and white linen shorts, hurrying herself before she could change her mind. She heard Jackson let himself out through the front door and allowed herself a moment to process the finality of his exit. She took in a deep breath, running a hand through her unbrushed hair and looked in the mirror to find that she was smiling.

*

She thought she might throw up as she turned onto Wampler Drive. The only thing that kept her from stopping was the knowledge that she had nothing left to lose. The Vespa vibrated above the rocks and sticks on Miles' driveway—her hands numb from gripping the handlebar so tightly.

The driveway opened up in time for Larken to see Miles tossing his duffle bag into the back of the old Ford, Uly's outline in the passenger seat. Miles took Thursdays off to mentally prepare for Friday's long surgery days—Larken's heart skipped when she realized she'd just barely missed him.

The old truck sputtered and moaned, drowning out the sound of Larken's arrival. Uly leapt out of the open driver's side door, running to greet Larken with long, excited strides. The dog let out a rare bark—Miles looking up to call him back, but finding Larken's face instead.

Larken's confidence wavered at the sight of him. Miles' eyes were vacant of emotion. He leaned back against the truck, the subtle movement enough to send it into a tremble that made the engine give out. The sudden silence was deafening.

"Miles Beckway," Larken said, making a fist. "I came to tell you I lied about something else, too." She took a few steps toward him. "I came to tell you that I love you."

Miles didn't say anything. His chest fell up and down with rhythmic breaths, but he did not move.

"I love you," Larken said again, walking closer. "And I want you to love me." She stood right in front of him, creek crickets singing in waves around them, their chirps like a million zippers. "I need you to love me." She felt the heat in her face spreading, her breath all but stopping as she waited for him to speak.

Miles bit the side of his cheek and looked at Larken—his brown eyes liquid in the shade of the trees. She felt like her heart was in a vice, each second that he did not speak another squeeze.

Miles reached his arms out and pulled her to him, kissing her like he had before, righting all of the wrongs between them. She felt like a ragdoll in his arms, his hold inescapable.

"I can't do anything but love you," Miles finally said, pulling back to look at her.

Larken drew him close again, a separation of any kind too much now that they felt like one body together.

"So this is what it's supposed to feel like," Larken said quietly into the nape of his neck, suddenly aware of the contentment she felt in Miles' arms.

A deep laugh shook Miles' chest.

"What are you laughin' about?" Larken asked.

"I'm gonna' make you so happy, Larken Devereaux. And you don't even know it yet." He kissed her again, his hands clasped around her waist.

"What are we gonna do about the Oxendines?" Larken blurted out, suddenly remembering the family so dear to both of them.

Miles smirked. "Hmm. I underestimated Bunny... I thought she would have told you."

"Told me what?" Larken asked, looking up at him confused.

"I bought the land back a couple days ago," Miles said. "We offered the power company five hundred thousand dollars more than they bought it from Bunny for and no risk of a lawsuit for attempted displacement of native people... Bunny insisted on paying me back." Miles rubbed Larken's back, reassuring her.

Larken wondered why Bunny hadn't told her. She was typically so quick to praise herself.

"She said that you needed to work through some things," Miles explained. "Something about wanting to be sure you make your own decisions from now on."

Larken felt a weight lift off her at the news, the reign of Bunny finally resigned.

"She told me about the ultimatum she gave you, too," Miles said. "About what you gave up for the Oxendines." Miles pulled her in tightly, resting his chin on top of her head. "God, you're amazing, Larken. And now you're my amazing."

Larken closed her eyes, tears falling out at Miles' words. She breathed in the distinct scent of Sycamore and creek water as she'd done the first time she'd met him, her heart bursting with excitement for the life ahead of them.

"Now what?" Larken asked, wiping her eyes. "Can I get my old job back?" She looked at him—the thought of facing Hazel bringing a hollow feeling to the pit of her stomach.

"Ah." Miles grimaced. "Don't get mad, but Bunny did have *one* little condition…" He paused, bracing for Larken's reaction.

"Let me guess…" Larken smiled, closing her eyes as a breeze blew around them, sweet and warm, "…jewels on your crown."

The End

CPSIA information can be obtained
at www.ICGtesting.com
Printed in the USA
LVOW12s1920070917
547903LV00005B/977/P